PRAISE FOR
THE CHILD QUEEN

"THE CHILD QUEEN is a lovely story, a wonderfully human retelling of the Arthur and Guinevere legend, one touched with passion and enchantment."
—JENNIFER BLAKE

"A tale of enchantment. A love story like no other. You will be charmed. Surely Merlin's magic reached out to touch Nancy McKenzie's pen. Ms. McKenzie weaves a rich and powerful tapestry of words layered in legend and myth. Sit back and enjoy, for who of us would not wish to return to Camelot? Nancy McKenzie is going places!"
—ELAINE COFFMAN

"Guinevere comes alive—a strong, resourceful, and compassionate woman, accessible to modern folk ... McKenzie makes a quantum leap in defining the character of Guinevere as a real, flesh-and-blood woman. The Arthur-Guinevere-Lancelot triangle comes alive as well—believable, poignant, and bearing the seeds of tragedy. Nancy McKenzie is truly an important discovery of the year! My congratulations!"
—KATHERINE KURTZ

Look for these Del Rey Discoveries . . .
Because something new is always worth the risk!

THE CHILD QUEEN

THE TALE OF GUINEVERE AND KING ARTHUR

NANCY MCKENZIE

A Del Rey® Book
BALLANTINE BOOKS • NEW YORK

A Del Rey® Book
Published by Ballantine Books

Copyright © 1994 by Nancy Affleck McKenzie

All rights reserved under International and Pan-American Copyright Conventions. Published in the United States of America by Ballantine Books, a division of Random House, Inc., New York, and simultaneously in Canada by Random House of Canada Limited, Toronto.

Library of Congress Catalog Card Number: 94-94192

ISBN 0-345-38244-7

Printed in Canada

First Edition: August 1994

10 9 8 7 6 5 4 3 2

To Meg and Bruce

Anyone who has ever read any one of Mary Stewart's Merlin trilogy (*The Crystal Cave, The Hollow Hills, The Last Enchantment*) will know how much I owe to her vision of fifth-century Britain. These books, among others, inspired me to create my own tale about Guinevere, Arthur, Lancelot, and the real world these legendary people inhabit. I am indebted to many who have contributed to the Arthurian tradition, historians and storytellers alike. As I have built upon the works of others, so I hope some future writer might build upon mine. After all, that is the ultimate compliment—to be considered even a small part of the tradition surrounding this ancient, time-tested tale.

Special thanks are due to several people whose help and encouragement are directly responsible for the publication of this book. Meg Gossmann, my sister and first reader, went to a lot of trouble to convince me to find an agent; Bruce McKenzie, my husband, gave me the courage to try; Virginia Kidd, my agent, gave me good advice and dealt patiently with my questions; and Deborah Hogan, my editor, worked long and hard to give my story shape.

I thank also my friend Kate Delaney for her gift of Xenophon's *On Horsemanship*, and John Downey of the Andrus Planetarium, The Hudson River Museum, for his prompt answers to astronomical questions. Karen Kramer gave me invaluable support and advice about writing and editing; Caroline McKenzie helped me research White and Malory; Marsha Gorelick and Lydia Soifer provided me a constant source of excited and enthusiastic support, and Joellen Finnie listened patiently to hours of what must have been, in retrospect, boring detail.

I thank all of you for making this possible.

Nancy McKenzie
November, 1993

Arthur's Britain

PICTS
LOTHIAN
Dunpelder
LOTHIAN
STRATHCLYDE
North Sea
Eden River
Caer Eden
RHEGED
Galava
Caer Mord
York
IRELAND
Irish Sea
ELMET
ANGLES
BRITAIN
Isle of Mona
GWYNEDD
ANGLES
Pellinore's Castle
NORTHGALLIS
POWYS
EAST SAXONS
GUENT
DYFED
Severn River
Caerleon
Amesbury
Thames River
Rutupiae
Gwys Wiffin
Severn
Goat's Hole
SOUTH SAXONS
Constion
BRITONS
WEST SAXONS
CLODOMIR'S FRANKS
Tintagel
DUMNONIA
Camelot
Winchester
Scot's Bay
FRANKS
CORNWALL
Mt. Badon
Castle Dore
Narrow Sea
Potter's Bay
CHILDEBERT'S FRANKS
Benoic
BRITTANY
LANASCOL
LESS BRITAIN
BURGUNDIANS
Kerrec
Autun

GAUL

Map by S.T. Palmer

PROLOGUE

The night of my birth the famed witch Giselda, the ugliest woman in all Britain, came to see my father, the King of Northgallis. It was the last night in April, cold and blowing a fine, icy rain. My father and his drinking companions, such nobles and petty lords as could leave their lands in the hands of others, sat in the hall before a great log fire while the women attended my mother and brought him tidings as the night wore on.

The guard let her in, not knowing who she was. She was old and bent, her hands were crippled and swollen, and my father's hospitality to the poor and infirm was well known. But she would not stay to warm herself before the peat fire in the kitchen, where the cooks were heating water for the queen's birthing. She made for the hall and the king. When the guard would have stopped her, she lifted her hood and glared at him. The very sight of her face froze him to the spot where he stood, and she passed by.

Likewise, when she came into the hall, and the company turned to her in surprise and then protest, she silenced them all when she uncovered her head.

"King Leodegrance!" she cried.

My father faced her. He was always the bravest man among brave men. "I am he, witch. State your business and be gone. You come at a time of celebration, and we would not be interrupted! Know you not my young queen gives birth this night?" His companions cheered him, and he even smiled at the old witch. He was the father of five sons of fighting age and the new husband of the loveliest woman in Wales. He could afford to be magnanimous.

But the witch stared at him, trancelike, until the room was quiet and all eyes were on her. "Beware, King! Laugh not until the night is over! It is a night of wonders! The queenstar in the east

1

has fallen in a hail of light. And in its place burns a new star of wondrous brightness! The fairest in the heavens! These are portents of things to come. There is magic in the air this night. In this house."

My father was not a Christian, nor were the others in the room. He worshipped Mithra, the Bull-Slayer, when he was at war, along with all the other men who fought under the High King Uther Pendragon, and the Great Goddess when he was at peace. Yet he also believed in the ancient gods of his ancestors, the gods of roadways and rivers, of the storm winds, the low forests and the high hills, gods whom men had worshipped before ever the Romans came to Britain. To speak to him of magic was to touch him near the heart, and he was afraid.

"What do you mean, woman?" he demanded, hiding his fear in anger. "Where in this house?"

The witch grinned, showing black and broken teeth. Her voice fell into a low and vibrant monotone, and all strained to hear her words. "This night shall be born a daughter who shall rule the mightiest in the land." Her words fell on silence. The king, my father, stared. "She will be the fairest beauty the world has known and the highest lady in all the kingdoms of Britain. Her name will live on in the minds of men for ages to come. Through her will you reach glory." Here she paused and passed her tongue over dry, cracked lips. Someone handed her a cup of spiced wine, and she drank. "But she will bring you pain, King, before ever she brings you joy. Beloved of kings, she shall betray a king and be herself betrayed. Hers will be a fate no one will envy. She will be the white shadow over the brightest glory of Britain." Here she stopped, shook herself awake, and, doing my stunned father a low curtsy, hurried out of the house before any man had sense enough to stop her.

The room was at once alive with voices. Each man asked his neighbor what she had meant. Each man thought he knew what the prophecy foretold. All of them took it as wonderful news for my father, except my father himself. He sat frowning in his great chair, saying over and over "the white shadow. White shadow." He used the Celtic word the witch had spoken: *gwenhwyfar*.

Just before dawn the weather broke, and the wind softened. It was the first of May, a day sacred to the ancient Goddess, and the queen's labors were over. My father, asleep over his wine like his fellows, awoke with a start of premonition to find his chamberlain trembling at his elbow. He was charged with a dolorous message.

The good Queen Elen had brought forth a daughter, but had died thereof. With her last breath she had kissed me, and named me: Guinevere.

1 ✦ NORThGALLIS

My seventh year was my last one at home. It was not customary in those days for boys and girls of noble birth to spend their youth as pages and ladies-in-waiting in strangers' castles. Those were troubled times. The land was not at peace, and men did not trust one another. The law lay in the strongest sword. Outlaws lived among the hills, making travel treacherous. Even warriors undertook journeys only upon necessity, and that usually meant war.

And to tell truth, there were not many real "castles" in Wales. Our strongest buildings were fighting fortresses, where the king's troops slept on straw strewn over dirt flooring, and the walls of dressed stone were unadorned by the tapestries and weavings that kept the wind from our cozy rooms at home in the king's house. Caer Narvon, on our northern border, was the biggest fortress in Wales. It had been built by the Romans and then left to decay with the passing of centuries, but it was still in use as a fighting fortress and was our securest defense against the Irish raiders. With Y Wyddfa, the Snow Mountain, at its rear, and the Western Sea under its guarding eye, it was considered impregnable and was the pride of all Wales.

Nowadays, every petty king has a wonderful castle of quarried stone and plenty of tapestries and fine silks and cushions and carpets to adorn it, for the land has been at peace for twenty years and we have all had time, blessed time, to devote to the arts of peace. But in my childhood, the king's house was a simple enough dwelling. Welshmen have a devilish pride, and even the king's house could not outshine his soldiers' homes by much, else he have trouble on his hands.

My father's house at Cameliard was of wood and wattle, with a large meeting and drinking hall that had a hole cut in the roof to let out the firesmoke. Beautiful hangings adorned the walls, keeping out the winter winds, and beneath the fresh rushes on the floor were real Roman tiles. Cracked and faded as they were, the designs were still discernible. I remember a crouching panther, birds with bright feathers and long necks, and a golden lion, seated and serene, which was just in front of my chair, next to my father on the dais. He kept me by him all the time; I believe he was very lonely. During long audiences and even meetings with his men, I was beside him and amused myself by watching the animals on the floor and imagining that they moved and spoke. The men never bothered about me. They assumed I could understand nothing of their schemes and worries, and I never undeceived them.

Indeed, growing up without a mother had a few definite advantages. Instead of spending all my time with the queen's waiting women, learning needlework and the weaving of war cloaks, I was allowed to go where I would, with either my nurse Ailsa or some page of the king's as companion. I rode everywhere. In my youth, horses gave me freedom and independence; later, they were my comfort and solace. I have taken this to be a sign from God, that I should live in close harmony with these most honored of his creatures. With sturdy Welsh mountain ponies as my friends and teachers in childhood, I grew bold and free and as wild, they said, as any boy. Which is how, in the autumn of my seventh year, I caused trouble, lost my best friend, and learned an important lesson about friendship and power.

The king my father and all his sons and all their attendants were away on a boar hunt. Every year at the change in seasons, the king took his sport, and the men brought back venison and boar to be salted away for palace feasts all winter.

In the village women gathered the harvest of their gardens and small plots, foraged for berries and late herbs, prepared flax for winter's weaving and dyes for winter dyeing. Men went hunting, from the king and his courtiers down to the lowliest peasant; all the animals of the forests throughout Wales took heed; waterfowl fell to men's nets in the marshes, and fish to nets in the lakes and hill ponds. Everyone was busy, even the children. But as royal children, my cousins and I had it easier than most. We collected windfalls from the palace orchards, and when the gardeners were done with their other duties, we scrambled into the trees and shook off the ripening fruit for them to collect in their woven baskets.

I speak of my cousins, who were my playmates in these early

days, but actually they were my nephews. My father's sons by his first wife, Gwella, were grown men, with children of their own. My eldest brother, Gwarthgydd, was seven and twenty, a thick, powerful man with a thatch of black hair on his head and a mat of hair nearly as thick on his body. Most children feared him for his temper, but he had a ready smile and kind heart and was always good to me. His youngest son, Gwillim, was only a year older than me and was my best friend. There were not many girls in our family, and none of them was kind to me, for I did not look much like them, but took after my mother. Gwill's two older sisters were my chief tormenters. They insulted the memory of my mother, the affection of my father, whom I adored, the frailty of my body, which was not thick and dark and sturdy like their own, even the pale color of my hair, as if I could change it of my will. In my innocence, I did not understand it.

On a fine autumn day in the month of the Raven, Gwillim and I could not resist the chance to sneak away from work, only for an hour, to play in the wooded hills that encircled our valley. We pretended we were hunters, tracking our prey along the winding banks of a brook that led up through the hills to a spring in a mossy clearing. There we would flop on our stomachs to rest, drinking the clear water and pouring a small libation for the god of the place, for everyone knew that springs were holy. We could see the white shoulders of Y Wyddfa, the highest mountain in Wales, from that clearing. Its peak was always shrouded in mist, for gods lived there.

Sometimes, when I beat Gwill to the clearing, he would complain that I was cheating, for I was a girl and shouldn't have been there at all. Instead of a gown, I wore soft doeskin leggings better than his own, and as I was taller and my legs were longer than his, I ran faster and was more adept. He didn't really hold these things against me—he liked the challenge. But he disliked being taunted by his brothers and cousins that he played with girls and would grow up to be one. I don't blame him; they were cruel taunts, and I loved him more because he defended me to my enemies and took their abuse for my sake.

This day he reached the clearing first and was already on his knees pouring the libation when I arrived. We knelt together, mumbled our thanks to the god, and drank. Then we sat side by side and gazed at the distant heights of Y Wyddfa, which sparkled in the afternoon sun.

"Gwen, do you think anybody has ever seen a god?" he asked suddenly.

"Of course," I replied in surprise. "Holy men talk with them. Magicians and witches command them. They are everywhere, all about."

"Yes," he said slowly, his eyes on the mountain. "So men say. But if they are everywhere, why can't we see them?"

I was puzzled by his obtuseness. "Because you need special powers to see them," I patiently explained. "That's what makes holy men holy."

"Exactly," he said, turning to me eagerly. "What makes them holy is that they can see and talk to gods. But they can't see and talk to gods unless they are holy. You see?"

"See what?"

"Who's to prove or disprove it? It's their claim to be holy that makes them so. If I claim to be a wizard, it's my claim that makes me powerful, for no one can disprove that I talk to spirits."

"Gwill, do you mean that you don't—you don't believe in gods?"

"No. Of course not. Didn't we just pray to one? I mean, well—my mother fears a witch's curse because she believes the witch has power, and it's her believing that the witch has power that gives her the power she fears. Do you see?"

I was very impressed with his reasoning. But I had a more practical mind. "What witch has cursed her? What did she say?"

He looked a little embarrassed, and I guessed that he was not supposed to tell anyone.

"Swear by Mithra the foul fates," he commanded, and I solemnly swore by Mithra to bring devastation upon myself and my family and my descendants if ever a word that Gwill confided to me should pass my lips.

"Well," he said more easily, "Haggar of the Hills came by in the guise of a beggar as my mother and sisters were washing at the brook. She begged a drink of honey mead that they carried in their flask, for she was thirsty and dusty. Mother pointed out that the brook water was good enough for such as she, and my sisters claimed that common folk would fall ill drinking the mead of the royal house."

I grinned. Gwillim thought his mother insufferably snobbish about her connection to the royal house. Glynis had been the daughter of one of my father's minor nobles and not a good match for Gwarthgydd, but she had been lovely when young, and he had stood by her and married her when she got with child. In return for his kindness, she lorded her position over everyone around her and made everyone's life miserable if she could.

Someday, no doubt, if Gwarth lived, she would be queen, and she let no one forget it. But for all that, Gwill was devoted to her, and often rose well before dawn to fish the stream for speckled trout, which she adored. He was her favorite. All his transgressions she forgave him.

"Then Haggar revealed herself and called upon the powers of the air. My sisters say the sky darkened, but I do not believe this. I was not far away that day, and I saw nothing. She cursed my mother's vanity, saying that the highest shall be brought low and the least valued made high; that all my mother's hopes should come to naught, and her line should dwindle. That her home should be destroyed, and her husband die in a far-off land." He gulped and continued. "And that the Kingdom of Northgallis should be swallowed by a great dragon and disappear from the face of the earth forever."

I stared at him in horror. "Northgallis disappear?" I whispered. "Oh, Gwillim, no! What does it mean? Saxons?"

He shook his head. He was clearly more worried about the fate of his family than about the Kingdom of Northgallis. "Don't you see what my mother has done? She made the old woman mad, and now she believes every word she said. But what if the old woman isn't really a witch? I mean, what if everybody just thinks she is? Nothing need come to pass unless we make it so by believing it will."

I gazed at him with wonder and respect. "You are the bravest boy I know, Gwillim, son of Gwarthgydd. To think you can save Northgallis simply by believing you can—it's wonderful. Does this mean that the witch has no power over you?"

He flushed with pleasure and smiled. "She doesn't determine my future, Gwen, unless I believe that she does. That's what I think."

"And—and is this true also of other witches? And enchanters? What about the High King's enchanter? What about Merlin?"

He shivered at the name of the great magician, but bravely stuck to his belief. "Yes, it is also true of Merlin. But—but perhaps I might believe Merlin," he admitted, frowning. "He is wise as well as powerful. He is not afraid of kings."

The air around us had gone very still. The fleecy clouds hung motionless in the sky, and the birds fell silent in the trees. I realized suddenly that we were talking in whispers, and a thrill of foreboding ran up my spine.

"And the gods?" I breathed, wide-eyed. "Are they the same? Have they power only over those who worship them, so that

Mithra has power over warriors, and the Elder spirits over the common people and the hill people, and the new *Kyrios Christos* over the Christians?"

He stared at me. We hardly dared to breathe in the awful silence.

"You understand me," he whispered, and we were filled with terror at our sacrilege.

Suddenly we were not alone in the clearing; we felt the new presence before we heard or saw anything. For an instant time stood still, and we saw in each other's eyes the everlasting terror of perdition. Then I saw behind him, at the edge of the clearing, the soft brown eyes and pink nose of a wild mountain pony, and I exhaled with relief. We were not to be claimed by spirits after all! A small band of ponies had come to the spring to drink, that was all. Gwill turned slowly, flushing scarlet when he saw them, four of them, edging daintily toward the spring pool. We sat still, and they gathered courage and came forward, three of them lowering their pretty heads to drink, while the fourth eyed us warily.

Gwill was ashamed of his terror and needed to feel brave.

"They're very fine," he said softly. "And the leader is black. That's very rare. Let's see if we can catch two."

I was entranced. Ever since my father had placed me himself on a fat little pony at the age of three, I had loved horses. They spoke a language I somehow understood, and riding came effortlessly to me. At seven, I was already as good a rider as boys of eleven and twelve, who were ready for war training. And while Gwill was only slightly less skilled than I, catching wild ponies was a very different thing from riding trained ones and was a job for a group of mounted men and not for two children.

Nevertheless, I assented immediately and drew from my belt the windfalls I had brought along for our hunter's meal. Keeping movement to a minimum, I approached the nearest pony, a white one, offering the apple. While the other ponies scented danger and backed away, this one was overcome by curiosity and showed no fear. I fed him the apple and stroked his neck, lifting the heavy mane and scratching his withers. His eyes closed with pleasure, and Gwill whispered "Now!" In a single leap I was astride. The pony snorted in fear, spun around, and tore off through the woods. I buried my fists in his mane and clung to him for dear life, lying low on his back as we crashed through the brush, and branches whipped at my face and hair. I had a vague picture of Gwill grappling with the black one, his belt around its neck, but I could hear nothing behind me. The other ponies had bolted, too, but whether

Gwill was with them I had no idea. I spoke to the terrified pony in a low singsong, as we Welsh do, hoping he could hear me over the clatter of his hooves. Eventually he slowed, either calmed by the song or tired from his fruitless efforts. He cantered, then trotted, then came to a trembling halt. I stroked and comforted him but did not dismount. I let him feel my legs against his sides, gently, and then I sat up. As he got over his fear, he seemed to understand the messages my legs and body sent him. It is magic of a sort, speaking to horses, and a thrill I have never outgrown. We walked along a woodland track until he was calm and had got his breath back. Then, crooning to him all the while, I headed him back the way we had come, as well as I could judge. He was lathered with fear and sweat, his sides were slippery. So when, as we neared the spring, I heard my name suddenly shouted from the top of the ridge and the pony reared in fright, I slipped off as quickly as a raindrop from a downspout and fell hard against a tree. The last thing I remembered was the cry "Guinevere!" echoing among the hills, and then the world went black.

I began to hear voices, dimly, as if from a distance. I was warm and protected deep in my darkness, and the voices washed over me in gentle swells, gently rolling me this way and that. I was tired, too tired to move, so I lay still and listened to the coming and going of the voices.

Gradually I floated nearer the bright surface, and the voices came more clearly. There was a kind, deep voice that spoke in quiet desperation, and a higher-pitched voice that spat in angry whispers.

"It's not fair!" came the angry voice. "He has no right to kill the boy!"

"He has the right of the king," the deep voice replied slowly, wearily. "And he will not do it if she lives. So do your job and nurse her, Glynis. Enough of this argument."

"You listen to me, Gwarth! This girl is a curse to your house, to your family, and to your line. She was cursed on the night of her birth by the most powerful witch in Wales, do you not remember?"

"Hush, woman!"

Glynis lowered her voice, but her spite intensified. "She has brought nothing but trouble to Northgallis since that day. She killed her mother the queen with her birth. We had drought in her first year of life and a killing frost in her second. She is spoiled and petted by all the king's courtiers and servants. Even you! Yes,

even you, with fine children of your own, are kinder to her than
to them. She is a young witch, I tell you—"

"Woman, I will put you away! Hold your tongue!"

"She has woven a spell around Gwillim. He is enchanted, I tell
you! He follows her everywhere! And now, a week after the hill
witch's curse—"

"By the Bull! I am tired of hearing about that hag—"

"She said my house would be destroyed and my line diminished! And now this! This—this brazen witch leads my son into
the hills, gets herself hurt, and now the king your father will take
his life in vengeance! If that isn't diminishing my line, what is!
Gwarth, he is your son, too! Can't you stop it?"

The deep voice came nearer; it was very kind. "Glynis. Calm
yourself. Do your duty and poultice the girl. She is only a child.
This was an accident, my dear. Children are heir to them. She can
do you no harm unless she dies. You have seen your own children
recover from worse falls than this."

"Yes," Glynis continued, her fury unabated, "but they were
strong children, not dainty and pampered like this one. If it were
not for Gwillim, I would not try to save her! Oh, gods!" she cried,
choking. "Tell me, why does everyone love her so much?"

Gwarth was silent while Glynis sobbed noisily. "She is ugly!"
she blurted. "Such fairness—such pallor—is ugly! Her bones are
too small! She cannot work; she is useless! My daughters are
more worthy to be princesses of Northgallis! They are strong,
and—and . . . they are brown and healthy . . . I hate her! I hate
her!"

She must have sensed she had gone too far, for she began to
mumble an apology and flung a cloth across my brow.

For a long time Gwarthgydd said nothing. Then he spoke with
the voice of command. "*You* have destroyed your house. *You* will
diminish your line. I put you away. Take your brown daughters
with you, Glynis, and go."

The woman screamed, and pain shot through my head. I pulled
the quiet darkness around me with thanks and sank into its depths.

When I awoke it was early evening. I was in my own bedchamber, and a wood fire burned in the grate. The king's physician sat by my side, watching me eagerly. I was wrapped in warm
furs, and my head was bound in cool cloth. When I looked about
me, the outlines of things were murky, but soon my sight cleared,
and the physician uttered a prayer of thanks to Mithra.

I knew what I must do.

"Where is my father?" I asked him. "Is the king near? Bring him to me."

The physician nodded and patted my hand soothingly. "King Leodegrance is but waiting for word of your awakening." He snapped his fingers, and the page by the door hurried out. The physician poured some warm broth into a flat bowl and supported my head while I drank of it. It tasted of herbs and medicines, but it was warming and steadied my head.

"Please help me to sit up," I begged, but the physician insisted I lie quietly.

"If my father is coming, I will sit up," I commanded, using the voice I heard Gwarthgydd use, and the physician obeyed immediately. I was dizzy and my head felt several sizes too large, but I could hold myself erect.

"How long have I been here?"

"Since yesterday, my lady. You were brought to me in the evening."

"Please tell me what happened before the king comes. It is important that I know. I remember nothing of it."

He hesitated, but gave in to me. "When the king's hunting party returned, the palace was in an uproar because you could not be found. No one remembered having seen you since midday. In fear of their lives, the gardeners and house servants took to the hills to look for you."

"And Gwillim," I added, but he averted his eyes. "Yes, my lady. Ailsa fell down in a fit with brain fever. She is delirious still." Ailsa, my nurse, was a loving but lazy soul, who had attended me from birth. It was during one of her illicit naps in the garden that I had stolen away.

"I expect she will recover when she finds out I am all right."

The physician was doubtful. "It appears to be a serious case, my lady."

"Never mind. I will cure her. How did you find me? What of Gwillim?"

He looked uncomfortable when I said his name, and I began to be afraid.

"The king's son Gwarthgydd and his men found you, coming down from the hills across the back of a white pony, led by Gwillim," the physician said, frowning. "The lad was frantic. He thought you were dead. He told King Leodegrance he had led you away from the orchard and taken you to play with him in the hills. He said you had seen some wild ponies, and he dared you to catch one. He blamed himself for what happened. He said it was punishment for evil thoughts."

"Did the king believe him?" I whispered.

"We all believed him, my lady."

"And where is he now? Pray, quick! I hear the guards!"

"He is—he is in the king's dungeon, my lady. His family is disgraced."

"It was not his fault!" I cried hotly, but cut off my speech, for the door swung open, and my dear father strode into the room.

"Gwen!" He took me gently into his arms, and I hugged him and kissed his rough cheek. "Praise Mithra you are alive! How do you feel? Shouldn't you be lying down?"

"Not yet," I said, to forestall the physician. "I must speak with you first, dear Father. Can I see you alone?"

A wave of his hand sent the others out of the room, although the physician did not like to go.

"Father," I said, looking right into his eyes. "I owe my life to Gwillim. He saved me when I fell, and he brought me home. If it were not for Gwillim, I would be with Mother now. Can you send him to me, that I may thank him?"

The reference to my mother diffused his rising anger, and he grumbled a bit. "That is not what Gwillim says," he objected. "He admits that he endangered your life. He didn't claim he saved you."

I managed a blush and took his big, brown, callused hand between my own small white ones. "Well, what would you expect him to say? That your daughter behaved like an Irish hooligan? That she enticed him away from his chores and ran off to the hills to enjoy the day, knowing he would be forced to escort her? That she bragged she could catch and ride a wild pony, although he begged her not to risk it? And that when she was thrown and lay senseless, he found her and managed to tame the wild pony himself and bring her home upon its back? Would you have believed such a story?"

He glowered at me. "No, I would not. And I do not believe it now."

I sighed and inwardly took a deep breath. "Well, my dearest father, it is near the truth. I have behaved very badly, toward you and toward Gwillim. I humbly ask your forgiveness. I was thoughtless and selfish. I have caused Gwillim to lie to defend my honor, and I am ashamed."

He looked at me searchingly, but I withstood him. His uncertainty gave way at last to resignation. "Do you swear by the blood of the Bull this is the truth?"

"I swear it."

"Well," he said at length, "I am both grieved and relieved to hear it. I will send Gwillim to you after I have spoken to him, and when the physician says I may. You should be punished, Guinevere; but it is not in me to do it. And indeed, I believe Mithra will see to it in his own way, and in his own time."

"There is one other thing." He was getting up to go, and he turned warily, scenting deception. I put on the most guileless face I could summon.

"May I also have my nurse back? I dislike this physician near me. In my illness, I remember a light touch that comforted me. Would it be possible to send her back to me?"

He looked confused, but could not resist my supplication. "If you mean Glynis, she is gone from the house." As the ranking woman, after me, of the royal house, Gwarthgydd's wife would be appointed nurse to any royal patient.

"If she is gone because of Gwillim, can it not be put right?"

The king stood and looked down full upon me. "Guinevere, are you asking me to send you that jealous shrew? Do you really want her with you? Are your wits about you? You needn't—Gwillim is safe without that."

Safe, perhaps, but miserable and forever shamed without his mother. I trembled with the effort it cost me, but I lied. "She is a good nurse."

He stared at me and then shook his head. "All right. She is yours. But when you are well, my girl, you and I must talk about your future."

"Yes, Father," I said meekly.

Glynis returned the next morning. Her face was rough and blotched with the marks of blows and tears, and I guessed that Gwarth had lost his temper once again. There was no love in her face, no understanding, no gratitude; only fear. I was a witch; she was beholden to me, and she was afraid. I did not speak to her, but let her tend me and feed me with what tenderness she could muster, and we got along tolerably well.

In the evening Gwillim was brought to my door. Glynis would have embraced him, but Gwillim kept his eyes on the floor, and she crept out without a word.

I lay on the pillows and looked at Gwillim. He would not look at me. He was newly washed and dressed in clean clothes, but there were red marks on his wrists where they had bound him.

Bound him! What he had been through in the last two days, I could not guess. But what confounded me was his fear. He, too, was afraid of me and averted his eyes from my face.

"Gwillim," I whispered. "Kneel down so we can talk." He obeyed and waited. "Gwillim, I take responsibility. I am sorry they put you in prison. It wasn't fair." He said nothing.

"Gwillim, tell me what happened." It was a command, and he obeyed.

"I tried to come after you, but I lost the black pony. So I followed on foot. I could see where you went clearly enough, because the branches were bent and the undergrowth trampled. But of course I could not catch you. After a while I realized that if I followed you, I would never catch up. I figured you would circle back to the clearing. I knew you would be able to speak to him. I knew you would not come off unless—unless something scared you." So that was it. It was his voice that had startled the pony. "When at last I saw you returning, I could not control my joy, Gwen—I mean, my lady, and I shouted."

"I know about that part. Never mind. I'd have done the same. What happened after that? How on earth did you get me back on the pony?"

The ghost of a grin swept his face and was instantly hidden.

"I didn't know what to do. You were bleeding, my lady. There was lots of blood around your head. I thought you were dying. I sat down beside you and cried. And then—" His hushed voice sank so low I had to strain to hear it. "—then *the pony came back to you.* I was sitting there, and he came right out of the forest, right up to you, and nuzzled you. He let me put my belt around his neck. He let me lay you across his back. He let me lead him down the mountain, and he walked so carefully over the stones, you never even slid." There was awe in his voice, and in his face, and I realized with a shock of despair that Gwill had changed.

"The soldiers came and rescued you. They let me put the pony in the paddock before they took me to the king. He is there still. He didn't even try to get away." Suddenly his shyness fled, and he spoke eagerly. "Don't you see, Gwen? It's a sign. After the evil things we thought about by the spring, we were both punished, you immediately and me later on, and then the pony's coming all by himself. It's a sign from the god."

"From which god, Gwill?"

He looked pained. "Does it matter, my lady? It's the proof, you see."

"Proof of what?" My throat ached so it was hard to speak.

"I blasphemed," he said humbly, "and was given a sign. I have no doubts any longer."

"You believe because you saw a sign, but you saw the sign only because you believed."

"Don't," he said quickly. "Please, my lady. Don't say those awful things. You will be punished again."

"I am being punished now," I retorted. "Why do you address me as 'my lady'? I'm 'Gwen' to you, remember?"

He lowered his eyes, and I was instantly sorry I'd said it. I understood, of course. It was the risk I'd had to take to save his honor, but it was a bitter pill to swallow for a proud, brave boy.

"You are the king's daughter," he said slowly, addressing the coverlet. "And I am your servant. A word from your lips saved my mother and sisters from a cruel fate. For this I thank you. Even my father must be obedient to your command and take back what he had put away. The honor of our house is in your hands, my lady."

"Yes, w—well," I stammered, fighting back tears. "I saw no other way. You'd better go."

He rose with dignity, bowed, and turned away. I turned my face to the wall and wept.

2 GWYNEDD

On my eighth birthday I left my home forever.

My father called me to him one wretched night that winter and, with tears streaming unchecked into his beard, told me that come spring and my eighth birthday, he would send me away. It felt like death. Nothing he said could comfort me. I was not going far away, only into the next kingdom, by the Western Sea, to the house of my mother's sister, whose husband was lord of that land. But in those days, and at that age, it was across the world.

The reason was, he said, that it was the only place I would be safe.

I did not understand at first. He would not tell me that he had felt the first touch of the hand of Death. I thought he meant we should have war.

Wales had been quiet enough. Winter had closed the seas, and the Irish raiders kept to their own coasts. Of the inland fighting to the east and south against Angles and Saxons, news filtered in from time to time. But the names of the strange places and kings, of Cornwall, Strathclyde, Rheged, Lothian, of Cador, Ector, Urien, and Lot—these were foreign words, foreign lands, foreign princes. For the Kingdom of Northgallis was my country and Wales the limit of the civilized world.

When my father fell ill that winter, he called his sons to him. To the eldest, Gwarthgydd, he bequeathed the major part of his kingdom and the king's house at Cameliard. To the others he gave lands of their own to keep independently, provided, and he made this condition clear, that they follow and fight for the High King Uther Pendragon against his enemies.

For the king my father believed very strongly that the safety and, indeed, the future of Wales depended on the High King's desperate efforts to contain the Saxon invasions on eastern coasts.

And he knew whereof he spoke. He had been a young man when the High King Vortigern had invited the Saxons to Britain's shores to help him quell the rebellious Picts who threatened from the north. These Picts, a fierce and primitive race of thieves and bandits, had badgered the country incessantly and for generations, since the last Roman legions had left the land. But the Saxons were worse. At least the Picts had no organization and never stayed in the land they conquered, but retreated to their own homes to sing their victory paeans. The Saxons stayed. Vortigern found that, once he had invited them in, he could not make them leave and was forced to reward them with land in return for their service against the Picts. He gave them small plots along the southeastern shores and thought, the shortsighted fool, that that should content them. But within five years their families and all their relations had come to join them, and the Saxon colonies grew.

As everyone knows, their numbers increased until their lands could not hold them, and their war leaders Hengist and Horsa were a greater threat to King Vortigern than ever the Picts had been. Vortigern even married a Saxon queen, Hengist's daughter. After that no true Celt would follow him, and he lost his power to the Saxon horde. It was Ambrosius who saved us. Aurelius Ambrosius, brother of the rightful king whom Vortigern had murdered, invaded from Less Britain with an army of twenty thousand and fought Vortigern to a bloody victory. My father fought in that battle, where the old wolf and his Saxon queen were smoked out of their hill fort and burned alive. And he fought in the battle at Caer Konan, where Hengist was beaten, when Merlin himself appeared out of thin air to predict Ambrosius' victory. Had it not been for Ambrosius, we should all have been as degenerate as the Picts.

The great Ambrosius, and his younger brother Uther, gathered the many British kings together, from Lothian and Rheged to Dyfed and Dumnonia, and bound them with oaths of loyalty to the High King of Britain. Fighting together under a strong war leader was our only hope of stemming the Saxon tide, so my father was wont to exhort his warriors on cold winter nights, when war looked distant and glorious. But this my father deeply believed, even when he was called upon to take arms and fight in Uther's army. And he saw to it that his sons should follow his example.

Now, after fifteen years of vigilance and fighting constant small battles to hold the kingdoms together and give the people peace,

Uther was getting old. I thought my father foresaw war coming closer to home and was sending me temporarily to the coastal kingdom of Gwynedd to live under the care of King Pellinore and Queen Alyse, until Northgallis should be safe for me once more.

It was a sad leave-taking. I adored my father. He had not held my mother's death against me, and I think he loved me more tenderly because I reminded him of her. He was a good king and a strong one, but he never used his sword unnecessarily, nor took joy in killing. The worst I can say of him is that he spoiled me and knew it. I worshipped him.

"My little Gwen," he said, hugging me tightly as the escort made ready to leave early on the first of May. "I will come visit you at summer's end, the gods willing. You must make a place for yourself in your mother's family. You have a cousin for company, and they will give you book learning, which I cannot do here. You should know more than I do, my dear, if the witch is to be believed. King Pellinore is a wise man and has a scholar in his house. There are fine horses there, too, my sweet. You will not be without your favorite entertainment. Now dry those pretty eyes and be a brave princess. And always remember," he said under his breath, "always remember who you are and what you will be."

I was used to his references to the hag's prophecy and nodded obediently. Ever since the fortelling at my birth I was held to be a wonder by the Welsh. On more than one occasion I heard fantastic stories told about me that bore no relation to the truth, but that the people willingly believed. Thanks to Giselda, they expected me to bring them honor. This is a hard thing to live with, even now.

Thus I left Northgallis, but I never saw his dear face again, for he died when summer came and was buried before the news reached me.

My cousin Elaine was a gossip, even at seven. She befriended me on sight and made me feel at home from my first moment. She was eager to have a companion near her own age to talk to and play with, as her mother and the nurses were busy with three younger sons. I loved her for this. She was gay and warm-hearted, bold where I was shy, open and loving where I was reserved. I have never forgotten her sweetness to me at that time when it mattered most. For remembrance of this, I have struggled to forgive her cruel betrayal, for without her love and friendship in my childhood, I should not have had the courage to face what the fates have brought me.

While Ailsa unpacked my trunk and scant belongings in Elaine's room, Elaine took my arm and gave me a tour of her home. She showed me everything, from basement scullery to the turrets on the western tower, where the sentries kept watch all year for Irish pirates. She never stopped talking. She knew everything: reports of Saxon fighting to the east; which queens were witches, and which kings coveted another's land; who in the village was engaged to whom, and which of the kitchen slaves had given birth to an illegitimate child. I laughed to hear her tales, told with a gleam in her sky-blue eyes and a light in her happy face. Indeed, within an hour of my arrival, it was possible to forget, at least for a while, the hard two days' journey and my dear father's parting kiss.

When she took me to the sentry tower I had my first sight of the sea. It seemed to stretch on forever, away in the distance, low and gray and empty and immensely sad. Elaine was delighted at my amazement.

"Have you never seen the sea, then? Why, we ride upon the shore on holidays, or when Iakos gives us the day free. I have even been upon it, in a golden ship with silver sails! Well, it was pretty fancy, anyhow. My father sailed to Caer Narvon last September, and he let me come aboard before they departed. It was wonderful—the very floor I stood upon rolled this way and that, like a cradle, almost! I should love to have an adventure at sea!"

I smiled at her. "I would be afraid to feel the floor beneath me move so," I said. "But I should love to ride along the shore."

"Oh, yes! I have heard how you love horses. Let's go down to the stable, and I'll show you my pony. That is"—with a doubtful look at me—"if you're not too tired. Grannic says I mustn't tire you. She says we must take special care of you. Are you sickly, or something?"

"No, of course not. I think she means because I am your mother's sister's daughter, and kin to you. That's all."

But Elaine still looked uncertain. "But you're different from other people, aren't you?"

I seemed to feel a cold hand upon my neck. "Whatever do you mean?"

"Oh, now you're mad, Gwen. I'm really sorry. It's just something I overheard once. Nobody told me anything. I don't know anything about it."

"What did you overhear?"

"Promise that you won't be angry with me?"

"Elaine, I will not be angry with you. I promise."

"Well, didn't a witch put a spell on you at birth?" I gasped, but she went on. "Not a bad spell, a good spell. Aren't you going to marry a great king and rule over all of us someday?"

A cold shiver ran through me. I found myself furious that the prophecy had followed me even here. I wondered in sudden despair if there was anyone in all of wide Wales who had not heard it.

"I shall do no such thing, silly girl. My father is one among many kings. His lands are less wide than King Pellinore's. You believe in old wives' tales, and you a Christian? I thought your God frowned on magic."

Elaine was undaunted. "But *everybody* knows there are witches. And wizards, as well. Have you never heard of Merlin the Enchanter? He can see the future in a raindrop and vanish into thin air! All the world knows this."

"And many people who have no such power pass themselves off as witches with skill and luck. I am not different, Elaine. As my father is a king, no doubt in time he will marry me off to the finest Welsh lord he can find, but the rest is nonsense. Truly it is. Rule the land, indeed! I shall never rule over you, Elaine. Of that I am quite sure."

She grinned in relief. "Good, because I like being first." If I gave her ease, I am glad, but I was frightened. It was the first time I had voiced my own beliefs about the prophecy, and I was stunned to find how vehemently I resented old Giselda's interference. I was more unhappy to learn that people here knew and believed her words. It occurred to me for the first time, as I stood on the turret beside Elaine, looking out at the strange sea, that I might live under that cloud my whole life. I had insisted I was not different. But if everyone thought that I was, did that not make me so?

In the stables I forgot my fears. King Pellinore had many fine animals, all the sturdy mountain horses that breed freely in the hills of Wales. And Elaine had a pretty fat pony with a fine, dry face and great, dark eyes.

"His name is Petros. It means 'rock.' Iakos says it is a good name for a princess' pony. He's very lazy and does not like to move. This makes him safe to ride!" She laughed gaily at her jest and let me pat his warm neck and stroke the glossy coat. "Mother says you know how to ride already. Did you have your own pony in Northgallis?"

"Yes, a lovely white one. I found him running wild in the hills, and he let me ride him."

Elaine looked put out. "Did you bring him with you?"

"No, I—before I left, I let him go back into the hills. He belonged there."

She brightened again. "Well, Mother said you may take your pick of the next batch they bring in, as long as he gets along with Petros. That's a rare honor, you know. It's because she heard you were skilled."

I felt my face flush with pleasure. Perhaps having oneself talked about wasn't such a bad thing, after all. "I must thank her for the offer. And who is Iakos?"

"Iakos is my tutor—I mean *our* tutor. He is teaching me Latin and writing and figures, although not too much of that because I hate it. Also music. Leonora, the queen's woman, will teach us stitchery and weaving, and also housekeeping when we are older. There's a lot to learn to be a good queen, isn't there?"

She cocked her head sideways and looked up at me shrewdly. She seemed to me to be ready for anything, full of confidence and life, willing to try whatever came to her hand. I envied her enormously. I was completely untutored in any feminine skills. My childhood had been spent with my doting father and my rough, grown half-brothers. I could run, ride, shoot with bow and arrow, and hawk as well as any youth my age. For my fifth birthday Gwarth had given me a young falcon, fallen from his nest and saved just in time, to raise for my own. He had helped me to train it, and I learned to fashion jesses from worked leather and had made my own glove. But I instinctively kept these accomplishments a secret from Elaine, who I feared might despise them. Of embroidery and the weaving of war cloaks, tasks every woman of even moderate birth must learn in order to marry, I knew nothing.

And of her religion, the worship of the Christian God, I knew very little. But there was a priest among the household staff, and I knew I would be instructed in the new ways. This had been my father's only reservation in sending me to my mother's people. They had been Christians for two generations, ever since an Irish martyr landed upon their coast and with wit and charm persuaded them to turn their backs on the Elder spirits. Whether my father had thought it an inevitable consequence of his plans for me, or whether he recognized that the tide of change was sweeping the land, he had consented to my instruction. So I was brought into the fold of the jealous Christian God, my feet were set upon the True Path, and the little deities of hill and stream, rock and high place, were left behind.

* * *

It was a busy summer. Elaine's mother, Queen Alyse, kept us to our tasks and allowed us little time for mischief-making. As I was to find, her word was law. To her credit, she believed her daughter deserving of the same education she gave her sons and made no excuses to Iakos on our behalf. I tried my best to please her in everything, but it was not easy to accomplish. She was not unkind, but neither was she warm. Tall and beautifully featured, with the family's fairness and a majestic bearing, she did not welcome confidences from children. Even Pellinore was half afraid to cross her.

At our first meeting she looked me over carefully, placing her hand on my chin and turning my face toward the light.

"So you are Elen's daughter," she said thoughtfully, after I had made my speech of thanks for taking me in. "I pray you will be as well behaved. We will teach you manners here, Guinevere, and make a princess of you." I was tempted to retort that I was a princess already and that my father had taught me manners, but I held my tongue, afraid that to speak would give the lie to my assertion. "You would do well," she said coolly, "to follow Elaine in everything." It was advice I learned to take.

That summer the old High King, Uther Pendragon, who had held the kingdoms of Britain together for nearly fifteen years, began to fail. Messengers rode into the castle every week with news. It was said he could no longer sit a horse, but had to be carried to battle in a litter, like a woman. Some of the men scoffed at the rumor, denying that any soldier of mettle would follow an invalid war leader. Indeed, it was a shocking thought. But King Pellinore himself believed it, saying that Uther was the best warrior in the kingdoms, afoot, astride, or abed, and only a fool would be too proud to follow him. So the dissenters kept their grumbling quiet, sharpened their spears, polished their swords, and waited.

The Saxons were massing, they said, clogging the shores in the southeast, and Colgrin their leader was making alliances with the petty kings there, gathering strength for an attack on the High King. But weeks wore on, and no royal messenger came to summon King Pellinore and his men. What came instead were the rains. We had had drought all winter, and now, after a warm, dry spring, the skies opened over all Wales and drowned the fertile valleys. Crops rotted where they stood, the rich soil was scoured from the land by raging rivers, and sheep and horse foundered in the mired pastures. Ailsa muttered charms under her breath against evil spirits; the miller's boy went mad and threw himself in the sea; the queen's garden was spoiled, and the cooks complained bitterly; even the priest was seen to cross himself whenever the clouds grew black.

Every day brought news of some sort: local news of local catastrophes; distant news of discontent, uprisings, invasions, and assaults. A blight lay upon the land. Some said God was displeased that ignorant souls persisted in the worship of Mithra and would give no victories to pagan soldiers. But Elaine and I scoffed at that. Colgrin and his Saxons worshipped gods far more barbarous than Mithra! Some said the land was failing as the High King failed and that we would not recover until we had a new King. This argument was no longer whispered in corners between nervous warriors; it was spoken aloud at the king's supper table, after the women had left. Elaine and I heard it ourselves.

Of course, we were not in the hall. We were eavesdropping. Elaine showed me this secret in my first week there. Along the parapet between the east and south turrets was a smallish crack in the stone, and through this crack we could peer down into the smoky hall. This fissure was protected by the guardhouse wall from the east wind, else it would have been discovered when the rain blew in. But if we covered ourselves in our dark, hooded cloaks and crept up past the guardhouse when the sentries were warming themselves by the fire, or standing at their posts at either turret, we could crouch unseen by the crack and learn of the high matters young maids were never allowed to know.

To do the guards justice, they were good men and loyal to the king, but it never occurred to them that the young princesses were not abed past dark, or would be curious about what rough soldiers said in the drinking hall. But we were always curious and never afraid to listen when we knew a courier had come. Only the very worst weather could keep us away. Ailsa and Grannic, Elaine's nurse, slept outside our door, it is true. But they were loud snorers and deep sleepers, embarrassingly easy to deceive.

Thus we learned of the country's discontent, and the threat of war that loomed on the horizon, a war that would change our lives, whatever the outcome. All of King Pellinore's men were loyal to the Pendragon banner, and trained almost daily in the courtyard. But as the summer wore on and the crops and animals died, and men went mad from hunger and lack of sun, they were called to their lands to put down unrest among the farmers and oversee the care of their own families, so that the king's fighting force was scattered. There were barely enough men at court to get up a hunt, and no one cared to hawk when the gloom lay so heavy on the land. Talk at dinner invariably returned to one

theme: would not the High King at last recall his only son Arthur
from his secret fastness and reveal him to the lords and set him
to lead us against the Saxons?

Everyone in Britain knew this tale. I had been raised on it. Indeed, it was the one tale, in my father's country, which was better
known than mine. When Uther Pendragon was crowned High
King of Britain, he had fallen desperately in love with Ygraine,
wife of Gorolis, Duke of Cornwall. She was only twenty, and
Gorolis a grizzled warrior of fifty. Some said Merlin the Enchanter had put a spell on the King at his coronation feast, so that
as soon as he saw her, he had no peace of mind, but planned how
he could take her and yet not wreck the Kingdom by so doing.
Remembering stories of my dear father's infatuation for my
mother, I did not think that sudden love needed any supernatural
explanation, but I believed with the rest of the world, that the famous enchanter had been responsible for the clever plan that
brought Uther his heart's desire. Gorolis removed his wife from
the High King's reach as soon as etiquette permitted and brought
her to the impregnable fortress of Tintagel on the Cornwall coast.
He and his fighting men repaired to a fine fighting fortress that
guarded the route, in case the High King should follow. As soon
as the official feasting was over, Uther, and Merlin with him,
came with a large army and camped just out of bowshot. It looked
like the fragile kingdom would soon be split by war. But Merlin
changed the King by magic arts into the very likeness of Gorolis,
and thus disguised, he rode along the track to Tintagel and was
admitted by the guard, all unknowing. Men believe that the young
duchess was also deceived, but no woman I know believes this. It
is a known fact that Ygraine was a faithful and loving wife
to King Uther, obedient to his every wish to the end of their
days, as if the flame of love never died in her heart. I will leave
it there. During the night they were together, when Arthur was
conceived, Gorolis led his troops in a surprise attack against the
High King's army, which is treason, and the old duke was killed
in the fighting. Uther married Ygraine as soon as he decently
could, before her pregnancy began to show. But out of guilt for
the death of Gorolis, he refused to acknowledge the son that was
born, and three nights after his birth handed him to Merlin to safeguard and raise. Since then the boy had been in Merlin's keeping,
but no one knew where. Some said even Uther did not know.

King Uther and Queen Ygraine had no other sons in all the
years of their marriage. And now, with Uther ill and the Saxon
power growing in the east, men said it was time for the Prince to

be brought forth and for Uther to acknowledge him. Wales would rise for him, that was clear. But there were lands in the east, already menaced by the Saxons, that were less certain. King Lot of Lothian had met with Colgrin, and no one knew if he would support Uther when the time came or try to supplant him. Ambrosius' fragile kingdom might be split forever, if Prince Arthur did not soon appear.

Elaine and I were careful never to let slip any comment that would reveal how much we knew about events. But when news came, at midsummer, of my father's death, and Queen Alyse gave me a new pony of my own as a comfort gift, Elaine and I would ride along the shore, ahead of the escort, and have long conferences. Elaine could talk of little else but Arthur. No one had seen him, no one really knew if he even existed, but Elaine knew all about him. She even knew what he looked like.

"He's dark," she confided. "Black hair and blue eyes, the true Celt. And stronger than any man his age."

"Which is all of thirteen," I pointed out, grinning. We were five and six years younger, but girls could be married off at twelve, while boys had to wait until fifteen to be made warriors. Elaine was undaunted.

"He's a Christian, too, so the men will follow him."

"How can he be Christian if Merlin the Enchanter has raised him? Everyone knows Merlin is a pagan and a powerful one. It is said he speaks to the gods directly and has seen Mithra himself slaying the Bull."

Elaine crossed herself quickly, then made a sign against the ancient evil spirits that was not Christian at all. "Hush, Gwen, don't say such things! You're blaspheming, I know it! Have you no fear? Anyway, Queen Ygraine is a Christian, even if the High King is not, and she wouldn't have him raised by a pagan household. And how can he lead Christian soldiers if he isn't one himself?"

"King Uther does. I don't think soldiers care so much, as long as their leader is successful. And I don't know about Queen Ygraine. I mean, she can't be much of a mother if she was content to give her firstborn son away three days after she bore him. She may not care how he is raised." I saw I had hurt Elaine, who adored her image of Prince Arthur, and I was ashamed of myself. "Never mind, Elaine. You are probably right. I'm sure he's a devout Christian like Father Martin and handsome, as well. He can probably do everything." But as her humor was restored, I fell to teasing her again. "But perhaps he is fair. King Uther was red-headed in his youth, they say, although now he is gray."

Elaine was unmovable on this point. "You forget his descent. Uther's line is dark. Uther's brother Ambrosius was dark, and Constantius, their father, was dark, and so on back to the Emperor Maximus, founder of the line."

"Who was Iberian, and not Celt," I reminded her. "And black-eyed, to boot."

Elaine sniffed. "Dark hair can be Celt, too, and blue eyes certainly are. Maximus married a Welsh princess from our own country, Princess Elen, and she had blue eyes. She's famous for it. Dark, brilliant blue, like the sea in a summer storm. She's my kin." Then she stopped, remembering that she was related to the famous Elen through her mother's line, and therefore I was descended from her, too. She looked at me cautiously. I knew already what she saw, because the color of my eyes had been compared to the Princess Elen's all my life.

"Well," I said quickly, "it's no wonder we think so much of Prince Arthur, since we are both kin to him, if you go far enough back."

Elaine looked delighted. This was the kindest thing I had ever yet said about Arthur, and she took it as a victory. The truth was, I disparaged him only to tease Elaine; but the skeptical attitude, once adopted, stuck. From that summer on, I was always finding fault with him, if only because Elaine thought him so perfect.

The sun returned when September came, but it was too late. The smell of rotting growth and mud stank in the river valleys, and men and beasts died from mysterious fevers. Water lay everywhere on the ground, breeding insects and disease. We could not bury our dead for the mud, and burned them instead on funeral pyres like the dead of the Saxon savages. The queen kept us to the castle and forbade our rides upon the shore, fearing we would catch noxious vapors and fall ill. Indeed, the youngest of Elaine's brothers fell to the fever in September, and the queen was prostrate with grief. Men muttered under their breaths of omens and witchcraft; women wore charms against ancient evils, the Christian women secretly and others, like Ailsa, actually jingled and clicked as they walked from the jumble of talismans they carried. Small offerings were made daily at the wayside shrines. The village folk had not forgotten the Elders. King Pellinore, saddened and restless, called in his men from their homes and drilled them mercilessly in preparation for action, any action, to keep their minds from dwelling on the death and stagnation that enveloped Britain.

And then finally, toward the end of that interminable month, the royal courier arrived. Elaine and I were on the eastern wall when he rode up the valley on his tired horse, spattered with mud and so exhausted he could barely stay in his saddle. We knew who he was by the leather pouch at his belt, and we exchanged glances behind the sentry's back, knowing we would creep out that night to overhear the king's conference.

The news was thrilling indeed. King Uther Pendragon was gathering his forces at Caer Eden, a week's march north, and all loyal Britons were called to arm and join him there to meet the Saxon attack. The time had come. Cheering filled the hall. The men sounded wild with happiness, as if the courier were bringing them tidings of great joy. The king proposed a toast, and as the men turned to their tankards and the noise died down, we heard Arthur's name.

"Will Arthur be there?" "Yes, will the great Enchanter reveal him now?" "Will Uther acknowledge him, I wonder, and give him a command?" "He's just a boy—how could he?" "Ah, but he's the royal heir, with black magic behind him, and we'll follow him anywhere."

King Pellinore hushed them, looking fierce under his bushy black eyebrows, but the courier fidgeted nervously. He was not charged with any official message about the prince, but rumor had it—rumor, mind you—that Merlin had been sent for. And where Merlin was . . .

This was the best news to come to Wales in years, and within two days every able-bodied fighting man had marched north to fight the Saxons, confident in the certain victory that the fabled Arthur would bring. Elaine was beside herself with excitement, but I felt the loss of the men keenly. There was no more news, no more eavesdropping, no more feeling a part of events. We had shrunk to a household of women, and our chief occupations were putting the castle to rights, getting in what little harvest there was, weaving and sewing against the inevitable winter cold, and for me and Elaine, uninterrupted lessons with Father Martin and Iakos.

We did not hear about the battle for two whole months, when it was long over and the glory of the battlefield had faded in the minds of the wounded and maimed, who were the first to come home.

Queen Alyse organized a primitive hospital in the castle out-buildings. It was not primitive by the standards of the day, only by comparison to what I have seen since, for there were no learned men of healing in Gwynedd, no army physicians, no Merlin. We were a community of women with skill to heal minor wounds such as men get hunting. Those soldiers who made it back to us were grateful for our attentions, but they were halfway to recovery before ever setting foot in the sickrooms. The worst wounded had died in the field hospital at Caer Eden, and more on the road home.

Elaine and I were not allowed to treat the men directly on account of our youth, and I was grateful for this. Nursing repelled me; I had not the stomach for maimed limbs and open sores and the stench of sickness. We were happy to help the washing women hang the clean linens to dry and fold them away, sweet-smelling and herb-scented, until the nurses needed them. We helped to change the bedding on the palettes that lined the floor and were allowed to bring around cool water for the men to drink.

One day, as Elaine and I stood outside the sickrooms, folding linens, I began to hum, and then sing, an old Welsh song I had learned in Northgallis about the beauty of Wales, her fertile meadows where sheep grazed in summer, her shining ponds and white-frothed streams, her cool forests full of game, and the crown of her glory, glittering Snow Mountain, where the gods walked among the clouds. Elaine loved the song and begged me to teach it to her, so I repeated it for her sake. Then we brought our folded linens to Cissa, the queen's lady-in-waiting who was in charge of the washing. To my amazement, she curtsied low before me.

"The queen's compliments, Lady Guinevere," she said softly, "and would you be pleased to continue singing, for the men were quiet and restful just now, and seemed relieved of pain. The queen tells me they had tears in their eyes, and indeed, my lady, it was beautiful to hear."

I stared, astonished that the queen favored me with such attention, and assured Cissa I would be delighted to sing. From that day forward, singing to the men was my chief duty, and Queen Alyse had a cushioned chair brought for me and set just inside the door, so that all could hear the song, and yet I was not overcome by the sickroom vapors. To show their gratitude, the men began to call me the Lark of Gwynedd.

As men healed and were allowed to sit outside in the afternoon sun and take exercise on the grounds, Elaine and I learned from them all we wanted to know about the great things that had happened in the north. To be sure, King Pellinore had sent his queen a messenger bearing news of the glorious victory over Colgrin and his Saxon hordes, of Uther's death and of young Arthur's succession. With the kings of Britain united behind him, the new King pursued the Saxons eastward, and Pellinore went with him, leaving Gwynedd in the capable hands of Queen Alyse.

But these were dry facts, and we sought among the convalescing soldiers for those who could tell us what we really wanted to know. Finally we found Corwin, a twenty-year-old foot soldier who had suffered a broken leg. He was lucky that the bones had not pierced the skin. Merlin himself, he said, had splinted the leg and prophesied that it would knit cleanly and straight. He had since fashioned himself a pair of crutches and got about easily enough. He had a ready tongue, a bard's gift for exaggeration, and a lazy nature. He spun us tales by the hour, and we believed them all.

"Tell us about the battle!" Elaine cried, settling down at his feet, her face aglow. "Did Prince Arthur fight?"

"Did he indeed!" Corwin exclaimed, grinning. "Why, he won it for us, you may be sure, and proclaimed himself by the deed, even if he was the last to know it."

"What do you mean, the last to know it?"

Corwin laughed. "Why, just what I said, my lady. When he came to Caer Eden with Sir Ector of Galava, he was more a body servant to Ector's son Kay than a warrior. By rights, he's a year or two short of making a soldier. He'd no more idea of who he was than Kay did himself, or I, or any man there, excepting only Ector, King Uther and that sly fox Merlin. And as far as anyone could see, Merlin was there alone, standing silently with his arms folded into his sleeves and a face as dark as stormclouds, watching everything, saying nothing, keeping his own counsel. No one gave a second glance to Ector's fosterling."

"Ector's fosterling?" I wondered.

"Oh, never mind that now!" Elaine cut in. "Go on, Corwin, tell us about the battle!"

Corwin settled himself among the cushions we had brought him. He had a Welshman's love of a good tale, and this had all the earmarks of an afternoon's work. "It was midmorning when we saw them coming across the river plain. You should have seen them—thousands of Saxons—blond giants with paint on their faces and four-foot moustaches, whirling their two-headed axes over their heads in a mad frenzy of noise. Wild men, they were, screaming uncouth paeans—I don't mind admitting it to you girls, but my bones were shaking."

Elaine giggled. "You're no soldier, then. Soldiers are never afraid."

"Aren't they, my lady? Well, that's as may be. I can only speak for myself. And yet I'll wager there wasn't a man on the field who saw them coming who didn't wish he were safely home in bed."

Elaine was scandalized. "You call Prince Arthur a coward? And King Uther? And Pellinore, my father?"

Corwin shook his head quickly. "Certainly not, little princess. Brave men, all of them. But if a man has no fear to face and overcome, where is bravery? He is a fool, that's all."

"Oh, stuff and nonsense. You're just making excuses. Go on with the battle!"

"He was, until you interrupted," I pointed out, and was rewarded with a bold retort and an angry shake of her head.

"I'll tell you this," Corwin cut in. "They almost took us. We were all looking about for Prince Arthur when the trumpets sounded, but no one saw him anywhere. Half the men watched Uther, half watched Merlin. But Uther lay abed upon his litter, with his own guards in attendance, and Merlin busied himself in the field hospital, paying no attention to anyone. Men began to doubt the prince had come. When the Saxons attacked, we gave up hope and followed the High King's litter onto the field."

Corwin's voice fell into the singsong lilt of the storyteller, and we hugged our knees and listened, enraptured.

"The Saxons attacked at the center of the line, where the High King's litter was. So savage they were, we could not hold them, and fell back against the onslaught. They pressed hard, eager to get to Uther, a sick king, and have it over early. Now, Sir Ector of Galava led the right flank, and saw his chance to cut the Saxons off. Good soldier that he is! If Lot, who led the left, had had the sense to do the same, the villainous dogs would have been swallowed up and surrounded. But Lot stood his ground and looked the other way."

"I hope he was hanged for his treachery!" Elaine exclaimed hotly.

Corwin laughed. "On the contrary, brave lass, he rides at the side of the young King as they chase Colgrin toward the sea."

Elaine objected violently, but I said, "Since he is alive, it is the best place for him, where Arthur can keep an eye on him."

Corwin regarded me thoughtfully. "So many have said, my lady, and Merlin one of them, if rumors be true."

"Well, I'd have killed him myself if I were king!" Elaine cried emphatically. "But go on, Corwin, what happened next? Don't take all day."

"For God's sake, Elaine—" I began, but Corwin raised a hand. "Bide a bit, young ladies, and let me tell the tale. You will know it all, in time. Well, there we were, face to face with the stinking Saxon hordes. Had Lothian grown roots in the hill, that he could not move? Was he waiting, as some were saying, to see which way the battle went? If the Saxons got to the King, he could join them from the flank and cut *us* off—the lines wavered, uncertain. Good Ector led the charge from the right and drove deep, with his son Kay right at his side. But an ax got his leg and he lost his sword; he had to withdraw. Young Kay tried to take his place—he fought hard, he's a valiant soldier—but he had no sense of the battlefield, of the flow of things, of where he was. He was pushing too hard in the wrong place, and the seasoned warriors all knew it. The charge began to waver, the lines began to weave, the Saxons scented the kill; for a moment it seemed that all was lost—the charge, the Briton positions, the field, the day, the High King, the Kingdom. For a moment—the same moment—every man on the field knew it, wherever he was. It was one of those moments when time stops, when the balance between two futures—defeat and victory, death and life, evil and good fortune—lies on a thin edge of chance." Corwin paused. We could have heard a leaf fall in the silence. "But it was no chance the unknown boy rode forward, raised his sword, gave the orders in a voice that brooked no hesitation, and saved the day. Out of nowhere he came; but he knew what to do, and every man there followed him. I followed him myself, and I don't know why. I'd never seen him before. But he'd a cool head on his shoulders, and he fought a damned smart fight. Before old Colgrin knew what had happened, he found himself pushed hard against the hill where Lothian waited, and King Lot, forced to choose and seeing a new commander bidding fair to take his place at the King's right hand, cast his future with the British and attacked. That was the end of it, really. It was all over but the mopping up."

"And then?" Elaine asked excitedly. "Surely everyone knew by then? Surely King Uther proclaimed him?"

"No, my lady. It's a busy time, after battle, with the field to clear and the wounded to tend. We all found our own camps and took stock of who was left."

"But you must have wondered who he was," I said, "and where he had come from."

"Oh, he was the talk of the army, of course. Who was the new commander? No one knew his name or had seen his badge. The word went round he was a child, a dogsbody, a nameless lad who tagged along in Kay of Galava's wake. Ector's fosterling, they said, meaning Ector's bastard, born on the wrong side of the blanket and good only for errands and hard labor."

"No! How did they dare!"

"Who was to know? A few bright souls wondered if it might be Prince Arthur in disguise—such a disguise!—but no one knew, and no one liked to wager on such a long shot. All that long night we carried the dead from the field, dug the grave pits, sorted their belongings, and tended to our wounds. That's when I broke my leg, in a scuffle with a half-dead Saxon who attacked me when I took his armband. In the field hospital I saw my cousin Durwen— the bardling, we called him, because he wanted to be a bard, he had a gift for it. He was delirious with pain from a slice across his thigh, but he had already made a song about the battle. "The Wrath of the Nameless Prince" he called it. He had sung it for Merlin, he claimed, as he stitched his leg, and Merlin had smiled."

Elaine wrinkled her nose. "Ector's fosterling? No, Corwin, it's too ignoble. Tell us rather that Merlin raised him in the Magic Isles across the Western Sea and brought him forth just in time to save us from the Saxons!"

"I'm telling you what happened, if you'll be polite like your cousin and wait for me to get there." Corwin winked at me and took another pull from his flask. "When the work was done, the men who were well and whole caroused till dawn. There were plenty of girls in Caer Eden to toast our victory. Ah, those lovely northern lasses—" He stopped, recollecting where he was, and cleared his throat. "Beg pardon. But I cursed the misfortune of my leg, I can tell you that. At daybreak we gave thanks to Mithra in a formal ceremony, with King Uther in attendance, pale as a nether spirit. And that night there was to be a formal victory feast. Rumor had it he was going to bring forth the prince at last and name his heir—he was dying on his feet, anyone could see it. Men looked all about for Prince Arthur but could not find him. Meanwhile, Ector's fosterling was in the hospital with Merlin, visiting the wounded and offering his arm to Ector so the man could walk. By daylight you could see he was only a beardless boy, and hopes fell." Corwin paused. "These things I saw and can swear to. The rest I know only because the camp was alive with rumors, and I spoke with men who had been at the victory feast, and—and at what came after."

Elaine and I looked at each other. He was making the sign against enchantment behind his back, and we wondered why. We had certainly heard no rumors of magic from the men, only bragging about the battle itself.

"Then suddenly, toward sunset, talk began to go through camp the King was dying. Everyone fell still. The guard was doubled around Uther's tent, and all the lords gathered inside, including Ector with Kay and the fosterling, and Merlin, and the kings of Rheged, Strathclyde, Cornwall, Elmet, Lothian, and Gwynedd. I can't tell you just what happened, because I wasn't there, but word went round that Uther, on his deathbed, proclaimed the fosterling to be his own son by the queen Ygraine, named him his heir, and bade the kings follow him. The lords took it as well as they might: Ector pleased as punch; Cornwall, Rheged, Strathclyde, and our own good King Pellinore cheered the lad and swore him faith. But Lothian was furious. Lot had schemed for years to become High King, betrothing Uther's bastard daughter for the purpose. She was there, you know, the beautiful Morgause, to persuade her father to the choice. But they reckoned without Arthur, those two." He turned to spit, then recollected his audience and contented himself with a gruff rumble in his throat. "There might have been a brawl, except that in the middle of the fracas, Uther died. And that put an end to the celebrations." The sadness in Corwin's face bespoke his loyalty to Uther. I was moved to see it. "It's an uncommon bad omen, victory or no victory, the High King dying while the Saxons still lay encamped across the river. Why, the smoke from their funeral pyres kept us up coughing half the night. A new King had to be chosen, and fast. And while young Arthur had been proclaimed, no one felt easy about making a child a King with such a deadly enemy so near. In the interim, King Lot took charge."

"Traitor!" Elaine cried.

"No, my lady, not really. It needed the strong hand of an experienced warrior the soldiers trusted. It was best for everyone. And who else to turn to? Merlin might have stepped forward, but he did not. He returned to the field hospital, and young Arthur with him, looking dazed and grim. Lot announced we would hold the victory feast as planned, in Uther's honor, and that afterward a council of commanders could discuss the wisdom of Uther's recommendation and choose the next High King."

"Uther's recommendation!" Elaine bristled. "How dare he! It is treason!"

"Nonsense," I retorted, tired of her interruptions. "We are not Roman yet. Kings are still chosen by the lords who must serve them."

"If the king's son or his nephew are not worthy!" Elaine cried, beside herself. "But *Arthur* is the King's son! He *is* worthy! Were they blind? Hadn't he just won the battle for them?"

"Yes," I replied calmly, "it is easy enough to sit here safe in Wales and say so, but imagine being a soldier in the field. What Corwin says makes sense to me. They were all grown men, kings and lords and warriors; they did not want to serve a boy."

"Exactly so, my lady," Corwin said sadly. "It is ever the way of men not to see what is before their noses."

"What happened at the victory feast?" I asked.

Corwin frowned. "Well, they fell to arguing as soon as the wine went round. I have this from Durwen, who dragged himself from bed to accompany Pellinore. There were lords in the hall who were in league with Lothian and objected that a boy not yet fourteen was too young to lead a troop of seasoned warriors, much less a kingdom. Some argued long and loud on Lot's behalf: Cyndeg of Gore, the snake Aguisel, a few others. Lot himself said nothing. Be sure he had paid them well beforehand for their speeches. They said the High King's dying in the face of Saxons was an omen, and that Britain itself would die if we did not change the line."

"Had they already forgotten who brought them victory? What better omen could there be than that?" Elaine was shouting.

"Soldiers are superstitious," Corwin replied, "as you very well know. Black Celts from the hills of Wales are the worst of all. There was many a man in that hall who took it as a sign from the gods that Uther's line ended with Uther's death. There were cries of 'Lothian! Lot for High King!' from one side of the hall, and cries of 'Arthur!' from the other. And then, when the hall was near to erupting into open warfare, Merlin the Enchanter arose before the crowd. One look from him froze the wagging tongues, and when it was quiet, he spoke. It did not matter, he told them, what choice men made. This King had been ordained by gods a hundred years before his birth. He was the Light of Britain; his time had come. That day he had proved his prowess before them all. He was Chosen, and the gods that made men would prove it so, that very night. Lot stood up and objected—he has more courage than I have, to face Merlin in the midst of a pronouncement, I grant him that—Lot stood up and objected that an army of men needed a man to lead them, not a boy, and talk about gods and magic and foretelling was so much stuff and nonsense, to borrow my lady's phrase. Merlin, cool as ice, gestured toward the unarmed boy, and said that Arthur stood before them without a sword, for a reason. It was not Uther's sword that would bring him into Kingship, but one given by the gods themselves. That very night, in the presence of them all, they would give the Sword into his hand, the Sword that would protect Britain from her enemies for as long as Arthur held it." Corwin paused. "Now, Merlin, besides having power from the gods, besides being wise beyond the wisdom of men, Merlin is also a showman of the first class. He let the questions run through the hall like wind through a hayfield, and then he let the murmuring die down, until all was still. And then, when he commanded every eye and every ear, he told the history of the Sword. It was, he said, the Sword of the Emperor Maximus."

Elaine and I gasped. All Welsh children were brought up on the story of Macsen Wledig, as the Welsh called Maximus, but the tale of the Sword was new to us. Magnus Maximus had been the last Roman commander in Britain; when the Romans pulled out, Macsen stayed with his Welsh princess Elen and forged the hill tribes of Britain into a Kingdom. It was the Sword of Maximus that turned aside the Saxons, the Picts, and the Irish in the dark time men call the Flood Year. Romano-British civilization teetered on the edge of extinction then, but Maximus' disciplined troops beat back the savages and won for Britain a breathing space of peace. He was acclaimed Emperor of Britain by the people and kept the peace in the Roman way.

But at length his ambitions outstripped his judgment, and he declared war on the emperor in Rome. He led his loyal British troops across the Narrow Sea into Gaul and across Gaul into Italy.

Some say he defeated the Emperor of Rome, some say he was defeated by him; whatever happened, he died there in Aquilea, and his remaining troops brought home his armor and his Sword. Many men stayed in Gaul and settled along the edge of the Narrow Sea in what men call Less Britain. The rest returned to Wales. His son Constantius ruled after him and was the ancestor of Constans, who was murdered by Vortigern, and of Ambrosius, who was the first to reunite the kings of Britain, and of Uther, who just managed to hold the Saxons at bay, until Arthur should come.

"It was written in the stars, Merlin said in a soft voice that carried to every corner of the hall, that in the dark hour the Light of Britain should arise with a Sword of wondrous brilliance: Maximus' own Sword, hidden in darkness for a hundred years, waiting for the hand of Britain's greatest King to lift it once again into the light."

He stopped and let the silence hang.

"Corwin," I whispered, "you should be a bard."

He laughed. "I may have to be, unless my leg heals straight. Anyway, those are Merlin's words about the Sword. Durwen told me, and he was there with King Pellinore. He *was* studying to be a bard and had learned how to get things by heart in one hearing."

"Was?" I asked quickly.

Corwin sobered. "Yes, my lady. The poor lad died on the way home of his wound. It was stitched, but he opened it again by sitting a horse too soon, and against orders."

"But the Sword!" Elaine cried impatiently. "What can you tell us about that? Where was it? How did Prince Arthur get it? And when did they proclaim him King?"

"Merlin claimed the Sword lay under Lluden's Hill, where it had been left by Maximus' chief captain. He had brought it north from Wales when Elen, in her grief, banished it from her sight. It lay in darkness, Merlin said, protected by the god of the place, to be raised into the light by him who was born the rightful King of Britain. He invited all the lords present to ride there, that very night, and witness its lifting. What could Lot do? Every lord in the hall, from king to count to troop captain, would have given years off his life to witness Merlin's powers in person. Lot had no hope of being acclaimed King in that hall; his only hope was to join the throng on Lluden's Hill and hope that Arthur or Merlin would fail." He laughed and then slowly sobered. "King Pellinore took only Durwen with him, because, according to Durwen, he

felt that the anointing of a new king should be witnessed by a
bard. Now, I suppose, it is left to me to tell it."

He paused again and, closing his eyes, spoke softly. "So they
took to horse and rode upstream along the river Eden. In the dark
hours of the morning they came to the black island that sits hard
by the ford. Lluden's Hill, the locals call it; it has been a sacred
place time out of mind. Merlin led them up the slope to an old
tunnel, hidden by undergrowth, and through it into a gigantic
cave. So large it was, none could see its roof, nor its ending. Their
torches shed a dim and smoky light, enough to glimpse the cold
immensity of the place and feel the weight of dark shadows pressing down." Elaine and I shivered, in spite of ourselves, and made
the sign against enchantment, although we were Christians. "Forty
men had followed Merlin, and they all stood within the cave,
shuffling and whispering, hearing their own voices speak back to
them from the living rock; a place haunted, Durwen swore, with
the spirits of the Elder past. Merlin stood up before them, a black
shadow in the darkness. 'Look before you,' he cried, 'and see the
Sword of Maximus!' And there it was, in the middle of the vast
cavern, stuck into the cleft of a huge rock. There it was; where a
moment before they had seen nothing, now they saw the split
rock, the dark shaft rising, the dim glow of the hilt seeming to
float in the very air. Merlin beckoned, they moved closer, the
bravest among them trembling. The scabbard was of some ancient
silken fabric, embroidered with the crude marks of the Old
Tongue that Britons spoke before the Romans came. Merlin raised
high a torch that all might see the writing: 'WHOSO LIFTS THIS
SWORD FROM THE STONE IS RIGHTWISE BORN KING OF ALL THE BRIT-
ONS.' He read it out in a voice of dread, and the echoes circled,
chilling the soul. 'rightwise born ... rightwise born ... King of
all the Britons.' "

"Corwin!" Elaine quavered, gripping my arm.

His eyes were closed. He did not even hear her. "No one dared
to breathe. The Sword stood in its dark sheath, dull and cold, and
all around the air stank with the sweat of fear. 'Let him who dares
touch the Sword,' Merlin called out. But no one moved. At last
King Lot stepped forward. 'I am fitter than any man here to be
High King,' he proclaimed, 'but I distrust magicians.' Merlin
folded his hands into his sleeves. 'Sir,' he said, 'there is no magic
in this place but what the gods have bestowed in the Sword itself.
I am powerless before it. If the Sword is yours, take it.' The lords
held their breath as Lot reached out, put his hand to the hilt, and
pulled."

Corwin opened his eyes and stared at us. "Then was the sacred silence rent with a mighty yell, for the Sword did not budge an iota, but Lot's hand was burned, the flesh seared across the palm where it had held the hilt. He withdrew his hand, white-faced with pain, and cursed Merlin for a lying, two-faced bastard." Elaine and I both gasped at such outrageous foolhardiness, but Corwin hardly paused for breath. "The company shrank back, afrighted. Someone called out, 'Let the boy try! Where's Ector's fosterling?' Arthur was pushed forward, and seeing that there was no way out of it, he stood straight as a spear before Merlin the Enchanter. 'Is it for me?' he asked the great magician. 'If you tell me to, I shall try it.'

"Oh, how brave he is!" Elaine gasped.

"How so," I countered, "when he has known Merlin his entire life? If there is not trust between them yet—"

"Oh, shut up, Gwen! You ruin everything!"

"Merlin told him," Corwin went on, ignoring us both, " 'it is yours, my lord King. It was made for your hand, even before it was made for Maximus.' So the lad went forward and put his hand to the hilt, and the great Sword slid as sweetly out of the sheath as a knife through butter. The torchlight caught the blade, setting it aglow; as he lifted it into the light, the great jewel in the hilt blazed into life. A huge emerald, hidden in the dark, struck its green fire into every soul and brought them all to their knees. Life! it signaled. Victory! As Arthur held it aloft he seemed to grow taller before their eyes. His face shone in the reflected glory of the Sword, a face full of pride and fierce determination. 'I shall call it *Excalibur*,' he said, which in the Old Tongue means 'unconquered.' Then every lord came and knelt before him to pay homage and receive his blessing. Lot was last, but he spoke well and promised faithful service. So they made him their King in that sacred place, King of all the Britons, and carried him outside as dawn broke in the east. And behind in the cavern the rock lay split in two halves, and the scabbard crumbled into dust, when the Sword was freed."

Elaine's eyes were as large as goose eggs. The magnificence of her hero had been amply confirmed.

"That's not the end." Corwin smiled. "While Durwen was busy spinning phrases in his head to recite to me, others among the lords, including Cyndeg and Aguisel, were grumbling that the whole thing had been a setup. Merlin had done nothing but lead them to the Sword. They might have sworn to follow the boy who held that Sword, but they wanted proof that Merlin's powers were behind him. The lifting of the Sword was not enough; they wanted more."

"What fools men are!" I breathed.

"And Merlin heard them. As they made ready to depart, with the new King at their head, Merlin turned around in the saddle and raised his arms. A thunderous crack rent the sky, a flash of fire burst forth, and the hillside above the cave came down. Trees bent double, horses bolted and men bellowed in fear, but Merlin sat and calmly watched Lluden's Hill slide into a mountain of rubble. When the last stone had tumbled to a stop at Merlin's feet, he coolly turned and surveyed the doubters, who shook before his gaze. Then he reined in and rode behind Arthur back to camp."

We brought Corwin a flask of honey mead and thanked him sincerely for his tale. Elaine was speechless for a while, but soon she found her tongue.

"And what does King Arthur look like?" she asked eagerly. "Do tell us."

Corwin looked a little blank. "What do you mean, my lady?"

"I mean, is he dark or fair? Tall or short? Lean or heavy?"

Corwin smiled and said to me, "It seems the young princess is not without ambition." I winked at a scarlet Elaine as he continued. "Well, from what I saw of him, he is tall for his age and slender for a warrior, but he is young yet. He is an excellent swordsman, near the best I have seen. What else? Let me see, brown hair, brown eyes, a clear skin with a serious expression, well featured, with a look of Uther about him, and when he was young Uther was considered handsome by all the ladies of the land." Then Corwin's gaze grew distant, and his voice pensive. "But I think what is most impressive about him is something that I cannot put into words. Men call it poise, or inner peace, or wisdom, or strength, or grace of bearing, but it is all those and more; he is a man in harmony with himself. He has a mission. He knows who he is."

"He must be a born leader," I said thoughtfully, "for the men he commands are seasoned warriors and kings in their own right. Sword or no sword, men like King Pellinore and my brother Gwarthgydd would not follow a mere boy."

"Indeed," Corwin agreed. "And it isn't due to Merlin's magic, either. For Merlin disappeared after the lifting of the Sword and hasn't been seen since. Yet the army is off after Colgrin, with King Arthur at its head."

"He will beat the Saxons," Elaine said confidently, "and drive them from our shores forever."

"It will be a miracle indeed if he does that," Corwin replied. "The Saxons have been living on the Shore since Vortigern first invited them, fifty years ago. There are children your age, my young lady, whose grandfathers were born in Britain. Small wonder they consider it their home."

"But we were here first," Elaine objected.

"We Welsh?" I asked her. "Or we British? We are led by a descendant of Maximus, who was a Roman and a foreigner. The Celts were here before the Romans, and the Ancients before the Celts. No one knows who was here before the Ancients. Perhaps the Saxons are next."

"That's treason!" Elaine cried, tears springing to her eyes. "Gwen, I will never forgive you unless you take it back! How can you say such a thing?" Even Corwin looked shocked.

"If it isn't possible to drive the Saxons out—and where, indeed, can they go? —then it will be necessary to treat with them. Yes, I know the old saying: A treaty with a Saxon is smoke in the wind, but it seems to me it's the strongest sword that prevails. Perhaps what Merlin said is true and that Arthur's Sword is the strongest. Then we shall have peace with the Saxons." I could see that they both were calmer, and Elaine was on the verge of forgiving me. "Who knows? In two hundred years perhaps even the Saxons will be British."

Elaine gasped in horror and began to berate me; Corwin looked afraid.

"My lady Guinevere, it is not my place to say so, but these are not matters that should concern young maids. These are high matters, and beyond such as me; they are better left to the king's council chamber. You have a mind, my lady, which may bring you grief if you give it tongue. Such thoughts are better left unspoken."

It was good advice. I did not tell him that it was talk in the king's council chamber that had given rise to these thoughts, voiced here for the first time. I accepted his rebuke, apologized to Elaine, and kept my thoughts to myself thereafter. It was twenty years before I found a mind receptive to these thoughts: a man who accepted them and went beyond them, who believed in compromise and in the value of other cultures besides his own, a man who envisioned the entire civilized world as one community. That man was Mordred.

4 THE SIN

During the next five years King Pellinore was often from home while Arthur's new Kingdom fought for its fledgling life. The Saxons had been soundly defeated at Caer Eden, and Colgrin their leader had died of wounds received on that field. But there were other war leaders eager to fill Colgrin's place. Caelwin, Colgrin's second-in-command, organized the East Saxons, treated with the Angles, and with their combined forces fought to establish a new beachhead along the eastern shores. If Lot of Lothian treated with them, it would split Britain in two.

And along the Saxon Shore arose a youth who dared to call himself King of the West Saxons: Cerdic the Aetheling, Eosa's son, who promised his people freedoms and rule by law, should they conquer Britain. I wondered at his temerity—was not Roman law good enough for the likes of him?

But Arthur led his troops to victory after victory, with great losses on the Saxon side and few on his own. Young as he was, older men granted him their respect, and hardened warriors deferred to his opinions, for there is no talisman luckier than victory, and he did not seem able to lose. Everywhere they were attacked, Britons fought bravely, from king to foot soldier, knowing that the High King would come to their aid with his invincible Sword, Excalibur, and his companion force of trained warriors.

Without fail Arthur came and conquered. By the time I was ten he was already a legend in his own land. He never lost so much as a skirmish. His name was a password for victory, and men said he had only to appear on the horizon for the Saxons to turn and flee.

Elaine believed every word she heard about him, and I was forced to stop my teasing under the pressure of her adoration. She even fasted the whole day of his coronation, while everyone else feasted. He was no longer our hope, she told me with earnest passion, he was our savior. And truly, I could not in good grace quarrel with her, for the kings of Britain hastened to unite behind this fearless warrior, and for the first time in men's memories Wales, Cornwall, Rheged, Lothian, and scores of lesser kingdoms felt a kinship with one another—we were all part of one realm.

This took time to achieve. Indeed, for the first year of his reign, Arthur was busy fighting stop-gap battles in the east, north, and southeast. He had been High King for over six months before the Saxons left him enough breathing space to get himself crowned. It was a Christian ceremony, and he was anointed by a Christian priest at Pentecost, but it was held in the old fighting fortress of Caerleon with a minimum of ceremony, because, in the King's own words, there was little time. Most of his attendants were his troops and nobles, although all the lords and ladies of the land had been invited. King Pellinore and Queen Alyse attended, for Caerleon, lying on a hill above the Severn, was but four days' journey south. It was April, and spring was early that year, so the roads were clear and they made good time. According to Elaine, Pellinore had intended to take only his soldiers with him, but the queen refused to be left behind. She claimed she didn't care if she had to sleep in a tent; she wanted to see the young High King crowned.

When she returned, she was the center of all our attention, and one afternoon, in an expansive mood, she gathered us all around her: her waiting women, Elaine and me, and our nurses, and she told us all about it.

It was not grand, she said, more a meeting among war leaders than a social event, but the High King's mother, the lady Ygraine, had come up from Cornwall and had spent much time with Alyse, one of the few queens close enough to attempt the journey. Ygraine still grieved for her lost Uther and looked pale and wasted. Her physician traveled with her, but it was Merlin who concocted her a brew that brought color to her cheeks and allowed her to attend the ceremony without exciting her son's attention.

"Merlin!" Elaine cried. "Was he there? Did you really see Merlin the Enchanter, Mother? Were you in the room with him? What does he look like?"

Queen Alyse laughed gently. "You young ones grew up on the tales of his doings, I see, and to you he is a creature of fable. But he is real enough, I assure you. And free of arrogance, for such a powerful man. Without him, young Arthur would not now be King."

"Saints preserve us!" Grannic cried, crossing herself, and Ailsa clutched the amulet at her breast.

"Is he very fearful, Mother?" Elaine whispered. "Did you see him use magic?"

"No, child. He came often to visit Ygraine. They are old friends. But he used no magic except what he put in the broth that gave her the strength to see her son crowned."

"Is he ugly, Mama?"

"Goodness, no. He is tall, of course, and dark. Black hair and eyes. You would think him old, but I do not. He is slender and quiet and does not say much. He listens to everything. They say the young King loves him as a father and depends upon him greatly. Not for fighting, of course. By his own admission Merlin is no swordsman. But for matters of state, I should imagine he is the wisest advisor a king could have."

"What was the coronation like, Mother? Did you have to stay in a tent? Did you get to see King Arthur? Is he handsome and fierce? Tell us!"

Alyse laid a gentle hand on Elaine's head, and I watched her eyes. They looked through Elaine to something beyond. "We were lodged in a house next to Ygraine's. It was a high honor, for there are few private dwellings there yet, although I hear the High King has plans for the place. Yes, I saw the High King at the ceremony and afterward, when he greeted his guests. He is just fourteen, but already an experienced war leader. You could see it in his eyes, his bearing, his sureness. He is—he is—" she paused, searching for the words to describe the youth she saw in her mind's eye. "He is tall, but not too tall, he is handsome, but not to swooning point. He has a look of Uther about him, but not his temper, God be praised. And by all accounts he is moderate in his habits." No one needed to remind us of Uther's reputation for womanizing. It was a saying that he had never slept alone. "But one doesn't see him in that way. What you see is singleness of purpose, of youth and strength and joy. He was born for this, Merlin said to Ygraine, and it seems he knows it." She sighed and smiled gently. "As a mother, I would want him for my son. Were I a girl again, I would want him for my husband."

Elaine caught my eye and sighed in deep satisfaction. Alyse continued her account of her visit and the nobles she saw, but for Elaine the rest was chaff. She had her fantasy of Arthur confirmed and was happy to bursting point.

* * *

Those were good years, those early ones. While Elaine and I studied Latin and Greek and figuring, learned stitching and weaving and housekeeping, raced along the rocky beaches on our ponies, and listened in on the king's councils when we could, Arthur was busy repairing the Kingdom's defenses, building roads and fortresses, setting up communication links of signals fires from hilltop to tor top, refurbishing ransacked towns and castles, restoring life and trust to the land. He traveled constantly from kingdom to kingdom, renewing treaties and helping lords with their local problems in return for their pledge to come to his call. Around him he gathered the young men of the kingdoms, nobles' sons, and forged them, through friendship, into a close-knit group. With the help of a king's son from Less Britain, who was a consummate horseman, Arthur sent to Gaul for fine, swift horses and crossed them with the strong, native breeds to get warhorses unsurpassed in power, speed, and intelligence. Arthur's mounted Companions became a swift, mobile cavalry and one of his deadliest weapons.

But as they say in Wales, every sun has its shadow. No one is immune from slander, and one day I heard a tale that wove a dark thread of evil into the fabric of the new King's glory. I was in my horse's box, rubbing him down after a ride and grooming his silken coat, a job I preferred to do myself than leave to a groom, when I heard men talking.

One of Pellinore's men spoke carelessly as he handed over his sweated horse; I had lingered long after my ride and no doubt they thought I had returned to the castle with Elaine.

"Ho there, Stannic, how goes it?"

"Well, young master, thank you kindly. You made good time. We weren't expecting you before sundown."

"I hurried from York," the trooper replied, and then their voices became muffled as they went together into the horse's stall. I was about to straighten up and slip out, when I caught the High King's name and the word "massacre." Quickly I crouched in the corner of the box and kept as still as I could. The trooper came out and lounged nearby in the aisle, speaking with the voice of one who delights in bearing bad news.

"They are talking about it all over York," he gloated. "Two hundred babies, they say, all boys, all newborns, set adrift in a fishing craft with the sail lashed to the tiller and the course set for the rocks. I got it from a man who got it from his sister, and she lives in Dunpelder."

Dunpelder! The capital of Lothian. Lot's city.

"Oh, he was in a rare fury was King Lot. Put yourself in his shoes, Stannic. You're away campaigning with the High King, your bride of eight months tucked safely away in your castle, with guards aplenty. You have left her with child, but what do you find when you return for her lying-in? A slender wife, an empty crib, a thin tale of an early birthing and a quick death. And all the while the place is buzzing with the rumors of a strong boy born six weeks ago, looking no more like Lot than a dragon does an eagle!"

Stannic mumbled something, and the trooper laughed. I wondered what this common little tale had to do with the High King.

"Yes, there was a child, all right. But she hid him well. She's a witch, you know, a proper sorceress as well as a beauty. I'd say she was capable of anything. Seduction and deception would come as natural as breathing to her. Oh, it's not Lot's child, that's for sure. Lot beat her till she was well nigh senseless but could get no truth from her. All York is full of the news."

"Is that why he killed the children?" Stannic asked. "To find the boy?"

"Did I say it was Lot's doing? The babe had other enemies. Can't you guess whose child it was?"

"Her bath slave? The captain of the guard?"

The trooper paused, and I feared he would leave his tale unfinished, but he had only stopped to drain his hip flask, for I heard him push the stopper in and belch.

"Listen, Stannic," he continued, but very softly, and a curious, stealthy quality in his voice sent a shiver of fear down my spine; I crept to the front of the box to hear. "Can't you guess the reason for Lot's fury? No, no, if it had just been the queen's bastard, he'd have tossed it out, not sought to kill it. You never heard the rumors then? There was talk after Caer Eden about them. Morgause and Arthur, I mean. Before she was married to Lot, and before he was proclaimed King Uther's son." His voice fell to a hoarse whisper, and I strained to catch it. "The young prince shared her bed there, they say, his first woman, the night of his victory. And that she carried his child within her when she wed Lot soon after. You can be sure Lot had heard the rumors and wanted no Dragon chick in his nest, bastard or not."

"Does the High King know?" Stannic asked, coming out of the box.

"Well, that's the question of the hour, isn't it? Someone's troops invaded the city and slayed every newborn male child. Every house was searched. Babies dragged from their mothers' breasts, lifted sleeping from their cradles, and thrown into an open boat. They said you could hear the cries of those babies for hours after the boat was out of sight, and of course the wailings of the mothers for days on end . . . No, none survived. The bodies all came in on the tide three days ago."

"Are you suggesting—" Stannic's voice was shaking, "—are you suggesting they were *royal* troops?"

"Who knows? They wore no badge. And it stands to reason the King would want to kill the child. What a hostage to his future that would be, a bastard son raised by the Witch of Lothian!"

"Not this King," Stannic whispered. "He's but a youth yet. He's no evil in him."

"And who stands behind him at his right hand but Merlin the Enchanter, master of the black arts? Don't tell me, my man, it isn't possible. With kings, anything is possible. The north country is already laying the blame at Arthur's door. York is divided. In the south, they'll probably blame Lot."

"I blame the Witch herself!" Stannic cried, and the trooper laughed.

"Well, no doubt, she is the root of all the trouble. So beautiful, they say, she turns men's wits. But would she give the order to murder innocent children?"

"She might, to safeguard the boy. Bastards have come to power before now. Didn't you say Lot had beaten her in a temper? Well, I've known women who would do any evil thing to cover the tracks of a lie. If she'd hidden the baby well, as you said, she could slay the city's children and keep her dangerous son safe. That would cool the king's anger and still the wagging tongues."

"Hmmm. Perhaps, if you think a woman capable of murdering children. I don't know. But it was a terrible, black deed, and the blame for it must settle somewhere."

"I pray the Goddess it does not settle on the young King."

"Even if it doesn't, he will suffer for it. How would you like a crafty wolf like Lot murdering a host of innocents just to kill yours? Leave you with a bad taste in your mouth, wouldn't it? Leave you feeling a little unclean?"

I believe I screamed in horror, but my hands were over my mouth, and they were walking away together, so they did not hear me. The trooper left, but Stannic came back and walked down the aisle, checking the horses. I was pressed frozen against the door, and he did not see me. He doused the oil lamp, closed the door, and went out. I went to my dozing horse and wrapped my arms around his neck, burying my face in his rough mane to hide my tears.

I knew, as the trooper told the story, that there was more to it than he was telling, or perhaps than he knew, and when he said the word "unclean" I knew suddenly what it was. Morgause was Uther's bastard daughter, born before he married the Queen Ygraine. *She was Uther's daughter. Arthur's sister.* I crossed myself quickly as I thought the unclean thought. It had been a sin time out of mind. Could it be true? Could the High King have done such a thing? I remembered the tales that had circulated among the returning wounded at that time, that the prince was kept ignorant of his birth, at Uther's wish, until Uther proclaimed him on his deathbed. That was the day after the battle, when they celebrated the victory. Was it possible, then, that when he went to Morgause he did not know who he was?

But if he sinned in innocence, he must have realized the truth the next day, when Uther acknowledged him. Hadn't Corwin described him as dazed and grim soon after the announcement? Here was a motive for murder stronger than any the trooper had named. Such a son would be a blight upon his honor, a smear across his good name, as well as a threat to his power. Lesser men had done greater evil for smaller sins than that!

I found myself shaking badly. There seemed no way out of the dilemma. Either Arthur was guilty of incest or of murder, and perhaps of both. Our new King, our stainless, shining hope, would bear forever the taint of evil, once the news got out.

I realized suddenly that the trooper had come home to tell the news at the council table, and I straightened and stilled my trembling. I would dampen my clothing in the horse's trough and feign illness, so Elaine could not persuade me to go out on the turret and eavesdrop tonight. Someday she might find out, and if the story of the massacre was spreading across Britain with the speed it was spreading across Wales, then it was likely she would hear it from someone, but it wasn't going to be me. Elaine was my only friend, and I was going to keep her Arthur untarnished for her.

5 THE GIFT

Queen Alyse and her ladies-in-waiting sat stitching and dozing in the queen's garden, enjoying the soft sea breeze and the warming sun of midmorning. The winter had been a hard one, and more than one of the women nursed a lingering cough. It was luxury to spend the day outside the cold castle walls, delighting in the sun, the smells of new growth, and the early birdsong.

It was the first of May and my thirteenth birthday. Father Martin released us early from our lessons, praising our progress and pretending he didn't know it was my birthday. There were celebrations in the village, where maids plaited wildflowers into their hair and danced with the young men, and the smoke from their feast fires drifted up the hill to our castle. This was Beltane, a day sacred to the Goddess, and while King Pellinore and Queen Alyse kept a Christian household, most Welshmen honored the Mother as well as Christ and observed her holy days.

I had been looking forward to this day for a long time, because I was sure that on this day God would make me a woman. I had prayed so hard and tried so earnestly to keep all His commandments, obeying even the most stringent of the rules set down by Queen Alyse for ladylike behavior.

And more than that, I had learned, at great cost to my pride, to take my appointed place in Elaine's shadow. When she was willful I did not thwart her, but found some politic way, if I could, to temper her headstrong ways and yet avoid her anger. When I failed, and her silly schemes ended in disaster, I learned to hold my tongue when I was blamed. Once when Elaine and I sneaked down to the buttery to steal the new cream from jugs just set out, the cook caught us and scolded us roundly for our greed. Knowing from long experience whose idea it was, she chided Elaine for her appetite and threatened to tell the queen. That very morning

49

Alyse had lectured Elaine about her fondness for sweets and cream, so Elaine turned around and blamed the adventure on me. Because I knew I would pay for it well if I denied it, I confessed, and from then on Alyse concluded that it was I who was responsible for every lump of sugar that went missing from the storerooms.

When there was punishment, I took it. Afterward, Elaine would give me a sweet apology and a promise of better behavior. And if Alyse frowned and scowled and called me a young fool, I could always rely on Pellinore's forgiveness. He could not bear to see me out of temper and would tease me back to good humor with all the good-hearted boisterousness in his generous nature.

For these sacrifices, I was sure God would answer my prayer. Although Elaine was a year younger than I was, she had already grown round breasts and hips and had passed her menarche. All I had done was grow taller. I was taller now than Queen Alyse, but straight as a boy, with no sign that my body would ever change. But I was sure God had heard my prayers. Father Martin said He paid special attention to the requests of virgins.

Queen Alyse and her ladies had made us each a new dress to celebrate the day, and we hurried to change into them. Elaine's was made of a sky-blue cloth, soft and fine, that matched her eyes exactly. It had a high belt and rounded throat, accentuating her budding figure. She looked beautiful. Mine was a soft, spring green, the color of new leaves cut out of silk that must have come from the warm lands far to the south. The lace at the throat was a sign of love and honor, for lace was rare in Britain and very costly. But the dress fit like a glove and could not hide the straightness of my frame. Next to Elaine, I looked like one of Alyse's garden scarecrows.

"Gwen!" Elaine gasped. I turned to find her staring at me in distress.

"What's the matter?"

She shook her head angrily. "You have no right to outshine me!" she blurted. "Change your dress!"

"What? What are you talking about?"

"You know full well what I am talking about! You have been admiring yourself in the bronze half the morning! I mean it, I will not be outdone!"

"Outdone, indeed!" I retorted. "It ill becomes you to mock me, Elaine. Just because you look like a woman of twenty, and I—I—I will grow a shape someday and find a husband, just wait and see!"

"Too soon for me!" she cried, in tears.

"Good heavens, Elaine! Are you blind? Come and look at yourself! You look fit to be courted by one of the High King's Companions!"

This was the highest compliment I could think of, for the King's Companions were the finest men in all the land. But it did not please her; she scowled and turned away. I did not dream, then, of Elaine's ambition.

"Fat chance I shall have of ever courting anybody, Gwen, until you are married. Who will look at little Elaine, standing in Guinevere's shadow?"

I grabbed her arm. "What nonsense is this? You are Pellinore's daughter! Have some sense, Elaine!"

But she pulled away angrily. "Leave me alone! You'd just better leave me alone!" And she fled out the door and down the corridor before I could stop her.

"What have I done?" I cried to Ailsa, who bent to retrieve the comb Elaine had thrown aside. "What did I say? Do you know what is the matter?"

"Indeed"—she smiled—"but pay it no mind, my lady. It's an illness without a cure."

"Well, whatever is amiss?" I demanded. "Tell me!"

She looked up slowly, her eyes narrowing in laughter. "Be easy, my lady. If you don't know yet, time will tell you. Go on down to her now and be kind to her. You can bring her around, if you try."

I composed myself as best I could and went down to the garden, where I knew the queen was waiting for us. Elaine was there before me, but she kept her eyes in her lap and did not greet me. The conversation centered on the big event of the day, which was Pellinore's return from King Arthur's court. He was bringing me a special birthday gift, the messenger had said, but it was a great secret. Not even Alyse knew what it was.

Pellinore had been gone three months with his troops of fighting men, helping the High King repair the defenses along the Saxon Shore. Rumor had it they had been with Arthur when they defeated a Saxon force newly landed in longboats. The Saxons had been many in number, and the High King's force was small, only Pellinore's foot soldiers and those of two lesser lords of the Summer Country, but the Saxons had been without horses, and Arthur's Companions had demolished them. The young knight from Less Britain, Lancelot of Lanascol, who had bred and trained the horses, had been honored at the victory feast. The

High King graciously gave him credit for the victory and made him first among the Companions, his second-in-command. The fact is, he already was in all but name, for having no kin in Britain, he of necessity lodged and traveled with the High King, and they had become close friends.

Now the messenger had said the King had moved north to York, and Pellinore was coming home for what we all hoped was a long stay, bringing with him a surprise.

I picked up the piece of stitchery I was working on and listened almost absentmindedly to the women talking, my thoughts full of womanhood and distress at Elaine's sudden temper. Would she never cease her childish sulking and be my friend again?

"Melwas is King of the Summer Country," Alyse was saying, "although they say it is his sister Seulte who rules there. She claims to be a witch, but those who live there on Ynys Witrin say her foul temper is only bitterness at her inability to find a husband." Leave it to Alyse, I thought, to touch unerringly on Elaine's sorest spot.

"Isn't there a shrine to the Good Goddess on Ynys Witrin?" Elaine asked swiftly, to divert her mother. "I'm sure I heard it somewhere, but I thought there was a monastery there, too. How can there be both?"

"My goodness, Elaine, how do you get your information? You have never been to the Summer Country, and I am sure I did not know anything about it until Pellinore spent so much time there in the last year."

Of course we had got the information by eavesdropping. I caught Elaine's quick, warning glance and hid a smile. She turned an innocent face to her mother. "I don't know, Mother, I must have picked it up at the stables, I guess. Sometimes the men talk when they don't know young maids are about."

A chill of horror shot through me, and I almost gasped, reminded of the trooper from York. Was it possible Elaine knew the wretched tale, or had it merely been an arrow in the dark? I bent low over my work to hide my face.

"Ah, well, little pitchers have big ears. Yes, Avalon lies on Ynys Witrin below Melwas' fortress, the Christian monastery farther up the Tor. The monks and the Ladies of the Lake get along well enough. They are all in the service of the Divine. The priestesses are skilled in the healing arts, as the monks are in prayer and meditation. There has been no trouble there, at any rate. The trouble has all come from Melwas. He is young and handsome and is a likable enough fellow, I gather, but he has rather an eye for the girls in training. I understand he has ruined more than one pretty acolyte, and he is only twenty."

"Perhaps," one of her ladies said, "it is time for him to marry."

"No doubt it is, Cissa. But his sister stands in his way. No one is good enough for the lady Seulte, although I daresay Melwas himself is not so choosy. But he will not cross his sister, who feeds him full of praise and ambition, and so he bides by her will. Pellinore fears there will be more trouble in that quarter for some time."

"But at least it's only woman trouble," Leonora said.

"Perhaps," said Cissa, "he should look farther north for his bride." She turned and smiled at Elaine, who colored. I shot Elaine a triumphant glance, but she ignored me.

Alyse paused and looked at both of us thoughtfully. "Perhaps," she said, "but there is time yet. And I haven't told you the big news." She put down her work and gathered our attention. "I expect we will hear the details when King Pellinore comes home tonight, but I don't see why I can't tell you now what I know of it. As you know, the High King has been looking to build a fortress for his troops for some time. Caerleon, reinforced though it is, is not big enough. He has collected many men who follow him, not to mention the horses, and there are no hill forts large enough to accommodate his household. So a month ago they broke ground at a new site."

This set the ladies chattering with delight. At last the kingdom would have a center, a court that did not have to migrate from kingdom to kingdom, a place Arthur could call his own.

"It is in the Summer Country, which is what made me think of Melwas," Alyse continued. "On a high tor, flat-topped and long-sloped, within sight of the signal fires on Ynys Witrin. It sits near the river Camel, and there is a spring near the summit. It is rumored that before winter the fortifications will be complete, and lodging for the troops and horses ready. The castle, of course, will take longer."

What need had Arthur of a castle, I thought to myself, if he had good fortifications and lodgings for troops and horses? For five years he had done without either consistently and was still victorious wherever he raised his Sword.

"This is good news indeed, my lady," Cissa cried. "And perhaps, in two or three years, when he has built a home to bring a bride to, the High King will marry at last." It had long been a worry among my lady's maids, and I suspect among many of the ladies of the land, that the young King had not yet given a thought to marriage. He was now eighteen, well grown, well favored, war-hardened, and beyond all doubt the most eligible bachelor in the land.

Queen Alyse laughed in delight. "Cissa, my dear, you anticipate me. The new court at Caer Camel was but half my news. Hear this. The High King is betrothed and will wed come September."

I happened to be looking at Elaine and saw her blanch. She bent her head quickly, but I had seen tears forming in her eyes. With the swiftness of a lighting flash, I understood at last.

"Who is it, my lady?" the ladies were asking with eagerness. "Who backed her? What is her family?"

Queen Alyse took time to hush them, and Elaine struggled valiantly to compose her features. "She is the daughter of the Earl of Ifray, who was killed in battle at Duke Cador's side four years ago. Her mother died at her birth, and she has been raised in Cador's household since her father's death. Remember that the High King made Cador of Cornwall his heir until a prince should be born. And Cador is on excellent terms with his stepmother, the queen Ygraine." The women nodded solemnly to one another. There were no stronger backers in the land than the High King's mother and his heir-apparent, excepting only Merlin.

"She is sixteen," the queen continued, "and quite pretty, by all accounts. She has had speech once or twice with the High King." At least they know one another." Alyse had married Pellinore for love, which was almost unheard of at that time, and firmly believed that young maids should not be given in marriage to strangers. "And her name," Alyse said, "is Guenwyvar." They all gasped in surprise and then looked at me sidelong, as if I had lost by a near miss.

"Lord be praised," Leonora murmured. "At last we shall have a Queen and Arthur's line shall be established."

"Yes," the queen continued. "And it has been in my mind, that after the building at Caer Camel is finished, the High King and his Queen will want company at court, and his Companions may want wives, if the wars allow. It may be we shall move to the Summer Country in two years' time." The ladies looked at us and smiled knowingly.

Elaine's misery was heartbreaking to see, but no one seemed to notice it but I. As soon as I could, I made some excuse to leave, and Elaine followed me willingly. We fled to our room, and Elaine burst into sobs upon her bed. I sat beside her and stroked her fair hair. It was the color of ripe grain, dark gold and glowing.

Much lovelier, to my mind, than my white-gold hair, a childhood color I had yet to outgrow, and which always made strangers stare.

"I'm sorry, Elaine. I had no idea. I knew you idolized him; he has been your hero since tales about him first started to go round. But I never knew you really—expected to—"

"Oh, stop!" Elaine sobbed. "I knew it was hopeless, but I couldn't help it! I knew this would happen! And now Mother thinks to marry us off to his Companions!"

"Would that not be an honor?" I asked her. "Surely any maid chosen by the Companions would be among the first in Britain."

"I don't care! Oh, Gwen, it would be too awful! To be there in the High King's court and married to someone else. I couldn't stand it! And I don't *want* to marry anyone else! I shall never marry! Never!"

I tried to soothe her and calm her, but she so enjoyed her weeping fit that she ceased to fight for control and grew hysterical. It took Grannic and Ailsa both to calm her, with cold cloths to her head and warm blankets on her body. This was Elaine at her most tiresome; she often enjoyed the complete release of her emotions, always suffering dreadfully for it afterward, with headaches that could last days, but in a strange way I did not understand, she enjoyed the suffering, too.

I left her to the nurses, who calmed her to sleep, and went to the stables. My brown gelding Peleth was beyond his best years, which is why King Pellinore had taken him from a trooper and given him to me. But he was willing and had been an athlete in his prime, and I had taught him a new skill in his old age: I had taught him to jump. We had begun with natural barriers on the woodland trails: downed trees, rain-washed boulders, low walls, but these became easy with practice, and lately I had secretly built obstacles from branches, rocks, and greens, some wide and some tall, and he learned to take them all with ease. It was a wonderful feeling, flying through the air with the wind whipping my hair, and Peleth loved it.

I was not yet a woman; I checked before I went out, but the day was only half spent, and there was still time. We practiced jumping until he took all his fences perfectly, and then went for a gallop along the beach. The day was mild and clear, and the sea spray cold. We returned as the sun dipped toward the hilltops, splashed with seawater, sand, and mud, and very tired and happy. I did not go in the stable, but left him with the groom, for I knew I was late and had probably been missed.

Ailsa was in a panic. "My lady, where in the name of all the saints and devils have you been? King Pellinore has returned, and we are bidden to dinner! And look at you! You've torn your tunic, God knows on what"—she crossed herself quickly—"and your leggings are filthy!"

I laughed as she tugged the tunic off. "This is nothing, Ailsa. You should see Peleth!"

"What will become of you!" she wailed. "You're as wild as an Irish elf and shall never find a husband!"

She had touched inadvertently on my innermost fear, and I felt the gaiety drain from my body.

Ailsa saw it and began to croon lovingly. "That's just my way of talking, my lady. Don't pay any heed to a silly old woman. You're as lovely as a summer's eve, and as soon as the Good Lady blesses you with your monthlies, there's not a prince in the land who won't be knocking at King Pellinore's door for your hand. Mark my words, my lady. Remember what the witch foretold. First in the land will you be."

A sob rose in my throat, but I swallowed it back. Giselda's prophecy! It was clear to me now. The witch had been right. I might be flat-chested forever, a spinster and a burden in my old age, but no matter. The first in the land bore my name.

I had missed King Pellinore's arrival, and remembering that the feast tonight was held in my honor, I lifted my skirts and raced down to the greeting hall. I was surprised to see that Elaine had recovered enough to join the ladies seated about the great log fire. Usually she was long abed after such weeping. I supposed she had been made to join the birthday celebration; she looked pale and unhappy.

King Pellinore stood beside the queen's chair, holding Alyse's hand. His affection for her was a true one, and he never strove to hide it. He had two visitors with him, a man and a youth, but they stood with their backs to me, facing the fire, so I came upon them unawares.

"Ah, here's Gwen!" the king cried, smiling kindly at me.

I curtsied low before him. "Please forgive me, gracious king. We are so happy to see you safely returned to us, and I did not mean to be late. It was—"

He laughed and raised me, hugging me warmly. "The horses, no doubt. What else? Come, see who I have brought back with me from court."

I turned and faced two tanned, black-haired warriors, no taller than myself, with thick, strong bodies and dark pelts of hair along their arms. The younger of the two, after a wide-eyed glance at me, studied the floor; the elder grinned at me, his black eyes sparkling.

"Gwarthgydd!" I gasped, throwing myself into his arms. "Oh, Gwarthgydd, my brother!"

He laughed and swung me around. "Little Guinevere, I'd not have known you! Look at you, taller than me, by Mithra! You are a beauty, Gwen, there's no denying it." He turned to the youth beside him. "This will be something to tell your mother, Gwillim, won't it?"

"Gwillim!" I cried, staring at him. I had not recognized him at all. Of course he was taller, but that wasn't it. He was fourteen, had grown a beard and moustache, and looked at me with the eyes of a stranger. But I hugged him nevertheless. We had been playmates once. He stiffened and nearly fell to one knee, but restrained himself.

"Oh, Gwillim, I am so glad to see you! How came you to be here? Have you been with the High King? Did you not stop at Northgallis? Did you come on to see me?"

Gwillim was clearly speechless, so Gwarthgydd replied. "To see you, dear sister, and to honor King Pellinore, who invited us most kindly. And to show Gwillim his first sight of the sea." His glance flicked ever so slightly toward the moody Elaine, and I noticed that Pellinore was smiling at Alyse. "And to show Gwillim the beauties of Gwynedd," he finished politely. I understood instantly. They had come to inspect Elaine.

King Pellinore was clearly delighted, but Queen Alyse did not return his smiles. After the conversation in the garden I understood she had much higher ambitions for her daughter than marriage to a Welsh lord. Everyone was polite, of course, and conversation never lagged. King Pellinore's table was unlike any other I had heard of—it was round. The beauty of this arrangement was that it allowed everyone to see and talk to everyone else. There were long trestle tables and benches, as well, which were used to feast troops after victories of importance, or on high holy days, but always the family sat at the round table.

There was much toasting my health, and conversation about the Saxon wars, which was supposed to be above the ladies' heads, but which I listened to avidly. Elaine kept her eyes on her plate like any shy, young maid being courted for the first time. But I knew it was not modesty but misery that was blanketing her high spirits. And Gwillim, who should at least have shown some interest, if only curiosity, about the girl his father offered for, either looked at his own plate or looked at me. Try though I might, I could not engage him in conversation. He only responded "Yes, my lady" or "No, my lady" or, when I referred to the time we had found the wild ponies, "I pray you won't mention it, my lady." What could one do? At least Gwarthgydd had news of home. He and all his brothers were in the High King's service now, and he had nothing but praise for Arthur. What a leader! Calm, wise, purposeful, never a hasty move or an unplanned foray; gentle with women, just with men, ruthless with his enemies. He was full of laughter and good humor; men feared his rare anger; he fought not with heat but with unswerving, cold purpose.

When I could get him off the subject of Arthur, he told me of home. He had married two of his daughters off and seemed glad to be rid of them. His brothers had large families, more than the King's house at Cameliard could hold, and lived on their own lands. That left him with Glynis, two young daughters, Gwillim and his two older sons, who took turns soldiering and tending the kingdom of Northgallis. I was still remembered there, he said. Never had the black Celts of our family produced anyone so fair. I nodded toward the blond Alyse, my mother's sister, and her daughter, the fair Elaine. Gwarth smiled. Yes, he said, everyone knew where it came from, and he wouldn't mind at all having another fair maid in Northgallis. I felt obliged to tell him it looked unlikely. He glanced unhappily at Gwillim and agreed.

"King Pellinore seems pleased with the match, though."

"Probably because it means his precious daughter would be next door," I told him. "But I assure you, Gwarth, the queen feels strongly that her daughter will not be forced into a marriage against her will—and the lady Elaine has a strong will."

"Hmmmm. Well, I expect you're right. I can't say Gwill cares at all. Perhaps it's just as well. He won't look at anyone but you, Gwen. He never has."

I blushed. It was absurd. Gwillim was my nephew! I told Gwarth how happy I was to see them both and that King Pellinore could not have brought me a better birthday present.

He laughed aloud. "We're not your present, Gwen. King Pellinore has brought you a rare gift, more precious than any Welsh prince could ever be to you."

Pellinore heard him and rose. "I confess that the High King Arthur has done me a great honor. In return for my services in the last battle, he asked me to name anything I wished, and if it was in his power to give it me, he would." I saw heads turn and nod at this extraordinary generosity. King Pellinore smiled. "I thought of the young lass I keep in my care and told the High King I wished to bring a birthday gift to my ward. I asked him for a mare from his own stables."

I gasped, and everyone stared. Such a gift was unheard of! All of the fine horses young Lancelot imported from Gaul, and their colts and fillies, were kept for training or for breeding stock. None had ever left the High King's stables. And mares were prized above all. I stared at Pellinore in amazement.

"Did—did he agree?" I whispered.

Pellinore laughed. "The mare is in the stables now," he said gently. "The High King keeps his promises."

I could barely contain my excitement. If she'd been stabled as soon as Pellinore arrived, she must have been in the barn when Peleth and I returned from our ride! I berated myself for not having gone in to tend the horse myself—I could have seen her then. As it was, I would not be allowed to go out until morning.

"Oh, dearest Pellinore!" I cried, jumping from my seat and running into his arms. "How can I ever thank you enough! What is she like? Her color, her stride, her spirits? Did anyone ride her on the journey home? Where is he, that I may ask?"

King Pellinore laughed and sat me on his lap, just the way my father had been wont to do when I was small. "No one rode her, young lady. She is yours. She's a filly, but two years old, and a dark dappled gray. But she will be as white as the High King's charger one day, you may be sure. She is not fully trained—I leave that to you—but what lessons she has had, she has had from the best. Young Lancelot bred her and trained her himself, and a finer hand with a horse I never hope to see. He hated to part with her and was sure I was exaggerating your skill." He pinched my cheek. "I told him you rode bareback, as he does himself, and flew like the west wind over whatever lay in your path." I blushed violently; I had thought my jumping was a secret. "He said to me, 'There's a maid after my own heart' and let me take the mare. You may see her in the morning, Gwen. Happy birthday."

I was beside myself with joy and anticipation. When dinner was over, I kissed Gwarth and Gwillim good night, paid my respects to Queen Alyse, and flew upstairs to my room. Elaine was sullen, whether with jealousy over my great gift or with a headache from her weeping, I knew not, and I cared not. A mare from the High King's stables! It was too wonderful to be true! I said my evening prayers in a hurry. God had not made me a woman that day, after all, but now I hardly cared.

* * *

I was up at dawn, dressed quietly in my doeskin leggings, crept out without waking Elaine or the nurses, and raced to the stables.

Stannic was up, and he grinned to see me, not surprised. "This way, my lady. I gave her the corner box. It's the biggest and she can look out over the meadow."

I stopped at the door and held my breath. She was a beauty! Tall, slender, straight legs, long, arched neck, flat croup, tail held high. She was looking out her window when I came up but, hearing my step, swung around to see me. Her face was lovely: broad in the forehead but narrow in the muzzle, with fine, large dark eyes.

"Sweet Mary," I whispered, opening the door a crack and slipping in. She was taller than I was, much taller than the Welsh mountain ponies I had grown up on, but lighter and finer than Peleth. Her coat was a dark dappled gray, with black legs, black mane and tail, and dark muzzle. I spoke to her softly, crooning an old Welsh tune, and held out my hand. She was nervous at first, but then stood calmly and let me approach. When I was near, she lowered her head and put her soft muzzle in my hand. Clearly, she had been brought up with no fear of men, which meant she had been well treated always. I stroked her gently, and she nuzzled me in return.

I slipped a halter on her and led her from the stall. She moved daintily, careful where she put her feet. I guessed she would be surefooted on rough ground. She did not look heavy enough to carry a soldier, but she must at least have carried Lancelot, so I was not afraid to mount her. I refused the bridle Stannic proffered, although it was very fine, with silver worked on the browband. She was only two, and likely tender-mouthed.

"Give me a leg up, Stannic."

"My lady," he protested, "surely you're not going to try her without a bridle. You'll not have control!"

"I have the halter and the rope. I can spin her in a circle if she looks to bolt. Have no fear."

My eagerness made me impatient, and I was ready to climb the fence to mount her, but Stannic helped me against his better judgment.

How can I describe what it felt like to be astride of her? She was light and quick, she felt every shift of my seat, every touch of my leg. She quivered with eagerness, but when I stroked her neck and talked to her, she calmed under my touch. I let her walk around the stableyard and then onto the track that led down the gentle valley toward the sea road. It was a lovely spring morning, with dew on the grass and a cool mist rising. The sun was up, rose pink through the haze, and the hills were alive with birdsong. The filly danced along the track, swinging this way and that, pulling at the rope, wanting her head. I denied it to her, and she did not fight me, but bent her neck gracefully and walked on. She had been handled, I could see, with consummate gentleness; she responded to the lightest touch. When we reached the valley floor, the track widened, and I let her move out a bit. What a fluid, ground-covering canter she had! It was easier to sit than the queen's chair that rocked back and forth on curved braces. She tossed her head and snatched again at the rope, but I held her, and she obeyed. But I felt the power in her hindquarters and the desire to run that coursed through her. I had not intended to run her at all, not the first time, but she was convincing me. Before I could do it, I had to know if she would stop. I sat up and pulled back on the rope, squeezing my leg. She came back to me at once, slowed to a trot, and stopped. But she trembled in frustration.

"Oh, good girl, my beauty, my pretty, my love. For that you shall have your gallop on the beach."

We trotted down the sea road and turned off along a woodland path that ran down to the shore. Suddenly, as the trees thinned out, the filly shied, screamed, and reared. I grabbed her mane to keep from sliding off, she whirled and tried to bolt back the way we had come, but I turned her and made her stand, facing the sea. She must never have seen the sea before! It must be as amazing to her as it was to me the first time I saw it. I stroked her neck, wet with the sweat of fear, and gradually she calmed.

I turned her away, and we rode along the dry shingle, where the sand is firm.

"All right, my lovely one, now let's see what you can do." And I gave her her head. She exploded out from under me so swiftly, I'd have fallen if I hadn't buried my hands in her whipping mane. I clung there, bent over her withers, as the ground flew by and the salt spray stung my cheeks and the west wind brought tears to my eyes. She fairly flew over the ground—I felt nothing but speed, like a spear flying. She raced past the place where Peleth always slowed down, winded, and past the last trail up from the beach. I pulled the rope in vain; when she felt the pressure, she leaned against it, increasing her speed. The trees became blurs, the sea a pounding accompaniment to her hooves. There were treacherous rocks ahead, I knew, sharp, black boulders that protruded from the soft sand like wolf's teeth—The Fangs they were called—and there was no way around them. They were a natural boundary. Fighting my panic so the mare would not sense it, I sang to her again, steadying my gulping breath, and straightened up as much as I could. Whether it was my song or the motion of my body I know not, but at last she slackened her pace, and by the time The Fangs came into view she was cantering easily, tossing her head, enjoying herself.

I brought her to a halt and turned her around. Her nostrils were flared wide, and her sides heaved, but she did not seem tired. She was not even lathered; any other horse I knew would have been dead.

"Well, my pretty one," I said, patting her neck and her rump as we started the walk back, "you are in wonderful condition. You have been loved by someone who loves horses, that is easy to see. I think I must make it a goal of mine to someday meet this knight who raised you and thank him for this gift. Yes, when Elaine goes to Caer Camel, I shall go with her, to thank him. For while you are the High King's gift, it was Lancelot who made you what you are. And I have a name for you now. I will name you Zephyr, after the west wind, for you fly as swiftly as the wind and yet are as gentle as the sea breeze. Someday I shall meet this great Sir Lancelot and thank him for my Zephyr."

Gwillim's visit was the first of many by Welsh princes. We had one or two a month, I believe, come to offer for Elaine's hand. Alyse and Pellinore were proud and happy but they were guided by Elaine's decision, and she always refused her suitors. At first she was barely polite, but as time wore on she, too, was flattered by the attention and grew condescendingly courteous. No one offered for me and in time Elaine passed from gloating into a genuine sorrow for my condition. I did not much mind the absence of suitors; my head was much too full of Zephyr to have room for men.

But Elaine's pity nearly drove me to distraction. "I am ten times the rider she is," I railed at Ailsa when we were alone, "and twice the seamstress! I can do figures in my head and read as well as anyone, and speak better Latin than most! And even though she is beautiful, she is vain about it, as if her beauty were something she had earned herself and not a gift of God! How can she be so cruel to me? In her eyes I am a poor, impoverished orphan—like Cam, the cripple—just because she has grown a bosom and I have not!"

Good Ailsa hugged me and calmed my weeping and told me, in her motherly way, that things would change as the wheel of time went round. The last would become first, she crooned, and the low made high. I frowned and looked at her askance: Where had I heard those words before?

In the month of the Raven near the autumn equinox, almost five years to the day after his victory at Caer Eden, King Arthur wed Guenwyvar of Ifray. There had been much fighting during the summer, but the High King managed to find three weeks of peace in which to marry. Then, with his bride bedded and the elders satisfied, he went back to war. His young Queen was left in

Caerleon, protected by his soldiers, with all the people daily watching her waistline to see if the High King had bred his heir in her. Elaine envied her, but I cannot say that I did.

King Arthur's victories continued, and work continued on the new fortress of Caer Camel. One Gaius Marcellus, grandson of Ambrosius' chief engineer, designed it—the fortifications, the groundwork, the buildings, and the open places. He had even given directions for the quarrying of the stone. The fortress was to be the biggest, strongest, and best defended in all the kingdoms, a gathering place for Britons, a warning to Saxons, a symbol to all of the High King's power. And after the bishop of Caerleon had blessed the cornerstone, it was whispered behind doors, Merlin the Enchanter, in a ceremony of his own, had looked into the flames, foreseen a glorious future, and sanctioned its building. After that, Arthur gave the orders to proceed.

Merlin was at Caerleon for the High King's wedding and stayed behind when Arthur and his troops rode north. He was the most trusted member of Arthur's household, and the most feared, as well. The King's sister Morgan was promised in marriage to Urien of Rheged, and since fighting in the east near Elmet required the High King's presence, Merlin was left to escort the princess and her train to Rheged for her wedding. They left on a hot day in October and traveled north through Wales.

King Pellinore and Queen Alyse had attended the High King's wedding but had not taken Elaine and me, much as we had begged to go. As a guilt gift, perhaps, they agreed to let us accompany them to meet the princess Morgan's train and pay homage to her. Elaine and I were beside ourselves with excitement. Elaine and Queen Alyse were going to ride in a litter, and they thought it only right that I should, too, but I begged and pleaded with good King Pellinore to be allowed to ride my new mare. It was not unknown for ladies, especially when young, to travel on horseback; I was sure the only reason Elaine chose the litter was because she did not have a mount as fine as mine. When she had complained to her father that she had outgrown Welsh ponies he had given her Peleth, but she could barely handle him, old though he was. Pellinore at last gave in and said I could ride, but only if I rode Peleth. With tears of frustration, I begged him to allow me to ride Zephyr. He thought her too young, too flighty, but I convinced him by giving him a demonstration. In five months she had learned a lot and would do anything I asked. At the end of my demonstration, he was silent for a while, stroking her neck and looking up at me. At last he nodded.

"Use a saddle, for form's sake," was all he said.

We started out on a brilliant, crisp day, with sixty troopers in our party and twelve pack mules with all the tents, gear, and bridal gifts. I rode between King Pellinore and the litter, where he thought I was safest. In obedience to his wishes, I had on my best tunic of a dark, forest green, with a light-green mantle for warmth. I had woven threads of green and blue into Zephyr's bridle and into her braided mane. I wondered if there would be anyone in the princess' party who had known the filly. If so, I wanted to make sure a good report reached the knight who had trained her.

With the cool weather and the crowd of horses, she was very excited, and harder to sit than I expected. King Pellinore shot me a look from under his bushy brows, but I only smiled in return and quietly sang to the mare. She settled down, as I knew she would, and by midday was perfectly calm and well behaved. On the evening of the third day we reached the meeting of the roads from Caerleon and Glevum. We had been there only an hour when the royal escort came in sight. From our tent, we watched them set up camp, admiring the fine horses and trying to see if we could distinguish any of the royal party. Elaine and I shared a tent with Ailsa, Grannic, Leonora, and Cissa—we were all in a fever, as eager to catch a glimpse of Merlin the Enchanter as of the princess Morgan. But it was many hours before we were called to audience. We changed into our finest gowns and followed King Pellinore and Queen Alyse through the crowd of troopers, courtiers, and guards, to the royal tent. The servants followed, bearing our gifts.

The princess Morgan, daughter of King Uther and Ygraine his Queen, sat on a gilded chair, dressed in a heavy red gown. Her hair was dark brown and decked with a circlet of red gold; around her neck and wrists hung jewels of every color, and on her fingers she wore rings of ruby, pearl, and sapphire. She was only fifteen—she looked twenty. Her eyes were a golden brown that did not suit her coloring; she was not pretty, really, but rather proud and distant. Now she was about to wed a major king, a man with lands wider than Lot's or Pellinore's, but a man old enough to be her father. No doubt her future had been a matter of negotiation among Arthur, Urien, and Queen Ygraine. I wondered if she dreaded going to it. I shuddered involuntarily. It was not fair that happiness in a woman's life should depend so completely upon a man.

Courtiers crowded around her at a respectful distance while the servants laid our gifts at her feet, and King Pellinore performed the introductions. She smiled as Elaine made her curtsy, but at me she only stared and barely nodded. I flushed with embarrassment—it was almost a slight! What had I done?

Among the gifts we had brought, goblets and carved platters, thick warm blankets woven from good Welsh fleece, and ornaments of beaten silver from the mines near Snowdon, were several silken hangings for the new queen's chamber. Alyse and her ladies had sewn them and then we all had stitched decorative patterns in different colors of thread. One of these, of white silk with a mare's head in the center and colts frolicking in fields of green at each corner, caught her attention. She motioned for the servant to hold it up to the light.

"This one is most unusual," she said. "The stitching is very fine and the use of color shows an eye for beauty. I thank you, Queen Alyse, I shall use this for my bridal bed."

Queen Alyse curtsied low.

"Thank you, gracious Princess. But I cannot take credit for the workmanship. That silk was done by my ward, Guinevere of Northgallis."

Princess Morgan turned to stare at me, and her eyes grew cold. The smile left her lips, but her breeding held. "This is fine work indeed, for so young a maid. Thank you, Guinevere. I shall remember it."

Something moved in the darkness behind her stool—I felt eyes on me suddenly, and my flesh crept on my bones. There was a man behind her, come from nowhere it seemed, although I suppose the truth was that I simply had not noticed him before. He was tall and thin, with black hair and beard, skin as ageless as oak bark and much the same color, and black, fathomless eyes that glared at me with intense, unwavering, malignant hatred. I began to tremble violently, trapped like an insect in the web of his gaze; conversation went on around me, it seemed no one noticed. He was wrapped in a black cloak from shoulder to boot and clutched a staff in his left hand. I knew him at once. He was Merlin.

Elaine took my arm and drew me away, as Pellinore and Alyse moved off. I was shaking so hard I could barely walk and tears stung my eyes.

"Gwen! What's wrong? Why are you shaking so?"

"Why does he hate me, Elaine? What have I done?"

"Whatever are you talking about? Who hates you?"

"Merlin."

She gasped. "Merlin! How do you know? What makes you think so?"

"Didn't you see the way he looked at me?"

She stopped and stared at me, looking puzzled and a little frightened.

"Yes, I saw him," she said finally in a halting voice, "but he wasn't looking at you. He was just watching us present the gifts. He looked kindly, I thought."

Now it was my turn to stare. I thought she was teasing me at first, but then I understood her astonishment was genuine. No one, not Pellinore, Alyse, Cissa, or Leonora, had noticed anything unusual. Was it possible I had imagined it? But I knew I had not.

I kept my thoughts to myself and did not tell Ailsa. For Merlin was perhaps the most powerful man in all Britain, and an enchanter, as well. It would not do to have him as an enemy, and my dear, superstitious nurse would die a thousand deaths, yes, and clutch her amulets forever, if I shared my fears with her. I composed myself for sleep that night as usual, but sleep did not come. I lay awake, uneasy and full of fear, until the dark time at moonset. Then I seemed to feel a heaviness come upon my spirit, and I sank into sleep. Almost at once I saw Merlin's face again—not angry this time, but sorrowful. His black eyes bored through me with urgency and feeling, with beseeching, almost, but I knew not for what. I sensed longing, desperation, and then a breath, a catspaw touch of deep love. At last, his quest unsatisfied, he seemed to sigh with a sorrow from the depths of the earth. He nodded kindly, as if in benediction, and turned sadly away. As I drifted into forgetfulness, I knew even in my sleep that it was not a dream; I knew that Merlin's power had reached me where I lay, that he had seen something in me that had broken his heart and left him desolate.

In the morning, everything was packed and made ready for departure, but no one could leave until the royal party left first. I was ill with fatigue and fear and would have remained in the tent until all the farewells were said, but the tents were struck early and I had nowhere to hide. Elaine kept near Queen Alyse and Leonora, but I slipped away when no one was looking. It was very busy, with servants and soldiers bustling everywhere, everyone wanting to get an early start. I went to the horse lines and took an apple to Zephyr. She nickered a greeting and daintily took the fruit from my hand. The grooms had already saddled her, but I readjusted her saddle cloths and her girth, for I knew how she liked them best. Then I rebraided her mane, crooning to her all the while and keeping well out of sight. But I knew that I could not hide from a magician. Magic was in the air that morning, all about me, the still, awful dread I had known by the spring pool in Northgallis. I was amazed that no one else seemed to notice it. Everyone was bustling about his chores, calling out morning greetings, exchanging bawdy jokes, laughing and grunting, moving and working. Only I, it seemed, was caught in this bright web of stillness, where the very air I breathed was alive with the whisperings of phantoms.

Quite suddenly, he was beside me. I had not heard a footfall of his approach. He was plainly dressed; only the gold and red enamel Dragon brooch at his shoulder gave a clue to his identity. I believe I gasped as I sank to my curtsy.

"My lord Merlin."

He reached out and took my hands, raising me quickly. To my surprise, his flesh was warm and comforting. He did not let go of my hands, but held them in his own and looked at me with kind, deep eyes. I was shaking, and the air around me positively sang with voices, but he stilled them. I saw him do it. He gave his head a quick shake, and the world went quiet.

"Do not be afraid," he said simply.

I could not speak. Neither could I take my eyes from his face.

"Your heart's desire will be granted in six months," he said. "After that, it is with the gods. You cannot change your fate, my dear, and neither can I."

"You—you don't hate me, my lord?"

Something flashed in the eyes then, and the corners of his thin mouth moved. "For his sake, I cannot. Glory and greatness are built on love. What will be, will be. Let it be so."

He dropped my hands then, as pounding filled my ears, and he actually bowed to me before he left. The last thing I heard as the world went dark was a groom calling out in panic, "The lady Guinevere has fainted!"

King Pellinore made me ride home in the litter with Elaine, convinced I was ill. Or course I told Elaine all about it, and her eyes went wide with astonishment that Merlin the Enchanter should single me out to speak to.

"But is that all he said? What does it mean?"

"I have no idea what it means."

"But it was a blessing, wasn't it, and not a curse?"

I went cold inside at the thought. "I don't know, Elaine. Would he have held my hands while he cursed me? Would he have bowed? Why did he come to find me in the midst of the bustle of departure, just to tell me not to be afraid? How could he possibly think I would not be afraid?"

"But you are brave, Gwen. I've seen you—flying through the air with Zephyr. It makes me weak with fear to watch you!"

"Nonsense. I'm not afraid of Zephyr. I think you have to be afraid in order to be brave. And I am truly afraid of Merlin. Do you believe—a pagan enchanter has power over a Christian?" I was reminded of my conversation with Gwillim, long ago. Did he command real powers, or just my thoughts and dreams? If I did not believe he had power over me—but that was the trouble. Christian or not, I did believe it. I knew it.

"Ask Father Martin," Elaine advised. "He will know. He speaks to God."

When we were home, and I had convinced Queen Alyse that I had recovered from my faintness, I sought out Father Martin. He was a robust and comely man of about thirty who enjoyed the company of peasants and low folk as much as that of Pellinore's nobles. He was not a scholar like Iakos, but he was warm and approachable. I found him in his garden, surrounded by group of dirty, brown-skinned children in ragged clothing. They were listening open-mouthed to the story of Jonah and the Whale. I wondered if any of them were sons of fisher-folk and what would happen when they next went out upon the sea.

Father Martin rose when he saw me and smiled. The children filed out, eyes downcast, and then we heard them running down to the village, hollering and shouting, and Father Martin laughed. "To have such energy! I would I could be young again. Well, my lady Guinevere, to what do I owe the honor of this visit?"

"I wish to know the answer to a question, Father, and I think only you can answer it."

He paused and led me to a stone bench among the pear trees. "I will certainly answer it if I can, my lady."

"Do pagan enchanters have powers over spirits, or only God?"

I don't know what he was expecting, but it wasn't that. He stared a moment and then almost smiled. "Are you referring to any pagan enchanter in particular, my lady?"

"Yes. To Merlin."

He cleared his throat then, and looked away. "Ahhh. Merlin." He studied the clouds for a while and then turned to me. "May I know what brought this on, my lady? Has something happened that concerns Merlin?"

"Y—yes, Father. I met him. He spoke to me."

"And he frightened you."

"He told me not to be afraid. But he—he did frighten me."

Father Martin took both my hands, as Merlin had done, but the effect was not the same. There was nothing in them. They were human hands.

"You know, Guinevere, that the Lord God is the True God. He loves His children, especially the innocent. He protects you, child, He protects you daily. You have nothing to fear from Merlin while God's Hand is over you."

"Then Merlin has no power? Or is it that God's is stronger?"

Father Martin looked uncomfortable. "There are many kinds of power, child. There is the kind of power the High King wields against his enemies. There is the kind of power the soothsayers and hill witches have over the minds of simple folk. But the kind of power God grants is greater than all of them. It is the power of love."

I did not understand him. "Do you class Merlin with the soothsayers, then? Does he only have power over those who believe in him? Is it so with God, also?"

Father Martin crossed himself quickly, shocked. "Hush, my sweet child, it's blasphemy to say such a thing. That God's holy power could depend on something as frail as the will of a human! No, no, never think it. No matter what you believe, my dear girl, God will love you and protect you. His love is everlasting."

"Forgive me, Father. I did not mean to blaspheme. It's only—I want to know if Merlin has power or not."

Father Martin sighed and struggled with his words. "I do not know the man myself," he said at last. "But I have heard of his many doings. I will not deny that he has power. But they say his power has always been used for the good, for building and making. It is God's power, though even Merlin may not know it."

I wanted to believe him, but I did not. Jesus had never come to me in my sleep the way that Merlin had.

"What, if I may ask, my lady, did Merlin say to you?"

Now it was my turn to look away and feel nervous. "He—he spoke of the future, I think, but it was very unclear. I mean, I didn't understand him. He said what will be, will be. He said glory and greatness are built on love. But he seemed very sorry about it. It was the way he said it. As if he could see my future and it broke his heart."

Father Martin looked relieved and a little awed. Merlin's words, even secondhand, could strike awe into the heart of a Christian priest.

"He has told you the truth about the power of love," Father

Martin said. "It is a thing a wise man knows. And if Merlin the Enchanter is concerned about your future, Lady Guinevere, it must be a mighty future indeed."

I rose. I had learned what I came to learn. Father Martin believed every word out of Merlin's mouth. He was even staring at me with wonder. I wanted to cry.

"Thank you for your time, Father Martin," I managed, gulping. "I must—I must get back. The queen—" I choked on the words and turned away.

He rose hastily. "Whatever happens, my lady, God will protect you. Do not be afraid."

I shook my head as I hurried toward the gate, brushing tears from my eyes.

Poor Father Martin tried again. "Merlin cannot hurt you, now or ever."

I turned as I opened the gate and looked up into his worried face. With an effort I found my voice, and to my surprise, it sounded calm. "Perhaps not. But he will never forgive me, either, for whatever it is I am to do."

In bed that night, I told Elaine everything that had passed. It did not surprise her that Father Martin believed in Merlin's powers. Only a fool would not believe in them, so well known were they. I was the one she found puzzling.

"But what did you expect, Gwen? You never doubted Merlin's power. You felt it yourself, you said so. So why do you think Father Martin has let you down? What does God have to do with Merlin?"

"Can Merlin see the future, Elaine? Truly, do you think he can?"

"Of course. He sees what he wills to see. If he has seen yours, you may be sure it is important somehow." She paused. "If your future is important, it must mean you will be a great lady someday. Perhaps you will follow me to the High King's court. Perhaps you will marry one of the Companions."

"Elaine, you must know by now that is not my ambition."

Elaine smiled slyly. "What about the other thing he said? What is your heart's desire, Gwen? To marry a prince?"

"No, by Mithra. Just to be a woman, like you. The older I get the less I think I ever want to be married."

Elaine was scandalized. "You can't mean you want to be a spinster! And you shouldn't swear by Mithra now that you've been baptized. Gwen, what's the matter with you? Don't you want to be a queen someday and have lands of your own?"

"They won't be lands of my own. They'll be my husband's lands. He'll want to manage them all by himself, because he's the man and I'm just the keeper of his house. He won't even discuss what's going on in the world because 'it's not a fit subject for young maids.' Whether I'm happy or not will depend completely upon him, and not at all upon me. I tell you, Elaine, I hate the thought of it."

"Well, you don't have to marry anyone like that. Mother says so. She's let me refuse all the young men, even when Father is so furious, because she says it's only right that both husband and wife should want the same thing. And she'll do the same for you. I'm sure she will."

"Oh, Elaine, do you really think she would? Even though Gwarthgydd and Pellinore might want it differently? Would she really require my consent? I tell you now, I don't think I ever want to go near Caer Camel, or see the King's Companions. Not if Merlin is nearby." And I shivered.

Elaine put her arms around me and hugged me warmly. "You will come with me. I will protect you. You are meant for someone special, that much is clear. One of the Companions, without a doubt, cousin. Perhaps that young knight with the foreign name who trained your horse. Just wait and see. You'll love it at court."

Two weeks later Merlin disappeared. Princess Morgan had married King Urien, the wedding feast had lasted a week, the guests had departed. Merlin stayed on in conference with the aging bridegroom, discussing defense strategy. Lot's queen, Morgause, Morgan's half-sister stayed on waiting for a fair wind to sail back to the Orkney Isles. While her body had grown thick with child-bearing, she was still the most beautiful woman at the wedding and far outshone the bride. With her was a red-headed boy of three, Lot's firstborn son, Gawaine. She had other sons at home in Orkney; one of them, the whispers went, was older than Gawaine, "the dark prince" she had left at home, but I did not believe the talk. Lot, of all people, surely would not allow the Queen to raise her bastard side by side with his own sons. At any rate, on the day Morgause sailed for Orkney, Merlin disappeared. No one could explain it. He was gone, and he left no trace.

People laughed at first and said the King's enchanter was up to his old tricks again, but as time went on faces grew sober. Always before when Merlin disappeared in one place, he reappeared somewhere else; the people always knew the enchanter was there when Arthur wanted him. But this time even Arthur could not find him. The King's troops scoured the wood where he had vanished, visited his cold hilltop cave in south Wales, hunted around Caer Camel and anywhere else they could think of, but Merlin was not there. Winter winds closed the seas, early snows blanketed the land, covering the woodland tracks, and the search parties were called off. Now King Arthur was alone.

News came from Caerleon that the young Queen was with child of the royal heir, and bonfires were lit throughout the land in celebration. King Pellinore held a feast on All Hallow's Eve in honor of the event. Elaine was green with envy, but I told her what a dreary life it would be, married to the High King.

"You'd only be a broodmare to him," I said. "That would be your foremost duty. Bear his children as fast as you could and see that they're all sons. Forget having a companion, he would never be there. Even Alyse only sees Pellinore six months of the year, and he's a homebody compared to the High King. He must always travel about the Kingdom. You would never really know him. There wouldn't be time. You would be miserable." I succeeded only in convincing myself. I never convinced Elaine. She was completely and thoroughly in love with Arthur, and there seemed to be nothing anyone could do about it.

Then, as the first snows fell, the High Queen began to ail. All Caerleon was thrown into confusion. Priests, physicians, witches, and enchanters passed in a steady stream through the young Queen's chamber. Arthur promised gold to any who could stay her bleeding and turned no one away who offered help. King Pellinore went to court to see what he could do, but, as he told us later, there was nothing anyone could do. Neither Mithra, nor Christ, nor Bilis, Eroth, Llyr nor Lluden, nor the Great Goddess of Avalon could prevent the horror that followed. Merlin might have saved the child, it was thought, but Merlin was not there. Arthur was beside himself with grief. And that poor girl, only seventeen and still a bride, died on Arthur's birthday in desperate agony, with the High King weeping at her bedside. When it was over Arthur shut himself away and for three weeks spoke to no one. Finally his officers threatened to beat down his door. Word had reached the Saxons of the King's grief, and they were massing for an attack along the great river Thames, as far west as Amesbury. This news aroused the King, but he came out from his fastness a changed man. Gone was the gaiety and exuberance of youth; this was a man quick to anger and dangerous to cross. The Saxons retreated before his fury as before a wall of flame.

The entire Kingdom of Britain grieved with Arthur, all except

Elaine. Elaine alone was serene, at peace again. He was free once more, and she was biding her time. She tired me with her fantasies and her ambition, or perhaps it was the long, dreary winter days and nights within the castle that tired me. When the midwinter thaw finally came, I spent all the daylight hours out riding. It felt so wonderful to be free again! I pitied the High King, if he could not find joy in the freedom of a horse.

One clear, bright January morning I rose early, slipped into my doeskin leggings and a warm cloak, and took Zephyr down to the shore. Her favorite run was along the beach, and afterward she was relaxed and ready for practice jumping fences. Her prowess amazed me; she could fly over any obstacle I put before her with plenty of room to spare, and she seemed to love it. She was eager that morning, tossing her head and snatching playfully at the bit, urging me to hurry. But she came back to my hand the instant I asked her and obediently walked down the track to the sea. It was a fine morning, cold and clear, the last traces of dawn painted pink streaks on the gray sea. I caressed the mare, who trembled in anticipation, and, hooking a fist in her mane, gave her her head. She shot forward, and the shore sped past in a blur. I loosened my hair with my free hand and let it whip in the wind. I felt free of everything then—the Kingdom with its constant wars, Wales with its jealous lords, and castle routine with daily lessons and strictures—all were left behind me at that moment. I was as free as the seabirds, and as wild. The future lay before me, unknown and therefore bright and beckoning. As icy air filled my lungs, I shouted aloud with joy. Zephyr responded by quickening her thundering pace, and we flew up the beach, only slowing when The Fangs came into view. As we turned and trotted back, I hugged the mare in exhilaration.

"Oh, my proud beauty, what happiness you bring me! I shall never part with you, my Zephyr. We shall always ride together!"

She nodded her head exactly as if she understood, and we cantered slowly back the way we had come. I headed her toward a track that left the beach toward the jumping field, when suddenly she started, shying violently, and almost threw me. I grabbed her mane, and only just kept her from whirling and bolting. She was shaking like a leaf in an autumn storm, and though I sang and spoke to her, she did not settle.

"What is it, my beauty? What have you sensed?"

The beach was deserted, the sea quiet. I saw no movement anywhere. But the mare was frantic and would not advance. I slid off her back and held her head close to my body. When I wrapped her nostrils in my cloak, she calmed a little, and I knew then it was something she had smelled. The light land breeze still blew at that hour, so I looked inland, up the track, searching the sparse gorse bushes that grew in the sand, toward the line of bare hardwoods that marked the edge of the woods. And I saw something. Underneath our own footprints the sand had been disturbed. It looked like something heavy had been dragged up the track, and something small and white fluttered ahead under the bushes, just short of the trees.

"Come on, my sweet, let's find out what it is." Frightened as she was, the filly followed me up the track, but as we neared the trees she snorted once and screamed. A low moan answered from the bushes, and to my amazement, the filly blew once and was quiet. The mystery was solved for her: it was human, and therefore a friend. I tied her to a sapling and left her standing peacefully while I went to see who lay half concealed and moaning in the sand.

He was a stranger. There was dark blood caked in his bright hair, and his left leg was bent at an unnatural angle. His tunic was torn, but the cloth was fine. I saw no cloak anywhere. His face was blue with cold and pain, and his eyes were closed. I drew off my cloak and covered him. He shivered violently. I laid a hand to his forehead. He was very cold. The light touch seemed to revive him, for his eyes fluttered open and he looked right at me. His eyes were a brilliant green in color, with honey-colored flecks around their dark centers; I found it impossible to look away as he stared at me.

"Forgive me my sins," he mumbled, and then he sank into unconsciousness.

I ran to the filly, beginning to shiver myself, and jumped on her back. His speech had been in Latin, but his accent was foreign. I was sure he was not Welsh, perhaps not even British. He lay on the sand by the Irish Sea. My heart pounded in time with the filly's galloping strides as we raced back to the castle. Was he one of the Irish devils all good Welsh children had been taught to fear?

I roused the castle with the news, and King Pellinore sent troops with a litter down to fetch the stranger, but he would not let me show them the way. He ordered the grooms to care for Zephyr, and he roused Leonora, who took one look at me and threw me into a hot bath. Queen Alyse scolded me for parting with my cloak and made me go back to bed with hot bricks at my feet. I was furious with frustration, for I felt perfectly fine, only cold, and I wanted news of the stranger.

Thank goodness Elaine was adept at eavesdropping, for she tripped in and out of my room all day with whatever news she picked up. When they found the stranger he was delirious and half dead with cold. He was not expected to live, so they did not put him in the dungeon, but in a guest chamber near the guard tower. They bathed him and placed hot bricks wrapped in herb-soaked towels around his body. King Pellinore's physician set his leg and bandaged his head, and Father Martin gave him the last rites, for it was clear he was a Christian. In his delirium he called upon the Christian God and his angels to save him. But most of the time he rambled in a tongue no one could understand.

By nightfall he was hot with fever and still delirious. An Irish kitchen slave, captured in a thwarted raid upon our shores eight years before, was brought into the room to see if he could understand the stranger's delirious speech. The man broke into tears at hearing once more the lilting Gaelic of his homeland.

"And so," Elaine announced, perched on my coverlet, "he is Irish, just as you thought, Gwen. If he lives he will be a prisoner, and if he is a lord of some kind, a hostage, which could bring Father some Irish gold. They say he is young, not over twenty. What does he look like?"

I saw again the white, drawn face with the matted gold hair and the mesmerizing eyes. "He's the handsomest man I've ever seen."

Elaine giggled. "You'd better not fall in love with an Irish prince, Gwen. I don't think Mother would let you go to Ireland for all the gold in Rome. She saw his clothes, you know, and said they were of good quality. So he might be someone important. Isn't it exciting?"

"But how did he come to be lying on our beach?"

"I don't know yet. But I'll know before dinner is over."

I was not allowed up for dinner, but Ailsa brought me a meal in bed and fixed me a hot posset. I did not protest this care, for my throat was beginning to feel raw, and I knew I would be abed for two days with the usual winter chills. But Elaine was as good as her word and had all the news by bedtime.

"There was a raid last night," she confided, eyes shining. "The thaw has opened the seas, and Father has had the beach patrolled for the last five days. Last night a ship was sighted, and four boatloads of ruffians came ashore, led by a young hothead, or so the soldiers say. They didn't get far, and most of them escaped back to their ship, but the fighting was fierce, and many were wounded.

The soldiers rounded them up and they're in the dungeon now, but I guess they missed this one. I wonder if he's the leader."

"From your description of the raid, he can't be much of a leader."

Elaine laughed. "Well, he's no Arthur. But the Irish aren't thinking fighters. They never have been. They fight from passion. Show them cold steel, and they turn and flee."

I grinned at her. "If he lives, I'll be sure to let our stranger know your good opinion of him."

"I don't care what he thinks of me," she retorted. "He will always be an Irishman, and I'm going to be a British queen."

At least, I thought later, as I drew the covers around me and fell towards sleep, she didn't say "Queen of Britain."

I lay abed a week with fever and chills. I was nursed and cosseted, but given no news and forbidden to ask questions. An air of secrecy seemed to envelop the castle. Elaine was with me often, but turned the conversation from any topic of interest except King Arthur and his doings. He was doing much, it seemed, even in the winter snows. Tales of courageous deeds and of murderous rages were told and retold; he was no longer referred to as a youth. He was nineteen now and a man. Wherever he raised Excalibur in the defense of Britain he was victorious. Ten major battles and thousands of skirmishes lay behind him; he had never received so much as a scratch from a Saxon weapon. Yet in the midst of his glory he grieved, for his lost wife, his lost child, and his lost friend, the great enchanter. His tread was heavier; his smiles were rarer. He got on with the business of defeating his enemies and unifying the kingdoms with a cold determination that made his own men afraid of him.

Of the Irish stranger, Elaine would say nothing except that he still lived. But her eyes sparkled, and she winked at me when Ailsa or Grannic's back was turned. Finally my strength returned, and I grew weary of convalescence. I insisted on getting up to sit by the fire, or taking short walks on Ailsa's arm. When after two weeks I was fully recovered, the wild winter weather set in, and we were snowbound. I couldn't even get to the barn to visit Zephyr. I had to spend my days with the rest of the women in the weaving room, spinning, weaving, sewing, talking. We joined the men at meals in the dining hall, but otherwise we were cloistered together. It was the dreadful winter routine. People got fractious without exercise in the sun, and personalities began to rub one another into irritation. All this I knew and expected, but this winter was better than most. The Queen's ladies were often in buoyant spirits, teasing each other and laughing, singing new songs, even weaving new patterns—and all because of our stranger.

His name was Fion. He was, it seemed, quite a catch. He was certainly an Irish prince, and if the kitchen slave who served as translator was to be believed, he was *the* Prince of Ireland, son of Gilomar the King. He had lived through a three-day fever, survived two leechings and the setting of his leg, and was fast recovering from a chest cold. He ate like a young wolf and sang like a bard. He had already picked up enough Welsh to carry on a conversation, and he flirted with the ladies, even Queen Alyse, from dawn until dusk. He showed no fear and bore no grudge against his captors. He was a hostage, and he knew it. But he appeared to be in no hurry to return to his native land. As long as there was a woman in his room, he spouted poetry, sang songs, teased, admired, cajoled, and flirted. He had captivated every woman in the palace, from queen to cook, and although he was rapidly recovering his health, there was no talk of moving him into the dungeon with his fellows. The queen's ladies waited upon him themselves. King Pellinore seemed glad they had the diversion; everyone was in a better temper.

"Saints be praised," Cissa said as she sat spinning, "if the rascal didn't pinch me again this morning! And me old enough to be his mother!"

"He's a handsome rascal, to be sure," Leonora added. "And an amorous young devil. Do they breed them so in Ireland on purpose, to conquer our hearts?"

Queen Alyse laughed. "If he is on a mission to subdue Wales by winning its women, he is very likely to succeed. I have seen the way he looks at my daughter when he thinks I do not observe him."

Elaine blushed and I grinned. So this was what she had been hiding from me! She had an admirer, and this one, it seemed, she did not object to.

"Mother, please," Elaine protested. "He's a hooligan. A foreigner."

"Well, my dear," Alyse said smoothly as she bent over her stitching, "Welsh princesses have married foreigners before now. To be Queen of Ireland would be a great honor, would it not?"

I glanced quickly at Elaine. It was written on her face as clearly as the writing on any scroll that she wished only to be Queen of Britain.

"Mother!" Elaine cried. "I am British! I will never leave my homeland! I would rather be a British spinster than an Irish queen!"

All the ladies laughed and nodded approvingly, and I saw it had just been a leg-pull. Alyse had been teasing—indeed, I thought, she would be the last one to want to send her daughter across the sea where she might never see her again.

"Such poetry!" Cissa exclaimed. "And such good Latin he speaks. He's an educated man, you may be sure of it. This morning when I brought him his willow tea, he was on about the angel again."

"The Angel from Heaven who feeds his soul?" Leonora asked.

"He is on about her day and night. You would think a man lying half frozen on a winter beach would see devils and monsters, not angels. He has a vivid imagination."

"What is this about angels?" I asked. "I have not heard this story before. Is it an Irish tale?"

"No, my lady. The young man had a dream as he lay upon the shore. He claims he saw an Angel of God, a vision of loveliness with hair of white fire, who touched him just as life was about to expire and brought him back from the jaws of death." She smiled benevolently as my heart began to sink. "He claims he saw a halo of light around her head, the stars of Heaven in her eyes, and the joy of everlasting life in her smile. Oh, he has a way with words, that one. He had Cissa and me believing him, he did."

Elaine looked at me suddenly and made a face. "He's probably talking about Gwen. He's just dressing it up. After all, she saved him."

"Yes, and in addition to all our thanks, Prince Fion would like to thank you Guinevere when you have regained your strength," Alyse said. "But I warn you, he thinks we are playing upon his credulity. He does not believe a child could save his life. And he certainly does not believe any king or queen in their right minds would allow a ward of such tender years to venture forth alone on a frosty winter morning along a beach where raiders had been slain the night before."

It was meant as a rebuke, so I bowed my head and said nothing, but I resented it. How was I to know there had been a raid? They told us nothing, because we were young maids. If the weather had been warm, Elaine and I would have sneaked up to the tower wall and learned of the news ourselves, but I did not see how I was to be held responsible for my ignorance as things were. One thing was clear—gone was my freedom with Zephyr.

When Elaine and I went up to our room to change for dinner,

we walked in silence. I was hurt that Queen Alyse had referred to me as a child, and here I was only three months short of fourteen. It was the old wound again, and sore still from constant bruising. It was not until we were in our chamber and half undressed that Elaine spoke to me.

"Gwen, if you take him from me, I will never forgive you."

I simply stared at her. "What on earth are you talking about?"

"Mother will take you to see Fion, and once he looks at you he will never again look at me."

"Oh, please be sensible, Elaine. Do not start this again. You are Pellinore's daughter. You're a woman, and I'm a child. Your own mother said so."

Elaine was smiling, but her eyes were unhappy. "Mother hasn't seen you in your undergarments recently." She came up to me; she was a full head shorter. "Your shape is changing. Didn't you even know it?"

She led me to the polished bronze we kept by the window, and I looked at my reflection in some astonishment. I had not known it. I had not felt it. But there it was. My breasts were swelling, and my waist looked smaller because my hips, always as narrow as a boy's, were widening ever so slightly. At last I looked like a young girl on the verge of womanhood, the way Elaine had looked at ten.

"Elaine!" I cried, and hugged her, as the tears streamed down my cheeks. "Oh, Elaine, perhaps old Merlin was right, God rest his soul. Perhaps I shall be a woman at last!"

Elaine did not return my embrace.

"You will be too beautiful to bear when it happens," she said slowly. "I know already what will happen. Every man who looks at you will love you."

"Nonsense," I said, taking her hand. "You underestimate yourself. You are pretty, Elaine, and are the king's daughter. I am an orphan. Anyway, I don't want Fion. You don't, either, if it comes to that. Why should it matter what he thinks?"

Elaine would not look at me. "I'm not talking just about Fion."

But I did not understand her. "Come, I will guarantee you that after I have met him, his admiration for you will be undiminished. Shall we place a wager on it?"

"I am not such a fool as that."

Her good humor had vanished, but mine simply grew and expanded like a giant bubble, filling all the space between us and gradually, as it enveloped her, she acquiesced to its power and joined me, at least outwardly, in my happiness.

I did not forget Merlin the Enchanter in my prayers that night. Whether he was alive or dead, I prayed to God to be merciful to him, to save his soul, for what he had foretold was coming to pass, and in three swift months I should have my heart's desire.

"Come, Guinevere, and bring the basket of new bread." Obediently I fell into the train of waiting women burdened with clean linens, fine silks, and bowls of dried fruit and nuts, who followed Queen Alyse up the staircase to the prisoner's chambers.

The guard at the door smiled and shook his head when he saw us and, bowing to Queen Alyse, let us pass.

The chamber was large, with a narrow window facing the sea, and a log fire burning merrily in the grate. Fion sat on the window seat, bathed and dressed in a fine linen shirt, loose leather leggings, and wrapped in a warm, russet cloak. His splinted leg he held straight before him, and as we entered he rose, leaning on a stout staff.

"Welcome, my fair ladies, my morning nymphs." He spoke Welsh with a charming lilt to his voice and put a softness to the rough word-sounds that was foreign, and yet pleasing, to our ears. He was tall and handsome, standing there in his dark cloak with his bright hair falling across his brilliant eyes. He made me want to smile, and my heart beat faster. I pulled the hood of my cloak around my face and turned away with the others to place my basket upon the table. Queen Alyse was greeting him formally, as her husband's prisoner, but she used the tone of voice she might have used for a son. One by one the waiting women curtsied to him and left, until only Leonora and I remained. Queen Alyse signaled me to come forward, and as I rose from my curtsy my hood fell back, and I looked up into his eyes.

He gasped and fell back on the window seat, wincing with pain.

"Dear Lord in Heaven!" he cried in Latin. "Angel of God! 'Tis thee in the flesh! O Lord, have mercy upon my soul!" And he crossed himself reverently.

"My dear prince Fion," Alyse began smoothly, "may I present my ward, my sister's daughter Guinevere of Northgallis. Guinevere, Prince Fion, son of Gilomar of Ireland."

I smiled at him and extended my hand. He took it between both of his and gazed into my face. Finally, as the silence began to be awkward, he spoke in Welsh. "You are real, my lady? You are flesh and blood, as I am? May the blessed saints be praised! An Angel of God and real to the touch." He lifted my hand to his lips, and from the corner of my eye I saw the queen's eyebrows rise.

"It was Guinevere," she said, "who found you on the beach and sent my husband's troops to find you. It is she you must thank for your life."

Fion turned to her in amazement. "My beautiful Alyse, I thought you said a child had found me." And his brilliant eyes traveled from my face slowly down my gown and back up again, while I turned scarlet, and he held my hand firmly in his own.

Queen Alyse smiled. "She is at an age when every day makes a difference in a maid. It seems I have not been paying close enough attention."

She turned away, and I hastily withdrew my hand and followed, but at the door she stopped.

"Leonora," she said, "stay with the lady Guinevere awhile. I am sure our foreign prince would like to ease his conscience and thank her for the gift of life. Come to me in an hour." And she left us there.

I was dumbfounded. Leonora, with a secret smile, settled herself before the fire and began stitching a silk shirt, no doubt for Fion. I whirled around. The Irishman had risen, clutching his staff, and held out his hand to me. It was all too, too clear. He was not good enough for Elaine, of course. The mother's ambition lagged not far behind the daughter's. But he was perfect for me. She had waited until I had my health and color back before she brought me to him, for *his* sake, not for mine. By leaving us alone with only Leonora for chaperone, she was giving her consent to his courtship as clearly as if she had spoken it aloud. Alyse was no fool. It would suit her purposes very well to see me married and settled in Ireland. Pellinore would have friends across the Irish Sea, and they could stop worrying that I would somehow cast a shadow across Elaine's future.

Poor Fion seemed unaware of all that had passed. He simply stared at me with his glorious eyes and blessed aloud the luck that had brought him to Wales. I walked demurely to the settle on the other side of the fire and took up some embroidery.

"We are pleased to see you looking so well, Prince Fion," I said, in just the tone Alyse had used. "Our clean Welsh air seems to do you good."

He hobbled over to the hearth and stood with his back to the fire, looking from one of us to the other.

"The air here is very fine indeed, my lady. And I have been nursed by the loveliest gentlewomen in all Britain, I am sure.

How could I not return swiftly to health under such care?" His tone was very cool. I glanced up. His face, before so expressive, was masked like a courtier's, and he nodded gravely to me. "I would know, if my lady would not think it impertinent of a stranger, and a hostage one at that, where Northgallis is? And what fortunate king names you as his daughter?"

I put down my needlework and looked up at him. "Sir, I am an orphan. My mother died at my birth. My father was King Leodegrance of Northgallis, who sent me here to live with my kin before he died. Northgallis lies a day's hard ride eastward, a small kingdom in North Wales."

He smiled gently. "My sympathies for such misfortune. And I? Do you wish to know what manner of hooligan, as I think you Welsh call it, you have in your midst?"

I smiled back. "If you are a hooligan, my lord, at least you are an educated one, a Christian one, and at the moment, a tamed one."

He grinned, and his face lit. Leonora raised an eyebrow.

"Indeed," he replied. "Tamed and caged. And completely at your service, Guinevere of Northgallis." He bowed deeply and made it look graceful, although it was obviously difficult with his splinted leg and staff. "If my good Leonora will permit me to sit at her side?" He made an obeisance to Leonora, who blushed and hastily made room for him on the bench.

"You don't fool me, my young lord. You sit here not for my company, but so you may better see young Guinevere."

He laughed and kissed her cheek quickly. "And could you blame me now? Is there a lass in all the Northern Isles to match her? Would she not grace any king's hall?"

I bowed my head as he jabbered on and picked up my stitching. But I noted that his position on the bench enabled him to stretch his injured leg out straight upon it, and this seemed to afford him some relief. It had not occurred to me before, but he must have been all the time in some pain. I decided to be direct.

"And now, Fion, son of Gilomar. What manner of man are you? Did I do my foster father a disservice by bringing you into our midst? You came to raid us—are you now a spy?"

He looked up swiftly and with new interest. "I have been here three weeks. You are the first person to ask me a serious question." He paused. "My father calls himself King of Ireland. But if you know aught of Ireland you know we have ten or twenty such kings with ten or twenty such claims. We are a proud race and like not to bend the knee. Thus we waste our strength in petty quarrels and cannot unite. The rest of the known world thinks of us only as pirates." He paused, and I struggled to keep the truth of his statement from showing on my face. "I am Gilomar's youngest son, and the last living. All my brothers were hotheads, like my father, who threw themselves at the first foe they could find. When my father was my age, and the great Ambrosius lay dying, Merlinus came to Ireland to find the standing stones to bedeck his grave. He was protected by a small force led by Uther Pendragon. My father had five hundred men at his back, but it took Uther only three hours to repel his attack and send him fleeing. You have not heard this story? It is true. I tell it to illustrate the great difference between you British and we Irish. My father has not changed. My brothers were just like him. I am not. When my father insisted that I show my mettle and lead a raid upon your shores, I resolved to do it for one reason only. I wanted to see Britain. I want to meet this son of Uther's who knows how to rule men. Whether I go as a hostage or as a free man, I wish to see Arthur Pendragon and judge him for myself." He was looking into the fire as he spoke, and the passion of his feeling gave strength to his face. "If he is a true man, I will pledge my allegiance to him. And then perhaps in time my Ireland may become part of the civilized world."

In the silence the snapping of the burning logs was the only sound. I was moved. He had dealt straight with me and had spoken to me as if I were his peer. "I am sure you will get your wish, my lord."

He slowly came out of his deep thoughts and smiled again. "That's as may be. Being a hostage can be chancy. You must stay on the good side of your host and not wear out your hospitality. Pray let me recite you a poem from one of our famous bards."

He regaled us for a long time. He had a lovely speaking voice and an accurate memory. Leonora warmed willow bark tea for us at the hearth, and we all partook of the fruit we had brought him. At length he touched Leonora's arm.

"Your hour is up, good Leonora, and your duty done. Take the queen's ward away and the light out of my life."

Leonora did not know what to say. "Good sir, I beg your pardon. We may stay as long as we will, I am sure, unless we tire you."

"Heard you not the queen's orders? They struck fire in my young princess. I have no wish to force myself upon you longer than I must. You are free to go."

Leonora turned to me beseechingly.

"Fion." I rose. "It is true I was angry. But I am no longer. Time passes quickly with you, and I was pleased. If this is to be daily repeated—" I glanced at Leonora, who nodded, "—then I pray you will not dread it on my account, for I assure you that I am content to be here. That is—" I fumbled suddenly and looked away from him, "—that is, if you understand."

"I understand, Guinevere." His voice was very gentle as he slipped into Latin. "Thou art not for me."

I looked up at him gratefully and was surprised to catch him gazing at me with longing. To cover, he added hastily, "Please, my lady, if there are any books in the place, bring them that I may read aloud to you."

"I'll bring them and read them aloud to you, Prince Fion."

He stared in amazement. "What! You know your letters? Can you write, as well?" He came close to me then, his back to Leonora and grasped my hands. "For whom are you being groomed?" he demanded softly.

My bewilderment must have shown, for he released me at once and stepped back.

"Queen Alyse believes all young ladies of breeding should know reading and writing," Leonora stated, bundling up her needlework. "The lady Elaine and Guinevere have studied with a Greek scholar right along with Pellinore's sons. Someday they will make good wives to the High King's Companions, if God wills."

Fion looked thoughtful. "I see," he said. "Perhaps."

He kissed my hand before we left and begged me to give his love, his undying devotion, and his limitless admiration to the lady Elaine.

"Be sure you bring her tomorrow," he whispered. "The apple-cart must not be upset."

It occurred to me, as I followed Leonora down the hall, that in three weeks he had learned a great deal more about us than we had learned about him.

I went daily to see him at the queen's direction, and as often as she could manage it, Elaine accompanied me. She was determined to come every day, but Alyse preferred that the prince spend as much time alone with me as propriety would allow. I did not mind, for Fion and I were friends, and if Leonora chose to take our conversations as flirting and report to the queen that everything was progressing nicely, no harm was done. But Elaine could hardly bear it and was always cross when she was kept from him.

She dared not face her mother with her displeasure, so instead she grew angry and sullen with me. At bedtime, when we used to share our thoughts and hopes and secrets, she either berated me for my brazen attempts to attach Fion or refused to speak to me altogether.

"Who do you think you are?" she would snap as Ailsa brushed out my hair. "What right have you to take up all his time? He must be sick to death of all your pestering!"

"Elaine, you know perfectly well it is your own mother who commands it—"

"Fah! Don't give me that! You're disobedient enough whenever it suits you! Who went riding on the beach the morning after the raid, against orders? Who—"

"How was I to know there had been a raid on the beach? No one—"

"You're a guest in this house, Gwen, don't forget it! You can tell her no, you can feign illness, you can insult Fion, you can do a thousand things to prevent it!"

In the end, I had to apologize for my forwardness, for there was no winning an argument with Elaine. But apologies did little to improve her temper. The only time she was happy was when she went to see Fion.

Usually when Elaine was with us, Fion asked for the Story of Arthur, because she told it with such feeling. This was not a tale they told in Ireland, I suppose for obvious reasons, although they tell it now. He got the tale by heart, then retold it to us one day, with some embellishments of his own. I thought it well done, but Elaine was shocked.

"But, Fion, it is a true tale. The bits you have added are make-believe, of course, and you mustn't do it. The tale is true."

Fion looked amused. "Indeed? Dragons flying over Tintagel, King Uther changed by magic arts into the very Duke Gorolis? The prince hidden in the Enchanted Isles?" Elaine nodded, and he turned to me. "Do you believe this, Guinevere?"

It was awkward, for I had not expressed doubts about Arthur to Elaine for a long time, and I did not wish to arouse her temper, but I told Fion the truth. "It is a manner of speaking, my lord. I believe it was Merlin's plan and that he disguised King Uther and the disguise worked. I believe he protected Prince Arthur throughout his youth, and no one knows where, so one tale will do as well as another."

Fion nodded. "And that while Merlin may be a wise man, he is not—"

"Sir, make no mistake about Merlin." I met his eyes squarely. "He is an enchanter of the first order. He has power. Believe the tales you hear of Prince Merlin."

Fion's eyes widened. "*You* believe, my lady?"

Elaine jumped to my defense. "She knows it for a fact. Prince Merlin singled her out to speak to."

Fion looked thoughtful. "Did he indeed? And what did he say, if I am permitted to ask?"

"Why, nothing much," I replied, suddenly flustered because he was so intent. "He spoke about the future, but he didn't say anything specific. He told me not to be afraid."

"And right after that he disappeared," Elaine continued, "and no one has seen him since. Not even the High King. And although King Arthur has needed him desperately, he has not returned. Why, even the Saxons know and have attacked all winter, thinking King Arthur vulnerable without him, but—"

But Fion was hardly listening. He leaned upon his staff and stared thoughtfully into the fire. Elaine ended with the most recent account of Arthur's victory and of his decisive revenge. She spoke of him proudly, as if he were already her husband. I blushed for her boldness, and I thought Fion noticed it, too. He turned to her.

"And what does this prove, my pretty Elaine? Either that Merlin's magic is working still, or that he is a very wise man."

She misunderstood and tossed her head impatiently. "It proves King Arthur does not need a magician at his back to win battles or hold power."

"Precisely," Fion agreed, smiling benevolently. "He is a man now. And would the world ever have known that, had not Merlin disappeared?"

Elaine looked puzzled. Fion turned to me. "What say you, Guinevere?"

"It is true. Whether it is magic or wisdom, I know not, but I believe that Merlin's disappearance at least in this respect, has done the Kingdom good."

"Ah. Well, you might be right. This confirms me in my desire to meet the High King. Tell me, how old is he?"

"Nineteen last Christmas Eve," Elaine supplied. Fion looked shocked.

"Nineteen! I am twenty myself!" He laughed then, at himself, and shook his head. "He has led a Kingdom for six years already, and what have I done? Studied poetry and music until my father threatened to disown me, and got myself shipwrecked upon Arthur's coast."

"Pellinore's coast," Elaine corrected. Again Fion looked surprised.

"And is not Pellinore Arthur's servant? Is this Britain or Wales? You surprise me, my lady. I thought Britain was a Kingdom and a civilized land."

Elaine squirmed, aware she had erred, but not caring to demote her father.

"It is both," I replied. "This is Wales, part of Britain. These are Pellinore's ancestral lands, but he holds them for Arthur. You may ask him yourself."

Fion smiled and bowed to me. "You are a born diplomat, my lady. I knew I was in a civilized land. I must meet your King."

Elaine glanced at Leonora, who was fast asleep and snoring gently, lulled by the heat of the fire. "You may as soon as you are ransomed, whenever that will be," she said softly, tilting her head and looking coyly up at him. "But perhaps there is a quicker way."

Fion grinned. "I'm much too well bred to escape."

I giggled, but Elaine ignored me. "Offer for the hand of a maiden. If she is highborn, Pellinore must free you to avoid dishonor, and he must have the High King's consent, seeing who you are, I think."

Fion stood quite still, looking at neither of us. I glared at Elaine. How bold! How foolishly direct! It was clear she referred to herself, although she did not want him for a husband. And I knew from the careful way he guarded his expression that he was thinking of me, not of her. Merlin's words came back to me: "What will be, will be." Would it be so hard to have this handsome prince for a husband, even if it were in Ireland? He was amusing, educated, and he spoke to me about important matters, and he valued the things I valued. I could do much worse very easily. Perhaps this was my future. I did not mind. But I knew, as Fion turned toward me with a grave tenderness on his face and desire in his luminous eyes, that I did not love him.

"Perhaps," Fion said softly, "you have hit upon the solution, Lady Elaine."

Elaine flushed angrily, watching his face. Her ruse had backfired; against her will she had played into her mother's hands. A knock came at the door, and Cissa stuck her head in.

"Lady Elaine, the queen your mother requires your presence in the weaving room."

"Leave me, Cissa!" Elaine retorted. "I am not at leisure!"

"Nonsense, you know very well I'd never take such a message

to your mother. You're doing naught but flirting with Prince Fion, and that can certainly wait until later. Come, my lady, she dislikes to be kept waiting."

Elaine shrugged gracelessly. Her manners always left her when she was out of temper. She stalked past Cissa, who leaned toward me with a sly wink and whispered, "The queen's orders, my lady, to stay with the prince awhile. No need to wake up Leonora." She closed the door firmly behind her.

I studied the floor tiles carefully, my heart pounding fearfully as Fion stepped close to me. He placed his hand on my waist and drew me closer. "Guinevere, look at me." Obediently I raised my face to him, and he kissed me. Then he sighed most dolefully and backed away.

"Fion, I cannot marry you—"

"I know."

I was about to finish "because I am not yet a woman" but stopped in midbreath, astonished.

He smiled a thin, bitter smile. "I would fall to one knee if I were able, Guinevere, and beg your forgiveness for my forwardness. But, you see, I love you. I thought if I did not kiss you, I would perish of the desire." He motioned me to sit, and I collapsed gratefully into the chair. My knees were jelly. Leonora was still asleep.

"I am not a fool," he said after a long silence. "I can see your future plain enough, even if you cannot. Queen Alyse sees it, too, you know. That's why she throws you to me every day, hoping my hothead heritage will overcome my civilized veneer, and I will take you, willingly or not—"

"No!" I gasped. "She would not!"

"And then," he continued, "you would be forced to come to Ireland. And you are mistaken about the queen. She would. Do you think she would entrust her precious daughter to a chaperone who sleeps? Whenever Elaine is alone with me, there are three of them, at least."

I buried my face in my hands. "What are you talking about, Fion? You sound like Merlin, so sure and so garbled. What do you see for me? Why should they fear me so?"

"Ah. Merlin. It takes no magician's eyes to see your promise, Guinevere." He took my hand and raised me, walking me to the door. "You will come to fame and glory, as surely as the stars wheel about the heavens. In two years' time—well, I only hope I shall see it." He kissed my hand and pressed it to his cheek. "Come again tomorrow. Can you sing? Let me teach you a song.

And now leave me here with Leonora and let me spin her a yarn when she awakes."

I left him, but so troubled that I slept not at all that night, and felt ill the next day. And although my illness kept me from him, Elaine did not speak to me for almost a week. Finally I tired of her sulks and faced her. "Elaine, for heaven's sake, try to remember who you are. This behavior becomes a scullery drudge better than Pellinore's daughter."

"How dare you speak to me so!" she retorted. "You forget yourself! Your father was naught but a petty lord, a black Celt whose forefathers were hill men!"

I gasped. "How dare you insult my father! He was wise and brave and kind-hearted, and besides, there's not a Celt in Wales, including Pellinore, who is not descended from the Ancients, and you are a pin-headed hussy to think otherwise!"

Elaine screamed in fury and stamped her foot. "Stop this instant! I forbid you to speak to me ever again! I hate you, Gwen! I wish—I wish—Oh! How I wish you were ugly!" She burst into tears and threw herself upon the bed. I stood silent, stunned into speechlessness by her unexpected words.

"But, Elaine," I ventured lamely, "this is foolishness. I do not want Fion. And he does not want me. Why do you fear me so?"

"He does! He does!" She sobbed into her pillows. "It's plain as day—if you take him from me, I will kill you—I will have you turned out—sent back to your black brothers—I will—" She blubbered on unintelligibly and her distress confused me. Fighting anger, I stood looking down at her shaking body.

"Do you want him? Truly? To marry? Come, Elaine, control yourself just for the smallest second. Tell me your heart. Is Queen of Ireland your ambition?"

But she did not answer and shrugged away my hand. She did not want him. All she wanted was his admiration. Her weeping was hideous, and she did not strive to control it. Grannic hurried in, clucking and fussing, with Ailsa behind her.

"Oh, Lady Guinevere, what have you done to distress her so? Oh, dear, the poor child! Come, Ailsa, help me with her. Oh, dear!"

"Poor child indeed." I snorted in contempt. "She loves weeping better than sense, that's all."

"Guinevere!"

"I will not take insults from her any longer!"

"The lady Elaine would not insult you," Grannic protested, stroking Elaine's hair with tenderness.

"Of course not," I said bitterly. "Within the hour she will have you all believing it was *I* who insulted *her*. I don't care. Elaine, you are an ass."

"Guinevere!" they shrieked, as Elaine howled in rage, but I had already closed the door behind me.

Eventually we were made to apologize to one another, and at length we were allowed to return to Fion, but he must have guessed the trouble, for he never spoke personally to me again. When he discovered I could sing, he was delighted and taught me songs and ballads, sang with me, or just sat by the window, looking out at the Irish Sea and listening as I sang to him. And I sang to him often, to spite Elaine, who had not the voice for it.

So winter passed, and the spring rains came and washed the woods of snow. Messengers arrived from Ireland demanding ransom for the prince, and negotiations took place, week upon week, while the sun warmed the earth into bud and green grass sprang from the mud. Zephyr and I went out daily, but the beach was forbidden us now. Queen Alyse, thinking Fion's courtship progressed nicely, was graciousness itself toward me. She reminded me of a cat preening. Elaine could be no more than civil, but she was pleased that he no longer singled me out for his admiration.

Of the High King we heard only that he still grieved for his lost queen and that he still grieved for Merlin. The anguish of his grief had settled into a kind of grim despair, which worried his Companions. But his judgment of men, his justice, and his prowess as a warrior never faltered. The building on Caer Camel was nearly finished, and he planned to take possession of the fortress by midsummer. But the Saxons would not give him rest. Every time a leader fell, a younger, more eager, more bloodthirsty one rose to take his place, and the attacks continued.

A royal messenger arrived near the end of April. There were Angles and Saxons in the Caledonian Forest. Lot was marching to hem them in from the north; King Arthur was riding north and would pass through Wales in two days. Pellinore was summoned to gather troops and join him.

Negotiations for the return of Fion were nearly completed. It was time, Alyse said, he made his move.

We feasted the royal courier that night at the round table, and Elaine and I were allowed to stay and listen as the men talked about the wars. King Pellinore seemed delighted to be escaping the confines of the castle and taking to horse. He spoke eagerly of the upcoming action, and also of the Irish gold he expected to help finance the expedition. This was the first the courier had heard of an Irish prisoner, and he listened attentively as Pellinore told the story of his capture and convalescence. Of course Pellinore left women out of the story and, in so doing, missed most of what had actually happened. Elaine and I kept our faces straight, but her eyes were bright with merriment.

At the end of the story, the king's chamberlain approached and announced that the hostage, Prince Fion, begged audience of the king in the presence of the royal messenger. Pellinore was surprised and looked over at Alyse for advice. She nodded complacently, and he shrugged.

"Very well. Bring him. Let's see what he wants."

Fion entered in his best clothes. There was the fine, white blouse of Irish linen Elaine and I had repaired for him, new leggings of soft leather, and a dark-green mantle of good Welsh wool. He walked without a splint now, and the leg had knit straight, although it pained him to wear a boot on it for long.

He bowed low before King Pellinore, and then before the ladies, and last before the royal courier.

"Good King Pellinore, I have been a prisoner and hostage in your home for three months now, and I have been treated like an honored guest. Such hospitality is amazing to one such as I, bred in a less sophisticated land, especially as I know well I have done nothing to deserve it. I feel I must do something for you, my lord, besides allow my relations to send you gold." He paused, to judge how it was going. King Pellinore seemed pleased and the courier stunned. Queen Alyse waited expectantly.

"There is not much that is in my power to do, I admit. But I am young, I am unwed, and promised to no woman. I am my father's only heir. It would please me, and I hope do you honor, to make one of your household my wife and future Queen of Ireland."

King Pellinore's jaw dropped, and then he grinned broadly. "I call that a handsome offer, lad. Which one of them do you want?"

Fion bowed low. "Sir, with humble respect, I ask for the hand of your daughter, the beautiful Elaine."

Elaine gasped. Alyse looked scandalized. With an effort, I made my face an expressionless mask—it was best; everyone expected me to look hurt, while I could barely contain my laughter. King Pellinore had opened his mouth to accept him when Alyse cut in.

"Pellinore, this is not a thing to be taken lightly, nor discussed in public. It is up to Elaine to decide, and she should be given time. She is young to leave home. I—I would have thought, sir," she addressed herself coolly to Fion, "that there are those among the king's household of a riper age for marriage than my daughter. Honor would still be conferred."

"Perhaps so, gracious lady," Fion replied with a glint in his eye, "but none but Princess Elaine could I ask to be my wife." He left it at that, and there was nothing Alyse could say. But Pellinore was slower to catch on. He motioned Fion over to him and lowered his voice until he thought I could not hear him.

"If she's too young, what about my ward, Guinevere? She's as pretty as the other, if I do say it myself, and a mite older. Wouldn't she do as well, my lord?"

"With all due respect for yourself, sire, and with all respect and admiration for your ward, whose beauty has not passed unnoticed, I assure you, I can only offer for the Lady Elaine. I would be false to my heart to do otherwise."

"Well, well," Pellinore grumbled, pleased as punch at his reply, and tickled pink, I could see, at the thought of Elaine's being Queen of Ireland, "I'll not stand in your way. But it's up to my daughter, you know, and the queen seems not to favor it. Let me speak with them awhile."

"Thank you, my lord. There is—one more thing. I wonder if you would present me to King Arthur."

"If my daughter accepts you, you may be sure I shall. If not, on what grounds? You are my hostage, not his."

"So I am aware, my lord. But as I am to be King of Ireland, it is meet I should know the man with whom I shall have to deal. It matters not to me whether I come to him as hostage or free man, and I can't see that it would matter to him."

"Hmmm. I shall consider it. There is something in the suggestion. I leave day after tomorrow to join him; perhaps I shall discuss it with him then, if the Saxons give us leave."

Dinner ended swiftly after Fion left, and Alyse called us both into her chamber for a conference.

"Did you know about this, Guinevere?" she asked angrily.

"No, madam, indeed I did not."

"Why are you angry with Gwen, Mother? She has done nothing but been publicly spurned," Elaine protested, slipping an arm around my waist. "How can you blame her? She is to be pitied. Oh, Gwen, I'm so sorry I was jealous. All this time I thought he loved you, not me."

I shrugged. "There's no need for pity."

Alyse paced furiously across the chamber.

"I don't believe it for a minute," she snapped. "It's a clever plot, very clever. I've harbored a viper in my nest. The scoundrel! How dare he?"

Leonora and Cissa backed against the drapes. I kept my eyes on the floor.

"Mother!" Elaine cried. "Are you insulted at his proposal? You act so, and yet you want it for Gwen. I thought you would be proud."

Alyse shook her head. "Oh, Elaine, my dear. You cannot understand. It was an honorable enough proposal. I accuse him of being insincere. He offered for you because he knows you will reject him." A wave of fear swept her face. "You *will* reject him, Elaine."

"Yes, Mother."

"Had he offered for Gwen, he might have been accepted."

"I would not have accepted," I said quietly, to the floor.

"You are my ward. I might have accepted for you," Alyse replied, stiffening.

I looked up then. So she would not allow me my choice, after all. I think I had suspected it all along. I met her eyes squarely, and the relationship between us subtly changed and hardened into battle lines. "You could not have accepted for me."

Alyse bristled. "I am queen and your guardian. Tell my why I could not have accepted for you. It is the best you could ever do."

"Because," I said, the words dropping into the silence like stones into a still pool, "I am not yet a woman."

Alyse stared, then threw up her hands in resignation.

"Then perhaps it is just as well. You are old enough to be betrothed, and marriage could wait six months or longer. It cannot be that far off, at the rate you are growing. But as it stands, he has not offered, so I cannot accept."

"If you had accepted, I would not go."

The women gasped and held their breaths as Alyse flushed darkly. "You would go. Else you would be horsewhipped."

"I shall not leave Britain." I spoke with certainty, although it was only a blind faith in Fion's visions.

Alyse came up to me. I noticed that I was taller by a handspan and that there were gray hairs among the gold on her head. "Until you come into womanhood, niece, you will do exactly as I tell you. And when that blessed day arrives, I shall marry you off to the very first lord who looks at you twice. See if I don't. You are dismissed."

Back in our chamber, Elaine embraced me. "Gwen, I apologize for my mother. And I apologize for all my rude behavior. I have said things—you know which things—I did not mean. But I thought, all this time, that he loved you."

I lowered my eyes. "Thank you, Elaine. But he has not hurt my feelings, as everyone thinks. I knew he would not offer for me. So you see, I have lost nothing by it. And you have gained much. You have turned down the King of Ireland!"

She brightened and hugged me again. "Let's make a pact. We will swear by the Virgin never to fall in love with the same man. Is it agreed?"

The mischievous glint in her eye made me laugh. "Whoever sees him first, you mean? If I am ever to find a husband with you about, Elaine, I see I must practice my sprints!"

We laughed together, but I knew in my heart what she meant. I must take care from now on to keep well away from anyone Elaine admired. I was never again to be first in anyone's eyes. She would not forgive me twice.

Alyse and Pellinore did not sleep at all that night, by the look of them in the morning. And their arguments continued for the next two days. Pellinore was heard to exclaim that he didn't give a——if Elaine liked the lad or not. Queen of Ireland was good enough for him, and therefore good enough for her. If she persisted in refusing every suitor who came to her door, he would take matters into his own hands and contract her, sight unseen, to a lord of his choosing. Queen Alyse got round him somehow, though, for he was resigned to it by the time he left to meet Arthur.

Fion was left behind to nurse his disappointment. What he really thought we did not know, for we were forbidden to visit him any longer. But when we rode beneath his window, sometimes we heard him singing.

8 BETROTHAL

A week after my fourteenth birthday, Merlin's prophecy was fulfilled, and I began to bleed. I shared my excitement only with Elaine, and together, with Ailsa's help, we kept it secret from Alyse. For although her anger had passed, she was not kind to me any longer, and all of us who had heard her threaten me believed her. King Pellinore, her only master, was still away at war; while he was gone her power was absolute.

Fion was kept to his room, and I missed his company. Even when I was out with Zephyr, which was where I loved best to be, I thought of him, now a true prisoner, with pity and regret. I even toyed with the idea of telling Alyse I would marry him if he asked me—he was a good companion, I knew he cared for me, and Ireland could not be so bad. Almost anything was better than this tension at home. But I knew, in my heart, he would not take me. By some strange logic he had convinced himself I was meant for something else. It made me want to laugh, had it not been so sad.

Then in the month of the summer solstice we had a messenger from King Pellinore. The fighting was done, and the Saxons turned back in a great victory. King Lot of Lothian had received his death blow there, and Merlin the Enchanter had been found living in a cave in the Caledonian Forest within a stone's throw of the battleground. King Pellinore would be home with his troops in a week's time, and we were to send messages to Ireland to bring gold for Fion's ransom and take him away.

The palace was thrown into sudden activity. Everything was made ready at once. The castle was cleaned from top to bottom, a great feast was prepared, hunts were organized for fresh game, wild flowering herbs were gathered and fashioned into wreaths, which we hung in every room to sweeten the air. In all the bustle I managed to visit Fion twice without being noticed.

The first time I went to thank him properly for his offer for Elaine. He kissed my cheek and replied it was the least he could do for the princess who saved his life. When I told him the great news, that the High King had been victorious and Merlin had been found alive, he replied that he had never doubted either event. The second time I went to see him was the day before Pellinore's return and his own departure. He was very solemn then, and excited, also. We said good-bye.

"I shall see you again, sweet Guinevere," he promised. "I shall come to your wedding."

I shuddered. "Don't talk about weddings, I pray you." And I told him what Queen Alyse had said.

He only smiled. "She can't do it. You will see. There are forces at work in this land that not even Queen Alyse can command. Open your eyes."

"What will you do when you are free?"

"To Ireland, I suppose, since the High King is away. And you?"

"What I always do in summer. Ride away from the castle as often as I can, on whatever excuse I can fashion."

"You should get yourself a falcon. That's all the excuse you need. Oh, Guinevere, this parting is more difficult than I expected."

He reached for me and pulled me up against him. He kissed my throat, and then my lips, and hugged me tightly. "Never forget you have a friend in Ireland. You need only send a word, and I will come to your aid."

His countrymen sailed in that evening and were reunited with him. King Pellinore arrived the next day with much fanfare. Everyone attended a great feast in the hall that night. The room was crowded with extra benches, and between the press of bodies and the flaring torches, it grew very warm.

The first piece of business was the ransoming of Fion. This was accomplished with great ceremony, and when it was done, and Fion was a free man, he was offered and accepted a seat of honor at the round table. Then King Pellinore gave an account of the battle against the Saxons and the finding of Merlin.

"He was wandering about fringes of the battlefield, his wits quite gone, giving directions to the soldiers. One of the captains bound him to a tree to keep him out of harm's way, but at battle's end when they went back to release him, he was gone, although the rope was there, with all the knots still tied. The soldiers were convinced he was an apparition, but the captain was not so sure.

He had been calling out the names of Ector, Kay, and Bedwyr, and Arthur's childhood name. When the High King heard this story, he left off his pursuit of Saxon stragglers and raced back to scour the forest."

The story Pellinore told of Arthur's reunion with his friend touched the heart of everyone in the hall. He found Merlin in a small, damp cave, dressed in skins, aged twenty years, gray-haired and feeble, and never left his side from the moment he arrived until the great magician opened his eyes and spoke his name, three days later. Then he wept and kissed him, and fed him broth with his own hands. Merlin recovered his wits, but had no recollection of what had happened to him last autumn, or of the time in between. Some said the rigors of the Caledonian winter had robbed him of his youth and vigor; some said it had to be the work of poison; others maintained this was just another shape that Merlin took, by his own choosing. So as things stood, no one knew why or how Merlin had disappeared, and Merlin himself said nothing.

There followed many toasts to King Arthur and some to Fion, and the hall began to get rowdy. Queen Alyse rose to lead the ladies out. But before we left, I heard Pellinore advise Fion that the High King was traveling south to Caerleon before going on to invest Caer Camel and would be passing along the eastern border of Wales in the next day or two. Fion's features lit with joy, and he thanked Pellinore for ransoming him, that he might meet the High King of Britain as a free man. He left the next day to catch the King along the Glevum road. What he thought of our young King we did not learn that season, for he returned along the northern route to Caer Narvon and took sail from there. But I heard later that within a day of their meeting, Prince Fion had sworn the future allegiance of Ireland to Arthur, and Arthur had sworn the present friendship and protection of Britain to the Gaels.

Caer Camel was invested that summer, and at last Britain had a center, a fighting fortress for her King and his fighting men. It lay in the middle of the Summer Country, the land of gently rolling downs and soft breezes where sheep graze year round, the air smells faintly of the salt marshes, and the signal fires on hill and tor give long warning of an enemy's approach. The Saxon hordes were quiet that summer. Rumor had it they were finally defeated or, on the other hand, that they were regrouping for one last desperate attack. Arthur of the Eleven Battles was ready for them. He spent that year reinforcing his defenses, reestablishing contact with all his vassal lords, settling territory disputes, and gathering to his side young men of fighting age who wished to join the King's Companions.

I followed Fion's suggestion and persuaded Pellinore to let me hawk. I think he pitied me, after my public rejection by Fion, and sensing the queen's mistrust of me afterward, determined to do me a kindness. He was a soft-hearted man, though his speech was blunt and his manner gruff. His falconer found me a young bird, which I trained as Gwarthgydd had taught me. I fashioned its jesses myself out of soft worked leather and then, to my consternation, discovered that Zephyr was terrified of the thing. It took two whole months to get her to accept the bird and to get her accustomed to being ridden without reins and following leg signals only. But eventually we three worked as a team, and my young falcon Ebon provided many a fat dove for the queen's supper, whether she knew it or not.

The next time I saw Fion was in the autumn of my fourteenth year. Gilomar had died that summer, and Fion was now King. He was on his way to Caer Camel to a meeting of all of Arthur's nobles and his allies, called by the Companions for the purpose of finding Arthur a wife. Pellinore himself was going and stayed his departure to wait for Fion and travel down with him to the Summer Country. The news of this great meeting spread like wildfire throughout the kingdoms, and every king who attended carried instructions from his lady to propose his daughter, or his granddaughter, or his niece or whomever among his kin was the most eligible. Bards were hired to sing poems extolling the beauties of this maid and that. Family lineages were hunted up and extended back to Roman governors, or Maximus if it was possible. Bargains were made among families for backing; friendships of long standing were broken in the heat of competition.

The only two people in the Kingdom who stood aloof from this frenzy were, oddly, the High King and myself. By all reports Arthur had no desire to remarry, but was aware of the necessity to produce an heir, and thus yielded to the pressure brought by his Companions. He was content to let his subjects make the choice for him. All he required in a bride, he had said, was an honest tongue and a soft voice. As for myself, even if I had had Elaine's ambition, which I did not, there was no one to speak for me. My parents were dead. My brothers had daughters of their own. My guardians were the parents of one of the most eligible maidens in the land, and one who desired nothing more than the very position that needed filling. At last, it seemed, the world was marching to

Elaine's tune. This, she told me in secret, as if it were news, was what she had been born for. She was sure of it.

Indeed, in the new gown she wore to Fion's welcome feast, she looked every inch a queen. With her dark gold hair bound with flowers, her dancing, sky-blue eyes, her milky skin, and willowy figure, she could have passed for a woman of twenty, although she was but thirteen. Even Fion stared. He was still unmarried, but it was too late to renew his suit for Elaine. The only topic at dinner that night was the searching of Britain for Arthur's bride, and Elaine positively glowed. When Pellinore announced his intention to propose Elaine to the High King, the hall stood up and cheered. Elaine squeezed my hand hard under the table, and although she cast down her eyes as a maid should, her look was triumphant. I kissed her cheek affectionately and caught Fion looking at us thoughtfully.

When the noise in the hall had abated somewhat, I turned to Fion. "My lord Fion, the last time we saw you, you were on your way to make your peace with our King. Pray tell us how you found him: Were you treated honorably? Did you get fair hearing?"

"I have never met a more honorable man, fair lady," Fion replied solemnly. "Your King was graciousness itself. He heard me out until I had nothing more to say. He knew who I was, but he did not hold my father's sins against me. By the questions he asked, I saw he had a thorough knowledge of our shore defenses and knew something of the rivalries among our petty kings. I do not know how he gets his information, or how he has the time to think of Ireland with the Saxons at his back, but he understood how the land lay all about him, and he welcomed me most honorably. He made me feel like a brother." He paused. Pellinore was nodding with a broad smile on his face, and Elaine's eyes were shining. "He speaks to the lowliest of his servants with consideration. Every man has respect at Arthur's table. Were my heart not in Ireland, I would lay it at his feet."

Every man in the hall rose cheering, and there were many shouts of "Arthur!" and "Fion!" I was moved by his testimonial. Elaine was beside herself with excitement.

"You see, Gwen," she whispered to me, "he really is what he is supposed to be! I have known it my entire life!"

So she had. Elaine had never lost her faith in Arthur. She had believed every wondrous tale she had heard about him, and Fion's words were only fuel to her fire. I prayed hard that night that God would grant her her wish, even if it meant Alyse took us all to live at court.

Everyone knows what happened, of course. It is difficult to look back over the span of years and remember the uproar of those days. The meeting, which had been planned to last a week in order that everyone could speak, stretched to two weeks, and then three. There were too many candidates, and a consensus could not be found. Every leading family in the land had a daughter or a niece of marriageable age. Every maid had a flawless lineage, flawless complexion, flawless eyes of black, brown, blue, green, gray; flawless hair of gold, brown, black, red; features of surpassing beauty, an honest tongue and a lovely voice. Even Arthur wearied of it and went hawking. Feuds developed, powerful leaders backed one family and then another as the offers of gold increased. Happy was the man who had nothing to gain or lose by the King's decision. And throughout it all, Merlin sat by the High King's chair, old and frail, his black eyes watching it all, saying nothing.

At last, his patience near an end, King Arthur commanded the meeting to close. He would not divide his Kingdom over a woman, he said. He would rather die unwed. Only then did a young man rise from the rear of the Welsh delegation and, having received permission to speak, addressed the High King in a trembling voice. Just as silver was found threaded into black rock deep within the earth, he began, just as gold was sprinkled sparsely over pebbled sands, so all treasures worth pursuing did not come easy; the brightest jewel often lay buried in the darkest clay. As he overcame his fear, his voice fell into the sweet singsong of the storyteller, and the Welshmen in the hall settled back comfortably to hear his tale. It was, it seems, the tale of the emperor Maximus and how he found his Elen, the famous Welsh beauty with sapphire eyes whom Maximus wed and for whom he forswore allegiance to Rome. She was, he sang, fairer than the stars among the heavens, more constant than the sun in his course across the sky, sweeter than wildflowers that grace the summer meadows, and ever a true companion to the king. In all his endeavors she was beside him; she brought him luck and victory; he never lost a battle until he left Britain, where she could not follow. The singer paused—Welshmen were wont to attribute Maximus' prowess to the virtues of his Welsh wife, but it was unwise to expect this descendant of Maximus to believe it—he claimed, instead, that hidden in the dark Welsh mountains lay a jewel as bright as Elen, a girl as beautiful, as wise and steadfast, as Maximus' own bride. Like a vein of precious metal lying undiscovered in the hills, she awaited the High King's notice; a word from him could bring her gold to light. A king's daughter she was, descended from Elen, with hair of starlight and the voice of a nightingale. And Gwillim, for it was my old childhood companion who had risen to speak before them all, took a deep breath and held hard to his courage. The maiden's name, he said, was Guinevere.

There was a shocked silence. The Companions froze. Arthur's face was a mask. Merlin closed his eyes. Then the throng found their voices, and angry protests arose on all sides. "How dare the boy?" "What maid is this? I have heard no tell of her." "That he should mention the name before the king!" Then Gwarthgydd rose and clapped a hand on Gwillim's shoulder.

"My lords," he said, and his deep rumbling voice got their attention. "The lad speaks of my half-sister, Guinevere of Northgallis. In his later years, my father the King of Northgallis wed Elen of Gwynedd, a beauty of renown. She died giving birth to the lady in question, who was a childhood friend of Gwillim's here. She is now the ward of King Pellinore and Queen Alyse and lives in Gwynedd. Gwillim likes a good tale, but all he has said is true enough."

"Is that the Lark of Gwynedd?" someone asked. "I have heard of her."

"Isn't that the maid the old witch prophesied about, the night of her birth? You remember Giselda—"

"A curse, I thought it was, a spell—"

"Oh, no, she prophesied great beauty and great fame—"

"Has anyone seen her?" one of the Companions asked. "Where is Pellinore? Who can attest to the lad's claims?"

But Pellinore, weary of words, was out hunting. It was Fion who stood.

That winter lasted forever. Elaine lay abed with an illness born of disappointment and envy, and Alyse could barely tolerate the sight of me. Pellinore was proud and conscious of his new status in the High King's inner circle, but he never came to the women's quarters, wishing to avoid Alyse's cold fury at his betrayal, and I saw him only at dinner in the evenings. The queen's ladies kept aloof at the queen's wishes. Only Ailsa, of all the women in the castle, was thoroughly excited on my behalf.

"Just think of it! Wouldn't your dear mother be proud! Her little Gwen to be King Arthur's Queen! Why, I just pinch myself when I think of it! How lucky you are, my lady! How happy you will be!"

But I could not see how this unexpected event could make me happy. Already it seemed to have cost me Elaine's friendship, and she was the only real friend I had ever had. Proud as I was to be chosen out of all the maids in Britain, I could not envision happiness ahead. I was to be married to a man I had never met, and because he was who he was, there was no possible way out of it. I did not feel the thrill all Britain expected me to feel; I felt only apprehension and a nagging regret that I had not married Fion.

However much she suffered at the sight of me, Alyse knew her duty. She set all her ladies to work on my wardrobe, and we sat together all winter sewing my wedding clothes, fashioning new gowns, weaving bed linens and chamber hangings. Dear Pellinore ended up spending Fion's ransom on my trousseau. For if I did not go to Arthur surrounded by the most luxurious finery in the kingdom, I would shame Wales. We had the long winter to get ready, for in the spring the King would come himself to take me out of Wales.

I put this from my mind, for I shook with fear at the very thought of it. Wales was the only home I knew. I remembered every word I had ever spoken to Elaine about how dreadful it would be to be Arthur's Queen—well, I thought, I was justly served. That horrible witch had been proved right. And poor Gwillim, who I am sure thought he was doing me the finest service of his life, had been the unwitting instrument of my undoing. But there was nothing to do but face it. If I opened my mouth in complaint, I would shame Alyse and Pellinore, I would shame Northgallis, I would shame Wales. So I said very little and let the people take my silence for maidenly modesty if they chose.

In the month before the equinox Elaine finally rose from her bed. She was thin and pale and took the chair closest to the fire, but at least she joined us.

"Gwen," she said on our first night together in four months, "please forgive me for my grief. I wish you all happiness, you know that. I hated you for a while, but that was my unruly jealousy. I have remembered the prophecy at your birth, and also Merlin's prophecy, and I know that it is you who were born for this, and not I. Please forgive me."

"Oh, Elaine!" I threw my arms around her and we cried together for a long time. "Dear cousin, I would give anything in the world to change places with you and give you your heart's desire!

Can you think for one moment I would not, knowing how you feel? Oh, Elaine, I do not want to leave Wales!"

"You will not have to go alone," she said. "Mother says we shall all accompany you to court and see you married."

"Bless you!" I cried.

"And although Mother must return, I will stay if you like. Surely you may have your own friends there, as the High King has his."

"Oh, thank you, Elaine. You warm my heart, truly. You would give up your home for *me*? Dear Elaine, marry one of his Companions and stay with me always!" But I should not have spoken of marriage. She went pale and trembled.

"I will never marry. Never."

A cold breath seemed to blow upon my neck, and I shivered. "You will not always feel so, I am sure. Listen, Elaine, once you see the King himself you will not be so enamored of him. He cannot be the dream you cherish any more than he can be the ogre I fear." But she did not answer.

Wedding gifts began to arrive in Gwynedd and Caer Camel. King Fion sent yards of the finest, snow-white linen—no one on earth makes finer linen than the Irish, and this must have been bleached and beaten two hundred times to get such softness and luster. Alyse declared it perfect for the marriage bed and would not let me touch it, but set her ladies to do the embroidery, although my needlework was finer. Fion also sent quantities of jewelry for Elaine and Queen Alyse as well as myself, all silver and enamel, worked in the intricate way of the Gaels, with interlocking vines and queer nested squares. And he sent me as his personal gift a pair of silver earrings worked around dark blue sapphires that caught the firelight and reminded one of the color of the sea in a summer storm. "To wear," said his note, "with sapphire eyes." I missed him dreadfully.

King Pellinore's carpenters were hard at work building wagons to carry all the gifts and all the luggage to Caer Camel. Horses had to be bought from neighboring lands and trained to pull them, and his stable had to be enlarged to hold them. Food had to be bought from other kingdoms, even from Less Britain, for the High King would stay with us a month, and everyone in his train had to be fed, yes, and housed. Barracks were erected, and more temporary stables. The place was a riot of feverish activity. Men worked through snow and frost, day and night; no one rested. I used to stand by my window and watch them, amazed that this was all for me. At such times I felt the crushing weight of Britain's expectation. I was the chosen of Arthur—I could be no less than perfect. Whatever flaw they found with me would be magnified a thousand times. And there would be many—all the relatives and friends of the maids he had not chosen—looking to find fault. I could take no wrong step, say no hasty speech, or I would cast a shadow across the glory of Britain. These fears usually sent me into a fit of weeping, but the women only nodded to one another and winked behind my back. Even Ailsa said once in my hearing that all I needed was a good bedding and my fears would take care of themselves. I fainted when I heard it, and after that the women were more careful in their speech.

The truth was, I had never stopped to think that I was marrying a man. At twenty, Arthur was already a legend, even among the Saxons. He was an idea, not flesh and blood. I should have to bear him princes, but exactly what that meant I had not considered. As the rains of April fell, and Elaine grew quieter, and the women stitched away madly at the King's wedding sheets, it began to be real to me. And I was terrified.

I escaped to the stables on dry days and took Zephyr out on the hills, or flew Ebon, or dallied on the beach. They let me go wherever I chose, although I had a chaperone of troopers. Nothing could be allowed to happen to me. I was no longer merely Guinevere; I was King Arthur's betrothed. It angered me sometimes that the word of a single man I had not even met could so change my life. And it frightened me, also. What was the High King expecting? An ornament to his court? A broodmare? Surely he must realize that Gwillim's words were poetry and never meant to describe a woman of flesh and blood! Suppose—suppose he frowned on women riding horses? Should I have to take a litter, like Alyse? Oh, I wept in frustration and pounded my poor mare over the hills in desperate attempts to escape such thoughts, but they were always there when I returned.

Father Martin was useless as a confidant. He could barely hear my confession, so ready was he to bend the knee to me. I prayed to the Virgin, helpmate of women, to give me the strength to endure what was coming. But when I closed my eyes at night, all that came to me was Merlin's face and the gentle, ghostly voice repeating "what will be, will be."

My fifteenth birthday came and went, barely noticed in the frantic bustle, and three days later a royal courier arrived. Elaine and I gripped each other on the staircase as we strained to hear him give his message to Pellinore in the hall. Spring had brought new longboats to the eastern shores, and the northern kings could not hold their defenses against an attack of such numbers, should it come. King Arthur was required to show his face there and deal with them and could not come to take his bride to Caer Camel. But not wishing to delay the wedding, which was set for the summer solstice, he was sending in his stead three of his closest Companions and a troop of horses to take me to Caer Camel to await his arrival there.

Elaine and I turned to each other. On her face was writ her disappointment; on mine was sheer relief. The men would be arriving in three days and would stay until such time as we felt ready to depart. This was wonderful news! The building could cease, the cooks could rest, and everyone except the queen's ladies could be sure that the preparations they had already made would be sufficient. But a trousseau is never finished. There is always one more cushion to stuff, one more gown to stitch, one more slipper to line.

Elaine had made me a nightgown, entirely of her own design and working, of creamy linen lined with silk, and edged with costly laces. On the morning of the third day she bade me try it on for a final fitting. It was a lovely thing, with loose, flowing lines and a low throat. But Elaine was unhappy with the bodice, which she felt should be tighter. She gripped the cloth at the back until it was tight, and then placed her hand upon my bosom to get the shape. Then an odd thing happened. She hesitated and met my eyes. We both thought, at exactly the same moment, of where this gown would be worn, and that a man's large, brown hand would be where her small, white one lay, and she jumped away as I gasped, and we both turned scarlet.

"Oh, Gwen, I can't bear the thought of it!" she cried, tears welling in her eyes.

"Neither can I!" I wailed, as we fell weeping into each other's arms. This is but one illustration among many of the state we were in.

Unable to stand the castle any longer, I dressed in my doeskin leggings and soft boots and my old green mantle and went to the stable. I asked no one's permission. Today was the long-awaited day, and everyone was too busy to notice me. I took Ebon on my arm, hopped on Zephyr, and rode bareback up into the hills. The King's men were not expected until nightfall, and I should be back, bathed, perfumed, and gowned before they saw me.

It was a glorious day in May, golden and soft, and the forests were full of birds returning to their summer homes. We had a good gallop, and then we had wonderful hunting, one exciting chase after another, with five kills to Ebon's credit by midafternoon, when I hooded him because the pouch was full. He could have filled a saddlebag that magic day, had I brought one with me. We stopped at a stream for Zephyr to drink, and I felt it suddenly—the thrill of excitement, the throbbing expectancy of something marvelous that lay ahead and was coming. It was a wonderful day to be alive. For the first time in months my spirit lifted, and I felt like singing. We stood in the silence of the forest with dappled sunlight falling all about, while cool water dripped from the mare's muzzle and small creatures rustled in the underbrush. In the blessed stillness, the birds began to sing, tentatively at first, and then in full-throated song. The hawk sat hooded and quiet on my arm as the budding treetops came alive with music. I whistled in imitation and then joined in their chorus, and they let me.

The mare walked gently down the forest track while I sang to the birds, happy to be young and alive, glorying in the magic brightness of that special day. We came upon a clearing, and suddenly the mare stopped, threw up her head, and nickered. I looked about, but it was several moments before I saw the young man on the black horse. They stood under the trees where the track left the clearing, and he was staring at me. As I noticed him, he slid from his horse and took two steps forward. He cleared his throat, but no sound came out. He just stood in the clearing as if he had been there always, and my heart began to pound. He wore a strange device on his cloak, and his clothes were cut a little oddly, but that he was a knight there was no doubt. Black hair fell across his brow and shaded his eyes. His face had good lines and would have been handsome if his nose had not been broken and set slightly crooked. It gave an oddness to his face that set his features apart from those of other men. I could not explain why my spirit soared as I looked at him. He was a stranger, yet he set me trembling. He took another step forward and tried again to speak. I went weak inside, as if I would melt like butter in the sun.

"Are you—are you a vision or are you real?" he whispered. The question, spoken low and almost out of hearing, did not seem out of place, for I had wondered the same about him.

"I am no vision, my lord. Where—who—what badge is that you bear? You are no Welshman."

He bent one knee and sank down on the new grass. "Forgive such forwardness, my lady. I am a poor knight from foreign parts, and this badge is the badge of my homeland. My name is Lancelot."

9 Lancelot

"Your manners commend you, good Lancelot. Welcome to Gwynedd. My name is Guinevere. My guardian King Pellinore is lord of this land. We are not far from his castle. If there is aught that you require—food or rest or fodder for your horse, I—I am sure he would provide it."

His eyes widened. They were clear and cool and liquid gray. I stopped speaking. The silence around us seemed to breathe.

"Gracious lady," he said at last, his voice husky. "I have been there. It is you I seek, if you are Guinevere of Northgallis."

I was trembling so hard that Ebon shifted on my arm. The pressure of his grip brought me back to myself. "Please rise, my lord. I am the one you seek."

He stood and came toward me. Then Zephyr did an unexpected thing. She lowered her head and shoved him gently in the chest. He looked at the mare.

"Fina!" he cried. "Is it you, my girl? Dear God, it is!" Then he turned to me, and his smile robbed me of breath. "*You* are the one! Pellinore's ward! I remember it now!"

I feared lest he touch me, and I lose my seat on the horse. But he did not. He backed away a pace.

"You—you are the knight who bred and trained her? I—I had forgotten the name. I had always hoped to meet you and thank you for bringing so much pleasure into my life."

He flushed scarlet. "It gives me great joy to do you the smallest service."

His lashes were long and dark and lent his eyes a beauty that is usually a woman's gift. He was tall and slenderly built, with a sword hanging in a much-used, plain leather scabbard from his belt. As I looked at him, and he looked at me, the birds took up their interrupted song, and I knew in my soul that he was the magic behind the day. I believe I smiled at him; I know his face lit with happiness.

"What service may this humble maid perform for Lancelot, to repay the debt?" I asked him softly.

He caught his breath in surprise and then sobered suddenly, tapped on the shoulder by the finger of remembrance. He straightened and bowed. "My lady Guinevere, I have come to take you to Arthur."

It was a cloud across the sun; the cold shadow passed over, and the day darkened. Only then did I see two other horsemen in the trees behind him, waiting patiently. They wore swords and badges, and an indefinable air of self-importance. Of course. They were the King's Companions, they and Lancelot, who was foremost among them. As I watched, they rode forward into the clearing and, unsheathing their swords, touched the blades to their foreheads in salute.

"Princess Guinevere," Lancelot said formally, "these are two of the King's Companions, Kay of Galava, son of Ector, and Bedwyr of Brydwell, son of Boad. Gentlemen, Princess Guinevere of Northgallis."

They performed their formal greetings, as I did mine. Bedwyr looked worriedly at Lancelot, and Kay looked in some alarm at the hooded falcon on my arm.

"No doubt you could outride us at will," Lancelot said smiling, "so I beg you will lead us a decorous pace back to the castle, else we lose our way. We are supposed to be your escort."

I returned his smile, and for a moment there seemed to be only the two of us in the whole world. "Far be it from me to bring shame upon any who serve King Arthur. Have no fear. I shall be ladylike."

He grinned, and I could see the others were pleased by my response. Lancelot turned and whistled for his stallion, who trotted up and stood patiently while he mounted.

Zephyr nickered, and the stallion's ears shot forward.

"Not now, Nestor." Lancelot laughed. "Maybe next year." And he signaled me to take my place at his side for the ride back.

"That is a trick you must teach me, my lord," I said to him. "I can see that it would be useful."

"It would be an honor and a pleasure, my lady. But if my eyes deceive me not, there is not much I could teach you about a horse. You speak their language."

I was thinking the same thing about him. One can tell a born rider simply by watching the way he sits his horse. Lancelot's stallion was interested in the mare, but he controlled the animal effortlessly, without thought, with legs and seat and hand, as fluidly and as softly as the horse himself moved. It must give pleasure to the horse, I thought, to be ridden with such skill.

As we approached the castle, the woods gave way to fields, and I glanced mischievously at Lancelot. "Would my lord care to follow me? I know a shorter way back, but there are obstacles."

He hesitated, aware of the challenge. "Obstacles for a horse, my lady, or obstacles for a man?"

I laughed. "Follow me, my lord, and find out."

He glanced swiftly behind him and nodded. "Lead on."

I took them to my jumping field where I had, over time, fashioned a formidable series of obstacles. I settled Ebon on my arm and sang softly to him for reassurance, for this was new to him. Then I put Zephyr into a light gallop, and we flew over the obstacles. I gloried in the sensation of hurtling through the air, with the salt sea breeze in my face and my hair whipping behind me. I felt like a prisoner granted a last day of freedom before execution, and this was it—my last taste of girlhood. At the top of the field, I cantered the mare in a circle and then brought her to a halt. All three knights were standing where I had left them, watching me. I waited. It had been easy for us, we had done it before. But although the fences were new to them, the animals they rode were trained warhorses, stronger than Zephyr and as nimble, who knew maneuvers on a field of battle and could be a third weapon under a good rider. Lancelot was a horseman. We should see about the others.

Lancelot gathered his stallion and cantered toward the first fence. The stallion shied, but then obeyed and pushed himself over. At the next brush pile he took off too far out and barely missed landing upon it. By the third fence Lancelot had learned to judge the distance, and every obstacle thereafter was an improvement upon the one before. At length he drew up beside me, breathing hard, eyes shining.

"By heaven, that is a sport for kings! My compliments to Pellinore for building it, and to your own skill, my lady—the bird never stirred from your arm!"

"Pellinore had nothing to do with it," I retorted. "It was my own idea. I like to jump. And as for Ebon, he trusts me."

He stared. "My compliments to you, then, Lady Guinevere. But surely he built it for you."

"Certainly not. He disapproves of my jumping. I built it myself."

"By God!" he cried, his eyes dancing, "You are one woman in a thousand!"

I looked away to avoid looking into his eyes. "Am I odd, then? I do not wish to be."

"You are perfect! Perfectly suited to the High King, I mean." I was watching the others when he spoke, and heard in his voice the tenderness I had seen already in his face. I wished with all my heart that he would stop reminding me of Arthur. I did not know then that he was reminding himself.

Bedwyr made a good attempt. His horse refused the obstacle at first, but he persevered and got him over. All was then well until he came to the hen coop, where the stallion slid to a stop at the last moment and tossed Bedwyr over. Kay, who refused the challenge altogether, cantered over to him.

"What manner of man is Kay of Galava?"

Lancelot smiled. "He's old for his age and always has been. He's Arthur's seneschal. His place is at Caer Camel, and he misses it. He worries about it every minute he's away. Since he was injured at Caer Eden his sword arm is weak, and as he cannot take the field for Arthur, he holds his fortress in readiness. It is his service, and he is devoted."

It was clear from his tone of voice that Kay was valued for his devotion.

"He frowns upon my hawking."

Lancelot shrugged. "He believes that women should ride litters, not horses, and should be rocking cradles, not hunting falcons. It is his way."

I plucked nervously at Zephyr's mane. "And the High King?"

"What about the High King?"

"Does he disapprove of women hawking?"

Lancelot turned toward me, amused. "Do I hear aright? Are you actually frightened of Arthur?"

I raised my chin in defiance. "Do you blame me, my lord? I have heard so much and know so little."

He laughed outright, and I bit my lip, blushing. "My dear Guinevere, Pendragon may be feared by Saxons, and rightly so, but *you* have no need to be afraid. Do you imagine him a cruel tyrant? He is the kindest man in all the kingdoms. Why, Arthur would no sooner keep you from hawking or doing whatever it was you pleased than he would cut off his nose to spite his face. He would laugh at the very idea!"

He filled me with relief. "Then I shall be allowed to keep Zephyr? Is this truth, Lancelot? It has worried me a long time."

He began to look astonished. "Of course you may keep her. He is not a monster, Guinevere. Your doubts disturb me. Is not the High King known among his people here in Wales?"

"How a King treats his people is one thing. How a man treats his—his wife may be quite another."

He grew instantly grave and nodded. "That is true. I forgot myself, my lady. But with Arthur it is the same thing. The man and the King are one."

I looked into his face and saw his own devotion there. Clearly Arthur was a great leader, to inspire love in such different men as Kay and Lancelot.

Bedwyr rode up then, with Kay behind him, and I apologized sincerely for putting them through my little game. It had been a long winter, I told them, with nothing for maids to do but sew and listen to women's gossip. The high spirits of spring had to be played out in some fashion. They forgave me like the gentlemen they were; no one reminded me of my promise to be ladylike; and we approached the castle yard as princess and royal escort, much to Kay's relief.

Elaine was aghast. "Oh, Gwen, how could you! All these months we have been preparing for this visit, and their first sight of you is bareback upon your horse, in those filthy leggings! And your hair is flying everywhere! Oh, what must they think?"

I grinned at her as Ailsa pulled the shift down over my head. "My leggings are not filthy. I brush them well after every ride."

"Oh, don't, Gwen. Think of the report will they send to King Arthur!"

Ailsa sat me on the stool and began to brush my hair. I took Elaine's hand.

"Forgive me. I see this affects you deeply. But truly," I said, smiling as I thought of Lancelot standing rooted in the clearing, "I am not worried about the report they will send to King Arthur."

She looked puzzled. "I see you are not. But for goodness' sake, why not?"

"Never mind. I am bathed and clean now, dear Elaine, and Ailsa will dress my hair, and I shall wear the blue gown you embroidered with wildflowers, and I promise I will be a lady and try to make a good impression."

"I should hope so," she said crossly. "It's important to Mother. And to me. You must be—that is, you must try to be—"

"Perfect," I finished for her, sadly. "As everyone says Arthur is."

She nodded. "I guess so. I suppose it's a lot to ask."

I fought off panic as the weight of responsibility descended upon me once again. "It's far too much to ask. And everyone in Britain expects it. But at least I shall not be alone." I was thinking of Lancelot, who had become my friend so quickly.

Elaine kissed my cheek. "I shall be there as long as you are, Gwen. Rely on it."

Startled, I thanked her, and covered my confusion with some question about the progress of the trousseau. She answered with eagerness and filled me in on all the things I had missed while I was out—principally the arrival of the King's men. I listened, but my thoughts drifted back to the clearing, and to the jumping field, and to a pair of clear gray eyes and serious black brows.

"Dress my hair with the little pearls and bluebells, Ailsa," I said suddenly. "I wish to look my best tonight."

Ailsa looked at me sharply, and Elaine smiled.

"Now I know what's different about you today," she said. "You are finally happy. You have been happy ever since you came in."

"Have I?" I avoided Ailsa's eyes. "Well, perhaps so. It was a glorious day."

Queen Alyse led us into the greeting hall, where Pellinore waited with the King's Companions. The mellow evening light filtered in through the open windows and picked out the jewels the men wore on shoulder, belt, and wrist. They were weaponless, for Pellinore followed the High King's practice of leaving all weapons outside the meeting hall, except for the short dagger needed to cut food. King Pellinore presented Queen Alyse and Elaine; the courtiers bowed low. Lancelot wore a dark blue tunic of plain, fine wool. The silver buckle on his belt was worked in the shape of a hawk with wings outspread. He stood half a head taller than Pellinore, who was not considered a small man. Even as I looked at him, he dipped one knee to the floor and kissed my hand.

"King Arthur's compliments, my lady," he said formally. "He has sent us poor soldiers in his stead, not because he did not want to come, but because he could not."

"So I understand, my lord."

"He has sent me with words of greeting and begs for your forgiveness of his most untimely absence."

"He is High King. My lord, I understand."

"He would rather be here in Wales with you, my lady, than riding north to look at Saxons. He told me this himself."

"Where Britain needs him most, there must the High King go," I replied. "My lord may tell him he is forgiven." At last, it seemed, I had said the right thing. Kay and Bedwyr were nodding, pleased.

"And he bade me present you with this gift," Lancelot continued, "in the hope that it might ease your anger toward him and incline you to look favorably upon him."

Lancelot proffered a small packet, wrapped in soft linen. But I forbore to take it from him.

"Good Sir Lancelot. You speak as if Pendragon were one suitor among many. I do assure you, my lord, that I look with favor upon the High King so long as he holds the Saxons at bay. There is no cause for anger. He need send no gifts to win me. I know wherein my duty lies."

Kay and Bedwyr were positively beaming. Alyse looked at me in wonder, hardly able to credit me capable of a diplomatic word.

When he spoke, Lancelot's voice was low and gentle. "Will my lady not accept it, then, as a token of the King's esteem?"

I smiled at him. "I would be honored to accept a token of the King's esteem, my lord."

Lancelot opened the soft wrappings and lifted from them a single sapphire set in silver, the size of a robin's egg, and hung from a silver chain. It glowed in the evening light, dark blue and deep and clear. Lancelot came up to me and put his arms around my shoulders as he fastened it behind my neck. By sheer effort of will I stilled my trembling and stared hard past his shoulder at Kay, but I felt his breath on my skin, and then the warm touch of his hands as he struggled with the clasp. I felt it then for the first time—the hot lick of fire that set me ablaze with an emotion I did not then understand. He hesitated and leaned closer. "It is the color of your eyes," he whispered in my ear, and stepped back slowly. I sank to the floor in a low curtsy, shaking, which sent light glittering off the great sapphire.

"Please—please tell King Arthur I am overwhelmed," I managed.

Elaine and Alyse crowded round to view the stone and chatter in admiration. I was glad for their protection while I recovered my composure. I could not meet his eyes; it was like looking into flame. At last Pellinore offered me his arm and took me into dinner. Lancelot followed with Queen Alyse, and Kay with Elaine. At dinner, Pellinore placed me beside Lancelot, his foremost guest of honor.

As the wine was passed around, Bedwyr gave what news there was of the state of the Kingdom, but for once I was not attentive. I looked everywhere about me, at the troopers, Pellinore's and the

High King's, eating together in the hall, at the bowl of jonquils and bluebells at the center of the round table, at the bodice of Elaine's yellow gown, which I had embroidered with stars. Look where I might, I was conscious only of the man beside me, of the grip of his long fingers around the winecup, the turning of his head toward the speaker, the stillness of his body in his chair.

King Pellinore was proposing a series of hunts for the Companions to keep them busy while we finished the trousseau. To this Kay and Bedwyr readily agreed.

Then Lancelot spoke. "I have one favor to ask of you, Pellinore. Give me two hours each day to spend with the young princesses. The High King appreciates that leaving home to marry a man one has never seen may be hard on a young maid and he does not wish to meet Lady Guinevere as a stranger. He has instructed me to tell her aught she wishes to know about him and the life we lead at Caer Camel. If the young ladies are willing, I beg your permission to fulfill the High King's desire."

Kay and Bedwyr looked surprised, and it made me wonder if Lancelot had made the whole thing up. But Elaine looked ecstatic, and Pellinore of course agreed, so it was settled.

As dinner progressed and conversation became general, I gathered my courage and turned to Lancelot. "Forgive my impertinence, my lord, but did you speak the truth about the High King just now?"

He smiled. "Does my lady suspect me of inventing ways to spend more time in her presence?"

I flushed scarlet, I could feel the heat in my face, but his look was tender.

"It was truth, my lady. He spoke so only to me, but it is truly his desire to ease what fears you have of him. And I know now that you have them." He lowered his gaze to his plate, and his voice went low. "But had he not said so, I would have invented it. Your suspicions are just."

I felt triumphant and weak all at once and struggled to keep my voice steady. "I am glad you included Elaine. She is a great admirer of Arthur's."

He raised his eyes to me then and looked at me long and directly. "And so will you be, Guinevere, in time."

I bowed my head.

Lancelot kept his word. Whatever the men were doing, hunting, hawking, drilling troops, he took time out every day to spend with Elaine and me. In the beginning all the queen's ladies crowded round him to hear him speak of Arthur, but eventually, as the day of departure grew near and the trousseau lay unfinished, they kept to the sewing room, and we had just Leonora for chaperone. Elaine was almost always with me. On the four or five occasions when Lancelot and I went riding, we took several of Pellinore's men along for escort and said very little to one another. And every time we spoke, Lancelot was careful to bring King Arthur between us, gently and firmly. In my mind's eye I saw him as our guardian, and in this I was not far off the mark.

When we sat together, usually in the queen's garden, it was always Elaine who asked about Arthur.

"What is the truth of his birth?" Elaine wanted to know. "Why did no one ever see him? Where did Merlin hide him?"

Lancelot smiled. "In spite of the rumors that I know run rampant, Merlin did not spirit him away to a far-off land, nor change him into an eagle. He grew up in Galava, with Sir Ector as his foster father and Kay his brother. No one noticed him because he was not specially treated. When he traveled with Ector, he went not as a prince of the land but as a minor noble's son in Ector's protection, with small escort and smaller fanfare. Ector, a brave soldier who fought with Ambrosius, and a kind man, took him into his household for fostering when he was just a baby. Arthur and Kay grew up as brothers." The source of Kay's devotion lay revealed, and also of his readiness to disapprove of me.

"But where was Merlin all this time?" Elaine wondered. "I thought he raised the King himself."

Lancelot smiled at her, but Elaine seemed unaffected. "So people say, but Merlin himself has never said so. And yet there is some truth in the claim. Behind the scenes, Merlin supervised the prince's education and kept track of him through the power of his Sight. He sometimes lived as a holy hermit in the forest above Count Ector's castle. There he would meet the boy and give him lessons and tell him the story of his begetting and his lineage, as if it all pertained to someone else. You might remember," Lancelot continued, "Uther Pendragon proclaimed throughout Britain that he would not acknowledge the son he begot at Tintagel. Thus neither Ector nor Merlin could in all fairness tell him who he was."

"But how was his true birth kept from him?" I asked. "I have always found that part of the tale difficult to believe. Sir Ector must have told him something."

"But it is true, my lady. He did not know. Ector told him his parents were of noble birth, but that they could not claim him. Ar-

thur assumed he was the bastard of some petty lord, and Kay his
superior in birth and breeding. He heard all the tales about Prince
Arthur that you have heard, but he never once thought they might
apply to him."

"But the name!" Elaine exclaimed. "And to have Merlin the
Enchanter as a teacher! I'd have guessed, if it had been me!"

"Ah, but 'Arthur' was not his name." Lancelot turned to me
and smiled. My breath caught in my throat. "Sometime when he
is deep in thought and not attending, call 'Emreis' softly, and
judge the truth yourself by the unthinking quickness of his response." I colored and looked down. "As for Merlin," Lancelot
continued gently, "he is a master at disguise. He transformed himself so completely into a wild holy man that Ector himself barely
knew him. As Arthur had never seen him, it really is no wonder
he did not guess."

"Well, why is Merlin so dear to him, then," Elaine objected,
with a shake of her bountiful curls, "if Sir Ector was his foster father?"

"Perhaps because he valued more the things that Merlin taught
him." Lancelot shrugged. "Or perhaps it is just the chance agreement of two personalities." He shot me a swift glance and looked
away. I blushed uncontrollably.

"It may have been so for his childhood," Elaine went on, "but
surely, by the time he went to Caer Eden to fight for the High
King, he must have guessed. Holy men are not so wise as Merlin
and never stay so long in one place."

Suddenly I saw what lay ahead and attempted to steer the conversation another way, but Elaine would not have it. She pressed
Lancelot to answer.

"Ah, but Arthur did not know that. Galava is a small place, and
his experience of wandering holy men was limited to one."

"Then surely he must have guessed when Ector armed him for
the battle. He was by rights too young to be a warrior."

Lancelot smiled, unaware of the bog ahead. "While it is true
that Ector brought him on Uther's orders, it does not surprise me
that Arthur did not guess. Think of the long years he had believed
himself to be only a fosterling. And Galava is not far from Caer
Eden. Had the Saxons won, his 'homeland' would have been directly threatened. He would have thought it strange had Ector *not*
taken every able-bodied man and boy at his command, especially
as Arthur, even at thirteen, was the best swordsman in Galava."

Elaine sighed in resignation. "Then it's true, after all, that Uther
waited until the last minute to declare him?"

Still Lancelot went on, unseeing. "I have heard it was Uther's intention to talk to the boy and reveal his identity to him before the battle, but the Saxons attacked unexpectedly, and there was no time."

I looked down at my hands, twisted together in my lap. "And when, my lord, did he learn the truth?"

There was a long silence, and at last I glanced up. Lancelot looked stricken, having seen the pitfall too late. Elaine, in her innocence, merely waited for his answer. He cleared his throat and spoke stiffly.

"Uther told him the next day he was his father, in a public declaration, as he lay dying." When it was too late, I thought bitterly, *after* he had lain with his half-sister. Lancelot's eyes met mine, and he saw that I knew the tale, and I saw that the tale was true. If I felt grief, it was nothing to what Lancelot felt, having brought it upon me. Elaine continued unawares.

"You speak as if you were there, my lord. Did you attend, or did you hear these things from King Arthur?"

"I—I was there, my lady. I was young for it, just fourteen. I accompanied my father. He was convinced that our future lay with Britain, and he brought me over to fight at his side for Uther. He was wounded in the battle and, when he recovered, went home. I stayed to serve the new King." He spoke absently, his attention focused on what he had not said.

The conversation lagged, for we had heard about the battle, and at length Elaine excused herself. Leonora sat nodding in the sun. I leaned toward Lancelot.

"These are heavy matters, Lancelot," I whispered. "What has the High King said to you about it?"

Lancelot took a deep breath. "He has never spoken about it to anyone at all. Unless to Merlin. It is a subject the whole court avoids. I—I did not know you knew."

"I have heard rumors only. I have told no one."

He met my eyes. "Can you forgive him this, Guinevere? It is a great sin. It would be within your right to refuse him for this. No one could hold it against you."

"But—then the whole Kingdom would know for certain," I said softly.

He nodded and touched my hand. "Yes. But Arthur would survive it."

I rose unsteadily and went to the parapet. Lancelot followed. "Before I answer, there is another question I must ask you. Since you love him, I know what you will say. But you must, you *must* tell me the truth."

Lancelot took both my hands in his. "I will not lie to you," he whispered. "I swear it by most holy God."

My whole body shook with fear at the risk I took, but somehow I found the courage to ask him. "Did Arthur kill the children at Dunpelder?"

Lancelot went white and stepped back, but his grip upon my hands was firm. "No. Never."

"Everyone thinks he did."

"No one who knows him thinks so."

"That is not an answer. Perhaps you do not know him well enough."

Anger darkened his eyes. "I know him better than I know myself. It is not in him. He did not do it."

"Has he said so? To you?"

"Yes."

"Who did the deed, then?"

"He does not know. But it must have been either Lot or Morgause herself." He spoke the woman's name reluctantly, as if it left a bad taste in his mouth.

"Then why do the rumors persist, if he is innocent?"

Lancelot shrugged. His face was cold. "Blame must land somewhere. The Witch of Orkney has seen to it that it fell on him."

I struggled to hold back the final accusation, but it was a moment of truth between us, and it came out. "He stood to gain so much."

Lancelot's features twisted in revulsion; still, he held my hands. "No one ever gains by killing children. The crime itself leaves a stain upon the soul. Had Arthur done it, he would not be the man he is now."

I exhaled in relief, and warmth returned to his face. "But this other evil—you admit his guilt. Has that deed not left a mark upon his soul?"

Lancelot's hands tightened around my own. "Indeed it has. So deep a mark, he will never be healed of it. That is why he cannot bear to hear her mentioned, though she is his kin. If you dare, you can make him talk about the massacre at Dunpelder. But you will never hear him speak the name 'Morgause.' " Lancelot paused and dropped my hands. "You must decide, Gwen, if you can forgive him. You must decide now. If you wish to withdraw, I must get the word out soon."

I looked down, hopelessly torn. Lancelot had offered me a way out, had opened the door, and now stood aside like a gentleman to let me go through, if I would. But what was beyond that door, I could not see. A tarnished Arthur, for certain. What would the people of Britain do when they knew the truth as I now knew it? What would Lancelot think of me if I refused? I felt a sob rise in my throat and squeezed my eyes shut. I knew what I must do.

I gathered my courage and met his eyes again, clear and gray and trusting. "It was done in ignorance," I whispered. "One should not be punished for ignorance. I know I feel it is unjust when it is done to me. So I should not be honest with myself if I held it against the High King."

Lancelot flung himself to his knees and clutched my hand, pressing it to his lips. "O noble heart!" he cried. "What forbearance is this in one so young and unworldly? May God in His Heaven bless you, I believe you are worthy of him!"

"What's this? What's this?" Leonora cried, waking suddenly. "What's happened here?"

Lancelot jumped to his feet, coloring, and bowed in her direction. "If I am out of turn, good Leonora, please forgive me. Lady Guinevere has just revealed her noble soul, and I have thanked her on the King's behalf."

Then he turned and fled. Leonora looked at me in bewilderment.

"Don't ask," I said wearily. "It's too much to tell. Come, let's get in out of this hot sun."

10 ✸ The parting

The day of departure approached. I noted that Ailsa said very little to me and clutched her amulets a great deal. Even Elaine, whom I expected to show increasing excitement, watched me worriedly. I had no idea what about me concerned them.

On the last day of May I finished the bridegroom's gift. I had thought long and hard over what I could give a King who had gifts beyond counting, and finally decided that it must be something I made myself. I took some fine white wool, lined it with white silk, and fashioned it into a day robe, such as King Pellinore wore when illness or bad weather kept him indoors. But I wanted to make it finer and more comfortable, for surely warriors must enjoy a change from leather and mail. This was a plain shift, warm enough for all but the coldest days, with soft silk next to the skin. It could be worn loose or belted and was edged in dark blue so as not to show dirt. Over the left breast I embroidered a design of my own invention: interlocking squares in the Celtic pattern, stitched in blue, forming a square turned on end; and within, the Red Dragon of Britain standing on hind feet, clawing the air. And above it all, in the tiniest of stitches for which my work was best known, a silver star to represent the kingstar that had lighted in the west the night of Arthur's begetting. And that was all. The rest of the garment was without ornament, simple and fine. Elaine was after me for weeks to add some decoration to the sleeves, or along the hemline, but I refused. It would not be my gift, if it was not as I liked it.

I showed it to no one but Elaine and Ailsa. We packed it carefully in cloth wrappings, and then within a box, and it was placed with my traveling chests that were already in readiness. Then King Pellinore, who had been chuckling secretly for weeks, revealed his wedding gift to the High King. His carpenters had fashioned for Arthur another round table, three times as large as the one in Pellinore's hall. It broke down into sections for ease of transport and to enable it to be taken through doorways, but he displayed it proudly to us all before it was disassembled. It was made of white oak and sanded and polished until it shone like glass. It could easily seat thirty men and could do double duty as a dinner table, or in the council chamber. The Companions were impressed and complimented Pellinore until his poor head was swollen with pride. Alyse declared it would take months to get him back in line.

As the day of departure neared, I should have been nervous, but I felt instead both exhilarated and terrified. One evening Elaine and I took Lancelot up to the western tower to watch the sun set over the sea. The sky was aflame with light, and we watched in silence as the red streaks burned purple and the evening star blazed forth.

"I shall miss Wales," I said softly. Elaine turned to me, and I saw there were tears in her eyes.

"I've always lived in sight of the sea," she exclaimed. "I cannot imagine what life will be like without it."

"Caer Camel is not far from the sea," Lancelot offered. "You cannot see it from the towers, but you can see the signal fires on the tor of Ynys Witrin, which sits on the Lake of Avalon, which is fed by the sea tides."

It was not the same, but no one said so. Lancelot seemed subdued.

"Has there been any news from the north?" I asked

"There has been no fighting, my lady. The High King and his allies have shown the Saxons a strong front. I believe they are working on a treaty and on strengthening the line of defenses."

"There is no new word on when—when—" I could not finish, so Lancelot finished for me.

"No. My instructions are to take you to Caer Camel and there await him."

I nodded. In the darkness, Lancelot took my hand. Elaine had her handkerchief to her face, and Leonora had not wished to make the climb. I breathed out slowly as excitement and longing filled me. I now understood what I had only felt on the first day of his visit. In a month's time he had become more precious to me than life. His touch inflamed me, his smile robbed me of breath. Each night I dreamed I stood in his embrace, and each morning I awoke yearning for his kiss. And I knew that he felt the same. It was exhilarating, agonizing, thrilling, almost overwhelming, but it also hurt more than daggers, and all at the same time. So we stood in silence, hand in hand, in the beauty of the long June evening, loving without hope, and thinking of Arthur.

In bed that night, Elaine put her arms around me and said, "I know now, Gwen. I know why you've been so happy and so sad, and why you are not nervous about leaving, and why you so dread Arthur. You love Lancelot."

"Please, Elaine—"

"I shall never tell a soul. I was angry with you, though, until I saw that you could not help it, any more than I could. But what are we to do, Gwen?"

I gripped her by the wrists. "There is nothing to be done."

"Is there no way to talk to them and come to some agreement? That you may take Lancelot, and I Arthur?"

"No!" I cried, the tears that had been kept back at such cost all day finally bursting forth. "No, there is not! Think, Elaine! Arthur is High King of Britain, and Lancelot his second-in-command. The honor of all Britain is in our hands! Use your head! We are merely women."

"But—but it seems so unfair!"

"Yes. It is unfair. To you, to me, to Lancelot; most of all, to the King himself. But I truly don't see what is to be done about it. We must bear it. That is all."

"And if I can't bear it?" Elaine cried in despair.

"Elaine, you must!" I had a sudden prevision that filled me with horror. "Elaine, attend me! You must make me a promise—when we get to Caer Camel, you must behave as if you care nothing about the King. You must pretend that you dislike him. Be polite but always, always cool. Don't follow him with your eyes, don't put yourself in his way—you know what I mean. Everyone's honor depends on it. Will you promise?"

Elaine wept. "What you ask is impossible and you know it!"

"It is no more than I must do toward Lancelot. I know it is hard, but we are strong. You *have* to do it. It is the only way."

"You ask too much. I cannot promise."

"Then," I said slowly, "you cannot come."

She gasped. "You cannot prevent me! Mother has given me permission!"

"I can send you home with her when the celebrations are over. I will be Queen then. Even your mother must be obedient to my command."

Elaine went suddenly still and silent. Her tears dried but her body trembled. For a long time she said nothing. I waited in wretchedness, remembering Gwillim kneeling at my bed, sacrificing his friendship to my power. But I had no choice—it was the Kingdom's honor!

"I see," she said at last in a different voice. "Very well. I promise."

"You will be discreet? And engage in no embarrassing display?"

"I promise."

"And you will stay out of his way, as much as is in your power, and never let him know what is in your heart?"

"I promise."

I exhaled slowly. "And I will hold you to it. I have sworn to do the same with Lancelot. If we break these vows, we shame ourselves, and Wales, and Britain. I know it makes the future bleak, when it should be bright. But somehow, the future must be borne."

Suddenly the day was upon us. The castle yard was filled with loaded wagons, servants scurried everywhere to fetch packages and search for last-minute, forgotten items. The troops stood by their mounts, surrounding the caravan. Goods and gifts were bundled onto pack mules. A stableboy held Zephyr's bridle in one hand and Nestor's in another, and he had his hands full. The women's litters were just behind, and from my window I saw Leonora taking charge of the women's arrangements, while Kay supervised the troops and the loading procedures. He was good at his job, patient and exacting, organized and able to keep track in his head of a thousand details. Everyone who needed information came to him, and he knew where everything was, or where it was headed, or when it would be needed, and whose responsibility it was to tend.

"Come, Guinevere," Alyse commanded. "It is time."

Lancelot appeared at the doorway and made a low obeisance to the queen. "The litters are prepared, my lady. King Pellinore is mounted and ready to be off."

"Thank you, Lancelot. We are ready. I suppose, Guinevere, you will choose to ride like a man again?"

Lancelot was shocked at her tone, but I was not. To Alyse, I was still her sister's daughter and her ward. I was not yet her Queen.

"No, madam. On this journey I shall ride in the litter with Elaine. But I should like to ride into Caer Camel when we get there."

And to everyone's surprise, I consented to be carried, while my mare walked alongside, unbridled. But I thought there might be people who would come out at crossroads to see the girl the High King had chosen to wed, and I wished to appear to them as they wished to see me. But once we got to Caer Camel, I wished to be myself. Before the people who would live with me, I wanted no false impressions. Also, to tell truth, I both dreaded and craved Lancelot's company. It was easier in the litter with Elaine, who knew my secret, than it would be riding by his side, with my face a mask and my heart in turmoil.

I was right about the people's interest in their new Queen. Not just at crossroads, but along every highway people stopped their labors and came out to watch the caravan go by. Elaine and I kept the sides of the litter open since the weather was fine, and people threw us flowers and called to us as we passed. As I got used to it, I waved to them, and they cried out their blessings and good wishes. It became a real procession, all the way through Wales, past Caerleon, across the Severn, and down into the Summer Country. Every night we stopped and set up tents, and for three hours or so received the good folk who lived round about, and accepted gifts of all kinds. I sat in a little gilded chair, with Queen Alyse on one hand, and Elaine on the other, Lancelot behind me, Bedwyr to one side, and Pellinore to the other. Kay stood at the door and let well-wishers in by twos and threes. They all brought gifts, from carved tools to woven stuffs, to trinkets to hens, vegetables and fresh eggs. One village maiden brought a yellow songbird she had trained to sing, and this caught my fancy. She kept it in a little cage of willow reeds, and it sang joyful melodies all day. Everyone who came was kind, and blessed me, and everyone seemed to go away pleased and satisfied. The farther south we went, the more people crowded to see us. Bedwyr, who was a quiet man with a shy manner, grinned at me one night as he handed me a goblet.

"My lady, you were born for this," he said proudly. "I wish Arthur could see it."

"You may be sure," Kay answered, "that he will hear about it."

Early in the mornings and very late at night I spent time with Zephyr, grooming her, crooning to her, occasionally riding her. Lancelot came with me for escort at these times, but he kept his distance. Eyes were upon us, it seemed to me.

On the tenth day we camped in sight of the signal fires of Ynys Witrin, the Isle of Glass, the Holy Hill, and knew that the next day would bring us to Caer Camel. Kay left us that night to ride on to the fortress, for he was frantic with worry that his lieutenant had not carried out his instructions, and he felt strongly that nothing should go amiss the day that Arthur's bride came to his home. Since we were so close to Caer Camel, messengers came and went constantly. The High King was still in the north, but expected well before the solstice. In his stead, I was to be welcomed by Melwas, King of the Summer Country. There was to be a ceremony, everything would be formal, stiff and endless, and I did not look forward to it. For one thing, it meant the end of Lancelot's company. For another, it meant the beginning of yet another period of preparation and waiting that would end only with the High King's arrival. All I could see ahead was one trial after another.

Hundreds of people came that night to pay their respects, and Bedwyr had to send to Caer Camel to have more carts brought up before morning to carry all the gifts the kind people brought. The people themselves truly amazed me. Arthur was a person to them, not just their war leader who kept their lands from the Saxons. He was more real to them than he was to me, and they were intensely curious about the girl he had chosen to marry. They came from every walk of life, not just lords' domains, many old and poor, some of them in good health, some in bad. Everyone wanted just a few minutes of my time, and when I saw that Bedwyr was ready to quit after three hours, I signaled him to continue. I excused Alyse and Elaine, since they were tired from the journey and wanted to rest, but I continued to see the people myself.

"My lady Guinevere," Lancelot murmured after four hours had passed, "are you not tired? Should you not take rest for tomorrow?"

"Yes, my lord, I am, and I should. But look at the people outside. Think of the distance they have come, and for what? Just to greet me and wish me good health and long life. How can I turn them away?"

Lancelot glanced at Bedwyr, who smiled and shrugged. "You can do nothing, Lancelot. It's just what Arthur would say." Lancelot nodded. The people kept coming.

The morning broke cool and cloudy, with a rose-pink haze across the sun, and the meadowlands swathed in fog. I was up early to tend Zephyr, whom I would ride today, and to have some time to myself for contemplation. I was alone in the horse lines, but people were up and about, for I heard the voices of grooms and cooks, although I could not see them. Zephyr did not like the fog, and it made her a little edgy. She moved restlessly and tossed her head while I tried to braid her mane. Then suddenly she calmed and stood quietly. My heart began to race. Lancelot's face appeared like magic in the mist across her shoulder.

"Lancelot!"

"Guinevere."

We stood and looked at each other. The longing on his face broke my heart, but there was nothing to be done.

"I came to tell you," he began, and then stopped. He cleared his throat. "How much I have enjoyed your company. I think you are the bravest woman I have ever known, and the kindest and the truest. I know you look at what is to come as a trial to be endured, but I want to assure you—Gwen, you will come to love him, as we all do. You won't be able to help it, any more than I was able to help—you know I love you, Guinevere, and I will always be at your service, whatever happens. But for Arthur's sake, we cannot—"

"Oh, Lancelot!" I whispered "It will kill me to say farewell! And I couldn't help it, either! Lancelot, I will love you till I die." I gasped as the words came out; they were the last words I had meant to say! Lancelot ducked under the mare's head and took me in his arms. Thank God the mist lay heavy around us, for he kissed me with passion, and I returned his love. Then he was gone, and I collapsed breathless against the mare's body, shaken to my soul. How the future was to be borne, I did not know. I had no protection against Lancelot.

By midmorning the mist had lifted, and the sun shone forth in splendor. Lancelot rode at my side, stone-faced and silent, wearing his sword in its ceremonial scabbard of silver set with jewels. We rode slowly, for we still had litters, and I was content to walk along, wave to the crowds who lined the road, and let the time pass. It was lovely country we rode through, rolling green hills where sheep grazed, fertile farmland, thick woods full of game. In the west from Ynys Witrin the marsh birds came in flocks, wheeling overhead and calling, and then soaring back to the Lake of Avalon. It was a rich land compared to stony Wales, soft and green and full of life.

In early afternoon Caer Camel came into view. I caught my breath at the sight of it, and Lancelot finally smiled. "There it is, Guinevere. Your new home."

There were twelve turrets, each with a flag flying gaily in the summer breeze. The castle looked huge, even from this distance, and I knew from the soldiers' talk that there was a triple ring of fortifications around it. The sandstone walls shone golden in the sun, and it looked lovely set upon its green hill. The closer we got, the steeper I realized were the sides of this hill. Only the lower shoulders were forested. Most of it was sheep meadow and open, so as to see the enemy's approach. But the fortress itself was gigantic. At one end of the flat-topped hill stood the castle, at the other a sizable woodland, all within the ring of fortifications. A city would grow there in time, although in those days there were only workmen's huts outside the castle. As we approached along the western road, we saw the great, sweeping thoroughfare that ran up to the studded double gates: the entrance to Caer Camel. This road was wide enough for ten men riding abreast, and the steep sections were paved with rough stones so the turf would never wash away in the spring rains. This was the road down which Arthur's fearful cavalry flew at a moment's notice, swooping down upon the enemy almost before he had the time to draw his sword.

"Will Merlin be there?" I asked Lancelot suddenly.

"No, my lady. Probably not."

"Why not?"

"He is old, Gwen. He has retired to a small house in the forest east of here, where he lives with an apprentice. Arthur rides out to visit him every now and again, but Merlin seldom comes to Caer Camel."

"Won't he come for the—the wedding?"

"If Arthur wants him, he will be there. But I shouldn't say it's likely."

"What has Merlin advised the King about this match?"

Lancelot eyed me warily. "It's odd that you ask. He was there when your name was proposed and said nothing. When Arthur asked him for his advice, he simply said 'what will be, will be.' No one knows how he truly feels."

I shuddered suddenly, remembering my audience with Princess Morgan. "*I* know how he feels."

Slowly the procession climbed the great roadway. Sentries saluted Lancelot, and he gave the word to open the fortress gates. Within stood King Melwas, a huge, blond man with hard, light eyes, and beside him, old white-robed Nimue of Avalon, Lady of the Lake, and Landrum, Caer Camel's Christian bishop, overdressed. A crowd of people stood behind them, and as we rode up, they broke into cheering and shouting.

Lancelot dismounted, then came around to help me down. I slid off the mare into his arms, and he recoiled as if he had been burned. We took up our positions, my hand upon his arm, and faced King Melwas. He bowed low, the Lady curtsied, the bishop nodded. They each made a speech, welcoming me to Caer Camel on King Arthur's behalf. Melwas was brief enough but the Lady went on at length, praising the Good Goddess, describing Arthur's virility and strength with a light in her eye, blessing me with fertility and talking hungrily about procreation until I began to blush. Melwas, who stood half the time staring at me open-mouthed, and the other half glaring at Lancelot, finally interrupted and brought her back to the subject at hand. I was most grateful for this. Beneath my hand, Lancelot's arm was trembling.

Then Bishop Landrum stepped forward, lavishly bedecked in gold and crimson robes, with an ornate jeweled cross hung on his breast. He began a long tirade upon the banishment of heathens and the anathema of pagan ways in a civilized land. Clearly he was enraged at the inclusion of the Lady in the welcoming ceremonies and was determined not to be outdone. But the old priestess had been included by Arthur's order, it was certain. I began to see an even-handedness here that without doubt was not shared by any of the participants.

At length, the bishop finished, and Lancelot and I both knelt to receive his blessing. Then Lancelot led me forward, followed by King Melwas and the Lady, and the bishop and Bedwyr, down the street of workmen's huts where swordsmiths, blacksmiths, armorers, coopers, carpenters, and tanners all stood outside and bowed as we went by. There was nothing there yet that was not devoted to the arts of war. At last we came to the marble steps that led to the doors of the castle. Kay was there, smiling proudly at me, and I was mightily glad to see him. As Arthur's seneschal, the castle was his domain. He thanked Lancelot formally for bringing Arthur's bride safe and virgin from Wales, and Lancelot rather stiffly replied that anything done in the High King's service was his pleasure to perform. Then Kay took me into the castle and led me to my quarters. The halls were cool and dark after the bright June sunshine, and by the time my eyes adjusted to the dim light, we were at a wide oak door carved with the Dragon of Britain and guarded by two sentries.

Beyond this door were the Queen's quarters, which had never been occupied. At long last, after many thanks and assurances, Kay left and it was over. Alyse, Elaine, and I stood in the round foyer, with Leonora, Cissa, Grannic, and Ailsa huddled by the door, and we looked about us. The place was a fighting fortress, with smooth stone walls, narrow windows, dirt floors, and stone benches. Some attempt had been made to make it fit for women. Straw was strewn across the dirt, and tapestries, touched by moth around the edges, hung on the walls.

"Well!" Alyse exclaimed. "I am glad we brought so much with us from Wales. I thought before we were burdening ourselves needlessly, but now I wonder if we brought enough."

But I found the situation amusing and rather touching. "There have been no women here. We are the first." From this central foyer branched hallways with spacious rooms. My own chambers were somewhat more elaborately furnished. There were three rooms below: two sitting rooms and a maid's chamber with wide, glazed windows that looked out upon a terrace and a lovely, walled garden. From the maid's chamber rose a stairway to my sleeping chamber. The sitting rooms were floored with colored tiles in the Roman style, depicting animals and surrounded by flowers. The walls were hung with imported carpets in rich reds and blues. Blue and gold cushions adorned plain wood benches. Someone had gone to great lengths to make these rooms habitable for women, but that someone had most definitely been a man.

Alyse began to give orders to her women as to the hangings and coverings we would need. I turned to face her. "I will give the directions as to the furnishings of my home, Alyse."

She stopped, shocked. I saw the realization sink into them all, one by one. This *was* my home now, and not theirs. Within days I would be their sovereign Queen. And one by one they sank into a curtsy, even Elaine, and last Alyse.

I went alone up the stairs into the sleeping chamber. It was a large, octagonal room, opening on a terrace, flagged in stone, that overlooked the garden. The bed was large and made of carved fruitwood, hung with silk hangings of light blue, with golden trimmings. It looked old, and the workmanship was very fine. I later learned it was Ygraine's and had come from Tintagel. It was the bed where Arthur himself was conceived and born, and where Ygraine had died. The floor tiles were blue and gold and white and covered with a soft carpet of blue, gold, and rose, so thick and rich I knew it must be one of those imported from the East. A bowl of roses sat on a slender-legged table by the window, and an old chest, made of pearwood and carved all over with flowers and vines, stood at the foot of the bed. It was a simple room, but the touches were fine; it was beautiful.

There was only one other doorway, and this was covered with a heavy leather flap. I lifted it tentatively and, hearing nothing on the other side, went in. It was another bedchamber, the twin of mine in shape and size, but plain and completely different in style and taste. The floor was polished wood, without coverings. The windows were unglazed. The bed was large, carved of some dark, shining wood I did not know, and covered with a thick blanket of stitched bearskins. There was an oak chest in one corner and a marble-topped writing table beside a triple-flamed lamp. The bed itself stood on a low dais, and on the wall at its head hung an old silk banner, much worn, of the Red Dragon of Britain clawing at a field of gold.

My heart thudded painfully in my chest, and my palms began to sweat. This was the High King's bedchamber. There could be no doubt of it. Why had I imagined that his rooms would be in another part of the castle? But they were not. This was his room, and it spoke to me about the man himself. It was a soldier's room, bare of all ornament except the banner. He wrote here, or read. He slept here, dressed here, and that was all. It was clean and quiet and calm. I went to the window. It looked west, as mine did, and in the far distance I fancied I could see the dim shadow of Ynys Witrin. Of course the King would want to be able to see the signal fires, just in case the sentry slept. Aside from the entrance to my own chamber, there was only one other door, and it led to a staircase. No doubt his chamberlain slept in the room below. I turned and walked slowly to the great bed. The bearskins were soft to my touch. I wondered about them until I recalled that his name came from "Artos," which meant "Bear." They were probably a gift. Under the bearskins the bed sheets were fine and white and clean, but not nearly so fine as the ones we had brought him. This lifted my spirits, and I looked around the room again in satisfaction. It was a restful place, and if it suited Arthur, it was a good sign.

I returned to my own chamber and sat upon the bed, thinking hard. I thought I could bear any kind of husband, even a slovenly or domineering one, provided he was fair. It would be impossible to live with a man whose respect could not be won. I was prepared to do anything the High King desired to make him think well of me and not regret his choice. If he was at all fair, the future might be endured. Somehow, seeing his room gave me hope. Next to his skill as a war leader, King Arthur was renowned for his fairness. "Arthur's justice" was a by-word for fair treatment. If so, if so, perhaps Lancelot was right, and it might not be the trial I dreaded.

But how, dear God, how was Lancelot himself to be endured?

He could not leave court—Arthur needed him—and I would die if he left. But how was I to stand it if he stayed? The utter hopelessness of it all swept over me in a wave, and at last I gave in and wept, burying my head in the cushions, sobbing like a child. I did not care. I was alone for the first time in months.

At least, I thought I was alone. But by and by I felt eyes upon me, and when I looked up, I saw a thin youth in a servant's tunic peeking in through the leather curtain.

He looked dreadfully frightened, and his eyes darted all about. He tried to look anywhere but at me.

"Is—is my lady all right?" he asked timidly. "Is there aught that I can do?"

I smiled, wiping my eyes. "There is nothing wrong that time will not heal. I am homesick."

"Ah." He plucked nervously at his shirt. "Would you care for honey mead, or perhaps wine?"

"Who are you?"

He bowed low, and kept his eyes down. "My name is Bran, my lady. I am the High King's body servant."

"If you are the King's body servant, why are you not with the King?"

He flushed hotly and stammered. "I—I—I am an apprentice, really. Varric is the chamberlain. He went with the King. I—I came up to straighten the room and set the coals in the grate. Then I heard weeping."

"Straighten the room?" I cried, incredulous. "There is nothing to straighten!" I gasped as I realized what I had revealed, as Bran looked up and grinned. I burst out laughing then, and he laughed with me. He was about my age.

"Please, Bran, apprentice chamberlain, do not tell the High King you found me weeping in here on the day of my arrival. The last thing he should have to worry about is a foolish, homesick girl."

"If I know my lord, he will understand it. I was homesick, too, when I first came here. He caught me weeping more than once."

"And what happened? Did you get a whipping?"

His jaw dropped and he stared. "A whipping? From the High King?" He did not know how to respond; clearly he took me for an idiot.

"Never mind. I see you did not. Does the High King never anger, then?"

"My lady, I have not seen it. But I have heard that he does not like his time wasted."

I smiled. "Who does? Where do you come from, Bran, and how long have you served King Arthur?"

"From Less Britain, my lady. I have been with him five years."

"You are content to stay? You don't miss your home?"

He straightened. "I wish to be nowhere else but here." Then he smiled. "You will get used to it in time. There's a lot going on. Kings and princes in and out, knights coming to offer service, knights riding out to adventures, priests and enchanters everywhere—" He stopped as I shuddered.

"And old Merlin lurking about the corridors, no doubt."

Bran looked sideways out of his eyes, and lowered his voice. "Do not let the High King hear you call him old, my lady. Merlin will not confess what it was that aged him, but the High King believes it was poison."

Now it was my turn to stare. "Surely your life will be longer if you keep such things to yourself, Bran."

"I can trust you, my lady," he said simply, with all the certainty in the world. "Would you like some mulled wine? We have a special way of making it here—"

"No, thank you, Bran. I would like a drink of water."

"I will bring you a carafe. We have a spring on Caer Camel with the sweetest water in Britain." He darted back through the curtain and then popped his head through once more.

"You might as well know, my lady. I came up here to set the room to rights because we have just had news. The High King is on his way and will arrive the day after tomorrow."

11 ✿ The Bride

I had no time to be nervous. If we thought we had been busy packing, it was nothing to the unpacking. Good Kay lent us all the hands we wanted, and there was a constant flow of people, laden with furniture, hangings, cushions, and sundry necessities to and from the women's quarters. Elaine's rooms rapidly became the most luxurious, and what excess trappings she could not use, she found use for in my sitting rooms. Ailsa established herself in the small sleeping chamber at the foot of my stair. My own bedchamber I left the way I found it except for two things. I hung the singing yellow bird in its willow cage in the corner by the window, and I brought up the small carved bench that I had brought with me from Northgallis when I went to Gwynedd. It had belonged to my mother, and she had covered the bench cushion with needlework of her own design, showing the blue sea, the white stag of Northgallis, and the gray wolf of Gwynedd, with snowcapped Y Wyddfa behind. This bench I set upon the little terrace, so that I could sit there of an evening and watch the setting of the sun as I used to do on the towers of Pellinore's castle.

The rest of the castle was also thrown into an uproar by the news of Arthur's coming. The wedding gifts were all laid out, the hundreds of gifts we had collected on our journey were displayed, along with those brought by the lords and nobles who daily arrived and set up tents upon the open fields, come to see the wedding. King Pellinore's round table was set up in the dining hall, which was the only room big enough for it. All these people who flooded into Caer Camel had to be fed, and there were daily hunting parties into the woodlands for game and to the salt marshes for fowl. All the horses that carried the good folk and pulled their wagons had to be housed and tended to. All these things Kay oversaw, and although he was pressed to fuming point, he never lost his temper or said an unkind word to anyone.

Lancelot kept to the stables, which was part of his responsibility as Arthur's Master of the Horse, and with Bedwyr he drilled the guard troops daily. I saw him once or twice from Elaine's window, exercising Zephyr, and it was a rare pleasure to watch my mare's elegant paces, which I had felt but never seen. Elaine was beside herself with joy and excitement. At long last she was going to see King Arthur in the flesh. She kept pinching herself to be sure that it was not a dream. She could not decide which gown to wear when we were presented to him. I sat upon her cushioned chair and stared out her window, which faced east toward the open meadows and beyond to the wood. The meadows were alive with tents of every description, with lords and ladies from every corner of Britain. I was thankful the weather was dry for there was no mud. As it was, the meadows were so trodden down I wondered if the grass would ever come back.

"Gwen, you're not attending! I've asked you three times if I should wear the yellow or the blue."

"Wear what pleases you, Elaine."

"But what are you wearing? I don't want to wear the same."

"I don't know. I haven't given it thought."

"But you must!" She gasped. "He arrives tomorrow!"

It was an effort to turn away from the window and concentrate on clothing. "What is your mother wearing?"

"The gold." One should have expected it.

"Then wear the yellow, and I shall wear the blue. I must wear the sapphire, remember."

"Yes, and have Ailsa dress your hair with the seed pearls and bluebells again, as you did the night the Companions arrived. That was wonderful."

"There aren't any bluebells. It's June."

"Well, cornflowers then. I know I saw blue flowers in the meadows as we approached King's Gate. Send Kay to get some."

I sighed and turned back to the roiling throng that jammed the road from the valley below. "Poor Kay. I suppose I might ask Bran."

"Who's Bran?"

"The King's apprentice chamberlain."

Her eyebrows rose. "And how did you meet him?"

"Come sleep with me tonight, and I'll show you. Oh, Elaine, you will be with me tonight, won't you? Why didn't you come up to me last night?"

Elaine shook her head. "Mother forbids it. It's bad luck. The bride must sleep alone until—after you're married I can."

"But after I'm married—" I stopped, beginning to shake. The truth was, I had no idea what to expect. No one had ever spoken to me about what arrangements obtained between husband and wife. And everyone might be different. How was I to know what to do?

"I mean, when the King's away, of course," Elaine said hastily, coloring. It was too late. Arthur the man had intruded into the conversation, and we could not be comfortable with each other now. I left her shaking out the yellow gown and went to my rooms to help Ailsa unpack my wardrobe.

He came at sundown. The thundering of cavalry could be heard for miles, and I raced down from my chamber to Elaine's room and huddled with her by the window. Lancelot had troops lining the street from King's Gate, keeping back the crowds. I saw him sitting quietly on Nestor, and Bedwyr was there on his big chestnut, as twilight darkened to night. All the men had torches, and when the King came, he rode down a tunnel of light. His stallion was white and bunched his haunches to come to a sliding stop right at the castle steps. The King slid off in an easy motion as the groom stepped up to grasp the reins. He was too distant to see his features, but we could see his actions well enough. He went to Lancelot, who dismounted and saluted, but the King placed his hands upon his shoulders, said something, and then hugged him warmly.

"He is as tall as Lancelot," Elaine breathed in my ear. "But how broad his shoulders are!"

"Hush, Elaine."

He greeted Bedwyr likewise, then mounted the castle steps where Kay saluted at the door. Kay gave a long report and nodded in response to the King's questions. Then the King embraced him and slapped him on the back. He signaled to the guards, who moved to let the crowd of people into the forecourt, and they gathered at the steps. The King addressed them, but we could not hear his voice, for Elaine's window was glazed. Then the people raised a great cheer, which we heard even though the glazing, and the King turned and entered his castle. Lancelot glanced swiftly in our direction before he followed.

Elaine and I sat back and exhaled.

"Well!" Elaine exclaimed, glowing. "He's here at last! And every inch a warrior king. You don't suppose he would call an audience tonight, do you? After we are all dressed for bed?"

"I shouldn't think so. He's been away two months. There must be a lot to catch up on."

She raised an eyebrow. "I bet most of it's about you. He's probably grilling Lancelot right now."

I turned away, unable to bear the thought of it. "Won't you come up with me, Elaine? Just for a while?"

"Oh, Gwen, I'd love to! Just to peek into his chamber—but Mother would have my hide. I dare not do it. You'll be all right. Sit with Ailsa a while and have a hot posset."

I followed her advice. Ailsa and I sat together in her anteroom, talking about old times in Northgallis, and she sent for a warm drink, fragrant with spices. There must have been a sleeping potion in it, for soon I grew weary, and when she took me upstairs and tucked me into the great bed, I fell asleep instantly.

I awoke quite suddenly in the night. I heard voices. I looked toward the leather curtain and saw the soft glow of lamplight around the edges. He was there. I clutched the coverlet about my throat and held my breath, listening. I could hear his heavy tread on the floorboards and heard him speaking to someone, probably Varric or Bran, but I could not hear the words. It was a warm voice, pleasant in tone and deep. I heard muffled responses, and quite suddenly the lamp went out, and all was quiet. I lay there for what seemed like a long time, but I heard nothing. At last, toward dawn, I drifted back to sleep.

I awoke with sunlight streaming in through the terrace doorway. He was gone. I rose and donned my robe, then tiptoed to the curtain.

"Bran?" I called softly, hoping it was not Varric I heard stirring coals in the grate.

"My lady?" He came to the curtain and drew it aside. He looked tired but, in some indefinable way, satisfied. His King was back.

"Bran, were you up late last night?"

"Yes, my lady. We put the King to bed."

"Did—did he say anything about—"

Bran smiled. "Oh, yes, my lady. Of course he knew you had arrived safely. He got the full report from Sir Lancelot. But when he discovered I had met you—I did not tell him I heard you weeping, my lady. I said it was by accident."

"Oh, thank you, Bran. I am in your debt."

"Not at all, my lady. When he discovered I had met you, he asked me if I liked you."

"He did? Does he value your opinion so?"

"I could not say, my lady. But he knows that I am near your age, perhaps that was why he asked."

"What did you say?"

Bran's eyes widened. "Why, I told him the truth, of course. I said yes. He asked me why, and I told him you were without affectation. That seemed to please him."

I felt heat rise to my face. Bran looked suddenly shy and cast down his eyes, but I reached out and touched his arm. "Thank you, Bran. I think you have done me a great service."

"I told him the truth, my lady, as everyone does who knows him."

I drew back into my chamber and left him to his tasks. It boded well, that the High King was somewhat curious about me. It meant, perhaps, with luck, that he would treat me as a person. I did not want to hope too much; for if it were not so—and who could blame the High King of Britain if he had more important matters to think about than the thoughts and feelings of a girl?—I should be the more disappointed. I wondered how much Lancelot had told him. Had the King been able to see the truth behind his praise of me? I called Ailsa to me then, to occupy my mind with other thoughts.

Our audience was set for noon. People thronged all morning in the forecourt, waiting for the great doors to open. I sat with Elaine at her window, while Ailsa and Grannic dressed our hair, and watched them. Once again I noticed that people of every station were assembled, lords and ladies in fine clothes, knights and ladies-in-waiting, workmen, servants, peasants, and poor folk with only rags to wear. They all came, and they were all admitted.

Sometime later a page came to our door and brought the message that the High King was in court and waited upon our leisure. The time had come. Elaine and Ailsa put last-minute touches to my hair and gown. It was the smoke-blue gown Elaine had embroidered, and the High King's sapphire was round my neck, and Fion's earrings on my ears. Someone had gathered early cornflowers for my hair, which Ailsa dressed with seed pearls, braiding in the flowers to frame my face, and letting the long tresses hang loose down my back. In summer the sun turned my hair almost white, like a child's hair, much to my dismay. The gown itself was of heavy silk, and the day was warm, but I was shivering and my fingertips were ice.

Elaine gripped my arm, trembling. "Oh, Gwen, take care what you say! The honor of Wales is in your hands!"

As if I could forget it! With these helpful words ringing in my ears, I was led to the outer door. Lancelot was there, with Pellinore and Bedwyr, and I was never so glad to see him in my life. They led us through the long halls, where sentries snapped to attention at their posts, and slid their eyes sideways as we passed, watching. We came to the gilded doors of the Hall of Meeting and stopped. Lancelot looked down at me. My hand upon his arm trembled visibly.

"Courage, Gwen," he whispered, and I took a deep breath and stilled myself. He nodded to the guards, and the doors swung open. The babble of conversation stilled as the throng divided to let us pass, silent except for the occasional gasp and sigh. The High King's chair was on a dais at the end of the hall, and I gathered my courage and dragged my eyes off the tiles to look at him as we approached. He was standing, looking at me. It was a good face, of straight planes marked by dark brows, dark eyes, and straight lips. It was a rugged, handsome face, which one might expect of a warrior who was Uther's son. What caught me by surprise were his eyes. They were a rich, warm brown in color, glowing with a joyful light that seemed to come from within himself. He stood easily, waiting, not at all stiff or nervous, not shaking like a leaf in the winter wind, but calm and serene, and sure.

I dropped my eyes hastily and felt color rise to my face. I held on to Lancelot's arm for dear life and fought to collect my wits. The procession halted before the dais, and the High King came down the step to greet us.

"My lord Arthur," I heard Lancelot's voice dimly, "it is my pleasure to present to you the bravest, truest, loveliest maid in all Britain, Guinevere of Northgallis."

I sank helplessly into a curtsy at his feet. He extended a hand, brown from the sun, and raised me. He must have felt me shaking, for his voice was very kind.

"So this is the lass who has taken my Kingdom by storm." I glanced up quickly and saw he was smiling. "Since I left the north country, I have heard nothing but tales of your great beauty and your unflagging generosity to my people. I thank you, Guinevere of Northgallis, for this service. You are welcome here."

I tried to speak, but could not. He gently squeezed my hand and brought me to stand beside him, then turned to greet Queen Alyse and Elaine. I never heard what he said to them, for my head was whirling. His flesh was warm and dry and comforting somehow.

He imparted strength and ease of heart to me, I know not how. It was always so in his presence. It was his gift.

When the greetings were over, King Arthur offered me his arm and led me to the small, gilded chair that stood next his own. He bowed over my hand, screening me for a moment from the throng.

"You need say nothing," he said softly. "We must greet all the people who have come, but you may let me do the talking."

"My lord is kind," I whispered.

"Thou art young," was his reply, and then he straightened. It reminded me suddenly of Fion, who had a habit of saying personal things in Latin.

It took hours. First the nobles came forward, lord and lady, and bowed and curtsied and welcomed the High King home and looked me over from head to toe and wished us well. Then came the common folk, and this took longer, for they were mostly tongue-tied, but determined to say their piece. Arthur was amazingly patient and kind, addressed some of them by name, and knew their wives and kinfolk; others he met for the first time and took time to inquire about their lives, the number of their cattle, and the success of their crops, or the death of their elders. I had sense enough to realize that there was military intelligence to be gleaned from these conversations, and I was sure he was filing away new facts in the back of his mind, but he also seemed genuinely interested in how his people lived and what they needed.

At last the greetings were over, but none made move to leave. Now the petitioners lined up before him. The business of the High King's court was about to begin. But first Arthur turned to me and looked somewhat anxiously into my face. "Are you tired, Guinevere? You need not stay for this. It happens every day. You may leave when you will."

By this time I was able to manage a smile. "No, my lord. I am not tired. Though it may happen every day, I have never seen it before. It would be my pleasure to see the running of the Kingdom at firsthand."

He looked at me a moment, and his gaze was utterly direct.

"By Heaven," he said softly, "Lancelot was right." Then he grinned as I colored. "You *are* one in a thousand."

So we sat for three hours while Arthur's justice was dispensed. He listened attentively to each case that was brought before him, and I thought the questions he asked were to the point and clever. He was quick to smoke out lies, and I began to understand why people told him truth. His decisions were even-handed, and although not all parties went away pleased, I heard no grumbling. And after three hours had passed and everyone had been seen, he seemed as fresh and eager as he had at the start. At last he gave the signal that the meeting was ended and rose, extending a hand and raising me as well. He led me through a door behind the dais into a small anteroom. Lancelot was there, standing stiffly, waiting. Arthur stretched his arms and sighed. It was the first sign of weariness he had shown.

"I could do with a workout, Lance. Is there any chance of it?"

"Sword practice in the library," Lancelot said, his eyes lighting. "Or mud wrestling in the sties. There are crowds everywhere else." Arthur threw back his head and laughed. It was a deep, honest, joyful laugh, and I could not keep from smiling.

"What would I not give to be able to do it!" the King cried. Then he took my hand and raised it to his lips.

"You have been an angel, Guinevere. It bodes well. I wish we had more time to spend together. When is the solstice? Three days? Perhaps we could ride out together. Lancelot tells me you are accomplished. But I fear we may be too busy. Too many people about, and more are coming. I shall see you at dinner, at least." He inclined his head. "Till then."

I curtsied. "My lord." Lancelot offered his arm, and I took it.

The King paused at the door, suddenly looking almost shy. "I don't wish to be bold, or to instruct you in matters that are none of my concern," he began, and I froze, fearful of what was coming. "But I like you in blue," he finished, and disappeared.

I was so relieved I laughed out loud, though Lancelot was silent. He escorted me back to the women's quarters and stood solemnly by the door.

"You see," he said.

I nodded. "Yes."

I was awake late that night when the King came to bed. I saw the lamplight creep around the curtain, heard voices, the King's and one other, and then the light died. But the King did not sleep. Instead, he paced the chamber, back and forth, and I listened, amused, until I fell asleep to the steady sound of his measured tread.

We did not have time for riding. Two days were hardly sufficient to prepare for an event the Kingdom had waited so long to see. Thousands of people came to Caer Camel and camped upon the slopes outside the fortress walls. Their bonfires lit the night sky, their dancing and games and hunting cries filled the day with noise. I was taken to be examined by Bishop Landrum, a sour stick of a man, who questioned me at great length and at close quarters, with lust in his eyes and garlic on his breath, before pronouncing me fit to wed a Christian prince.

"I pray I will never have any sins to confess," I cried to Elaine when I returned, "for, most certainly, I would not tell that man!"

She quieted me somehow, and we both longed for friendly Father Martin. I was fretful and restless, much to the amusement of Alyse and her ladies. I could not ride out, for the crowds. I could only walk in the Queen's garden, for the palace was thick with strangers. So I paced there by the hour, much as Arthur paced his room at night, as the time crawled by. Whoever had designed the garden knew what he was about. There were pear trees set against the wall where the morning sun warmed them and creeping vines that flowered in many colors. Roses grew along the walks, and wildflowers and sweet herbs along the walls. It was peaceful there, when everyone would leave me alone, and I blessed the gardener, whoever he was. All it needed was a fountain for the birds to play in. As I paced, Elaine kept up a steady stream of chatter.

"He has fine, strong hands and a dexterous touch. Have you noticed how he holds his head when he is listening? His concentration is tremendous. He listens with every fiber of his body. No wonder grown men twice his age tremble before him! I'll bet he is skilled at bending other wills to his purpose. And such handsome features! His face should be stamped upon a coin. What joy it would be to see him wield a sword! With shoulders like that— who could stand against him? I've never known a man with such a bearing, such a presence. And his stride is twice the length of Lancelot's—"

"Heavens, Elaine!" I cried. "Have you looked at no one else besides the King? What have you been doing?"

"Don't worry," she said lightly. "I've been discreet. I'll wager a copper coin no one's seen me watching. And I'll wager another you could describe Lancelot from head to toe."

"I could. But I won't."

"Well," she said with a defiant toss of her head, "you were wrong about his falling short of my expectations. He is everything a king should be, and more. And he *does* have beautiful hands."

"Oh, Elaine!"

She came up to me and gripped my arm until it pained me.

"Gwen," she whispered fiercely, "take care. You have never known a man like this. This is a powerful man."

"Well, of course, he is High—"

"I am not talking about kingship!" she said, leaning closer. "I am talking about the man himself. He has power of a kind you don't suspect. Take care you please him."

I felt heat rise slowly to my face as I trembled in her grip. I dared not ask her what she meant.

We took our meals in our quarters, by choice. But dinner was a public affair. The High King sat surrounded by his Companions, and I sat between Pellinore and Alyse, on his right hand. I was toasted every night and heard many speeches in my honor. Only Lancelot never looked my way. Every time I saw him he looked thinner and paler than the time before. Once or twice I saw Arthur look at him with compassion and felt a trickle of fear slide down my spine. I returned from this ordeal exhausted, for it was hot in the hall, what with the torches and the press of bodies. But sleep came hard. Ailsa mixed me potions, and on the night before the wedding, I sat on the floor with my head in her lap and cried. She stroked my hair and sang me songs as she had been wont to do in nursery days. But each night it was Arthur's restless pacing that lulled me finally to sleep.

The wedding day dawned cool and cloudy, with a fitful breeze. I knelt by my bed and prayed God to give me strength. I was up early, but Arthur was already up and about. Ailsa brought me tea, and we sat on my terrace and watched the morning mists rise off the distant meadows.

"It will clear," she predicted. "And be cool for the games. Never fear, my lady. 'Twill be a perfect day."

We were married at midmorning by the bishop in the church. King Pellinore was my escort, and as my guardian it was his right to give me to the King. I remember little of the preparations. My dress was white, and trimmed with laces. Arthur, too, was simply dressed in white. He wore a thin circlet of red gold on his head, and wonderful Excalibur hung from his jeweled belt. I remember the moment I first saw it, as King Pellinore led me down the aisle to where he stood. The scabbard was old, oiled leather, and very plain. But the hilt burned bright and deadly in the candlelight, while the dark emerald flashed once, as he turned toward me, and then lay quiet. It was a cold weapon, and dangerous, the Saxon-Slayer, and hugged his hip as if it were part of him. His Kingship sat upon him like a glowing mantle, and he wore it easily. He took my hand, and I sank in awe before him.

"My lord Arthur," I whispered.

We were married while the mists lifted, and as I left the church on his arm, the sun broke through the clouds and the throng of people cheered.

I sat beside him at the wedding breakfast, for it was now my place, while Elaine sat weeping between her parents. Lancelot, straight and pale on the King's right, never glanced my way. All the people who could fit into the dining hall were given seats, rich and poor alike, and shared the same food and drink that was served to the King. I noticed that while wine was served to all, Arthur and I drank water only. The hall was loud with the babble of a hundred tongues, and at some tables the people sang and danced. The High King walked about the room, stopping at every table to say some word of thanks, or endure a humorous remark, or greet a friend. He did not seem to weary of it. I remarked to Bedwyr, who sat next me, that he had a talent for making friends.

"He loves his people" was Bedwyr's reply. And they, it seemed, loved him. As Lancelot continued to stare moodily at his plate, I kept talking to Bedwyr to keep nervousness at bay.

"And where is Merlin? I would have thought he would be here, to see the High King wed."

Bedwyr smiled and shook his head. "Merlin dislikes weddings, and he is getting old. He sent to beg to be excused, for he suffers from a chest cold. He will be here in a few days, however, for the High King has called a Council meeting. And Merlin is his chief counsellor."

This was good news and bad news. I was mightily relieved the old enchanter was not there, but uneasy about his coming. Sooner or later, I knew, I must face him.

King Arthur returned to his place, gathered the hall with a look, and raised a toast in praise of me. Everyone drank and cheered. Then I stood, to his surprise, and raised a toast in praise of Arthur, who brought glory and honor to Northgallis and all of Wales, by choosing a Welsh maiden as his bride. This brought the house down, and there were shouts of "Northgallis!" and "Pendragon!" as men slammed their goblets on the tables and stomped their boots upon the floor.

Arthur said nothing, but kissed my hand to the cheering of the crowd.

Then we returned to the church in grand procession, this time for my coronation. Arthur himself took the slender silver crown set with amethysts and set it on my head, while the bishop blessed me.

"It was my mother's," he said softly as he came close. "May you wear it in good health and have long life, as she did."

Wearing Ygraine's crown and feeling overwhelmed, I was led at last to the open fields by the woodlands, where flags waved gaily in the breeze and stands had been constructed for the King's guests. We spent the brilliant afternoon watching Arthur's Companions compete at various skills for the honor of his notice. There was wrestling, and swordplay, and foot races, and horseracing. There were even contests to see who could throw a spear the farthest and whose horse could pull the most tree trunks the greatest distance. Nowhere, although I looked for him, did I see Lancelot. But finally, as the shadows began to lengthen in the long, June twilight, I saw Nestor's head through the crowd and then heard the stallion scream. Lancelot rode out alone upon the field.

He gathered Nestor under him and began to canter in a circle. With a fluid change of lead they changed direction and circled the other way. Then he cantered away in a straight line, changing leads every four strides, every three, every two, *every stride*—it was like dancing! I held my breath in excitement. What skill was this! Then he galloped the horse down the field, gathering speed, till they raced by in a blur of motion and came to a full sliding stop, the stallion sitting on his haunches and the clods flying. The horse whirled and reared, striking out with his forelegs, and when Lancelot set him down, he began to canter sideways, bent around the rider's leg, first one way and then the other. It was breathtaking! How I longed to get astride Zephyr and teach her those things!

"I see you are a horseman in your soul," Arthur whispered, smiling.

"Yes, my lord," I breathed, unable to take my eyes from the field.

Then the stallion reared again, holding it, standing on two legs in arrested motion, then coming down and trotting smoothly forward. Suddenly he leaped into the air and kicked out with his hind legs, like a deer in full flight, and the crowds gasped. They did it three times, Lancelot landing lightly, never stirring from the saddle, never tugging at the bit, hardly moving a leg. It was like magic. To wild applause, my own included, horse and rider came and stood before the King. Nestor ducked his proud head, as Lancelot touched his forehead with his sword.

Arthur was moved. He leaned over the railing and spoke to Lancelot. Above the roar of the crowd I could not hear what he said. Lancelot, white-faced, asked him something. The King paused and then assented. Lancelot saluted him once more, sheathed his sword, and rode away.

The competitions over, we all moved back indoors as dusk fell, to the great feast that awaited us. This time the wine that went around was not watered, and the men drank thirstily. Even the King partook of it, although I did not. Lancelot did not appear at dinner. When Bedwyr asked after him, the King replied without expression that he had asked to be excused, and after the demonstration he had given, he had not been refused.

"Is he ill?" Kay inquired, who overheard. "He looked well enough this morning. What ails him?"

Arthur turned slowly toward Kay. His eyes were dark and sorrowful, but his voice was hard. "It is something he has suffered from for weeks. He will be better in the morning."

Kay looked bewildered and shrugged. Bedwyr seemed to have lost something in his lap. The King could not mean what I thought he meant, I was certain, but I began to be uneasy. Suddenly Arthur downed the wine in his cup in a single gulp and signaled to bring on the bards.

Four bards sang for us that night, from the four corners of Britain. One of them was a Welshman with a melting tenor. We had all the King's favorite tales, and then the one about King Arthur that Merlin himself had devised. Several new tales had been composed for the occasion, one of them very lovely, accompanied by lap harp and flute. I enjoyed the music, and after the last bard had finished and been served his well-earned wine, I turned to Arthur to praise his choice.

I found him looking hard at me, seeing through me, in the way he had of judging men. It was a moment of testing, and I knew it even then. His color was high with the effects of wine, and his eyes were bright, but they pierced like a sword thrust and felt like cold steel. It took every ounce of courage I possessed to meet his gaze and hold it; this was in deadly earnest. There was no tenderness on his face. I saw suddenly that he knew everything, he who could judge a man's character to a hair's breadth and from whom few could keep secrets. He was wondering what manner of woman he had married. In that instant I felt his spirit reach out to me, and I felt his great need. I placed my hand upon his own as it rested in his lap.

"My lord."

"Art thou mine?" he asked in Latin, so low that only I could hear.

My throat ached, and I blinked back tears. I held onto his hand and from it drew strength. "King. I am thine."

He nodded and slowly lifted my hand to his cheek, where he held it resting against his face. At last he let me go and turned away. Released, I felt drained; strength had left me, and my hand shook as I reached for my water cup.

"Dearest Guinevere," Bedwyr whispered, leaning toward me and staring hard at his plate, "I bless you."

I shook my head, but I could not speak. There was no way to explain the turmoil of emotion I felt. The power of the man was real, and it was tremendous. And Elaine had known it before me.

Singers and jesters were circulating now, and the hour was growing late. Alyse kept looking at me expectantly. The songs grew bawdier and bawdier, and many of the men, who were drunk, started telling anecdotes and singing little ditties that reflected on the High King's prowess in more domestic fields of battle. Alyse's looks grew pointed, but she did not tell me what to do. At last I turned to Arthur, who was laughing. He had recovered his good spirits and looked at me kindly.

"Yes, I think it's time you went. It's only going to get rougher, and I see Alyse is already embarrassed. Take the ladies away. We will be hours yet." Then he caught me by the hand as I rose and kissed my upturned palm. "But I shall come to you before midnight."

I fled back to my rooms, Elaine close behind me, and fell quaking into Ailsa's lap. She was tipsy herself and giggled at my distress.

But Elaine understood. "Oh, Gwen, dear Gwen, don't go! I can't stand it!"

I hugged her tightly in my terror. Too much was happening, and too fast. He knew, I kept saying to myself, and yet when he had asked me the question I dreaded, I had told him the truth. It had been dragged out of me without my will, and it was true. It was true, and I had not known it until I said it. What kind of man was this?

Ailsa tempted me with honey mead, but I refused.

"You'll need something to calm your nerves, dear," she advised. "Lady Elaine, see if the queen has any of that sherry left."

But Alyse, who was on her way in with it, smiled kindly at me. "Guinevere is Queen now, Ailsa." And she dipped a curtsy to me.

"Oh, Aunt Alyse!" I cried, using the name I had not used since childhood. "I am so afraid!"

"Of course you are," she said easily, pouring a small glass and putting it into my hand. "Every girl is. I was terrified of Pellinore. But it passes."

"Let's see your crown," Elaine interrupted hastily.

I took off the silver circlet and let her hold it. "He told me it belonged to Queen Ygraine."

Alyse confirmed it, for she had seen Ygraine wear it. This led to stories of King Uther and Queen Ygraine, and between the two of us, Elaine and I kept her going for a long while. But it could not last forever. She happened to glance out of the window and saw how high the stars stood and cried out in anguish.

"Dear God, what devil has possessed me, on this night of all nights! Come, Gwen, Ailsa. You must be ready. You must be waiting when he comes."

They dressed me in the gown Elaine had made for me. The bodice fitted me now to perfection, but neither she nor I could look at it. Ailsa slipped my blue robe over my shoulders, and we all climbed the steps to my chamber. The leather curtain had been pulled aside and fastened against one wall. The lamps were lit in my room and the King's. There was no one there but us, and Alyse heaved a sigh of relief.

"I shall do penance tomorrow," she said fervently. I sat down on my bed and looked at them all unhappily.

"No, no!" Alyse cried, smiling, "not here, Guinevere. In there." And she pointed to the King's bedchamber.

I paled and gritted my teeth to keep my voice from shaking. "What must I do?"

Alyse came over and took my hand gently between her own. "Simply get into his bed. He will expect to find you there. Go in and close the curtain. No chamberlain will come in. Once the bride is there, no one goes in but the bridegroom. Don't shake so, child. He seems a kind man. He will not be long. It is near midnight now." She kissed me tenderly, as a mother would, and I clung to her. She hugged me once, then led her women back down the stairs.

Elaine, struggling against tears, embraced me. "Be obedient and please him," she whispered. "Just remember, I would give half a lifetime to be in your place!" Biting her lip, she whirled and raced for the stairs. Ailsa waited until I had gone in and pulled the flap across the doorway. Then she left.

12 ✻ THE KING

I stood in the center of the room, shaking. It was warm. A low coal fire burned in the grate, and the night breeze blew through the window, laden with scent. On one side of the bed stood a skin of wine hung over a low flame, and a small table with two silver goblets, one set with amethysts and one very plain. I went slowly to the bed and sat on the bearskins. They were soft and tickled my bare feet. I looked up at the Dragon of Britain above the bed and pinched myself on the arm. It was still there. I slipped out of my robe and folded it neatly, laying it on the oak chest in the corner. The thudding of my heart was the only sound. Tentatively I lifted the bearskins. The chamberlains had remade the bed with the sheets we had brought the King from Wales. I stroked the fine linen; it felt like silk. Holding my breath, I slipped in and pulled the bearskins tight around my chin.

Nothing happened. The lamp flared in the corner as the breeze passed, and then all was still. I tried closing my eyes, but it was pointless. It was so very quiet. There were no sounds from outside. I could not hear the rowdiness in the feasting hall. I knew they would give a great cheer when they finally sent the High King off to bed, but I did not hear it.

After what seemed like hours lying rigid on his sheets, I heard the King coming. There was laughter from the room below his stairs, and several voices wishing him good hunting. Then there were only two voices, his and Varric's. I heard the splash of water and the King's deep voice asking a question, and Varric's soft one giving an answer. Then there was silence. I heard no footfall on the stairs, but suddenly he was there, standing at the foot of the bed, watching me. He was wearing the day robe I had made him, and against his tanned skin it shone silver white. He came around to where I lay and sat down beside me. I had not realized I had a death grip on the bearskins, until he gently pried my fingers loose, one by one. He had washed his face and hair and looked scrubbed clean and rather boyish.

"Guinevere, sit up." Obediently I pushed myself up and sat against the headboard. He took the skin of warmed wine and poured a little into the jeweled cup and handed it to me.

It smelled enticing, heavy with sweet spices I did not know.

"Try it," he said gently. "It's mulled wine. We have a recipe here that comes all the way from the East. That wonderful smell is cinnamon, and there are rare cloves in it, also. It is not strong." The shadow of a smile crossed his face. "But I think you need to relax a little."

I obeyed him and drank. It was very good, sweet and fragrant and warming. Slowly my joints began to thaw.

"I don't know how much young maids are told about wedding nights," he said, holding my eyes. "But there really isn't much to fear. I promise not to frighten you, Gwen. I know you are brave, but this should not need courage." He poured some wine into the plain cup, sipped, and put it down. He reached out and took a strand of my hair and ran it through his fingers, watching it as the white-gold threads crossed his rough palm.

" 'Hair like light,' Bedwyr told me. Bedwyr is a poet, did you know? He's a skilled musician, as well. But he has a gift for words ... hair like light ... I have never seen hair so light as yours, nor blue eyes so dark."

I sipped the wine and watched him over the rim of the goblet. He was not drunk. He was not in a hurry. He looked as if he had all the time in the world. Such was his patience.

"Do—do you like your robe, my lord?"

"Indeed I do. It is the most comfortable thing I have ever worn. It was a gift from you, I am told. Did you design it?"

"My lord, I made it."

He looked surprised. "Yourself? And the emblem here? You stitched that? The work is very fine, Guinevere. Then the gift is doubly dear to me. I like the way you have done the Dragon. I was thinking of having it copied for a new banner in the Council chamber I am building. Would that please you?"

"Yes, my lord."

"Guinevere," he said, drawing closer. "My name is Arthur."

"My lord Arthur," I repeated in a whisper. I did not mean to shrink back as he leaned forward, I simply could not help it. He sat up and looked at me thoughtfully. I expected him to be annoyed, but he was not.

"There are ways around it, you know," he said calmly, watching me steadily. "It needn't be done tonight. I have no desire to force you. I will await your sign."

I stared at him wide-eyed. "But—but what about—the proof—"

Something flickered in the dark eyes. "There are ways around that, too. I know a few tricks." With a flick of the wrist he whipped back the bearskins. A dagger leaped to his hand, I know not from where, and he cut his fingertip, squeezing three drops of blood onto the sheet. "There," he said, binding up his finger in a handkerchief. "You see how easy it is?"

But I had jumped up and stood trembling beside him.

"No!" I cried. "I will not be shamed so! What you suggest is a disgrace to Wales and a disgrace to Britain!"

Arthur rose slowly, a look of great tenderness on his face. His shoulders were very broad. He took my face in his hands and kissed me.

"You pass every test with honor," he said softly, "and yet you fear me. I will not hurt you, Guinevere. Trust me for that. And I meant what I said. I will not take you against your will. I believe it's wrong. You must give the sign."

"I?" I quavered. "I do not know how."

"When you are ready, it will come to you. In the meantime—" He drew away and smiled down at me. "How much of the castle have you seen since you've been here?"

I think I gaped at him in shock. "The women's quarters."

"That's what I thought. Come on, put on your slippers. I want to show you something."

"What? Where are we going?"

He was already at the top of the stairs, whistling. "Varric! Get Kay! Send him here. Double march!"

He picked up my robe from the chest, fingering the fine cloth. "So soft. Will it keep you warm?"

"Is it cold where we are going?"

He laughed. "No. You'll be warm enough." He held out the robe, and I slipped it over my gown. He lifted my hair and held it in his hands a moment, then let it fall. As he took breath to speak, but then we heard running footsteps, and Kay's panicked voice.

"Arthur! My lord Arthur! What's amiss?" Kay bounded up the steps and into the room and stopped dead, staring.

"I want you to clear the way to the northwest tower. Minimum sentries. No lights. No passwords. Double guards on the entrances."

Kay's eyes widened. "*Now*, my lord?"

Arthur grinned. "Yes. Now, Kay. No questions."

Kay turned on his heel and was gone.

"We'll give him five minutes. He's a good man."

"What's in the northwest tower?"

"A sight not to be missed. And some clean air. It will do us both good."

He took my hand, and the torch from the wall sconce, and we sneaked out through the castle corridors like a couple of errant children. His glee was infectious, and I found myself enjoying the adventure immensely. The whole castle thought we were abed, and instead we were tiptoeing through the dark, hand in hand. Kay had doused the torches in the hall, and the sentries on guard snapped to attention, eyes forward, and said nothing. Eventually we reached the tower door. Two soldiers stood there. Arthur brought the torch down to his face, and they sprang aside, eyes averted. Not a word was spoken. Inside the stairs wound upward, slowly circling. He led me up cautiously. I began to giggle, and Arthur squeezed my hand.

"I feel as if we're stealing something," I whispered.

"We are," he whispered back. "Privacy."

Up and up we went, stopping once or twice so I could catch my breath. Arthur was not even winded. At last we came to an unguarded door, and Arthur pushed it open. At once I smelled the salt air and felt the light sea breeze in my hair.

"Arthur!" I cried. "The sea!" The northwest corner of Caer Camel was the highest part of the hill, and from the turrets of that tower the view was fabulous, miles in every direction. The full moon rode low in the western sky, and distant Ynys Witrin seemed close enough to touch.

I clung to the turret with the wind in my face, and Arthur stood beside me, leaning his arms on the parapet and pointing west.

"On a clear night when the moon is in the west, you can see the sea," he said. "Look for her reflection, that silver streak? That's the sea."

"It is? Oh, how wonderful! Are you sure it's not the Lake of Avalon?"

"I'm sure. I've checked it."

The wind blew steady like a sea breeze, and smelled of salt and salt marsh and new-mown hay. I breathed in great gulps of it, and felt at home.

"Have you ever sailed upon the sea?" he asked.

"No. I never have. But I have often wondered what it must be like, to be on a ship in the middle of the sea out of sight of land."

Arthur laughed softly. "It's heaven. I dream of it often." He was silent awhile. "I have been upon the sea three or four times as King, but the best time was the first time. I was six, I think. Ector took me. My guard let me spend time with the sailors when Ector was seasick. What a wonderful freedom that was! To be alone and unattended! I remember well standing in the bow and looking out upon the endless sea, rising and falling, all by myself."

"It must be hard to find ways to be alone as King."

He barked a short, bitter laugh. "It is impossible." He stared gloomily out at the distant sea. "I am never alone. Except in sleep." He turned to me quickly. "I beg your pardon, Guinevere. I did not mean—"

"No need my lord. I know what you meant. It's one of the reasons I love to ride so much. When I'm on a horse, I am alone with my thoughts, and free."

He nodded. "Then you understand. Some people, I think, are only happy in the company of others. But I, I could sometimes give my Kingdom for an hour's solitude!" He spoke vehemently, and stared back out toward the sea.

"You were constantly guarded, then, even as a child?" I asked, to divert his thoughts. Did everyone else in Galava know who you were?"

He shot me a swift glance and then smiled. "If you want to know whether it is true my birth was kept from me, the answer is yes. No one in Galava knew but Ector. He was as cautious as they come; he had Kay guarded as closely, so none guessed."

"When you were a boy, Arthur, did you not dream of being a king? I imagine it is a thing that boys do."

He sighed and gazed back at the distant Tor. "No. Not a king. That was out of my stars, I thought. But I wanted to be important. I felt it in my bones that there was something I must do. I could do so many difficult things more easily than other boys, I felt it was a sign. Not of anything so grand as kingship—you must believe me, Guinevere, it never crossed my mind it could be possible—but I wanted to make a difference."

His voice was tinged with melancholy again, and I did not understand it. I was not yet old enough to feel so, looking back upon youth. "Britain is whole," I said slowly. "And her enemies fear her power. That is a big difference from the way things were."

"But so many people have died," he said under his breath, bowing his head.

"Because of me. So many lives laid to my account." He lifted a hand before his face and slowly formed a fist. "It's the curse of Kingship. I command, and men die." His voice tightened. "No one ever thinks of that in the heat of battle, while the banner is waving and the paeans fill the air. No one thinks of it later, while we bury the dead and listen all night to the cries of the maimed and wounded. No one but I. And I grieve for every one of them." His hand dropped to his side and we stood together in silence. Suddenly he straightened and turned towards me. "Whatever am I saying? My dear Guinevere, I beg your pardon. I did not bring you up here to listen to my sorrows. Forgive my bad manners—it is unpardonable!" He reached for my hand and lifted it to his lips. "What a wretched bridegroom I am making!"

"Oh no, Arthur! Not at all!" I faced him and placed my hands against his chest. "I understand you, my lord. But you are just the kind of man a soldier wants to fight for—he knows you value his life and will not carelessly discard it; he knows that if he dies, the King will weep for him. My lord, you treat them like they are beloved—I have heard them say so. Because you grieve, my lord, they are eager to offer you service and die in your cause. And the people who live, live in a new world. . . . A safe world. We are now one country. I remember when I was a girl I thought Wales the extent of the civilized world. We were Welsh. Others were Cornish, Bretons, Lowlanders, Celts from the mountains of Rheged—now we are Britons, one and all. It is a miracle."

He looked down at me with tenderness on his face. "When you were a girl," he repeated softly, smiling. His arms came around me and he caressed my hair. "My sweet woman, I believe that you are jollying me back to good humor."

It was warm standing against him; the night breeze felt suddenly cold, and it was warm and safe in his arms. "Every word is true," I whispered, tentatively slipping my arms around his strong body. "If you will teach me how to please you, Arthur, I will try to keep you in good humor."

His smile broadened. "One in a thousand." He bent and kissed me very gently, and I felt the power of the man in his restraint. Excitement gripped me—pleasure at the feel of his lips and terror of the unknown merged into breathless excitement; I pressed closer and returned his kiss with sudden longing. His hands slid down my back and pulled me hard up against him as his lips moved on mine; my breathing quickened, my knees turned to jelly—so fast, so unforseen, like catching fire, my body spoke a language new to me, but that he understood at once. He sighed a great sigh and lifted me off my feet, carrying me in arms that felt like iron bands.

"I told you," he said huskily, "that it would come to you. Hang on." And he kicked open the tower door.

"Arthur! Who made this garden?"

It was the evening of our third day, and I stood on my terrace while Ailsa took down my hair and began unfastening my bodice. I could hear the King in his room, whistling.

He poked his head through the curtain, and Ailsa fell into a curtsy, eyes averted.

"Did you call me?" he asked.

"Who made this garden? It's so beautiful and done with such skill by a hand that knows plants. I would like to thank the gardener."

Arthur grinned, mischief in his eyes. He stepped into the room, and Ailsa, who had risen, flattened herself against the wall.

"You may meet him tomorrow. A master at his craft, as I should know better than anyone." He took the hairbrush from Ailsa's trembling hand and began brushing out my hair. He loved to hold it in his hands. It always gave him pleasure. He bent and kissed my neck, and I looked sideways at poor Ailsa.

"You may go, Ailsa. I'll call you if I need you—if there's anything the High King finds he cannot do himself."

Ailsa fled, and Arthur laughed warmly. "Was that kind?"

I turned to face him and kissed him lightly. "Kinder than keeping her here, I should say. Now about this gardener. Where shall I find him?"

Again his face lit with mischief. "Most likely on an old bay gelding, with saddlebags full of herbs he has stopped to gather along the way, coming down the road at a snail's pace. He does not like riding."

"The *gardener*?"

"Yes. The gardener. Merlin."

"*Merlin? Merlin* is the gardener?"

"Guinevere, you are pale. Do not be frightened of Merlin. He is a good man. Wait until you meet him."

"I have met him."

"*What?*"

"Years ago. When King Pellinore took us to pay homage to the princess Morgan on her way to Rheged."

"Ah, yes. I sent him as escort because I could not go myself. But you only had sight of him, not speech. You can't know a man from that."

I wanted to tell him about it, but the words would not come. It was as if my lips were sealed upon any word against Merlin. I managed a smile.

"You are right, of course. But I have wondered about the garden—all my favorite plants are there, and some that I did not know, but which please me greatly. It is peaceful and sweet and beautiful. There are even songbirds in the trees. It is as if it were designed for me alone and exactly to my liking."

He paused and looked thoughtful. "I will not say it is impossible," he said slowly. "With Merlin, anything is possible. But you are asking me to believe that he knew, even then, you would be my Queen."

"My lord, is he not famous for seeing into the future?"

Arthur shifted uncomfortably. "He does not talk to me about magic," he said a little gruffly, and I could easily believe it. Arthur definitely lived in the world he could see and touch. "Well," he said at last, with a shift of his shoulders, "I shall ask him tomorrow, if you like. He will tell me."

"No, let it go. It does not matter. But I will thank him for the garden."

"I wonder," he said softly. "I wonder if it is true. It would explain why he was not surprised to learn that my first—that Guenwyvar died, when it was he who had foreseen a lasting marriage."

"Perhaps, but I do not think he wanted it to be me," I blurted suddenly, and he looked at me sharply, startled.

"Why do you say that?"

But again my lips felt sealed, and I could only shake my head. "It was a feeling I had at the time, when I saw him."

"He lifted no hand to prevent it. He was there in the Council chamber when your name was raised."

"What will be, will be," I whispered.

Arthur gripped my arms. "What did you say? Never mind, I heard it. He has said it to me ten or twelve times, whenever I asked him for advice about you. I thought he was simply putting me off; he knows nothing about women. But perhaps he meant more by it. In the end he told me to follow my heart." He relaxed his grip, and I exhaled quietly.

"Why—why did you need advice, my lord? If Merlin knows nothing of women, you know a good deal more than he."

His eyes grew sad, and his lips thinned. "Because I feared another disaster."

"Ah." I sank onto the little bench and gently rubbed the places where his fingers had bruised me. "Arthur, will you talk about her? Can you? Was she pretty? Did—did you love her?"

He regarded me calmly and turned away, looking past the garden wall, past the fortress wall, to the distant darkness of the Tor.

"All right," he said gently, and then turned back to face me. "How odd that you should be the person I can tell." He took a deep breath. "She had not your beauty, Guinevere, but she was a pretty girl, and about your age. We had only three weeks together, a month perhaps. She was gay and bright and full of laughter. And in the end—she was so very brave." His jaw tightened, and the great vein in his neck stood forth. I reached for his hand. He sank to one knee, then, and took my hand between his own, holding hard. "The worst—the worst was the knowledge that I alone was responsible for her pain," he whispered. "Oh God, how she suffered! No soldier wounded in battle has endured what she endured. Dear Christ, there was so much blood!" He buried his face in my skirt, and his shoulders shook. That he, who was so strong, and from whom so many others drew strength, should reveal to me his weaknesses touched me near my heart. I stroked his head and spoke whatever words of comfort I could think of for a heart so burdened with woe. I sang softly a tune I had often sung to my mare, to calm her when she was frightened. It was an old Welsh melody, and the words had long been garbled beyond sense, but it had the power to comfort. He lifted his face to me, his eyes swimming, and I saw clearly his love, powerful and deep and uplifting, and my heart seemed to sing with joy. I sank to my knees beside him, clasped in his warm embrace.

"Oh, Arthur."

"My Guinevere."

"The King looks well, my lady," Bedwyr said. "It is the talk of the palace. He purrs like a well-fed cat."

I smiled at him. "He warned me you had a way with words, my lord Bedwyr."

He bowed and smiled shyly. "It is a fact, my lady, that in the past three days he has not denied anyone whatever has been asked of him. Kay is hard put to it to see advantage is not taken. Merlin noticed at once—you should have seen the look! His eyebrows touched his hairline! You have done for him what no one else could do. He is happy."

I colored and dropped my eyes. "I pray you will not attribute all this happiness to me, good Bedwyr. Put some of it down to his homecoming, after two months away at soldiering."

He laughed, amused. "Oh, no, my lady. I put it down to love."

He was one of Arthur's closest friends; he had the right to speak so, but I blushed horribly and could not control it. We were walking to the Council chamber. It was dusk, and the Council had just ended. The wine was going around, and Arthur had sent Bedwyr to fetch me, since he knew I wished to speak to Merlin.

"Do not blush so, my lady Queen. There is no shame in it. And we are all so grateful to you. All of us." And I knew what he was telling me.

We came to the door of the Council chamber, and I faced him. "How is he?" I asked quickly, and he knew that I did not mean Arthur.

He looked at me straight with his black eyes. "He is as well as he is ever going to be."

"Some things," I said, my voice trembling, wishing him to understand, "some things cannot be helped."

Bedwyr smiled, very kindly. "If anyone knows that, my lady, I should say Lancelot does." And he opened the door.

The men were standing in clusters, mostly around Arthur, talking and laughing, while servants went around with skins of wine. I looked briefly for Merlin but did not find him. Heads turned toward me; Arthur looked up, the smile of welcome on his lips, when suddenly a horn sounded, loud and insistent, and all movement stopped. Within seconds a guard came flying down the corridor, nearly knocking me down as he threw himself, breathless, at Arthur's feet.

"The Tor!" he cried. "My lord, the Tor is lit! And the fire on Bekan's Hill, southward!" He gulped, pausing for breath. He did not need to go on. Every man in the room knew what it meant. "Saxons, my lord!" In the small silence that followed, Arthur's features hardened, and his eyes grew cold. I could see his swift calculations as the men around him began to shift and mutter. He spun on his heel and pointed.

"You and you, to the barracks. I want Lukan, Vasavius, Gereint, Galgerin, and Lamorak. All companies at the ready, armed, provisions for a week, at King's Gate in one hour. Lancelot!"

"Here, my lord!"

"Take charge of the Companions. We'll need double mounts for Caesar-speed. We'll get there first, and let the army come up later. I give you fifteen minutes. Bedwyr!"

"Here, my lord!"

"You've heard the orders. Inform Kay. We'll need to resupply by week's end. He can meet us at Uther's Ford. Then send to Melwas. I want every man he has at the Camel road by moonrise. He can fall in with Gereint."

Bedwyr bent his knee and asked the question on everyone's lips. "Where are we headed, my lord?"

Arthur's eyes narrowed. "Badon."

I saw the stunned surprise on all their faces. Whispers ran round the walls. The young men did not believe it. Badon? They would never dare Badon, it was too far inland. The peace was settled, everyone agreed. But if the Saxons got to Mount Badon, someone pointed out, there was nothing to stop them—no, no, it was too far west. They wouldn't dare, even with longboats. But with the King just wedded, perhaps they thought—the arguments eddied past me. They mattered not. The men would go where the High King led them.

I watched Arthur. His face was white, and his eyes—his warm, loving eyes—were as cold and dull as slate. I shivered to see them; so he must look to his enemies, I thought, before the steel goes home. But there was a glow about him, an excitement, an authority that I recognized immediately, though I had only known him a week. He was the Unconquered King, called to battle, and he was exultant.

"Cerdic has landed his longboats and is heading for Badon. We will meet the courier upon the road and discover their landing point. We must get to Badon first, or Britain is lost." He spoke with certainty, and the whispers stopped. "Get me my Sword."

Men charged away; I could hear shouts throughout the castle and within minutes the jingle of bridles and the scrape of hooves on the paving stones outside. A page came running in with Arthur's mail. A young knight spoke up timidly behind the King.

"What about the Queen?"

Arthur frowned, all his concentration on his far-off enemy as his fingers worked the buckles of his corselet. "What queen?" He looked up suddenly and saw me in the shadows near the door, but his look was the unseeing gaze of a man in sleep. "Benwic's company shall stay to guard her. And Merlin is here." He looked vaguely about. "Somewhere. She's safe with Merlin." Then he spun, belting on his great Sword as he strode for the door.

"See to it," he snapped, to no one in particular, and left. The young knight smiled nervously at me and shrugged. I waved him away, to show I understood and did not take offense, and he ran out after Arthur.

Outside in the forecourt the cavalry were gathered, and I heard Arthur's stallion scream as the spurs went home, and they all thundered away. They were gone, and in so short a time! The room so recently alight and warm with voices stood cold and empty, the candles guttered. I drew a trembling breath and went out into the dark corridor. Someone had taken all the lamps from the sconces, no doubt to light the troops upon their way. I was not sure I knew my way back to my chamber in the dark. But an icy fear was breathing on my back, and I hurried away in whatever direction seemed most likely. I had not gone twenty paces when a cold hand reached out of the dark and grabbed me.

I believe I shrieked, and suddenly there was light. Merlin himself stood before me, with an oil lamp in his hand. A moment before he had not been there! I covered my mouth with my hand, stifling a gasp, and tried weakly to do him a reverence.

"Guinevere."

"My lord Merlin. I—I—you frightened me!"

"I beg your pardon." He hung the lamp in its place and stood quietly before me. He was one of those men who seemed always in repose. If he ever felt a nerve, he never showed it. His stillness had no edge to it; his patience was unending.

"You wanted to see me." It was a statement of fact; I did not know whether or not Arthur had told him.

"Yes, my lord."

"And I you."

I gulped. "I am at your service, my lord."

"I wished merely to offer you my congratulations," he said lightly. "You see how it has come to pass, Guinevere of Northgallis. You are Queen."

"Yes, my lord."

"Does it please you?"

"Being Queen? I hardly know. I have no desire for power."

"What then do you desire?"

Although spoken lightly, it was not an idle question, and I gave it thought. I suspected that it mattered much what I answered him, and I knew for certain that he would know a truth from a false-hood. "My lord, I wish Britain to be whole, and safe, forever. I wish her borders to contain one nation. One people."

Not a muscle on his face moved, but I fancied his eyes softened. I sensed that he was pleased. "There will be Saxons on our shores beyond your lifetime." He said it flatly. It was a known fact to him.

"Perhaps so, my lord. Still—"

"Still?"

"Perhaps in time they will be British, also." His focus sharpened, and I hurried on. "I was Welsh once. It was the world to me. Now I am British, yet Wales is still a part of me. Could not the same be true someday of a Saxon maid?"

He took in a quick breath and let it out slowly.

"You dream of civilization," he said quietly. "Perhaps it will be so. I have not seen. But it is not in Arthur's destiny. Remember that. He shall hold Britain until the day he dies, but it will be the Britain that you know tonight."

I trembled before those penetrating eyes. "Be it so, my lord. I am content."

He paused for so long, I thought he was finished with me, but I dared not leave until he dismissed me. "What did you want with me?" he said suddenly. "You have not asked your question."

How did he know I had a question? My courage deserted me. "I came to thank you for my garden. It has brought me so much pleasure, and Arthur only told me yesterday it was you who built it."

He bowed gracefully. "You are welcome for the garden. It needs only a fountain to complete it."

I stared in amazement. "Then you did design it for me? You knew, when you spoke to me, that—Arthur did not believe it."

A glimmer of a smile touched his lips. "Visions do not sit easily in the same room with Arthur. It was likewise with his father. What is the other thing?"

"What other thing, my lord?"

"The other thing you came to say to me."

"Oh." I looked away, suddenly frightened. "My lord, you are so kind to me tonight. And yet when we met, two years ago, you were so angry. I—I wish to know why my lord was angry, and—and disappointed. What have I done? Or what am I to do?"

He considered this plea and frowned. "It is not a thing for a maid to know."

"Please, my lord. I am afraid—I am only afraid I may bring some dishonor upon the King. If I am to do something dreadful—if you have seen it in the stars—please tell me that I may take pains to prevent it, or take myself away where I cannot be a danger to him."

"You cannot prevent it," he said gently. "You are a noble child, and I was wrong ever to doubt it. But you would do better to go on your way unknowing."

"Oh, please, my lord! At least tell me if I shall somehow wound him! Tell me at least something of what you have seen!"

He paused, and when he spoke, his voice was very kind. "You will come to glory with Arthur. This I have seen. If you leave him, his glory will be less bright; his death will come sooner. Britain will suffer. If you stay, your name will live on the lips of men for beyond a thousand years. Do not ask me for more. There is suffering ahead for you; you will be torn two ways. You must live with that. I think perhaps you are brave enough."

"But my lord Merlin! You hated me once! Please, oh please, tell me why!"

"I was wrong to hate. Even to feel anger. You will fail the High King, Guinevere, although it will not be of your will, and it will grieve you more than it grieves him. I was hurt for Arthur's sake, and therefore angry. But what will be, will be. Perhaps it is for the best. He will stand alone in glory. Nothing will take from it."

I did not understand his words, but I could see that he had done his best to answer me. The gray hair upon his head trembled in the light.

"My lord, I thank you for your patience with me."

He smiled wearily. "No thanks are due me. Everything I do is done in Arthur's service." He lifted a long arm and pointed behind me. "Your chamber lies that way."

"Truly? Thank you. I fear I do not yet know my way about."

He handed me the lamp, and as I took it, the light shone fiercely upon his face. He looked human suddenly, like a grandfather doing a kindness for a child. The fear that had gripped me since the sounding of the horn found voice. "Will he live? Will he be injured? Will he return?"

Merlin smiled. "I have just prophesied a glory lasting past a thousand years, and you are afraid the Saxons will harm him. No, child. He will come back to you unblemished and, when he comes, will stay. This is the last battle. At Badon, he will break the back of the Saxon snake."

13 ✹ CAMELOT

All the world knows what happened at Badon Hill. The Saxons, pushed by the pressure of their growing numbers, made one last and desperately bloodthirsty attempt to take the south of Britain for their own. They landed in longboats in great number and pushed toward Badon with speed, murdering villagers and setting fire to the land as they went. But before they came to the hill itself, which would have given them command of the country roundabout, Arthur and his chosen troops swooped down on them in the darkness of early morning, completely unexpected, like a horde of murderous spirits from the Otherworld, silent and deadly, and destroyed them before they ever knew what happened. At dawn the signal fires flamed across Britain: the Saxon force was broken. For a generation after, Saxon children were raised on the stories of the Demon King, whose white steed could fly on silent wings and snatch them from their beds in the still predawn if they were naughty. As for the Saxon kings, they were resigned at last to peace behind the borders Arthur set them and turned their energies to the arts of peace: government, husbandry, and music.

It was a grand summer. After celebrating the great victory at Badon, Arthur gave himself time to honeymoon before the real building of his Kingdom began. No one could deny he had earned it. All Britain, it seemed, joined in the celebrations of his victory and his wedding. As for the King himself, he attended games and competitions among his knights and feasted with them nightly. He kept me near him always and seemed to enjoy my conversation. He never tired of my questions and gave me leave to explore the castle from towers to kitchens to stables. And when I willed, I could sit beside him in the audience chamber and listen to the petitions brought by the people. The first time that he asked for my opinion, I colored to the roots of my hair, unable to say a word.

164

That he should care what I thought! The second time I was not so shy, and answered him. But the third time, I ventured my opinion when he had not yet asked me, for the cause concerned me. A villager sued for his wife's return from her mother's, whither she had gone when he had beaten her so badly she had lost the babe she carried. The King had heard the man's complaint with solemn face, and I feared in my heart that being after all a man, he might require the poor woman to be sent back to her husband, as was the law. I laid my hand upon the King's arm, and he turned to me at once, signaling the petitioners to fall back.

"My lord," I whispered urgently, "I know you are an honorable man and wish to keep the law, but consider this poor woman. You consign her to death if you return her to him. He has murdered her unborn child; if he had hate in his heart then, how much more will he have now, that she has fled from him? My lord, consider—what if I were in her place? I believe in the sacredness of the marriage vow, but this man has sinned against God in his treatment of his wife. Women should not stand outside the law, for we need its protection even more than men." I ended in a rush, amazed at my own temerity, and saw the faintest of smiles cross his lips. But his face remained solemn. After a moment, he took my hand in his and, facing the room, beckoned the villager closer. His voice, steady and low, never wavered, and all who attended that day were amazed by his words.

"Gilgarth, hear my judgment. The laws of my Kingdom are based on respect, honor, and trust. The vows of marriage are sacred. You have violated these vows by treating your own wife, who should be dearer to you than any in the land, as if she were a scoundrel. She is your wife; you may take no other. But you treat her not like a wife; therefore she need not share your house nor your bed. You have murdered your unborn child. For this you shall spend three months in my dungeons. The killing of children is a sin against God and a crime against Britain, whose future lies in her children's hands. When you are freed, you shall reform your life, else you will face my wrath. Your wife may return to you when and if she wills. She shall not be forced. And I tell you now, that all may know it, that in Britain we honor women, and my laws shall protect them." He dismissed the stricken man with a wave of his hand, and I slid from my chair and sank to my knees at his feet.

"My lord Arthur!" I gasped, overcome. There was silence in the hall.

He raised me quickly. "These are not tears of distress, Guinevere, I hope."

"Oh no, my lord, I am—I am amazed by your generosity."

"Do not mistake me," he said softly. "I did not speak solely on your account. But you were right. And it would ill become me to deny it. As far as women needing the protection of the law, though I had not thought of it before, it is only just. By setting an example, we shall make it so."

This was power, and I trembled to think of the magnitude of what I had done.

"And I am pleased," the King continued with a glimmer of a smile, "to hear that you value marriage vows as much as I."

One night at dinner Lancelot proposed a hawking party for the following day, as the weather promised fair. Lancelot had seemed more at ease with the King since the victory at Badon, in which he had played a major part. I was glad to see their good fellowship restored, for it was clear to everyone who knew them that their love was deep, if unspoken, and cherished by them both.

The King readily assented, and they began to plan the outing. I waited anxiously to see whether Arthur would think to include me in the party, but they were deep into talk about horses and terrain. I recalled Kay's dislike of what he called my "forwardness" and I remembered that Arthur had been raised in Kay's household. Perhaps, I thought, Lancelot's assurances had been more expressive of his own attitude than of the High King's. On the thought, Arthur turned to me.

"And you, Guinevere, shall ride Zephyr and fly Ebon. Have you any among your women who might attend you? We shall be out the entire day. The best hunting is south and west of here."

I simply stared at him in wonder. "May I truly come? My lord is very kind to ask me. I—I would love nothing more."

Arthur smiled. "I would not go without you. We will leave after breakfast, and Kay will send along a midday meal to Nob's Hill. Do you think the lady Elaine might attend you?"

I looked at him in surprise, and I hope I kept my face straight. "I expect so, my lord."

"Good," he said heartily. "Then Kay might come himself, who knows?" And he turned back to Lancelot.

I was kept busy digesting this piece of news. So Kay was an admirer of Elaine's! That a man so conservative and unchanging in his views should be interested in a willfull, headstrong girl like Elaine surprised me. But I knew well she would never accept him.

As I knew well she would come hawking, even though it meant riding the whole day, to be near the King.

I was up at dawn and in the stables before breakfast, grooming Zephyr myself and checking Ebon's jesses. The mare was happy to see me and greeted me with a soft nicker. If Lancelot was around, he did not come near. But one of the grooms, a boy named Petri, brought me a thick leather strap, well oiled and soft, and gave me to know that Sir Lancelot thought that, as I rode without a saddle, it might save the King worry if I made the mare wear it. I did not have to use it, Petri recited carefully, but as the High King had never seen me ride, it would be very natural if he feared for my safety. I laughed, taking the hint, and bade him thank Lancelot for the advice. I would use the neck strap.

I hurried back to my quarters to change into my doeskin leggings and my old green hunting mantle. Dear Lancelot! Encouraging me to be myself! He was right, of course. The pattern of our life together would be set in these few weeks, and it would be well to hide nothing from the King.

But Elaine, who was dressed down to her fingertips in fine cloth and trimmings, was furious at the sight of me in my old, comfortable hunting clothes.

"You just can't do it, Gwen! You can't go out like that! Think of who you are! You will shame King Arthur before all his Companions! You can't mean to ride bareback in those old leggings! Oh, Gwen! It isn't done!"

I wanted to laugh, but her distress was genuine, and it was, after all, on Arthur's behalf. "It will be done, Elaine, once I do it."

"But—but you are Queen, Gwen! You cannot!"

"It is because I am Queen," I said gently, "that I *can*. Who will say me nay?"

"The King himself, I'm sure!" she cried, in tears.

I shook my head. "I don't think so. Anyway, I mean to find out now. If he objects, I will simply change. There won't be any scandal. He will not be dishonored. Wait and see."

But as I sat bareback on Zephyr and waited with my women in the courtyard, I wondered if Elaine might not be right. Would the King be insulted, or his pride be hurt? I had to trust Lancelot, who knew him better than anyone. I had to rely on his honor, and not for the last time.

With a clatter of shod hooves on stone, they came, the High King on a pretty bay mare, Lancelot, Bedwyr, Lamorak, Bellangere, Gereint, and some others behind him. He raised a hand in greeting and opened his mouth to speak; then he pulled up short, staring. I saw him glance swiftly at Lancelot, who also rode bareback, and then he gave that long, cool appraising stare for which he was known and feared. I sensed no anger in him, only concern. It was his duty, after all, as well as his right to protect me. It was an effort to meet those penetrating eyes, but I managed. At last he smiled.

"I yield, lady," he said, inclining his head. "Let us see what you can do." And we cantered out of King's Gate, side by side, followed by the host.

It was a glorious summer day and glorious country for hawking. The rolling downs promised fast galloping, the meadows were full of hare, and the woods to the south teemed with birds. We cantered along at a decorous pace down the long approach to Caer Camel and then let the horses out when we met the straight causeway south. It was along this road King Arthur had flown on his great war stallion countless times; now, pounding along beside me on the bay mare, he rode like a boy, relaxed and eager and full of the fun of life. To him horses were a tool of war or a means of transportation, nothing more. He acknowledged Lancelot the better horseman, just as he acknowledged Lancelot the finer swordsman. But this Lancelot disputed. While in sword play, man against man, Lancelot was the quicker, nimbler fighter, Lancelot himself maintained that in a real battle no one could touch Arthur. He had the great gift of calm in a heated fight. And, as everyone knew, he had the deadliest sword in the Kingdom. Wherever he raised Excalibur in the defense of Britain, he was victorious. So did Lancelot praise him to the young men who continually flocked to Caer Camel, hoping to be accepted into the High King's service.

As the King found I rode well, he increased his speed, and the party began to thin out, with some of the men reining in to keep pace with Elaine and the other women. The King was first to raise a hare and fly his hawk. The kill was swift and clean. Arthur honored me by offering it to me; I accepted it with thanks and had it stowed into my servant's pouch. Then Bedwyr flew his falcon at a hare. By this time the rest of the party had come up, and we all watched together. Elaine was looking breathless and unhappy, so I beckoned her to ride up next to me.

"Are you all right, Elaine? Isn't this exciting? Isn't it wonderful to be outside and free?"

She looked at me strangely and shrugged. "You always were wild as a boy. I don't see what's wrong with a cushioned seat in the garden and a piece of needlework. I have blisters on my leg, and I can prove it."

"That's what comes of saddles. The horse feels it more than you do, I assure you."

"Mmmm," she agreed absently, watching the King as he set his hawk free. "You seem to be enjoying yourself these days, Gwen, after all your fear. I suppose I ought not to ask you how you like married life."

I colored and said hastily, "Now that Alyse and Pellinore have returned to Wales, I know you must be very lonely. Let us spend time together every day from now on."

She turned toward me slowly. "But you are always with Arthur. Except in Council, you are always at his side or following him about. You don't even seem to see me, Gwen, and you ignore poor Lancelot. You are—it's as if you are dazzled by the sun."

I opened my mouth to speak, then closed it abruptly. It would serve no purpose to tell her that I was with Arthur because he wanted me there. He knew how short time was. Yet her remarks raised a host of emotions in me, and I could not speak of them. Ignore Lancelot! Could she not see that we looked away and kept apart on purpose? That we were always, always aware of each other's smallest movement, even in a crowd? I was certain the King knew it.

"Elaine, I don't mean to ignore anyone. But everything is so new. Once life settles into a routine again, things will be easier. Let some time pass."

Elaine's face grew stiff with the effort of control. She so seldom made the effort, I braced myself for what was coming. "Are you with child?"

My mouth dropped open. This was the last thing I expected. "How would I know, until I bleed?"

"How do you feel?"

"Fine."

Unless imagination deceived me, she was relieved. But this I did not want to believe, even of Elaine.

"I am sorry to hear it," she said flatly. "The whole court is waiting to hear the news."

I took a deep breath to steady my nerves. I should have known, I told myself bitterly, I should have known. Of course everyone was waiting for the prince to be conceived. It was, after all, why he had married me. Only I had been dazzled by the sun.

The silence grew heavy between us.

"Have you admirers among the Companions?" I asked finally, trying to think of something, anything to break the tension.

Elaine looked moodily away. "Five or six. Lamorak's all right. Kay's the worst."

"Well, be warned, then. The King has asked Kay to meet us at Nob's Hill for the midday meal."

"Oh, God," she groaned, watching as Arthur, Lancelot, and Bedwyr came galloping back to us, a pair of hares slung across the King's saddle.

But as the men approached, Elaine sat up straighter, and her eyes grew brighter, and color came back to her cheeks. The King's mare came to a sliding stop, and Arthur tossed the hares to a servant.

"Lady Elaine," he said politely, inclining his head.

Elaine's color deepened ever so slightly as she dropped her eyes. "My lord King."

"Guinevere." He turned to me, smiling. "That's five altogether. Shall we head toward the woodland and show Ebon some fat partridges?"

"Certainly, my lord, if we have enough hares to serve in hall tonight."

"We can always hunt for more on the way back. The game is so thick hereabouts it's hard not to trample it underfoot."

"Then by all means let's try the woods. Lancelot," I said, addressing him directly and seeing the startled look in his eyes, "perhaps you would fall back and ride with the lady Elaine?"

Lancelot bent from the waist. "Whatever my good Queen pleases," he replied, and obeyed. Arthur shot me a quick look but said nothing, and then we were off.

Hawking in woodland was difficult, but it was how I had learned in Wales. Everything I flew Ebon at, he killed, and he made us ride hard only once. Then, in a furious pursuit through the woodland tracks, Zephyr's training paid off. We flew over trees and brush in our path and landed both hawk and kill neatly. When Arthur, who had been close behind me until the last obstacle, came up, he found the falcon hooded on my arm and the partridge in my pouch, and Zephyr and I calmly awaiting him. He cantered up to me, took in the situation at a glance, and laughed aloud. Then he swung the mare's haunches into Zephyr's, threw an arm about my waist, and, half lifting me from the horse, kissed me.

"What a woman you are," he said roughly.

"My lord," I replied almost shyly, "it was nothing. We did it daily in Gwynedd, Ebon and Zephyr and I."

"You are a team, and no mistake. How did you teach your mare to jump so effortlessly? Could Lancelot teach our mounts, do you think?"

"I'm sure he could. I think all horses know how to do it; you just have to learn how to tell them, and then how to allow them."

"Is that all?" His smile was mischievous. Some way off we heard our closest followers fighting through the brush.

"Fly him again, Gwen! The escort can take care of themselves. How many can he take in a day?"

"Why, he caught five the day I met—" I stopped suddenly, frozen. "—the day your Companions came to Wales," I finished lamely, coloring deeply. I cast my eyes down, afraid to look at him. There was a long silence. I tried and tried to meet his eyes, but I could not. At length he spoke, and his voice was flat, without any anger, but without his warmth.

"Yes. Lancelot told me of your meeting."

My eyes flew up to his at that. "He did?"

His face was shuttered. I could read nothing in it, but it broke my heart to see it so.

"You sat in a clearing upon your white mare, with the black hawk hooded on your arm, your mantle thrown back, lovelier than a thousand springtimes, your eyes alight, and your cheeks glowing with youth and good health, and you sang to the birds in the trees, and they answered you."

He said it as if by rote, watching me steadily. The words were the words of a man in love, and the flat voice repeated that man's words, knowing them for what they were.

He waited. I seemed to feel his kiss still on my lips; I seemed to hear, beyond the realm of sound, a cry born of need. Then he spoke.

"He is my closest friend and first among the Companions. I made him knight. For me he has forsaken his home and his kin; he shall be by my side as long as I hold Britain. I shall not send him away."

I licked my dry lips and tried to keep my voice from shaking.

"My lord Arthur." It came out in a whisper. "I am no threat to the love you bear him, or that he bears you. I cannot come between you; do not fear it. I am but a woman."

I paused, and the King said, with a flicker of warmth, "Only a woman!"

"I would cut my wrist before I would bring dishonor to Britain. And what is a maid's life, or a man's, either, beside that?"

He moved at that; his chin lifted, the cold passed from his eyes. I moved Zephyr closer until we were knee to knee. Then I placed my hand upon his own and looked up into his eyes. "Arthur of Britain. I am thine."

He looked down at me, and his reserve left him suddenly. I was in his arms and he kissed me slowly, tenderly and long.

A horse nickered nearby, and he released me. I did not look up; I knew who it was. The escort was coming up, and I heard the King give the orders for moving off toward Nob Hill. Neither Lancelot nor Elaine could bring themselves to speak to me, so I rode beside Arthur, who wanted me near him. He knew, I thought helplessly, exactly what he was about. Again, I had been dazzled by the sun.

So life continued for six weeks, past midsummer. Every day brought a new adventure. Arthur's Companions accepted me, even Kay, and after the day of that first hawking party, there was even admiration in their bearing toward me. They drilled daily, held sword practice, tested their strength with wrestling and their aim with spears. As a group, they were a deadly fighting weapon in the King's hand, and the point had to be kept sharp.

Work on the Round Hall, which Arthur was building to hold the round table Pellinore had given him, went steadily forward. It was to be the Council chamber where all petitions would be heard and judgments given. I set my ladies to weaving a banner for the wall behind the King's chair, following the design upon his day robe. And I myself began work on a hanger for the King's great Sword.

I had twelve ladies-in-waiting by the time Arthur left. Now that there was a queen in Caer Camel, noble ladies from all over Britain sent their daughters to court, to serve the Queen and to get husbands from among the Companions. Young men from the four corners of Britain came to take service with Arthur and trained rigorously, hoping to be accepted some day as one of the King's Companions.

So our population grew, and so did the town's. The city that came to be called Camelot was begun that summer, as tradesmen, artisans, physicians, musicians, and skilled workmen of every sort came flocking to the castle grounds, and brought their families. Arthur, or perhaps Merlin, had foreseen this, and had a plan for the city. That summer the foundations were laid.

And the King began that summer the long and difficult work of binding the kingdoms into one Kingdom and keeping the nation together with justice and laws, now that the Saxons no longer threatened. As he told me himself, this was in some ways harder than fighting battles.

"That, at least, I was born for," he said slowly, his gaze far away. "Once I took the Sword of Britain into my hand, I knew it. Fighting was always easy for me. As natural as drawing breath. But this," he said, his eyes coming to focus on the four walls of the chamber, "this will be the real test. Peace makes men fractious. Can I hold them together? Will they follow a king who no longer leads them into battle?"

"They will follow *you*," I replied with complete certainty. He smiled.

"So at least you and Merlin are agreed," he said.

Of the great enchanter I saw nothing, and Arthur said no more about him, though he rode out two or three times to his house in the nearby hills to visit. Rumor had it the old magician was failing and doted upon his assistant, Niniane, whom he was training to take his place. I was astonished that he chose a woman to replace him. Wasn't this the man who had said to me, "It is not a thing for a maid to know?" But Arthur seemed not to mind, and I could not ask.

The High King called a council of kings in York for the first week in September to settle a territorial dispute that had arisen and to cement the federation of the northern lords. The night before he left, he stayed late at council. It had been his custom during that peaceful, carefree summer to retire shortly after I and my ladies had left hall, and to come to me in my chamber where we would talk long on the terrace, or stroll in my garden, before he came to my bed. Not since that first night had I set foot in his own room. I assumed that this was how he wished it, and I did not think to change the pattern. But that night, although I was awake when he finally came upstairs, he did not come in. I heard him say good night to Varric, and I saw the lamp turned low, and then I heard his restless pacing across the room and back. I fancied he stopped once at the curtain, and I waited expectantly, but he resumed his pacing and did not come in.

Silently I slipped out of bed and tiptoed to the curtain. I did not know whether my interruption would be welcomed, but there was something in the cadence of his tread, in the fitful pace and hesitations, that made me think he was not working out some problem but some turmoil of heart.

I lifted the edge of the curtain. "Arthur?"

He stopped at once and turned. "Gwen?"

"My lord, may I come in?"

"Of course you may come in. You are always welcome here."
He strode across the room and took me in his arms. "I thought
you were asleep, but I am glad you are not. We leave at dawn,
and I have things to say to you."

I nestled against his chest, and he hugged me, his hands caress-
ing my hair. For a moment we stood so, and then he led me to the
bed and sat me down upon it.

"I have not offended you, Arthur?"

He looked startled. "Offended me?"

"Why did you not come to me, but stayed in here, pacing?"

He laughed lightly. "My dear young Queen," he said, still smiling, "I thought you must be asleep. I have lain with you every
night for six weeks. It is enough. I thought I ought not to wake
you."

I stared at him, frankly astonished. "But, my lord, we are married!"

He looked puzzled and then, understanding, grinned broadly
and knelt at my feet. Protesting, I reached out to raise him, but he
just clasped my hands in his. The joy that lit his face delighted
me.

"What innocence! No one has told you anything about it, have
they? Do you imagine that Pellinore lies with Alyse every night?"

"I—I never thought of Alyse with—I never thought about it.
But I thought it was what *you* do, my lord."

He kissed my palms, close to laughter. "And so it has been, my
sweet. But I have so little time. We have each our own chamber
because we are entitled to privacy, at least when we sleep. You
are as free to come to me as I am to come to you, and we are
both just as free to stay apart the night. There should be no offense in it. There might be many reasons why I would not come:
If I were ill, or tired—"

"Or angry with me."

"Yes, it is possible. Should that happen, you may always come
to me to charm me out of ill humor. It would not take you long."

I smiled at the compliment, and his eyes blazed.

"Would you—I should be afraid you might refuse me if I came
in uninvited."

He took a deep breath and stilled himself. "Don't be afraid of
me, Guinevere. I might—it is not unheard of. But at this moment

I find it hard to envision. And you, likewise, are free to refuse me."

I stared at him in wonder. I thought this to be against the law. "I would never refuse you, my lord!"

He groaned softly and laid his head in my lap. "I believe you mean that," he whispered. I stroked his hair, which sprang up thick and soft between my fingers.

"Of course I mean it. I shall miss you, Arthur."

Still on his knees, he raised his face to me and let his soul speak in his eyes. "Thou hast my heart," he said softly in Latin. "Know this and take care."

For answer, I took his upturned face between my hands, leaned down, and kissed him.

At length he arose, walked to the table, pouring water from the carafe there, and drank. When he returned, he sat down beside me and with a solemn face placed his hand gently against my belly.

"Guinevere, I must ask you this, though the gods know how little it matters to me. I have lain with you every night for these six weeks and have not known you to bleed. Is it possible you carry my child?"

"I know not, my lord. I have no sickness."

"But you have not bled."

"Oh, but that is nothing. My bleeding comes only once in six months."

He sat silent, and as he looked at me I saw shock, anger, fear, and relief cross his face.

"No one told me," he said slowly.

"Is it so important, my lord?" I asked, bewildered. I had not known it was a matter for distress.

He shrugged. "In truth, I do not know. But I suspect so. No matter. For myself, I almost hope you are not with child. You are so young, and I could not bear—to be the cause of another disaster."

He looked in such pain that I leaned over to kiss his rough cheek. "What will be, will be, my lord."

But it was a mistake to remind him of Merlin. His face went white, and he rose quickly from the bed and took a turn about the room. At last, calmer, he came and stood before me, a very bitter smile upon his lips. "It is growing clearer," he said cryptically. "But let be. We shall know in time. As for more practical matters, I must tell you that, whereas before I was content to leave Caer Camel in Kay's hands whenever I left, he is my seneschal only, and not a fighting man. From now on I must leave in my place a knight who can protect you and who can represent me in council and hall alike. I have chosen Lancelot."

I saw it coming before he said it and schooled my face. Indeed, I knew not which was greater, my joy or my despair. "Has he consented to this, my lord?"

Arthur looked surprised and answered sharply. "I am his King. I did not ask for his consent."

"I meant—" I started, but he waved me silent.

"I know what you meant. He is the finest knight in all of Britain. In all truth, Guinevere, I could leave you in no safer hands. If you wish to know whether he is pleased or unhappy to be so appointed, I may tell you I think he is both. You are to sit at his side at table, and in the Hall of Meeting when you will. I have given orders that you are to be consulted if anything of importance arises, and in all cases of domestic disputes." The twinkle had returned to his eye, and I slowly let my breath out in relief.

"You are most generous, my lord."

"I hope," he said slowly, taking my hand and laying it against his cheek, "I hope I am also wise."

I met his eyes, then, and found them searching me once more. I rose and, going to the triple lamp, blew out the lights.

The King was gone four months. At first it was awkward seeing Lancelot so often, sitting by his side at meals, sitting by his side in the meeting hall. Our conversation, to Elaine's amusement, was so stiff and formal that several of the Companions who had been left behind thought Lancelot disliked me, and I him.

We went riding often, always with an escort of armed guards, and usually with some of my women, as well. For the first two months the elders frowned and clucked as I rode out, but as it gradually became clear I did not carry the King's child, they let me be and awaited Arthur's return.

Lancelot obeyed Arthur's instructions to the letter. He shared with me the news of every courier who came, received every visitor in the King's name with me at his side, discussed with me the judgments he was asked to pass, and in general treated me as a trusted counsellor. If, when he looked at me, he let his eyes linger, or when he inclined his head to hear my speech, he stayed so a little long, no one noticed but I. And if my dreams were haunted by a pair of cool, gray eyes and a solemn, full-lipped mouth, it was no one's business but my own.

Every evening before bedtime he took me to mass. He was, I discovered, a much more ardent Christian than Arthur. Ygraine had been devout, and she had had her son christened, but she had not raised him. Kay's household had been Christian, and as a boy Arthur had learned the ways of the Christian faith, but it was the pagan Merlin who had made him the man he was. I recalled his references to Mithra, the soldiers' god, the Light, and his calling upon older gods than that from time to time. But although he went to mass twice a week and worshipped no other God that I could see, and although for ceremony he wore an old enamel brooch of the Virgin set in copper Ygraine had bequeathed him,

I did not know which god held his spirit. It seemed to me that Lancelot's faith, while perhaps stronger, gave him less ease of heart. He prayed most fervently as we knelt side by side in the chapel, but seemed to find little relief in it.

I spent nearly half of every day with my women and the other half with Lancelot. While the builders were at work on the Round Hall I asked Lancelot if I might have two to build a fountain for my garden, and he sent them without delay. He denied me nothing.

Gradually we slipped into an easier friendship, for our interests lay together, but there was always a watchfulness between us. We took great care to observe the courtesies between Queen and courtier and to be always attended. Only once did we find ourselves alone, and that was Elaine's doing. I had taken both Lancelot and Elaine to the top of the northwest tower to show them they could really see the sea from Caer Camel. It was near sunset, and we stood side by side on the turret as the sun dipped below the level of the land and painted the sky with broad strokes of color. Slowly the light faded, and night drew down.

"I love it up here." I sighed, drawing my cloak closer. "It reminds me so of home. Arthur brought me up here on our wedding night, to see the sea. To put me at my ease. I guess he thought I was nervous."

A strangled cry escaped Lancelot, and when I turned in surprise I found him several paces off, white as a sheet and trembling from head to foot. Elaine was gone.

"Lancelot!" I cried. "What ails you? Are you ill?"

He would not meet my eyes, but looked away. "Guinevere."

"What is it? What have I done?"

"I beg of you," he said in a choked voice, "if you value my sanity, please do not—do not speak to me about Arthur. He is my friend and my liege lord. I can bear it if I think of him as my King. I cannot bear it, Guinevere, if I think of him as your husband."

His words stabbed me to the heart. Suddenly the tissue veil of courtesy was rent; I saw the depth of his passion and the enormity of his suffering. For the first time, I felt the deep pull of physical desire, and I shared his pain.

"Lancelot!" I whispered, and sank to my knees. "Oh, forgive me, do!"

He raised me quickly, but I clung to his hand.

"I forgive you. But do not speak of him again."

"Oh, my Lancelot, what has happened to us? Why can't it be the way it was?"

His grip tightened, and then he thrust himself away. "You know why. You have married the King."

"Did you want me to refuse him?" I cried, aghast.

"No," he whispered, running a hand through his hair in distraction. "No, of course not, Gwen. I only meant—where in God's name is Elaine?"

"Never mind Elaine," I cried, reaching for his hand and taking it between my own. "Speak your mind. What did you mean?"

He went very still, although his breath came fast, as if he had been running. "Only this," he said quietly. "We cannot be as we were because—you are not as you were. You have known a man. Now there is danger."

I stared at him and felt the heat rise to my face. I dropped his hand as if it burned my flesh. He was right. It made a difference. I no longer feared a man's touch; instead, I feared my own weakness. I tugged at the tower door, unable to see past my tears, and ran down the stairs away from him as fast as I could go.

The next day, as if by design, Arthur's courier arrived with orders to move the court to Caerleon for Christmas. We should be there by mid-December, and the High King would meet us there as soon as might be. Although we had ample time to prepare, this at least gave me an excuse to absent myself from some of the daily routine. But I discovered I could not absent myself for long, or the people began to wonder if I was ill. Illness in a bride meant to them only one thing, and to avoid renewing speculations of pregnancy, I had to show myself again.

Lancelot was perfectly behaved, and so I tried to be, that no one might suspect the turmoil in my soul. Only Elaine knew. She shared my bed, now that the King was away, and as I had in Wales, I shared with her my secret agony.

"Do not leave me alone with him again, Elaine!" I wept, holding her tightly. "It is too much for me to bear!"

"Why?" she asked quickly. "What happened?"

"Nothing. Only—it is so difficult to be near him!"

She gently stroked my hair and tried to soothe me. "You did not used to feel so, in Wales. Do you not love him anymore?"

"Oh, don't, Elaine! You know I do. But this is agony—we cannot, we *must* not dishonor the King!"

"Certainly you must not," she said calmly. "Did you feel tempted to?"

"Yes," I whispered, shaking. "Oh, yes."

"Well," she said after a moment. "I was only trying to give you joy."

Shortly before we made the move to Caerleon, King Melwas of the Summer Country invited me, and Lancelot as the King's proxy, to the Goddess' Harvest Festival celebrated at the Lady's shrine on Ynys Witrin. He was lord of the country thereabout, including the environs of Caer Camel, and since Arthur's ease of access to his own fortress depended upon good relations with Melwas, Lancelot did not like to refuse, although his Christian soul rebelled against the Mother's worship. I assured him that he would find nothing offensive in the ceremony; it was mainly an excuse for a feast. He was astounded to learn that I was familiar with the rites.

"Surely you know my father was a pagan. Wasn't it only a year ago my ancestry was publicly discussed in this very place?"

Lancelot flushed, and I placed my hand on his arm. He went very still.

"I meant only that I did not think it any secret. This used to be my favorite festival when I was a child, after Beltane, which was my birthday. I remember being disappointed when I went to Gwynedd that the Christians had no such celebration."

"Is there any part of the ceremony that requires my parting from you?" he asked, then added carefully, "I am responsible for your safety, my lady, even when I am not with you."

"There are rites that are sacred to the Goddess and that men may not attend. Actually, only initiates participate." I grinned at his worried expression. "I am not an initiate, Lancelot. I was six when I last bent a knee to the Goddess. Have no fear for me."

"Could you not plead to be excused? You are a Christian Queen."

"And offend Melwas? It is likely that he remembers my ancestry, even if you do not!" He smiled and took my teasing in good part. "And Arthur attends the rites of Mithra when it serves his purpose. You knew that, surely. How would it look if I refused?"

"Then are there any among your women who could attend you?" he insisted. "You must be guarded, Gwen. Please do not be annoyed, but understand. As Arthur's Queen you are a valuable hostage. Your capture, may Heaven forfend, gives your captor a hold on the High King of Britain. Think of what that might mean."

"Arthur would never submit to—" I began hotly, and then stopped, as memory recalled moments of great tenderness.

"If you are dear enough to him," Lancelot said quietly, "he might. So must I protect you to protect Britain. Now, is there anyone who can attend these pagan rites with you?"

In the end I took two attendants, a maiden named Alissa, sister to one Pelleas, King of the River Isles, and Ailsa, my own nurse, who believed in all gods as a matter of self-protection.

King Melwas received us royally. He was a big man, tall and tending to heaviness, with thick features and very light, cold eyes. Unlike Arthur and his Companions, who preferred clean-shaven faces, Melwas grew a short blond beard and moustache, which he kept neat and well combed. His palace was little more than a fighting fortress, for he was still unmarried, but he saw to it that we women were comfortably housed in the guest pavilion of the Lady's shrine. Melwas' sister, the lady Seulte, kept us company and ensured that we had everything we required. A hard-featured, proud woman, she spoke well of no one except her brother, but as I was polite to her, she took to me, and we got on well enough. Ailsa did not like her and told me that behind my back she came high and mighty with the servants, but of this behavior I saw nothing.

Lancelot was housed in Melwas' fortress with the escort, and with this he was not well pleased. Melwas' soldiers outnumbered the royal escort ten to one, but I told him not to be ridiculous. No one could get at me in the Lady's shrine. Her precincts were sacred, and the pain of violation was death. He did not like it, but in this he had no choice.

The ceremonies lasted most of the day. Melwas placed me at his left hand, next his sister, while Lancelot, representing the High King, he placed on his right. He thus stood between us at the public ceremonies and sat between us during the long feast that followed. There was much toasting and drinking and general good fellowship, and I took note that both King Melwas and his sister partook liberally of the unwatered wine. Melwas favored me with his attentions all evening, and he was scarcely intelligible by the time the bard came on. I had worn a gown of gold and blue, and Arthur's great sapphire, which seemed to bewitch Melwas. As his power of speech left him, he became unable to take his eyes off it, and seemed transfixed by its slow rise and fall upon my breast. I saw Lancelot getting restless, saw him color in annoyance, watched his anger slowly mount until I feared he would ruin everything by a display of temper. Quickly I turned to the lady Seulte, pleaded fatigue from the pleasures of the day, and begged to be excused with my women. She leered rather drunkenly at her brother, winked at him, and rose. All the women followed, and with relief we escaped the hall. She led the procession back to the shrine, where men were forbidden to enter, but I sent a page to ask Lancelot to meet me outside the gate in an hour. It took me that long to disentangle myself from Seulte's oversolicitous care, and when I slipped out at length, cloaked and hooded, I found him awaiting me, pacing anxiously back and forth.

"My lady!" he cried, pressing my fingers to his lips. "I knew we should not have come!"

"Shhh! You will do our cause no good by shouting. What do you mean we shouldn't have come?"

"Melwas is enamored of you, Guinevere. Couldn't you see it? Dear God, I nearly strangled him, the fat oaf!"

"Lancelot!"

"He was drooling! I swear it! Peering down your bodice and slobbering! Shall I never forget it!"

"Lancelot." I put out a hand to stop him and found it held hard between his own. "Do not let his subjects overhear you calling their king rude names," I whispered, smiling.

He shook his head impatiently.

"We are alone," he said. Then it was I who went quite still, but my heart was pounding.

"Let him look," I said at last. "The High King needs his friendship. If he admires the Queen, so much the better. It does not hurt me and furthers our cause."

"Ah," Lancelot said softly, "but it hurts *me*. You are his sovereign Queen, not one of the serving wenches he lusts after, to hear his soldiers talk. He will show you respect or he shall meet me on a field of honor."

"Good Lancelot, your words go to my heart. But he was in his cups. It is a compliment to the Bountiful Goddess to be so on this day. Everyone here understands. Do not fear for me so. You alone think I was insulted."

He looked at me, then, and I hoped he could not tell how I trembled. "Did you not feel insulted?"

"I—I did not like the way he looked at me," I admitted. "But I understand it."

"He wanted you."

"Yes."

"He had no right." Then I heard his quick intake of breath as he realized what he had said.

"It is no sin to want," I said slowly, "only to take."

He stood stiffly before me, pinned in place by his own spear.

"It is a sin to want," he said hoarsely.

I bowed my head and let the hood fall forward to hide my face.

"I asked you to come," I said desperately, "because I wish to leave at dawn. Make some excuse. I don't know what will be acceptable. If he presses you, tell him I have begun to bleed."

His hands gripped my shoulders firmly, for comfort. "Is this true, Guinevere?"

I raised my face to his, so near. "Oh, yes. He may verify it through his lady sister, if he doubts."

"I'll see him damned first," he whispered, and took me very gently in his arms, holding me lightly, while my tears welled up and my heart raced. "I am sorry," he said, and meant it. I shrugged and struggled to compose myself. Lancelot stepped away.

"I will send the escort at first light. Will you ride, or would you prefer a litter?"

"I would prefer to ride, but a litter is more diplomatic, surely. Have one prepared."

He inclined his head. "It will be done. Ought I—ought I to send a courier to the King?"

"No. I—I don't believe it will surprise him. Besides, anyone can wait three weeks to hear bad news."

So we left King Melwas in the morning. He saw us off with many smiles and gifts and protestations of goodwill, looking fully recovered from last night's debauch and ready to do it again. I don't know what excuse Lancelot made, but it wasn't the one I had given him, for Melwas' eyes were as hungry as ever, and I shuddered to think what must be in his heart.

We were at Caerleon only a week when the High King returned, four days before Christmas. After dinner I sat with Lancelot and several other knights before a log fire in the hall, waiting. Lancelot told us about his Breton boyhood, and his younger brother Galahantyn and his cousin Bors, and how he hoped to bring them both into Arthur's service in a few years' time. The words tumbled forth in a constant stream; this was so unlike him, I glanced at the other men, who watched Lancelot with compassion. Then I understood it was Arthur's coming that made him so anxious. As for myself, I dreaded the King's return. It wasn't that my daily visits with Lancelot were ended—for that, I was as thankful as I was sorry. But I felt ashamed of my failure as his Queen to conceive his heir. And this I had to tell him face to face.

I rose abruptly, made my excuses, and retired to the company of Ailsa and Elaine.

The King's dwelling at Caerleon was the villa of some long-dead Roman governor, and it stood outside the walled fortress itself. This fortress had been maintained since Roman times, enlarged by Uther, and expanded to include the city without its walls by early in Arthur's reign. We were safe enough, for the place was always well guarded. But this arrangement meant that the King could receive guests, hold council, and go about his daily business at a far remove from his house. Thus when Bedwyr knocked upon the chamber door and begged to inform me that the King had been back three hours, had bathed, dined, and met with his advisors, and now had sent for me, I was shocked. What ill omen was this? I wondered. Arthur back three hours and no word sent to me? Ailsa had dressed me for bed and unbound my hair, but I threw a cloak over my nightdress and went out to Bedwyr.

"Good Bedwyr, what news? He is returned? Safely? Thank God for that. Where is he now?"

"In the library, taking Lancelot's report. He would like to see you, after."

"By all means. Let me dress, and I shall be with you."

But Bedwyr put out a hand to stop me. "No need, my lady. The page reported you had retired to bed, and the King gave me to understand that this is the request of a husband and not the command of a King." Bedwyr smiled gently as he bowed, and I exhaled in relief.

"Bedwyr, tell me truly. He is not angry with me?"

His eyes widened. "He did not seem so, my lady." He looked at me with curiosity, but said no more.

"All right. I am ready then."

He led me toward the King's quarters, at the other side of the house. As we neared the library, the door opened, and Merlin appeared, followed by a slender, dark-haired, beautiful young woman. I was amazed. I had not known he was even in Caerleon. As they passed us, Merlin inclined his head to me; his black eyes were cold and flat, and his face held no expression whatsoever. But the woman stared at me as if she would devour me, and the anger in her eyes set me shaking with fear.

Bedwyr felt it, for he stopped me at the door and took my hands. "What is it, my lady? Are you cold?"

"Who—who was that with Merlin?"

"His assistant, Niniane."

"Does she have the Sight?"

"Aye, and power, also, the King tells me."

I felt cold terror in my bowels and fought to keep my voice steady. "Bedwyr, I fear her."

"I see that, my lady. But why? She can do you no harm. You have Arthur's protection. She is his servant, and so must serve your ends. Where is the cause for fear?"

I shook my head. "I don't know. She disapproves of me."

"If she does, she is the only one in all Britain," he replied gallantly. "Now come, compose yourself. Don't give the King cause to worry about you. He has enough on his mind."

Of course he was right, and for Arthur's sake I managed to still my trembling when Bedwyr pushed open the door.

Arthur and Lancelot stood before a great log fire, talking. They turned toward me as one, and I thought to myself as I sank into a deep curtsy, how welcoming they were, the brown eyes and the gray.

"My lord is welcome home," I said, as Arthur raised me.

"And glad to be here at last," he replied, smiling and looking at ease. "How have you been?" His very serenity calmed me, and I was suddenly extremely glad to see him.

"In perfect health, my lord."

He laughed and slipped an arm about my waist. "It is the gift of youth. I'm sorry to rouse you so late. Were you abed?"

"Not yet. Elaine and I were talking. We did not hear your arrival, or I would have been more ready to receive you."

"You're fine as you are. Thank you, Bedwyr." Bedwyr bowed and closed the door behind him. Arthur offered me a seat by the fire, and then stood, looking thoughtful.

"Lancelot has told me of your visit to King Melwas," he began, and I glanced swiftly at Lancelot, who kept his eyes on the flames.

"Yes, my lord?"

"I wish to know if your impressions of the king's behavior match his own."

I did not know how much Lancelot had told him, but it hardly mattered. One told Arthur the truth.

"He was very drunk, my lord. At the Harvest Feast it is acceptable, more so than at other times—"

"Yes. I know. Go on."

"And I think he wished for the old days when the festival sometimes led to—to—well, my lord, even in my father's day it led to orgies." I blushed, but the King was serious and intent.

"Yes. I know of it. Did Melwas suggest such a thing?"

"Oh, no, my lord! He was beyond speech."

One eyebrow lifted, and Lancelot shifted his weight to the other foot.

"Did he, by look, or gesture, indicate any such desire?"

The room was so still, the noise of the flames sounded like whip-cracks.

"Desire for an orgy? No, my lord."

A long pause.

"Desire for you, Guinevere. For your person."

I felt again Melwas' hot, sour breath on my cheek and neck, and his groping hand beneath the table. My lips felt dry and stiff, but there was no escaping the King's eyes and their demand.

"Yes, my lord. By look and gesture."

Lancelot looked up quickly at Arthur, triumphant and indignant. Arthur came over to me and took my hand. I could not meet his eyes, but I clung to him, and from his firm grip drew strength.

"For what you endured on my behalf, as my Queen, I sincerely thank you, Guinevere. Your going there served my cause, it is true. But I would not have it served thus, and it shall not happen twice. You will go there no more, even by invitation, and if he should come to Caer Camel, you will not receive him. Let Lancelot do it. I will deal with Melwas, in my own time." His voice, so gentle when he began, ended in a cold, flat tone that sent a shiver through me.

"Let me call him out!" Lancelot cried, hot with fury. "I will take him in three strokes!"

Arthur turned to him slowly, and, to my amazement, the cold was still in his voice. "On what grounds?"

Lancelot froze, then paled, then flushed.

"I will deal with him myself," Arthur repeated. It was a command.

"Perhaps he should marry," I ventured in a desperate attempt to ease the tension that fairly crackled between them. They both turned to me, Lancelot with a ghostly smile and Arthur with a warming of his features.

"No doubt you have put your finger on the problem," the King said. "But this I cannot do for him. We might have to wait until his sister dies or marries. She must have turned aside a hundred maids already, finding none good enough for her brother." He paused, then squared his shoulders in a familiar gesture half the Companions had copied. "At any rate, until he has said or done something publicly, I cannot come openly against him. But there are other ways."

He called for the servant to pour wine and handed me a goblet, and then Lancelot. They spoke together in low voices for some moments, and suddenly Lancelot lifted Arthur's hand and touched his lips to the great carved ruby on his finger. Arthur gripped his arm in the soldier's embrace, and then Lancelot left us.

The wine was warm and fragrant with spices, and I gladly yielded to its soothing powers. Arthur took a seat beside me and sat bent forward, his elbows upon his knees. "Are you tired, Gwen? Would you like to retire? It is past time, God knows."

I did not know if he meant this as dismissal or not, but I could not leave until I said what I had come to say.

"My—my lord Arthur." I sank to the floor at his feet and looked up into his face. "Please forgive me."

"Why, what is this?"

"My dear lord, I have—I have failed you."

He looked alarmed and set the wine aside to clasp my hands. "What is it, Gwen? What has happened?"

"Three weeks ago I bled," I blurted out.

He looked blank, and then comprehension came in a great rush of relief. "Dear Lord, you mean the heir! Oh, Gwen, don't look so tragic. I am in no hurry; there is time. What, did you think I would berate you?" He laughed at my expression and lifted me onto his lap. "Queen or no Queen, you're a girl yet," he said, and then grinned. "We are doing the best that we can, are we not? The rest is with God."

"But it is my duty," I whispered, feeling happy and safe in his arms, with my heavy burden lifted from me by his mere word.

"No. That is a broodmare's duty. Your duty is to be my companion. Stay at my side. Give me your company by day and the pleasure of your person at night, when you will. I am content."

I laughed for sudden joy. "Arthur, you are wonderful."

"The most welcome compliment I have ever had," he said gravely. "And now, little Queen, what is your pleasure? Back to your bed with Elaine, or will you come with me and keep sleep at bay awhile longer?"

I went with him.

15 ❁ THE RAPE

I pulled my cloak tighter around me against the icy rain and paced back across the garden. It was a cold April morning and the wind blew in fitful gusts, tossing rain against the castle walls and hurling dark clouds across the pale gray sky. I desperately wanted a good gallop, a day hawking, anything to escape Camelot. I was sure the weather would clear. It had that smell, that keen edge of promise. Any excuse for an outing would do—if I could only be alone!

The garden extended the length of the women's quarters. At one end, beyond a locked door in a solid wall, was my own garden, accessible now only by steps from my terrace. When I had closed it off to create a little sanctuary, I had had the larger garden built, that my women might take the air and walk any time they chose and not disturb my privacy. Six of them sat now in a little curved bay with windows looking out upon my walk. They had just come from breakfast and worked upon the needlework I had set them. I could see them clustered around Elaine in the window seat, and they could all see me. Alissa was there, Kay's wife, heavy with her second child, and dear Ailsa, of course, with her brow furrowed in worry at my bad temper. The youngest was a girl of fifteen named Hanna, whose parents had sent her to court to find a husband among the Companions. It was the same old story. They came in droves, acquired manners and refinement, married the King's Companions, and were carted off to bear sons to fight in Arthur's service. I bit my lip hard against new tears and lifted my face to the rain. Sometimes they stayed, but usually they left. In five years I must have said good-bye to twenty at least.

I found myself at the foot of the garden and stood for a moment, pulling my hood closer, reluctant to head back. I knew what they were saying in there. The lady Elaine, favorite of the Queen, was holding court. She would be gently explaining to Hanna, in her kindest tones, why the Queen was so bad-tempered lately. It is not in her nature, she would begin, carefully laying the groundwork. Normally she is the gaiest, gentlest, sweetest-tempered woman in the Kingdom. And how not? There is not a man in the High King's service who does not adore her. She has the admiration of all Britain. But you see, little Hanna, she cannot give the High King the one thing he most desires: a son of his body. It is the one thing her precious beauty cannot win for her. She has failed the High King Arthur as she has failed the people of Britain. She cannot conceive the heir.

If Hanna had courage, she might ask how it was known that the fault lay with the Queen and not with the High King himself. Elaine would remain composed and smile her sly, contented smile. Her reply, when it came, would be oversoft. It was known that the High King had fathered bastards here and there. He had acknowledged them and provided for the ones he knew about. There was a girl in Northumberland he had given a dowry to and had honored the knight who married her and gave a name to the child. He was, after all, away from court six to eight months out of the year, and even though he was known to be a man of moderate habits, well, if a pretty maid were willing, who could blame him? He saw to it she never suffered by it.

And then, if Hanna had any grasp of facts, she would ask Elaine if the High King meant to put the Queen away. Elaine would look slightly shocked, and afterward sorrowful, and take time to frame a reply. And in the meantime poor Hanna, who had only asked the question that lay on everyone's lips, would tremble in fear that she had overstepped the bounds of propriety.

One did not know, Elaine would answer gravely, what the High King might do. Whatever he did, it would be just, kind, and well thought out. He had spent four months with the High Queen this winter, at Caerleon and at Camelot, and when he left she had not bled and was feeling sickly. Everyone hoped that at last she might have conceived his child, but alas! Two weeks ago she bled, and afterward made herself ill with weeping. And now the High King was coming home; no one wanted to tell him the bad news; no one knew what he would do when he heard it.

I pressed my hands against my ears to stop the sound of words. This way lay madness. For five long years I had endured this humiliation before Arthur's subjects; had daily felt their eyes upon my waistline, daily heard their whispering behind my back. Even in my dreams they pursued me, with their frightful pity and their contempt. And everywhere I looked, I saw only bounty and increase. Camelot was growing; the streets were filled with pregnant women and the sound of infants crying. Among my own women, four had swollen bellies; in the last year, five had been delivered within my hearing. I, alone among them all, had failed to grow past childhood, was less than a woman and a wife. Alone among them all, I could not bear. And in failing, I failed the High King of Britain. I choked back a sob and wiped my eyes. I had to escape! Rain or no rain, I must get out. I was Queen. If I chose to go, I could go. None of them could stop me.

I ran back up the path and came in by the door that gave onto Elaine's rooms. I moved quietly, and they did not hear me. I meant to slip out into the hallway and so escape unnoticed to my own rooms, but when I came to the door I heard Lancelot's name.

"Do not worry, my dear. Lancelot will cure her. He always does. However low she is, he will make it right as rain. And only he can do it. We call it 'the Breton touch.'"

"Do you indeed?" I said coldly. Alissa gasped, and the others whirled, frightened. Elaine, who had spoken, did not even have the decency to blush.

"Yes, my lady, we do. It is intended as a compliment," she said airily.

I turned from her and addressed Alissa. "Send Kay to me. I will ride out this morning, and I wish to inform him of my plans."

Alissa was wise enough to keep her protests to herself, and she went at once. But the others had not acquired her wisdom.

"But, my lady, it's raining!"

"You'll catch your death of cold!"

"How can you go out in this storm?"

"Lancelot cannot accompany you. It is initiation for the new recruits." This last was from Elaine, and I turned back to her.

"I am aware of it. I will ride without him."

"He will not allow it." She was intent, excited about something but holding it in.

"I am his Queen," I told her angrily. "He cannot stop me." I knew she hated it when I pulled my rank, and I knew I would be ashamed of myself later, but at that moment it gave me great satisfaction to see her without an answer. "Breton touch, indeed," I muttered. Her curtsy was stiff, and I saw she was as angry as I.

"Any of you who wish may attend me," I said to the others, "but you need not come out unless you want to. There's a soaking rain now, but later it will clear."

No one volunteered. Kay was not pleased, but Alissa had

briefed him, and he soon saw it was useless to argue. I told him where I was going, and he grunted, which was as close as he could come to an assent. Of course, he informed Lancelot, who showed sense and sent a message saying he would join me when he could and begging me to be careful. He knew better than to cross me in my moods.

We rode west, toward the low hills that sank into the marshlands surrounding Ynys Witrin. Marsh birds had been arriving in great flocks for a month now, and the wetlands were full of fowl. My new hawk Dakar was a wonderful hunter of marsh birds, and besides, the hills were low and the woods thin: It was great country for galloping.

And gallop we did. My horse Pallas was too light-boned for a war stallion, thus had he been gelded and given to me, but he ran like the wind. I had to wait every mile or so for the escort to catch up.

Toward midmorning the rain lightened and dispersed into mist, which hid the valley bottoms and sent thin tendrils of damp fog snaking up into the hills. The captain of the escort cleared his throat and looked at me pointedly. Clearly, they could not protect me in a fog, and it was time to go. But anger still bit at me, and I sought some excuse to delay. At that moment a young egret rose squawking from the fringes of Avalon and flapped noisily southward. The hawk stirred on my arm.

"One more, good Ferron, and we shall call it a day. The bird is slow. This will take moments only." I was right, of course, and I was also Queen. He had no choice but to agree. I loosed the hawk, who rose in graceful circles and, spotting the distant bird, took off. As I put leg to my horse, I had a sudden forboding. If, at that moment, I had changed my mind, or the hawk had lost the bird in the mist, or Ferron's native caution had exerted itself, how much might we all have been saved! I have thought of it often, since; how so many futures may hang on a single thread of circumstance; how long a shadow that day cast over so many lives!

Against all expectation, the egret headed into the woods. The road narrowed to a track, and we slowed our pace. I lost sight of the hawk in the thickening mist, and whistled to him at last to call him back. We all heard then a bird's cry and the crashing of some heavy animal through the bracken. My only thought was to recover my precious hawk.

"This way!" I cried, and sent Pallas straight into the woods in the direction of the cry. If the soldiers shouted, I did not hear them. All my senses were attuned forward, to the trees looming up suddenly out of the mist, to fallen logs that must be jumped, although the distances were difficult to judge, toward where I hoped my hawk stood patiently above his prey. We reached the bank of one of the slow-moving rivers that fed the marsh and pulled up. It was very quiet. I could see only the shadowed shapes of trees on the opposite bank twelve feet away. I heard no voices, no hoofbeats, no movement through the underbrush. I realized with a jolt of fear that I was lost, and without my escort. But we were only a few leagues from Camelot, and Pallas could find the way home. He stood easily, his nostrils wide and his small ears swiveling in every direction. I waited, calming myself, very sorry now that I had acted so arrogantly. I was framing a suitable apology to Ferron and to Kay, when Pallas' ears shot forward and his head lifted. He had heard something downstream. As he did not nicker, I feared it could not be the escort, but perhaps it was the hawk, caught in some tree by his jesses, or the injured bird in the brush. We went slowly along the bank, unable to see, feeling our way. The fog thickened as the land sloped lower and caught in the nostrils and mouth like a cold cloth over the face. My cloak was damp, and the horse's body slippery with wet. Which is why, when out of the white mist on the water a gigantic dark shape suddenly arose before our very eyes and shouted, Pallas spun, reared, leaped sideways, bucked twice—and I fell.

I awoke slowly to darkness, to pain in my back, and to gentle rocking. Had it not been for the pain, which grew steadily more insistent, I might have fallen back to sleep, for the rocking was very soothing and made my head feel heavy.

"Please," I cried, "my back!" but it came out the barest whisper, and when I opened my eyes I saw nothing, only whiteness. Frightened, I shut them. Strong hands supported and lifted me, and the pain eased. Even in my dazed state I felt relief, knowing I was not injured, but only lay on something hard and sharp. I was slowly let down upon some cushion or soft stuff. The hands that had held me did not leave me at once, but cupped my shoulders and then slowly slid down my arms to take my hands, before folding the cloak around me. It was a slow, sensuous gesture, and I shivered, a frisson of horror sliding up my spine. Discomfort was forgotten. There was danger here. I looked vainly about but could see absolutely nothing. I had no clue to where I was, or with whom, except that I was still surrounded by fog and the gentle sounds of river and marsh.

"Who are you?" I asked. "Who art thou?" I tried in Latin. No one answered. But someone was there. I sensed movement and breathing. "Where is my horse, good sir? What has become of the hawk? My escort must be about—if you call, they would be pleased to find me and to reward you for my rescue."

"Please be still," a male voice said softly. "All is well." I had heard the voice before, although I could not remember where. Perhaps he was a knight, or a nobleman who had been at Arthur's court.

"Good sir," I whispered, "I know you are a gentleman. Return me to the King and he will well reward you. For I am Guinevere, his Queen."

There was a rough bark of laughter, followed by a sliding, dipping motion as a shadow loomed above me in the mist. I realized suddenly that I lay on the bottom of a coracle and that we were well out in the marshes. Hands gripped my body, and a bearded face bent low to mine.

"I know who you are," a gruff voice said, "and now you are mine." Thick lips pressed against mine, and I smelled old mead upon his clothes and the sweat of fear upon his body. Mercifully I fainted. For I recognized him. It was Melwas.

When I awoke from the faint I had the wits to keep my eyes closed and let him think I still slept. It was warmer, and a breeze eddied against my cheek. I guessed that we were now on open water, for the boat rocked, water gurgled near my ear, and the splash of oars came steadily. I heard no other sounds, not of men, or of animals, not even of birds. My heart raced with terror, but I kept my breathing slow. All I could think of were Lancelot's words to me, long ago, about how valuable a hostage I would be, and how I had to let myself be guarded.

My poor Lancelot! In my mind's eye I could see the panicked ride of the messenger back to the palace, the fearful confrontation with Lancelot, the averted face and bent knee as the message was delivered, and the horror and anger and—most undeservedly—the guilt that would show on Lancelot's face. What would he do? He might take every man in Camelot to the spot where I had last been seen, if they could find it, but it would avail them nothing. They might find the horse and the hawk, but they could not find me.

I steadied myself and pushed the tears away. What, then, of Melwas? How dared he? Arthur would kill him. And then in a flash I understood. I was no longer so valuable as a hostage; once, perhaps, but a childless queen? Melwas did not think to gain some advantage over the High King, he thought only of me. He dared not kill me—no, that would touch the High King's honor and put his own life in jeopardy. But if he merely took me—I forced myself to face it—for his pleasure, and soiled me in the eyes of Arthur's subjects, and in the King's own eyes, as well, he could plead any excuse he liked and beg to take me formally from the King. It would solve Arthur's problem for him. He could put me away, give me to Melwas, binding his neighbor to him, and leaving himself free to marry a woman who could bear him sons. Against my will a tear slipped out, and I shuddered to hide a sob.

Melwas grunted, but said nothing and rowed on. Where on earth could we be going? Somewhere on the Lake of Avalon, no doubt, but where? Not to his palace, surely, where I was known. But wherever it was, clearly he had planned this. For the stuff I lay on was soft and sweet scented, not the normal outfit for a river craft. He had been expecting me.

The oars stopped suddenly, and we jolted gently against solid ground. I opened my eyes. Melwas was tying the boat to a wooden platform built out upon the water. The mist was thinning fast as the day advanced, and I saw him clearly. He was a huge man, thickset, dressed in hunting clothes. When he turned and found me awake he looked uncomfortable. I was glad to see it. I hoped he might be frightened at what he had done; but he was a brave man, and his face was set. He extended his hand to me.

"Come, my lady. We have arrived."

I allowed him to help me onto the platform, where I chafed my hands and arms to restore their use. "Where are we, King Melwas?"

He smiled, and I found his smile revolting. "In my kingdom. Safe from Arthur's lads. Come and see my house. It is prepared."

He referred to a small, wooden structure half hidden by willows, which stood on a low rise near the edge of open water. As he took my arm and led me up the rough path, he boasted about the isolation of his hideaway. We were on an island, he said, with marsh grasses all around that screened us from the shore a quarter mile away. No one could see us, he declared, chuckling, and no one could approach us, except by boat. At low water there was a land bridge at the far end of the island, which had tempted would-be thieves from time to time. Should anyone try to come that way to rescue me, they should find the sharp surprise the thieves had found. He laughed wickedly under his breath, as if pleased at some jest he had made. I shivered at the sound, and he turned to me, smiling.

"Don't worry your pretty head, my lady Queen. No one will come. You are safe with me."

Safe indeed! I struggled to keep my fear from my face as he handed me up the step and into the crude dwelling. Whatever it had been built for I could not guess, but its present purpose was clear enough. He had furnished it as luxuriously as he knew how, with soft skins and cushions and a low, Roman couch. A hearth stood stacked with logs, and skins of wine hung nearby. There was only one other door.

"Your clothing is damp," Melwas said nervously. "Please, my lady, change in here." And he opened the door to reveal a sleeping chamber containing a great bed hung with crimson hangings and piled with furs. "There is a robe ready for you," he hurried on. "Hand out your clothes to me, and I will dry them before the fire."

I said nothing but went into the room and closed the door behind me. There was no lock. I heard him moving about in the other room, and went to the window. It was barred and looked out toward the shore across acres of reeds and a stretch of open water. I put my hand to the window and saw how it shook. It looked small and cold and white, a hand that belonged to someone else. It seemed a poor frightened, delicate thing, trembling as it gripped the iron bars. It moved at my command, yet did not feel a part of me. I pulled against the bars with all my strength until I fell back, gasping, on the bed. I could not budge them. But even if I could, what then? I could not swim. I did not know how to handle the boat, supposing I could have got to it unseen. And I did not know where I was, or in what direction help lay.

I stared at the soft bed furs in rising panic. It was all too clear what Melwas wanted. My only chance was to play him fair, fend him off, and wait for rescue. But I did not hold out much hope of it. Even if the King's men could find me, they would never be in time.

I began to undress but it was slow work. My fingers were cold and stiff with fear and took minutes to manage a single knotted lacing. The robe he had set out was a good one of soft, combed wool, dark blue with a silver border. But it was too big, and there was only one belt. I shrugged. I thought nothing; I felt nothing. I seemed to be somewhere else, watching myself, wondering what I would do, wondering what it was possible to do, wondering if death might not be preferable to what Melwas had in mind, and wondering how I could come by it.

At length Melwas knocked upon the door and bade me come

out. I obeyed him. He had a good fire going and two goblets of wine poured. He had not waited for me, but was on his second cup already. His greedy eyes ran over me with eagerness, and I blushed, turning away.

"My lord Melwas," I protested, surprised to hear my voice sounded natural as I handed him my damp riding clothes.

"Eh?" He looked up, fairly drooling, and it was all I could do to keep revulsion from showing in my face.

"You are a king, sir, and I a queen, and not the kitchen slave."

He seemed slightly embarrassed and licked his lips nervously. "Aye, madam. But you are the most beautiful woman I have ever seen. Such hair! Such eyes! Such skin!"

I lowered my eyes and took a seat on a stool by the fire. He hastily laid my garments near the hearth, but clearly he did not care whether or not they dried. "You are twenty, are you not? I have wanted you, Guinevere, since the day you came to Caer Camel at fifteen, and you now so far surpass in beauty that fifteen-year-old girl as a—as a full flower does an unopened bud. I tell you, I have been patient." He stopped for a gulp of wine.

"I belong to another," I said quietly. It was a mistake; his face grew dark with anger.

"Don't taunt me with that young pup! I'll not have it! For all his high and mighty ways, he's naught but a bastard of Uther Pendragon, and he's not master here!"

"No, my lord. Of course not. Pray forgive me. I will not mention him again."

He looked slightly mollified and poured himself another drink. "That's better. Where was I? Oh yes. I was patient, and do you know why? Because you are worth the wait, my beauty, and because I knew it would happen."

I looked up quickly, and he laughed loudly in delight. Clearly he did not worry about being overheard. I fed him his line. "How did you know?"

"The Lady of the Lake saw it in a vision. Not the witch that's there now. The old one. Nimue. She told Seulte about it years ago. That was why she would not let me marry. We were waiting for you."

I gasped and then tried to let my breath out slowly. "Your lady sister connived at this kidnapping?"

Melwas snorted rudely and then smiled. "I suppose it strikes you as kidnapping. I am only taking what I was meant to have. Your precious husband is finished with you. All the world knows that. You are to be mine. It is in the stars."

I was afraid if I shed tears he would try to comfort me, and the terror of it stopped their flow. Somehow I must try to keep him civilized until Lancelot—dearest Lancelot—he would leave no stone unturned! I glanced out the window. I could see the open waters of Lake Avalon and, in the far distance, the Tor. The veil of mist had lifted and it was, as I had known it would be, a clear day.

"Take what comes and live without complaint," I murmured. "Life is a woman's gift; death is God's. What will be, will be."

"What's that?" Melwas cried. "What are you saying about me?"

"Nothing about you, my lord," I replied wearily. "It's an old saying of Merlin's. And not very comforting."

"Forget Merlin. I fear him not. Drink up," he commanded, coming closer.

The cup I held shook horribly. I took a small sip, held hard to my courage, and faced him. "Are we to be married, sir?"

He stopped. Fair speech made him uncomfortable, I noted. I supposed he was well used to truculence.

"In time. Everything will be formalized in time."

I nodded and did my best to smile. "I knew you were a gentleman, King Melwas. See how you have prepared for all my wants. It shows forethought and consideration."

He glowed and preened under these shameless compliments like a young boy. He had no subtlety at all. "I am glad my lady is pleased. I promise you, Guinevere, I shall do my best to make you happy." The odd thing was, I believe he meant it.

"Do you have a book at hand, by chance?"

He gaped. "What for?"

What for, indeed, when he probably could not read! To hide my thought I smiled my sweetest smile. "That I might read to you, my lord, for your entertainment."

He snorted. "I've no use for reading, and as for entertainment, I've a much better idea—"

I moved quickly away as he came toward me and stood behind the supper couch. "Let me sing to you, then." I raised my winecup to him. "All things are better, my lord, if, like good wine, they are taken slowly."

He paused, astonished. I could see his thoughts run through his head. How much easier and more pleasant everything would be if I consented! And why not? He was a handsome enough man in middle years and king of a wide land. Not everyone would want Arthur's castoff. I could do much worse. As hope is ever the father of belief, no sooner had he thought it than he believed it. Complacently he settled his fat body on the couch and consented to be sung to.

At first, it was all I could do to open my throat, but after a while, my voice began to steady. I wondered if perhaps he was more frightened than he appeared. For all his brave talk, he must know that he had put his future in grave jeopardy. The High King was expected by week's end, and he did not take kindly to arrogance of any sort. But week's end would be too late. I would be this pirate's wife in all but name by then.

I sang him every song I knew, and some I made up on the spot. We had the best bards in Britain at Camelot, and I had learned something from every one of them. By midafternoon my throat was raw, and he was hungry. He brought out a tray of food he had prepared—soldier's rations with trimmings, little more—jerky, bread with honey, fruit, and pudding. And much more wine. I ate little, but I fed him everything, pretending all the while that I enjoyed thrusting biscuit and raisins into his mouth, and having my fingers kissed by sticky lips.

I made what small talk I could, as I had learned to do with visitors at Arthur's table. It seemed the old priestess of the shrine, who had made the prophecy about me, had died a year ago. The new Lady of the Lake was a young and powerful woman who disliked him. If she knew of Nimue's vision, she said nothing about it. Her allegiance, after the Goddess, was to Arthur. He and Seulte had planned secretly for twelve months how to take me; they had planned it all down to the last hair. That he feared and hated Arthur was clear, but I could not discover the reason.

He ate too much, of course, and drank more than most men did in a week. I bade him try the couch again, but he made me sit beside him, and held my hand. He looked at me like some adoring dog, but the greater beast was there, biding its time. Nevertheless, I sang to him, all the old Welsh lullabyes I had learned when I was young, and soon, as the afternoon turned golden and crept toward dusk, he slept. My clothes were dry; more than once I attempted to sneak away, but every time I moved my hand from his, he stirred and threatened to awaken. I dared not hazard a bold dash for the door. To flee or to fight him would only bring upon me the fate I dreaded. My best chance, I thought soberly, was to do as I had been doing, and string him along.

But a hooked fish cannot swim forever. At last he awoke and, grunting, rose and stretched his huge limbs. He lit candles and did not bother to draw the blinds. With sinking heart I realized he felt perfectly safe from any detection.

"Come, Guinevere," he said, towering above me and extending a hand. "It is time." My hand shook as he took it, and I found that I trembled so hard I could barely stand.

"King Melwas, I—I cannot give you children."

His great arms encompassed me, and he laughed. "I care not if you are barren. I do not want your children. It is you I want."

His lips sought mine and, held in his grip, I could not fight, but merely bore it. I dared not look ahead even to the next second.

"But, sir,—" I fumbled, my dazed thoughts running in circles. "—what will happen to your kingdom if you leave no sons behind you?"

He stood back for a moment, his eyes blazing. "Arthur will have it, the bitch's whelp! He is taking it from me now, what with harbor dues, raised every year, and road taxes. Your fancy boy, Lancelot, filled his head with lies about me, and he has set out to destroy me."

"Lancelot is not my fancy boy!" I cried hotly, but it was a great mistake to show resistance. His grip tightened, and his eyes filled with greedy lust.

"So," he said huskily, "that's how the land lies, does it? He will not find you here, my beauty." He released my belt and pressed his ugly lips to my neck, my shoulder, and, opening the robe, to my breasts. He made horrid noises, slurping and gurgling, and squeezed me with his big hands until he hurt me. But I would not give him the satisfaction of crying out. I simply wept, quietly and hopelessly. I could not stop the tears, once they started, but let them fall as he fondled me and sucked my flesh. He did not care that I could not respond, he was beyond any thought but the fulfillment of his desire. I looked over his shoulder, numbed, and in the blurred dimness beyond the window, I saw a light. It flickered and went out, then flashed on again.

"A light!" I gasped, pushing uselessly against his massive shoulders. His eager sighs and moans disgusted me, and I shuddered as his motions grew more frantic. "Sir, a light!"

He ignored me completely, and it was not until he straightened to whip off the thong that bound his leggings that he glanced out the window and saw it. He stared dumbly at the light and then broke into a stream of furious invective. I cowered against the wall as he pulled up his leggings and reached for his mantle. He got to the door and turned. I could not believe he was going. I could not imagine what the light meant.

"Don't bother trying to escape," he snarled. "I'm taking the only boat. And you'll never cross the bridge of swords alive." He paused, staring hungrily at me. "I'll be back," he said, and was gone.

I stood there, numbed and shaking and half dressed, while night descended and the fire burned low. I was aware of nothing. I reached for a cloth and began to wipe his slobber off my breasts. I wiped and wiped in a meaningless, steady motion without thought or feeling. I was dirty and feared I would never be clean. I don't know how long I stood there, dry-eyed and frozen in place, steadily wiping, but at length I heard a low grunt, the sound of gasping, and the hut began to shake. I believe I whimpered like a beast in pain, but I could not move. A loud thud, a cry of pain, an oath bitten off—the bedroom door flew open, and there stood Lancelot, dripping wet, bleeding from the knee and gripping a sword, white-fisted.

"Where is he?"

I stared dumbly at him, still wiping, and although I tried to speak, my lips made no sound. He turned left and right like a questing hound, and strode to the outer door, battering the bolt with his shoulder, kicking it down with his good leg, sword held ready.

"Melwas!" he shouted. He took a deep breath, collecting himself, and looked back at me. "Wait here," he said gently, as if I could have moved. I heard him outside, searching the little island, challenging Melwas in the King's name and, when he found the empty dock, calling him every sort of epithet. He returned with lowered sword.

"Is he gone? By boat?" I nodded, and began to shiver violently.

Lancelot came to me and took the cloth from my fingers. With the utmost gentleness he rearranged the robe, covered my nakedness, and tied the belt around my waist. Then he poured wine and held it to my lips and threw a woolen blanket about my shoulders. He gripped me firmly and made me look into his face.

"What happened?" Panic stiffened his face as his beautiful eyes searched mine. "Dear Christ, am I too late?"

I fumbled hopelessly for words. At last my grief and terror found vent, and I burst into sobs, crying with an abandonment I could not help, while he held me tightly and kissed my hair. At last I found my voice. "Oh, Lancelot! Thank God! Thank God!"

"My sweet Guinevere," he whispered, his lips against my ear. "It doesn't matter, my dearest love. You are alive, that's all that matters."

I buried my face against his shoulder. "Lancelot, he—he—"

"Never mind it, now. It's over. You are safe."

"He almost—he started to—but—"

He pulled away and looked down into my face, hope lighting his features. "He did not take you?"

"No," I cried with a shudder, "no, but he was five minutes from it. Less. Then he saw the light. On the Tor. I—I don't know—he just left me—as you found me."

"Thank God," he murmured softly. "That makes things easier. But you are safe, that's what matters. Take heart, my love. Your cruel ordeal is nearly over. You must dress, and quickly, and then I will find some way to get you across the water. Once ashore, we can get you home."

"We?" I repeated blankly. "Is someone with you?"

He lifted my clothing from the hearth and held it in his hands. "Merlin is with me."

"Merlin!" I gasped.

"He found you, Gwen, when we had been all day searching the woods and dragging the river, to no avail."

"You dragged the river?"

"Guinevere." He sounded impatient. "I love you. I would give my life for you. I feared you were dead—drowned, perhaps. I did everything I knew how to do in order to find you. When I saw it was beyond me, I sent for Merlin." I sat down slowly upon the stool and gazed at him unmoving. "He told me where to find you. In a vision he had heard your song." I gasped, and he reached for the winecup. "You were really singing?"

"Not—not for joy. I had to speak him fair," I whispered, "to keep him sweet. Every time I—I resisted, he—he—it was a challenge to him. He went mad." I swallowed hard, and Lancelot limped over to me and took my hand.

"I know the kind of man he is," he said gravely. "How you forestalled him an entire day I do not know."

"Lancelot, you are hurt! The blood on your leg!" Aghast, I saw suddenly a great pool of blood upon the floor. "It must be deep!"

"I have bound it. I will have it seen to. Listen, Gwen, we must hurry. I—"

"He isn't coming back?" I jumped to my feet, and he gripped my arms.

"No, he cannot. He must be at his palace to receive the King." I cried out, and he held me tighter. "What? Did you not know Arthur is back? His ships were sighted in the estuary three hours past. The light you saw must have been a signal to Melwas from some confederate on the Tor."

"The lady Seulte!" I whimpered, fighting rising panic.

"Truly?" He shook me gently. "Then both of them shall pay for this. Arthur will see to it. Hurry and dress, and I will take you to him. He will stay on Ynys Witrin tonight, with Melwas as his host."

"Dear God, no!" I cried. "So soon? Lancelot, no! I cannot do it! I cannot bear to face him!"

"Have you heard me, Gwen? Be still. No one knows what happened but Merlin and me. There will be no scandal. Your honor is unstained. And even so, you have nothing to fear from Arthur."

"What of his own honor? Have you thought of that? He will put me away."

"You do him an injustice."

"But I must tell him the truth. About what happened here."

"Yes."

"And after that? Oh, Lancelot, the—the monster touched me. He—he put his hands and lips on me. I am unclean."

Ever so gently, Lancelot kissed my lips and said, "I have done that, too." All at once it was more than I could stand, and I pressed against his wet and bleeding body and kissed him with passion. A sigh escaped him as his strong arms came around me and held me close. He bent my head back to kiss my neck, my throat, my breasts; his hands roamed my body with a deft and knowing touch, trailing fire. I clung to him, alive with excitement and desire.

"Lancelot! Oh, Lancelot!" I gasped. "Where is Merlin?"

He laughed shortly and pulled away from me, his face flushed, his gray eyes aflame. "My God, I had forgotten all about him." He passed a trembling hand across his face. "Take your clothes, Gwen, and dress in the other chamber."

"My dearest—"

"Hurry. We must both be there when Arthur hears Ferron's report."

One look at the bedchamber revealed how Lancelot had entered. The iron bars outside the window were bent wide, and the bedsheets all messed and bloody where he had fallen on them. It looked for all the world like the scene of a rape.

I felt much better back in my own clothing. Lancelot led me down a narrow path behind the hut toward the water.

"Is this how you came?" I asked him. "Over the land bridge?"

He grunted. "Over the bridge of swords, you mean? It is indeed."

"Swords! What swords?"

"Oh, he has set a neat trap in the middle of the bog. I was nearly caught, and I was expecting something of the sort. As it is, I got a blade in the leg. But there are bones about of others who were less nimble."

So that was Melwas' sharp surprise! "How then will we get back across?"

"Nestor will take us, if his training holds good."

At the water's edge he whistled for the stallion. We stood forty paces from the land bridge, now a bog in rising water. Within minutes we saw his dark head arrowing through the black water, swimming in a straight line toward us, safely past danger. He swam us both back, clinging to his mane. I was amazed at how little strength I had; twice my grip gave way. If Lancelot had not been holding me, I should have drowned.

Merlin sat on the bank, unmoving, on an old black horse. He nodded to me and spoke to Lancelot. "We have an hour, at most. Go quickly, and I will follow. Take her to Niniane."

I shivered. Lancelot bowed, holding me against his body with one firm arm.

"Sir," he said to Merlin, "on behalf of the High King, I thank you for the Queen's life."

I could see nothing of Merlin's face but the black eyes glinting in moonlight.

"It is to Arthur she owes it," he said.

16 AVALON

I did not, in fact, face Arthur that night. The day's exposure to damp and the aftereffects of terror took their toll, and I fell into a fever. Lancelot delivered me to the Lady's shrine, where I was washed and put to bed, already delirious. They tell me Arthur came to see me the next morning and stayed at my bedside half a day before returning to Camelot, but in my fever I knew him not. I do not remember it.

After a week I was strong enough to sit in the garden and take short walks in the lovely orchards the women cultivate. I was well tended. Of the Lady of the Lake who had allowed the High King entrance to the shrine, I saw nothing until ten days had passed. I had said very little to anyone, since we were a stone's throw from Melwas' castle, and I did not know what had transpired between him and the King. But I was treated with respect, so I deduced that I must still be Queen.

Then on the tenth day the Lady Queen came to me as I sat in the orchard, sunning. She wore the white robe of the Goddess' servant, but when she pushed back her hood to show her face, I found I knew her. It was Niniane, Merlin's pupil!

"Queen Guinevere." She made no obeisance, as I was not her sovereign. The Lady's shrine was under neither Arthur's protection nor Melwas', but belonged to itself, being an ancient sacred place. I inclined my head to her, for she was ruler here, and I her guest.

"Lady Niniane."

Her black eyes flickered. "You know me."

"I remember you."

"We have not met."

"No. But when I was a bride, I saw you once in Caerleon. With Merlin."

204

She looked down at me and paused. I could read no expression in her clear features. She was dark haired and light skinned, as slender as I was and a little older, but what distinguished her from ordinary beauty was an indefinable poise, a certainty, a wholeness. Arthur possessed it, and until now I had thought him to be the only one.

Because of this quality, the opening parry and thrust of our conversation filled me with dread. She did not like me, and she had power.

"Ahhhh, Merlin. My master and teacher. He has taught me everything he knows. And like every good pupil at training's end, I took flight. As you see." She glanced coolly about her. It occurred to me that in the year since she had become Lady of the Lake, we had not seen much of Merlin. "I do not recall seeing you in Caerleon. You have a good memory."

"I had occasion to remember it. You frightened me."

If I was not mistaken, the shadow of a smile touched her lips. "Did I? I beg forgiveness. It was not intentional."

"The fault was mine, Lady Niniane. I was very young."

She sat gracefully beside me on the bench. Introductions were over.

"You are recovered," she began. "In three days you will have your strength back."

"Thanks to the excellent care of your women," I murmured.

She accepted the thanks. "Yes. What do you wish to do when you are well?"

My eyes opened wide at that. What was she about? What had been going on? "I wish to go home, Lady, if it is permitted."

"To Camelot?"

"Of course. If—" The fear of it set me trembling. "—if it is still my home." There was no softening in her stern face. She accused me of some crime, yet I did not know what it was.

"Arthur is there."

I met her eyes. Here was the battleground. "I am glad to hear it. I wish to see him."

"He knows what happened."

"I should hope he does. It was not a small thing and affects him nearly. Please tell me, for I have heard nothing, what has become of Melwas?"

She regarded me closely, and I felt my thoughts probed by careful fingers. I was reminded of Merlin's visit in my sleep, years ago. That a woman could hold such power! On the thought, she spoke.

"Nothing yet."

"What! Is he not taken?" I cried in horror. "Am I not believed?" I shook with fear and saw the first sign of compassion in her.

She placed her hand upon my arm. "No one has formally accused him yet but Lancelot, and he was largely incoherent with pain and fever."

I grew instantly still, and she noted it. Compassion fled, she withdrew her hand, and when she next spoke her voice was remote. "You do not ask after Lancelot?"

"How fares my rescuer?" I asked obediently. But it had been a week since he had ridden in with me, and if he still could not accuse Melwas it meant he was very ill indeed—or worse. That was instantly clear to me. My eyes were lowered, and I waited, barely breathing, for the blow.

"He lies gravely ill in our house of healing. The wound he received in his knee has festered. It might be necessary to remove the leg to save him."

"Dear God!" I cried, and covered my face with my hands.

"He lies unconscious. The King is held at Camelot by visitors of state, and he has asked—commanded—me to make a difficult request."

I steadied myself and looked up. Something was coming. Niniane looked strained.

"Difficult for me to make, I should have said. I doubt you will find it difficult to obey. The King commands me to ask you to go to Lancelot and stay by him through his illness, to whatever end comes."

I stared at her. It was all I could do to keep my seat. She sat there looking hard at me, and I barely kept myself from commanding her to take me to him that instant. She read the flow of my thoughts, and her expression grew cold. It was intolerable. Even Arthur did not judge me so.

"Lady Niniane!" I reached out and clasped her hand between my own. "Do not set traps for me, I pray. I know you see the truth. Why try to catch me in a falsehood? Merlin was there. I can hide nothing and do not wish to. I will tell my lord the truth. He needs to know it."

"The whole truth?" she asked.

"Ah," I said sadly, "he knows already. Can you doubt it? He has known it a long time." I paused, and Niniane said nothing, but looked sorrowful herself. "Have you led such a blameless life, Niniane, that you cannot conceive of being rent in twain by love?"

She gasped, and to my amazement I saw her disconcerted. I did not know, then, that as her old master neared his end, she had lost her heart to a handsome king in Arthur's service, one Pelleas, Alissa's brother. I knew none of this, yet God guided my arrow and sent it home.

She blushed faintly. "I love and honor Merlin," she whispered.

"Yes," I said calmly, meeting her eyes directly, "and I love the King."

She nearly protested, then looked at me a long time, searching, and finally nodded. "I did not know it."

"Know it now. His honor is safe with me."

The corners of her mouth twitched into a smile. "So he has told me many times."

"Why is he sending me to Lancelot? Is this some test you have devised?"

"No, my lady. He fears for Lancelot's life. He only hopes that your presence there may strengthen his will to live."

"I will go, then. Let us pray he is right."

"I advised him against it," she confessed.

"He is wiser than you," I said gently. "And I do not care who talks. Lancelot saved me, and I owe him this."

She shook her head. "The gods saved you, Guinevere, God, if you like, who sent the fair wind that blew Arthur's ships into the estuary two days early."

"As you say. But it was Lancelot who got me off that island. Whatever happens now, I am forever in his debt."

She turned away and gazed across the orchard to the distant shimmer of the Lake. I fidgeted impatiently, thinking of Lancelot, who lay near death for my sake.

"Will he live, Niniane?" The question escaped me against my will, and I bit my lip, afraid of her answer.

"Lancelot's fate I have not seen," she said apologetically. "The stars do not foretell everyone's destiny."

"Wait!" I cried, although she had made no move to go. "One thing more I would know. I—I am afraid of it. If it concerns Arthur, you will know it, will you not?" At the mention of his name her attention focused on me sharply, and my voice wavered. "Everyone thinks—he will put me away. God knows he has cause. I know it better than anyone. Will he do it, Niniane? Oh, please, tell me if you know!"

Her eyes grew cold once more and although she did not move, I felt her withdraw. "Should you care overmuch? You would be free. And Lancelot is unwed."

I cried out and covered my face with trembling hands.

"I would rather die," I whispered brokenly. "I will kill myself first—I don't care if it means eternal damnation, I could not live with that shame, I could not, I could not. Oh, dear God, why must I bear this trial? Why can I not conceive the son he wants? What have I done to bring such shame upon him? I cannot bear it—"

At this point Niniane pressed her cool fingers against my temples and said some words in a low, calm monotone. My eyelids grew heavy and closed against my will.

"Rest, Queen Guinevere. I would help you if I could, but I do not know the answer to your question. Merlin has seen your end, but I have not. It is in Arthur's hands, and to him you shall go."

"May God have mercy upon my soul," I whispered.

"The gods have chosen you," she said quietly. "There is a reason. Perhaps you would do well to accept what life brings you."

"Take what comes and live without complaint," I said slowly. "What will be, will be."

"Life is a woman's gift; death is God's," she finished. "So you have heard Merlin's litany before."

I smiled and touched her hand. "Arthur says it to me every six months," I told her. "Thank you, Niniane. I feel better for your visit."

We rose together, and at last her smile was warm.

"You have great charm, Guinevere. All the world knows it, of course, but I thought—Arthur warned me I should not be proof against it. He was right."

I took her arm in mine. "Arthur is a very wise man."

I sat with Lancelot four days before the fever abated and he opened his eyes. As a nurse I was useless, except for applying cold compresses and fluffing pillows. I sat at his bedside holding his hand, and remembering my childhood role in the hospital of Gwynedd, I sang to him. I sang when the leeches were applied, I sang when they lanced an abscess and as it drained. I sang to keep myself from being sick and to ease my terror of the physician's art. I left his side only to eat and to sleep, and only then because Niniane insisted on it. A small service she would do Arthur, she said, if she allowed me to fall ill again. I obeyed her every command, and she seemed pleased with Lancelot's progress, although to me he looked deathly pale whenever he was not hot with fever.

That he was alive at all was something of a miracle. The night he brought me in, they told me, he had no sooner given me into the Lady's care than he had staggered into Melwas' fortress intent upon revenge. Hot with fever and so lame he could barely stand, he had burst in upon the kings at supper, sword drawn, and thrown himself at Melwas while the whole court sat frozen. Shouting accusations and half delirious, he had slipped in a pool of his own blood and missed his target, hit his head against the table and fallen senseless to the floor. Only Arthur's restraining hand on Melwas' arm had kept the two-faced coward from killing him then and there. While I had Arthur to thank that Lancelot lay struggling for life in the Lady's pavilion, Arthur was not there now.

On the fourth day Lancelot opened his eyes and knew me.

"Gwen!" he whispered.

"Hush!" I cried, and then "Nurse!" The attendant lifted water to his lips, and he took it eagerly.

"Gwen, my beloved," he said, and slipped back into sleep. I pressed his hand to my cheek and cried for joy.

For two more weeks I stayed with him, and each day he improved. As he gained strength, he talked to me, and talked and talked, as if words could take the place of sweet caresses. He told me of his Breton boyhood, his loneliness, his dreams of honor and glory, and his finding in Arthur the answer to his prayers. I held his hand throughout and touched his brow, and wept and laughed as he moved me to it. It was as if his illness had dissolved the reserve that had always been between us, and he shared his thoughts freely with me. We were always attended and observed, but it mattered not to us. In the world we inhabited only we two existed. He did not mention Melwas, and neither did I. We grew so close during that time, and shared such happiness, that often we did not need to speak at all, but only touch. The memory of his brief passion burned in my thoughts, and in his, also. He would lay his hand upon my arm, and look at me with hot gray eyes, and we were back there in the cabin, alive and ready for surrender. Then one of us would look away and break the spell. It had happened; we could not deny it; but it was past.

At last, when Lancelot was on his feet and could put weight on his leg with the help of a stout staff, Niniane brought me news that the King desired my return and was sending an escort the following day to take me back.

I looked at her anxiously. "Is it a bad sign, Niniane, that he does not come himself?"

"I think rather it is a test for Melwas, who must give the escort passage," she replied kindly. "You are in no danger, Guinevere. Should Melwas try to prevent your going, the King's Companions would be down upon him within the hour." She smiled lightly. "I hear that many of them are beside themselves with eagerness for war, to avenge your honor. The King gives Melwas a chance to save his life."

I broke the news to Lancelot that evening, and he looked puzzled at my distress.

"I shall hate to lose your company, Guinevere, but you belong in Camelot with Arthur. When I am well enough to ride I will follow."

"It's—it's not so much leaving as arriving that I fear."

"Fear arriving? Whatever for?"

I paced about his room nervously. The servant, flattened against the wall with wooden face, slipped out at my signal.

"I fear Arthur may—may see things as the world sees them and put me away. No one could blame him. Not even I. And now he has a perfect excuse."

"Guinevere." He spoke tenderly. I came to his bedside, and he took my hand. "Since I have known you, you have been afraid of Arthur. Has he ever given you cause?"

I shook my head. "I am not afraid, exactly. A little in awe, perhaps."

He smiled. "With Arthur, awe is easy. But I cannot believe you think he will do this. You are too entangled in your own fears. Think of how Arthur feels."

"But I am!" I cried. "How else could he feel, but betrayed by fate? He is High King, and he has no son."

Lancelot's face reflected only his loving kindness and his understanding. "Gwen," he said gently, "think of the man you know. He would as soon part with a limb as part with you. As I would."

"He would part with a limb readily enough to save Britain, and no one knows that better than you, Lancelot."

He smiled and kissed my hand.

"True enough. But is this a matter of saving Britain or of pleasing her King?"

"Arthur's seed is Britain's future."

"Perhaps. That's with God, surely. But don't pretend to me that Arthur treats you like his broodmare, because I won't believe it."

His words were so like something Arthur had said to me once that I started in surprise. "You really think he will keep me?"

"Yes," Lancelot said. "I do."

I sat down next his bed and gripped his hand. "Dear God, I hope you are right."

17 ❀ fIÒ ELITY AND BETRAYAL

The escort arrived with great pomp and flourish and not with a litter but with Pallas, dressed in a gilded bridle. The King had even sent new riding clothes so I could return to him in the style for which I had become well known.

Niniane's ladies dressed my hair, and Niniane herself as Lady of the Lake blessed me in public ceremony before I left the shrine. Outside, King Melwas' troops lined the road and saluted us as we rode by. Melwas himself was there, richly dressed and crowned, and, although I could scarcely credit it, still followed me with hungry eyes. I remembered he had spoken to me of visions fed him by the old Lady of the Lake. Perhaps, having come so close to his heart's desire, he could not bear to leave it and still had hope. I shuddered at the thought, and the captain of the escort, who rode beside me, guided his horse closer.

"Have no fear, my lady," he said in a low voice, "we shall be rid of Melwas soon."

I was surprised to recognize Ferron and saw in his very presence the touch of Arthur's hand. If the captain had been in disgrace as a result of my foolhardy behavior, he was being given the chance to redeem himself.

"Good Ferron," I greeted him, "how glad I am to see you here! I beg you will forgive my arrogance last time we met. I was wrong to ignore your good advice on that occasion and see now what it has cost us!"

He looked astonished and stuttered in reply. "Queen Guinevere, I—please do not—I beg you will not—the fault was mine, my lady. Were I half the horseman you are, I could have followed you in the fog!"

I laughed in delight, for his admiration was genuine and his

compliment, so unlooked for, pleased me greatly. The bright May
sun shone down upon us and my heart lifted.

"How does the King?" I asked him, knowing he had had an interview.

"The King is angry," he said stiffly, eyes straight ahead. And so
he should be, I thought, but nonetheless I felt apprehension grip
me. Soon after this we came to the end of the marshland causeway and met the open road to Caer Camel where, breaking into
a gallop, we had no time for further talk.

The trumpets sounded at King's Gate as we drew nigh, and all
of Arthur's troops came out to meet us. They lined the streets of
Camelot and every man of them cheered as I rode past. I was
overcome by such devotion, and when I dismounted in the castle
forecourt, my eyes were blurry with tears. Ferron led me up the
steps to the waiting party at the door. It was not until I sank into
my curtsy that I realized with cold shock that Arthur was not
there. Kay's hand raised me, and Kay's voice spoke the formal
greeting.

"Welcome home, Queen Guinevere."

Trembling, I took his arm. "Where is my lord?" I whispered.
"Kay, why is he not here? Take me to him!"

Kay grunted kindly and led me inside. "My orders, lady," he
said rather loudly, "are to take you to your rooms, where you may
await the King's command. He will send for you when he is at
leisure."

I glanced at him sharply, but his bland expression told me nothing. At leisure! What could he be doing now, with every one of
his men on the streets of Camelot? Kay escorted me through the
corridors to the door that gave onto the women's quarters. The
nearest sentry stood a good ten paces off. When he bowed over
my hand, he winked and said in a low voice, "He waits in your
garden, but let no one know."

I thanked him swiftly and ran to my rooms. Ailsa and all my
women were gathered in my sitting room, sunk in curtsies. I
barely paused to greet them as I hurried by.

"My lady!" Ailsa cried in distress.

"Later!" I called over my shoulder. "I wish to be alone. Await
my call." And I flew up the stairs to my bedchamber. Whether
they thought I suffered from anger, fear, or humiliation, I cared
not. I had to see Arthur. If he desired a private meeting he had
chosen the place well. My garden could be approached from my
bedchamber only, and no man could enter except through the
King's apartments. As I stepped onto my terrace I stopped and

took a deep breath to steady my nerves. So much depended on this interview!

Arthur stood at the end of the garden, half turned from me, watching the fountain play. I saw him suddenly as a stranger might, with that odd sight that is given to us at times to clear our senses and show us things anew. He was then in his twenty-fifth year, in the full flower of his manhood. He had been High King of Britain for eleven years, and kingship was part of the fabric of the man. He was tall and well made, with long limbs that moved with a natural grace. Clean shaven and clear-featured, he was a handsome man in a rugged, soldier's way. But what set him so apart from other men was something else: his inner light, his grace of bearing, his wholeness, his serenity. He knew who and what he was. He lived in his own time. This is what I saw that day, and it moved me deeply.

I came lightly down the stairway and crossed the garden toward him. The splash of the fountain hid the sound of my approach, and he did not see me until I was beside him. Thus I saw his true reaction and could judge his heart.

He turned and his face lit. "Guinevere!"

I sank to his feet and, taking his hand, pressed my lips to the great carved Pendragon ruby. "My lord Arthur!"

He lifted me with both arms and held me tightly, his hands in my hair, unbraiding it with practiced skill as he whispered endearments in my ear. "I have missed you so! Are you truly recovered from your ordeal? When you are able, I would like to hear everything you have to say."

"I shall tell you everything. But Arthur—"

He stopped my lips with his own, and I yielded to his ardor. I felt so safe in his arms. He was Britain, and my home.

"Ah, Gwen," he said at last, drawing away and allowing me breath, "can you forgive me for leaving you on Ynys Witrin? I've been through hell here, carrying on as if everything were normal, while you lay in Avalon surrounded by Melwas' troops. I wasn't sure he'd keep his promise to let you go. If I'd forced him—well, I'd have won the war, but risked losing the battle. I had to do what Merlin tells me you did and treat him like the gentleman he's not. If he thought I cared for nothing but your honor, he'd think he had less to lose by returning you. I had to sham indifference," he said with a touch of icy anger, "and give the coward hope."

I drew him to me and rested my head against his chest, where I closed my eyes and listened to the slow, strong beat of his heart.

"He told me," I said quietly, "that you would put me away. That all the world knew it." I felt his body tense, but I went on. "That was why he dared. That and some prophetic dream a priestess fed him. It matters not. But he is brave, Arthur. You were well advised to speak him fair and give him hope you would put me aside. Else I think he would have kept me and risked war."

He lifted my chin and looked down into my face. His eyes were dark and deep and warm. "Did you believe him?"

"I—I—I have feared it, my lord, before this. You have cause."

His face hardened, but his hand against my cheek was gentle.

"I shall not do it," he said roughly, holding my face in his hand and looking directly in my eyes. "I shall never do it, Guinevere. I swear it here before God. So long as I am King, you shall be Queen. At least I can spare you that horror."

Tears slid down my cheeks, and he kissed them, one by one. "Arthur," I whispered, choking back a sob, "I love you from my soul."

He closed his eyes at that and went quite still. "Mother of God!" he breathed. "That I should live to hear you say those words to me! And after what you have been through and where you have been!"

Then he laughed a joyous laugh and, sitting on the stone bench that flanked the fountain, pulled me onto his lap. "And how is Lancelot? I have had reports from Niniane, but you can tell me things that she cannot."

"He is impatient of return," I told him, "and furious that Melwas is still alive."

"Then he is nearly recovered. I do not worry about Lancelot with Melwas. There is not a man on Ynys Witrin who would willingly raise a sword against him. He is the finest swordsman in Britain."

I smiled at him. "He speaks highly of you, too."

"Besides, I brought his weapons home with me, for his own protection."

I laughed. "He did not tell me that."

"I think perhaps he owes you his life."

"But it was you who sent me to him. It was a noble gesture."

"It was a desperate one," he said gravely. "I wanted you here, but I cannot afford to lose him."

I slid my arms around his neck. "Arthur."

"Yes?"

"I must tell you. About Melwas."

"Ah, yes. Of what do you accuse him?"

"Of kidnapping."

"Is that everything? Not," he said, facing it, "of rape?"

"No. He did not take me. I escaped that fate—by minutes—but I escaped."

He let out a long, slow breath.

"Did no one tell you?" I cried. "Did they let you think—"

"No one knew, for certain. Lancelot lay senseless, and Merlin disappeared."

"But if you doubted—Arthur." I looked at him with awe. "Do you mean you vowed to keep me, even when you thought he had used me so?"

His face was grave, but his eyes were warm and comforting. "I do. Nothing Melwas could do could change what is between us. He would have to kill you to take you from me. As for the rest, it is simply fools' chatter. I have had, for years now, plenty of advice to put you aside—you know the reasons. But I cannot do it, Gwen. There is more to life than breeding children, and I do not wish to do without you." His arms about my waist tightened. "A King's life can be abominably lonely. I am away from home so often and so long, I feel I have the right to come back to the woman of my choice."

I kissed his throat and rested my head upon his shoulder. "You are the soul of generosity. You are the only man in Christendom to whom it would not make a difference."

"Oh, it makes a difference," he replied, with an edge to his voice. "But not to you. To Melwas. The difference between certain death and the chance to sue for mercy."

"What will you do to him?"

"I will charge him with the crime he has committed. We shall see how he responds. I have wanted to kill him, but it is not the best solution."

We sat silently awhile. I was wrestling with my conscience; Arthur looked at peace.

"My lord," I said at last. "There is more I should tell you about Melwas. Niniane told me you should hear it."

He waited. I could not tell from his face whether or not he already knew.

"I stalled him for as long as I could," I said slowly, forcing it out, "but eventually Melwas decided he could wait no longer. When it grew dark, he—he—Arthur, he put his hands and lips upon me, and half undressed me. Then he saw a light, a signal, from his confederate, and left. I should have covered myself, my lord, I know. But I was—frozen. I was so frightened I could not move."

"Yes," he said in a tight voice. "I have seen the same in men, after battle."

"I knew nothing. I did not feel time pass. I was still standing thus when—when Lancelot came in." My eyes were averted from his face, and I know I blushed. "He covered me, my lord, and took the unclean feeling from me."

His finger pressed against my lips to stop the words, and I was grateful. After a long silence, where neither of us looked at the other, he spoke. There was pain in his voice.

"He is my friend. He has done me a great service, and almost lost his life for my sake. If he—gave you ease of heart, Guinevere, I am glad of it."

Such generosity was beyond belief. I bowed my head and let the tears slip out. My heart ached for him.

"He told me," I whispered, "that you would not put me away."

"He knows me well."

I hugged him tightly and pressed my wet cheek to his face. "Sir, I would that it were not so. I would spare you this."

"Thank you, Gwen. But it cannot be helped. This we all three have known. It is the trust between us that matters."

"We shall never break it," I promised him, as I sat on his lap in the shaded garden with tears on my face and my heart too full for speech.

At length he lifted me and began his slow pacing to and fro before the fountain. I could not imagine what there was left to say.

"Guinevere," he said at last, "you have been brave and honest with me and told me things I did not like to hear. Now I am afraid that I must say such things to you."

"How so, my lord?"

"Recall I told you that I had to hide my anger from Melwas and feign indifference to your fate to give him hope, both by leaving you there so long, and by sending you to Lancelot."

"Yes."

"There was a double purpose in it. And in my sending Ferron in my place, and in my leaving Kay to greet you. I had to seem cold, not only to fool Melwas, but to fool his accomplice here in Camelot."

I gasped. "Accomplice?"

He glanced at me quickly, and he looked a different man. His eyes glinted hard and bright, and his face was set. I had never seen him so angry.

"How else was Melwas there? He was not fowling in the fog. He had information that you would be riding that way. More than that, he had information that if he were successful he might keep you, for I might put you away. God knows the palace gossip has found little else to talk about this year past." He shrugged it off quickly and moved on. "A courier was seen leaving King's Gate before your party left, and after you had told Kay your plans."

"You don't suspect Kay!"

"I will not unless I have to. Who could have overheard your instructions to him?"

I thought back carefully. My answer might amount to accusation. "Six of my women," I said at last, and named them.

"Ah," he said with satisfaction. "So Elaine was there."

"Arthur!" I cried, gripping his arm. "You cannot suspect Elaine!"

His look was very gentle. "You feel about her as I do about Kay. You grew up together. She is your sister. But think closely on this, Guinevere. Is the trust between you strong?"

"My lord, I—I have always thought so."

"I am not sure that it goes both ways," he said. The very gentleness of his voice frightened me.

"Something has happened," I said suddenly. "Tell me."

He sat me down upon the bench and stood before me, holding both my hands. "Do you know why Elaine has refused all offers, even from the finest of my Companions, and never married?"

I gasped and met his eyes. "Yes, my lord. But—do you?"

He nodded, and I sat speechless, waiting for what was coming.

"I found her in my bed," he said simply, "when you had been two weeks away. For a moment only, I thought it was you. She has the trick of imitating your voice. For a brief moment I imagined you had escaped and come to me secretly somehow." He smiled, a little shamefaced. "A dream born of longing. It was a moment only. I knew, as soon as I touched her hair. But in that moment—" He hesitated and I felt my face grow red with shame. I stared miserably at the paving stones and clung to his hands. "—she revealed her soul. She said things to me that will not bear repeating. In truth, I think she is not well."

I shook my head. "No, Arthur. It is only infatuation. She has always been so. It is not new."

"You will keep her away from me!" It burst out of him with force, and then he sighed and sat down beside me. "I am trying to tell you, Gwen, that I suspect her of grave disloyalty to you. Whatever the cause, I think she betrayed you to Melwas."

I said nothing. It was possible; I saw that. But I did not want to believe it of Elaine. That she loved Arthur, yes. That she would actually try to supplant me, no. But if she had really gone to the King's bed—

"Are you certain it was Elaine?" I asked desperately.

"Yes," he replied with sadness. "I lit the lamp."

"And this happened when?"

"A week ago. After I had sent you to Lancelot. To all the world it looked as if I had given in to fate and cared no more about you, which, may God forgive such deceit, was the plan." He passed a hand across his brow. "I did not suspect her until this happened, but I do now. What I wish to know, Gwen, is whether you want to handle this yourself, or if you want me to do it. I leave the choice to you."

"If it is Elaine—she does not know that you have forgiven me?"

"Forgiven you?" He smiled kindly and touched my cheek. "You have done naught to offend me."

"I mean—you have promised—she cannot know yet that you will not put me aside?"

"No. That has been one point of all this subterfuge, that the informer should not know my true feeling toward you. Thus I conspired to meet you privately, where not even Elaine could observe us."

"Then let me speak with her, my lord. I owe her that."

"I thought you might say that. It will not be pleasant, Guinevere."

I managed a smile. "Of a certainty. How was it left between you? Does she still feel as she did?"

For the first time I saw Arthur embarrassed. He knew not what to say. "It is my belief her feelings are unchanged," he admitted awkwardly. "For all that, she is angry with me."

"Of course she is, since you refused her. You need tell me no more. I know what line to take."

He rose then and took me in his arms, running his fingers through my loose hair. "Welcome home, my Queen. We missed your birthday. You are twenty now, and you are the most wonderful woman alive."

"Thank you, my lord."

"And you will be more careful of yourself from now on, for my sake, and not put my valuable captains through such tortures of soul?"

I smiled at him. "Yes, my lord."

"Whatever possessed you to take off that day, if I may ask?" I looked away, the smile gone. "Never mind," he said quickly. "I see it is as I thought."

"Take what comes and live without complaint, for what will be, will be," I said slowly, looking up at him again. "I will try to put it behind me, Arthur. I know I may never give you children. I can bear it, I think, if you can forgive it. Lend me your strength."

A deep sigh escaped him, as if something long held in had been freed at last.

"It is a day of miracles," he breathed, and kissed me. At length he loosed me and squared his shoulders.

"Let me leave first," he said, "that I may be in another part of the castle when you go to your quarters. Give me ten minutes. I shall see you at the feast tonight."

"What feast, my lord?"

His quick grin lit his face. "The Companions are throwing a great feast in the Queen's honor. You are their darling, did you not know? And there I shall publicly declare you my Queen for my life. In Council this afternoon I will charge Melwas. So you had better confront Elaine before that."

"As soon as you are gone, my lord."

"Brave woman." He saluted me, and left.

When I went in I called Ailsa to me and bade her shake out my blue gown, "for it is the King's favorite," and sat while she bathed me and brushed out my hair. She scented my gown with the jasmine scent the King had procured from southern lands and dressed my hair with seed pearls and a net of small sapphires, also the King's gift. When all these preparations were complete, I sat on my little needlepoint bench and bade Ailsa leave me, "for," I said, not untruthfully, "I await the King's command."

She had said very little to me, just chatted in the ordinary way, and asked no questions at all. But she looked pale and frightened, and I was sorry I could not relieve her fears. As she reached the door, I stopped her.

"Ailsa, if the lady Elaine is at leisure, and if she is so inclined, she may come to me. Keep everyone else away."

"Very good, my lady."

Elaine came up immediately. When she saw me sitting there in Arthur's favorite gown, dressed for a feast at midday, bathed and scented and waiting, her eyes lit, and my heart sank.

"Gwen!" she cried, running to me and hugging me lightly. "Oh, I am so glad you are back! Was it very horrible? Have you seen the King? Is he very angry?"

I had seated myself so my face was in shadow, and she put my nervousness down to fear of the King.

"I was hoping perhaps you could tell me that," I replied. "I—I have heard rumors."

"He is furious at Melwas, of course," she confided, seating herself upon a cushion at my feet. Light from the terrace doorway fell on her face, which was lifted to me. "It was an insult to his honor. But he shall be avenged." She paused. "What happened to you, Gwen? All we have heard here are rumors. That is, if you can bear to speak of it."

"What have you heard?"

"That Lancelot rescued you with Merlin's help, but that he was too late to save you from—the worst."

She watched me eagerly, and my flesh crept upon my bones.

"As far as it goes, that is true," I said, and the triumph on her face, quickly suppressed, was a knife in my heart. "But for Merlin's Sight and Lancelot's courage, I might still be—in that place. It was well hidden."

She had the grace to shudder. "And was Lancelot badly injured?" she went on. "They say he lay dying, until you went to his bedside and restored his will to live."

"They exaggerate," I replied.

"That must have been terribly hard, Gwen, to see him so near death, and for your sake."

"Yes. It was hard."

She took my hand to comfort me, and if she felt my trembling, she misconstrued it.

"Were you there when he regained his senses? Did you speak your heart?" she asked in a dreadful whisper. "It must have seemed like stolen time for both of you."

"Elaine," I said quickly, "what should I do? I have heard things about the King—that he is—that he might be ready to annul our marriage. Tell me it is not true! What can I do to regain his favor?"

She smiled. "You are off to a good start. It's well known he cannot resist you when you wear blue!" Then she rose and took a turn about the room. "Seriously, Gwen, I would be careful." She frowned. "I have had private speech with the King—" Here I stifled a gasp. "—and I tell you I think you are on dangerous ground. It is possible that he will put you away. He has spoken to the bishop about it."

It was a cool lie, and she told it without a flicker of hesitation.

"The bishop?" I whispered.

She turned to me. The excitement in her eyes belied the sorrow on her face. "Oh, Gwen, forgive me. I only meant—I don't know what will happen. I only tell you to prepare you. After all, what future has Britain unless the King has sons?" She came closer and reached for my hand. But I could not help myself, and I shrank from her touch.

"Are you so certain he has determined upon that course?"

"No. No one is sure. But Arthur indicated, when he spoke to me—" I blushed to hear her use his name so freely. "—that it was time to put the past behind him. Listen, Gwen." She sank to her knees and looked up at me earnestly. "Remember when we were girls in Wales? How happy you were with Lancelot, and how you longed to be his bride instead of Arthur's? It can be so—it can happen now with no disgrace! The King will charge Melwas with kidnapping and rape, and when he has avenged the slight to his honor, he will free you from this bond you never wanted. Lancelot will jump at the chance to wed you. Just think of it, Gwen! Your fondest dream can come true. You can marry your true love."

She came to a stop, breathless and excited, and I simply could not bear to look into her face. I rose and walked away, struggling to compose myself enough to speak.

"You have it all worked out, Elaine, do you not?" Her head went up at the tone of my voice, and she went suddenly still. "How did you make contact with Melwas? Was it after the Harvest Festival years ago when I told you how amorous he had been? Who was your go-between? The King will want to know."

She went white. "What are you talking about?"

"I have trusted you with secrets, Elaine, and loved you as a sister. What have you done to me?"

"Gwen," she whispered, "I am innocent."

I whirled and faced her.

"You should know," I said flatly, "that before I called you up here, I was with the King an hour."

She gasped. Then a subtle change came over her. Surprise left her features, along with every vestige of warmth and youth. She looked suddenly old and hard.

"Arthur made it clear to me, Elaine, very, very clear, that everything you have just said is false. You have made a grave mistake. He will not put me away. And he would not have you, even if he were free. Live with that."

It was cruel, and Elaine was never able to take a barb in silence.

"You do not deserve him!" she spat. "You are barren! Give him up and let him wed a fertile woman who will bear him sons!"

"That is his choice. But he will not do it. He has told me so."

"You are soiled!" she cried. "Do not stain his honor! Gwen, don't rob him of his future!"

"If I am soiled," I said levelly, "who set me up for it? How devoted to Arthur can you be, to conspire to defile his wife? What is wrong with you, Elaine?"

"I have done nothing!" she screamed. "You can prove nothing!"

"I can ask Melwas, when he faces judgment, who his informer was."

Her face flooded with color, and she stood to face me. "You dare not do it! You dare not expose your shame to public view!"

I regarded her with heartfelt pity. "So that is what you counted on to save you. I wondered." I found myself near the foot of my bed and gripped the bedpost for support. "I suppose now is the time to tell you that Melwas did not rape me."

"Coward!" she shrieked, then clapped a hand over her mouth as tears started to her eyes.

"He tried, God knows, but was prevented by circumstance. I have told the King what happened. I tell you now so you may know how hopeless is your defense."

"I will not bother to defend myself!" she cried hotly, and I saw with dismay that the floodgates had opened, and her words and tears tumbled forth together. "Go ahead and accuse me! I do not care! You are so high and mighty, you who were taken in as orphan by my mother, always spoiled and pampered—oh, God!— past bearing! Nothing was denied you! You took everything away from me, even that God-forsaken Irishman! Everything I ever wanted was given to you! It was I who honored Arthur from my youth, not you. It is I who should be his Queen, not you! I can breed sons aplenty—I know it—as my mother did before me. It is not fair! You will destroy him! You—he loves you for your beauty, which you have done nothing to deserve, and you love that—that broken-nosed Breton who always stinks of stables! Oh, God! I cannot bear it! Kill me and have done!"

She flung herself to the floor, weeping horribly, while I stood by, numb, and waited. But as no one came to cosset and tend her, at length her sobs diminished and died into rhythmic whimpers.

I found my voice. "Is *that* what lies at the bottom of all this?" I took a deep breath. "Have you learned nothing? Beauty may be a gift from God, but I thought by now you would have learned this lesson: that it is as hard to bear and as welcome as a double-edged sword that turns in the hand. You are a beautiful woman, Elaine—how can you not know this? Only see the cost we pay—you, Melwas, Lancelot, and even Arthur! It is the first thing anyone sees, and few ever try to get beyond it. To half of Britain, man and woman, I am a mask, an ornament, a prized possession, no more, made for the King's pleasure, to dispose of as he wills! If Arthur regarded me so, or Lancelot, I should throw myself into the Lake of Avalon and have it over! Dear God! I have thought so often, if I were plain and men did not admire me, how simple and how easy life would be! Even you, Elaine, who have known me from childhood, do not know me. *And to find that this is why!* Sweet Mary! What I would not give to be judged by words and deeds and not by my face!" I stopped, gulping, forcing back the tears. Elaine had covered her ears and was not even listening.

"I have done nothing," I said slowly, "to deserve such treatment at your hands. I have loved you as a sister. You have shared my bed, Elaine, and shared my pillow talk. These things I cannot forget. For your treachery, which grieves me to my heart, I banish you from court. I will send you back to Alyse and Pellinore as soon as arrangements can be made, and perhaps you can find a husband in some corner kingdom of Wales."

"Guinevere." She looked up, and I saw her swollen, puffy face and reddened eyes. "Do you not love Lancelot?"

I sat suddenly upon the bed, trembling. "You know I do."

"Then why do you throw away the only chance you will ever have to wed him? I have done you a great service, if you but knew it."

"Because," I said slowly, "it would dishonor Arthur. I don't know if I can explain it to you, Elaine. Without Arthur, Lancelot and I would not be who we are. The love we bear each other is—is also love for the King. I can't say it any plainer. But I knew it—we both knew it—back in Melwas' cabin when he found me all alone, and we could so easily—how easily!—have been lovers. Don't you see, Elaine? You talk about honor, but I don't believe you know what it is."

She sank to the floor once more, utterly defeated. "You cannot have them both," she mumbled. "It isn't fair."

"I will send for your parents," I said at length.

"Please, Gwen," she cried piteously, huddled on the floor, "please let me stay until the solstice. And send me home by escort. My father will be so angry to learn I have displeased you! Let me stay at court just until then."

"Displeased me? Elaine, you have betrayed me."

She shivered but did not deny it any longer.

"I should have you whipped. Melwas, your dupe, must take his punishment publicly, like it or not. It is not fair that you should escape so lightly. But—but you were once dear to me, Elaine, and I cannot forget it. You may stay until the solstice celebrations are over. The next day you must leave. But there is one condition." The sly smugness that had crept across her features slowly faded, and she waited in fear. She had some new plan afoot already, I saw, and my only thought was to protect the King.

"You will not come within sight or speech of the King or of myself. You shall take all your meals in your rooms. If either of us so much as sees your face, you are gone."

She blanched at that, but I saw relief in her face. "You are cruel," she whimpered, but she put no feeling in it. Her mind was already somewhere else.

"Go now. Tell Ailsa I will speak with Alissa."

So Elaine left, I thought forever. With Alissa I made arrangements for her confinement and surveillance.

Melwas was formally charged in the Round Hall with kidnapping the Queen and was bidden to show himself in three days' time in the Council chamber to answer the charge, else the High King would declare war against him and confiscate his lands.

I was worried about Lancelot's safety, but the King was not, which reassured me. When he met me before hall that night to take me into the feast, he asked after Elaine, and I told him what had happened and what I had done.

"My poor Gwen. I see you have suffered. I can imagine the kind of things she said."

"I did not know she had it in her."

"Sometimes those closest are the last to know. What will you do with her?"

"I will send her back to Wales after the solstice."

"Three weeks? That is generous indeed."

"She begged me so piteously to stay for that. And I could not forget what we have been."

He smiled. "You are kindhearted. Don't tell me she wants to celebrate our anniversary with us. She must have another reason. Look she does not take advantage of your lenience."

"In truth, my lord," I said slowly, "I do not want to send her back to Wales. It would break poor Pellinore's heart, and Alyse would never forgive her. If I know Elaine, in three weeks she will get herself a husband, and when she leaves, it will not be in disgrace. Pellinore and Alyse will be deceived, but you and I and Elaine will know the truth. I care not if she escapes public disgrace, so long as I never see her again."

He regarded me with approval. "A shrewd observation, Guinevere. Well done. Though but a girl, you are a diplomat."

"I am twenty, my lord!" I protested, grinning, pleased by his praise. "As old as you were when you married me. Did you think yourself a boy at this age, after six years as King?"

He laughed and slipped an arm about my waist. "But you are ageless, Gwen. Merlin says it is your fate. You will be as young at forty as you are today. You are my child Queen."

A childless queen was closer to the truth, I thought, but I did not speak it for Arthur's sake.

18 ✹ the traitor

Three days later King Melwas of the Summer Country rode into Camelot with a force of armed men and Lancelot. He was received by Kay and escorted to the Round Hall where he sat in the Chair of Complaint opposite the King. Bedwyr later told me everything that happened, sparing no details, for I was wild to know.

In response to the King's accusation of abduction, Melwas said he had rescued me when my horse slipped on the muddy bank and, hearing no one else about, had taken me to a hunting cabin where he could attend me. He had had no servant, but had dried my wet clothing and fed me with his own hands, and was on his way to Avalon to fetch attendants and a barge when Arthur had sailed into the estuary.

"Liar!" Lancelot cried, struggling to his feet. "You were still on the island when the ships were sighted! Your confederate signaled you from shore!"

"What confederate?" Melwas demanded.

"And it was no hunting cabin, my lord," Lancelot persisted, who did not wish to accuse the lady Seulte without proofs of her guilt, "but furnished with furs and wine and gilded candlesticks! He had prepared the place, my lord! He had planned to bring her there!"

The Companions muttered among themselves, watching Arthur's stony face and waiting for Melwas' reply.

Melwas rose. "You lie, Lancelot. I never touched the Queen. And the place is a ramshackle cabin, nothing more. Come, my lords all, and I will show it to you."

"No doubt it is so now!" Lancelot shouted. "You have had plenty of time to put it back to rights! But it was not thus the night of your arrival, my lord King! I was there!"

"Yes," Melwas sneered, his voice gone dangerously soft. "Let us not forget that you were there." He lifted a hand and signaled to his servant, who brought up a canvas satchel. Melwas faced Arthur boldly. "While I was gone for help, my lord," he said coolly, "this ardent hothead broke in upon the Queen." He reached into the satchel and brought forth an armful of wrinkled sheets, foul with bloodstains and reeking with old wine. "I found these on the bed the morning after. I swear by Llyr, by Lluden, by Bilis, by the Great Goddess herself, that I was not the one between these sheets! But I can tell you who was." He turned to Lancelot and snarled, "If there was rape done, sir, you did it! You are the one who was wounded and bleeding—you are the one who was there when I was gone, all alone with the Queen!" He whirled toward Arthur. "He has loved her beyond all sense for years, my lord King. It's about time you knew it. And here is proof he has betrayed you!" He raised high the bloody sheets; the Companions sat stunned; Arthur shot to his feet, gray-faced. Lancelot's strangled shriek rent the silence. He threw himself right across the Round Table at Melwas and caught him by the throat.

"Devil! Fiend! Liar! I shall have your life, you filthy blackguard!" Melwas crashed to the floor with Lancelot atop him, a wild man, raging incoherently, blind to his surroundings. Thank God Arthur banned all weapons from the Council chamber, or murder would have followed! The Companions came to their senses and pulled Lancelot away, holding Melwas back while the two men cursed and shouted at one another. Finally Arthur called for silence.

Lancelot fell to his knees, gasping in pain. "Arthur, Arthur, my most sovereign lord! I am innocent of his accusation! I swear it by the blood of Christ!"

Arthur came to where Lancelot knelt and extended his hand. "Rise, Lancelot. I know you are free of that sin. Neither you nor the Queen could hide it from me."

In the complete silence that followed his words, Melwas threw his glove upon the Round Table. "I will not be called a liar without redress! Arthur of Britain, I challenge you to make good your accusation! Meet me on a field of honor, on the day of your choosing. I will show you what justice is."

No one in the room dared to breathe. Lancelot kissed Arthur's ring and clutched his hand. "Let me fight him, Arthur! I can take him, wound and all! Oh, please, my lord! Let me clear her name!"

Arthur, as cold and pale as a stone carving, shrugged free of his grip. "On what grounds? The Queen's honor is mine to avenge." He turned to Melwas. "I accept the challenge, Melwas. On the morrow I will meet you. The Queen accuses you of her abduction. And I accuse you of slandering her good name. Kay, see to it."

Melwas bowed, satisfied, and strode out of the Council chamber. Then pandemonium broke loose. The Companions crowded around Arthur, all talking at once, protesting against the outrageous suggestion that the High King should put his person in jeopardy to satisfy the honor of such a scoundrel. Each of them beseeched the King to let him fight in the King's place. When the bedlam passed its height, the King answered them.

"I thank all my brave Companions for your offers. But I ask you to think what you would do, if you were I. The Queen's honor is mine to avenge. And no one else's."

Bedwyr wrote two songs about this Council meeting and what came after. The true tale he wrote for Arthur; but the other he wrote for Lancelot. Lancelot could not forgive himself for Melwas' accusing me of adultery in public; he was certain that it was his injury which prevented Arthur from allowing him to fight. To soothe his tormented spirit, Bedwyr remade the story to his liking and sang of Lancelot's great rage in Council, and his great defeat of Melwas in single combat; how he split his brains with a swordstroke and rid the Kingdom of an evil scourge. Lancelot delighted to hear it, and indeed, it was much the prettier song, although it was fiction. In later years I heard it retold by young men as if it were truth, but no one who ever knew Arthur thought so.

Everyone, myself included, was horrified that he should put himself at risk, but to Arthur it was a kind of a relief to be fighting again. His dislike of Melwas went deep, but more than that, he desired to show himself a warrior again after years of patient statesmanship as King. There were many young soldiers who had never seen the King's sword Excalibur lifted from its hanger in the Round Hall. To them the Sword of Britain was a symbol, for they could not remember the hard years of fighting, when Excalibur was raised against the Saxon terror, always victorious. So perhaps, I thought, it was a wise move. But it also brought the King joy.

The day dawned cloudy and cool, with the promise of rain. Every citizen of Camelot turned out to watch the King defend my honor; from the turrets I could see the press of people as they hurried through the streets, past closed shops and empty marketplace, to join the assembled throng at the Contest Field beyond the town. I spent the morning watching from the southeast tower, most of the time on my knees praying God to spare the life of my lord.

What Britain would do without him I could not conceive. The banners that usually flew so gaily over Camelot hung limply in the still, unmoving air. I feared we would have a thunderstorm before the day was out. It was a good day to die, I thought suddenly, and then crossed myself quickly.

Shaken, I descended to my quarters to await escort to the field. All the women were going, except Elaine. Alone of my household, I did not wish to go. But I had no choice. I was the cause of this disaster and must show my face. "Sweet Mary," I prayed, "save me from such arrogance again! That I should put my lord in jeopardy!" It was unbearable.

Lancelot came for me at noon, in a black humor, followed by a group of Companions to escort the women. The ride from Ynys Witrin and his attack on Melwas had inflamed his leg, and he walked with a stout staff and leaned upon my arm, but he was determined to go. Slowly we filed out of the palace and through the streets of the town toward the field, while people stared openly at us and made reverences.

He stumped along beside me, muttering under his breath, making no attempt at civility.

"I owe you thanks for your defense of me in Council," I ventured. "Bedwyr told me of Melwas' denial and your quick response. I am grateful, Lancelot, and not for the first time, you hold my honor so dear."

"Do not speak of it, I pray you," he retorted. "It is my fault Melwas had the courage to accuse you. Had I caught the lying bastard, had I not blundered around so—"

"Blundered!" I cried. "Is that what you call it? You rescued me from a fate I could not have borne! You insult me to think so little of it!"

That startled him out of his selfish sulks, and he looked at me quickly. "I did not mean it that way, Gwen. Surely you know my heart. But Melwas accused me—boldly accused me before Arthur himself and all the Companions—of the one sin I dread committing—"

"Arthur knew it was a lie."

"Yes, but—" His voice sank to a whisper and began to shake. "—it so nearly wasn't."

"Don't, I pray you. You are guiltless, and Arthur knows it."

"He accused me outright, and I cannot make him pay for it! Oh, God, I would give my right arm to fight him!" He clutched his sword hilt in distress. "But I must sit by helplessly while Arthur clears your name!"

"Lancelot," I said evenly. "He is my husband. It is his right."

"But—"

"Who do you think sent me to you on Ynys Witrin? Who has put your well-being first, at every step, before his own? He knows what he owes you."

"But I—"

"I pray you will be sensible! This public display is the best way to put things right between us all. He must do it."

"But, Gwen, I—"

"For the love of God!" I cried, clutching his arm. "Stop thinking about yourself and think of Arthur! King Melwas is twice his size!"

"Why, Guinevere!" Lancelot suddenly exclaimed. "You are shaking like a leaf in a storm! Surely you do not fear for the King?"

"Of course I do! Don't you?"

He looked amused. "Fear for Arthur? No, indeed. He cannot lose."

"How can you know that? He is mortal flesh, like other men."

"He will not lose to Melwas." He spoke with certainty. "Melwas knows the truth behind his lies. In his heart he expects to be defeated. He expects to die."

"May his expectations be fulfilled."

"Amen to that." Lancelot grunted. "Besides, if today were Arthur's deathday, Merlin would know of it and be here. But as you see, he is absent, so all is well." As he spoke the word "deathday" he crossed himself, and I shivered.

"You believe in the magic of the Sword, then? Well, so you should, I suppose. You have seen it used enough."

"Aye, it has saved me more than once from a Saxon ax. But he will not wield Excalibur today."

"What!" I stopped so suddenly he almost lost his balance, and only just saved himself from falling. "Not Excalibur? What madness is this?"

Lancelot saw my great distress and spoke with patience. "The Sword is meant to preserve Britain from her enemies. Melwas is a Briton himself. He—"

"He is an enemy of Arthur's," I said hotly, "and Arthur is Britain!"

Lancelot's mouth twitched in an effort to keep from grinning. "No one denies it. Relax just a little. Your fingers will leave bruises on my arm."

"I beg pardon," I said blushing, releasing my grip. "I am—not myself today. I had a premonition of disaster this morning and cannot shake the fear."

"Come, let us go on. We are holding up the others, and people are staring. Do not fear for Arthur, Gwen. He is twice the swordsman Melwas is, whatever sword he holds in his hand."

"And twice the rider, as well."

"Ahhh, well," Lancelot demurred, and I looked at him sharply. "What are you going to tell me now?" I cried. "Will they not fight on horseback?"

"It is already arranged, Gwen, you can do nothing about it. Arthur knows Melwas has no horses that compare to his own. We have bred them for ten years, and he catches his loose in the hills."

"He felt it would be unfair," I finished bitterly. "What has fairness got to do with it? This is revenge. I am surprised he does not tie one hand behind his back to compensate for his greater skill."

Lancelot said nothing, and gradually my temper cooled and I saw the injustice of my protest. Lancelot read my thoughts perfectly.

"His victory must be earned," he said slowly. "It is important for his honor in the eyes of the people, as well as in his own eyes. To make use of all the advantages he has would ill become him. It must be a fair fight."

"But Melwas is so big. And he is brave. I heard him say things that let me know he was not afraid of Arthur."

"Bravado. It is easy to be brave with one's lips."

"Yet he dared to take me."

"His lust was greater than his fear." He looked quickly away, and I knew what he was thinking. He was ever quick to condemn himself.

"Love is not lust," I murmured softly.

"Thank you, Gwen."

We walked in silence until the field came into view. A small pavilion had been built at one end of the field, with a dais for chairs and an awning above. Here was where the King and his household sat to watch the contests during celebrations throughout the year. The steps up to the platform were narrow, and as Lancelot bade me precede him, I was first upon the dais. The crowds broke into wild cheering and stomping, raising their arms in the air. Vainly I looked about for Arthur, but could not see him.

Lancelot, come up behind me, said, "Gwen, they are cheering for you."

Amazed, I looked upon the people. "The Queen! The Queen!"

they cried. Their faces were raised to me in joy, and their eyes
were alight. I felt both uplifted and unworthy, and bowed my head
and made them a deep reverence. The cheering only increased,
and I turned to Lancelot helplessly.

"What do they want of me? I know not what to do."

"They just want to look at you. You are dear to them, and they
nearly lost you. It is the way the King feels, too. And I."

I took my seat, my ladies filed in and sat on either side. Kay
stood behind me, and Lancelot sat in the King's empty chair as
his proxy while he was on the field. The Companions took their
places guarding the pavilion. When all was ready, the noise gradually subsided. From opposite ends of the field the combatants
suddenly appeared, each accompanied by his second, bearing
arms. Arthur wore his fighting armor, thick leather leggings and
boots, a heavy leather tunic studded with brass, and a leather hel-
met with a gold crown across the brow. That Melwas could look
at him and not bend his knee defied belief. Melwas, who loved a
rich display, was dressed as simply. He had come to fight.

Bedwyr and Arthur approached the center of the field. When
Melwas and his second came up, the King spoke, but we were too
distant to hear his words. Melwas' reply was short. Then he
turned to his second and grasped his sword and short dagger. Arthur turned to Bedwyr and did the same. Then the seconds left the
field, and Arthur faced Melwas alone.

A great roar went up from the assembled throng, and the two
men began circling, like rival dogs over a bitch in heat. I gripped
Lancelot's arm.

"Is there no way to stop this?" I whispered frantically.

He glanced at me swiftly. "He is your husband. It is his right."

"Damn you!" I gasped. "And may God protect him!"

"Amen. Relax, Gwen. See how they feint and dodge? He is
taking Melwas' measure."

And Melwas was taking his, I thought, but did not say it.
Growing up in a household among five brothers, I had seen plenty
of fights, but none between such skilled swordsmen. Pellinore's
men had been better trained, but their swordplay was only in practice. Never before had I seen two men face each other with the intent to kill. The difference in their styles was apparent before
either scored a stroke. Arthur moved with grace and assurance
and an inborn sense of timing. Melwas lunged with a boldness
born of rage or desperation. He was nearly twice Arthur's size,
and much the slower of the two, but any stroke that landed was
capable of killing.

Each man gripped his sword, feinting, swinging, blocking each other's strokes. It was slow, this testing, getting a feel of the weapon and the opponent. It ended suddenly. Melwas feinted one way and lunged another. Arthur dodged but fell back. The crowd roared, and I gripped Lancelot's hand. Melwas pressed his attack, swinging ferociously, always advancing. Arthur sidestepped him, first one way and then another, but always retreating. They were getting farther from us, but I could hear Melwas' loud grunts of effort.

"What is he doing?" I cried.

"Watch now," Lancelot said, his eyes never leaving his King. "He will turn him in a minute. This is child's play."

Melwas raised his sword once more, and Arthur ducked under it and ran past. Melwas whirled in fury.

Lancelot chuckled. "Did you see that?"

"I see no humor in it. The man could kill him."

"He could, Gwen, but he won't."

I wished I had his calm. Immediately Melwas' tactics changed. He feinted toward the King's body, then chopped swiftly from the side, shortening his backstroke so his movements were harder to read. Arthur matched him stroke for stroke, blocking his thrust and being himself blocked. Once or twice they locked swords and came face to face. I saw Arthur's lips moving and could not guess what words he had to say to Melwas, there in the middle of the field. Melwas' sheer weight bore the King down, and they advanced toward us. Suddenly Melwas leaped sideways with surprising swiftness and swung upward. I gasped aloud. Arthur proved as agile, avoiding the stroke with a twisting of his body as he jumped toward Melwas and knocked the sword away just shy of his hip.

"Dear God," I whispered, but Lancelot was excited.

"Did you see that? I taught him that move, but he has never done it so well with me. He must have been practicing."

"Lancelot, this is not a game!" I cried in earnest, and for my sake he recovered his gravity. And so they went, back and forth and in circles around the field, with the people shouting encouragement, and Melwas always the aggressor. To ease my fears, Lancelot told me about the sword the King fought with, how it was made here in Camelot by a swordsman from the far north, a man of great skill who could fashion a living blade from cold iron in four days. But he had worked a month on the King's weapon. The blade was supple and strong, heated by the hottest fires and chilled in water just melted from ice blocks cut in midwinter and stored carefully in straw. The grip was made for the King's hand and none other. The smith swore if the blade ever chipped or cracked, the King might kill him with the remnant. Lancelot succeeded in distracting me for a while, and when I returned my attention to the fight, I noted that the pace had picked up considerably and that Melwas was getting angry.

"He thinks the King is playing with him," I said at a guess. Lancelot did not reply, and when I glanced at him I saw him looking worriedly at the leaden sky. "What's wrong?"

He shrugged. "I hope it does not rain."

"Why?"

"The footing will be slippery."

"Will that favor one or the other?"

"It often favors the heavier man. Oh, no, Gwen, forgive me! I should not have spoken. Look how Melwas is tiring. That is why he presses. Melwas is past thirty and fond of good living. The King is fit. Please don't worry."

But it was too late for reassurance. I watched in agony while the strokes got short and vicious. Arthur drew first blood, a glancing cut on Melwas' upper arm. Enraged, Melwas struck out blindly, and the very unpredictability of his attack made him dangerous. Blood flowed freely from his wound and wet the ground. Dodging, the King's foot slipped, and Melwas' sword came down. I believe I cried out. Lancelot half rose from his seat. The crowd gasped as one man. But Arthur rolled away, and the blow landed spent in the muddy grass, just grazing his arm. Melwas' sword stuck for a moment in the turf, pinned by the weight of his downstroke, and the King leaped to his feet, sword raised. The people roared, ready for the kill. But Arthur only pointed his blade at Melwas' heart and spoke to him.

"What is he about?" Lancelot cried, finally as fearful as I was. "Finish him, Arthur, before the rain!"

Melwas freed his sword and backed away, crossing the King's blade. He shouted something defiant, and I saw Arthur's shoulders stiffen. Then the King went on the attack, but Melwas gave no ground. Thunder rumbled menacingly, and the crowd grew uneasy. Arthur worked hard, but Melwas fought in fear of his life and was as quick. There was blood on the King's sleeve. "It's not his sword arm," Lancelot said, as if that should comfort me. Both men were tiring. Melwas used his weight to lean against the King, knowing he could not support it for long. I began to cry, silently, helplessly. Then Melwas tripped him. Lancelot leaped to his feet, shouting, and all the Companions drew their swords. It was the act of a coward, and base. Melwas had to be desperate. The King went down, but as he fell he kicked out at Melwas' sword hand, and his blade flew wide. Melwas drew his dagger and threw it.

"Bedwyr!" Lancelot yelled. "To him!"

Bedwyr was already running onto the field. The dagger caught Arthur in the shoulder, and as his blood soaked through his tunic, the people cried out in dismay. To the astonishment of all, including Melwas, Arthur pulled himself to his knees and pointed his sword at his attacker. The big man stepped back quickly, too quickly, and one foot slipped a pace in the bloody grass. In that moment the King was on his feet, his sword at Melwas' throat. Every person watching held his breath. But again the King forbore to kill him and spoke instead. Melwas was now weaponless, defeated, and he listened. When the King finished speaking, Melwas nodded slowly and sank to one knee. The crowd screamed wildly for an execution, but they were disappointed, for it was an act of submission to authority, and as such it was accepted. Arthur laid the flat of his blade upon Melwas' shoulders and spoke the ritual words that bound a vassal to his liege lord. The whole time he did this, the hilt of Melwas' dagger stuck out straight from his tunic, and I wept to see it. I did not know, having always had a horror of hospitals, that it was only safe to leave it thus; it was in the removal of the weapon that life was threatened.

The King put out a hand to Melwas and raised him, then suddenly staggered. Melwas lifted him in his great arms and carried him off the field. The crowd parted nervously and let them pass. Lancelot's face went white as Melwas approached the pavilion with the unconscious King. The Companions surrounded him, swords drawn, but Melwas ignored them. He looked up at Lancelot.

"Where shall I take my lord?" he asked. "He needs attention."

The people who heard let out a great cheer, and others took it up. Lancelot's sigh of relief came from his soul.

"Follow Bedwyr, King Melwas. Kay will call the physicians." The clouds opened then, and the rain fell in a sheet, but no one noticed.

It is a fact that Melwas, having put the dagger in the King, waited by his bedside until he had recovered from its removal. Then he gathered his troops around him and went home in honor. From that day forward, he was Arthur's loyal ally, and his strongest supporter in the southwest. He would hear no word against the King, and men learned to watch their tongues in his presence. He never looked at me again.

Late that night, when the physicians were finished and the King lay wrapped in bandages and resting, Lancelot and I were allowed to go into him. He had been given a posset of some healing drug with a sedative and was sleepy.

Instead of congratulating Arthur on his victory, Lancelot was hot with indignation. "Why did you let him off? You had him, three times, and let him go. He might have killed you."

Arthur grinned. "It's good to see you again, too." Lancelot threw up his hands and turned away to hide his emotion. But I did not have to hide mine.

"Arthur!" I knelt near his head, and he reached for me with his good arm.

"Hello, Gwen. You have been crying."

I nodded and kissed his hand, unable to speak.

"Has she not!" Lancelot exclaimed. "All the world knows now where her heart lies." Then his expression softened, and he regarded Arthur with outright admiration. "What a King you are! With this day's work you have turned an enemy into an ally and set to rest the rumors that have been flying about the Kingdom. I congratulate you."

"It's about time." Arthur smiled, and yawned. "I made use of everything you taught me, did I not? And he never meant to kill me, or he would not have thrown so wide."

Lancelot shook his head, then came up to the bedside. "It was well done," he said gruffly.

They talked awhile about fighting strategy, while I held his hand and silently prayed my thanks to God. At length the King fell asleep, and Lancelot rose. He met my eyes.

"I will stay with him awhile," I said softly.

He nodded and went to the door, where he turned and looked back at Arthur, his eyes full of worship. "There is a King," he said.

19 ✷ The Solstice

Arthur's shoulder and Lancelot's knee healed together over the next weeks. By the solstice they were whole. All of Camelot was busy during this time, making preparations for the great day of celebration. The summer solstice had been a sacred day, time out of mind, and the people of Britain had not given up this feast day as the Christian God drove out the worship of older deities. Since the King and I had been married on this day, the bishop sanctified it as a holy day, and now Christian and pagan alike joined in the celebrations. Lords and ladies from all over Britain came to Camelot, if they could, and set up their tents, or built pavilions, on the open fields.

There were to be contests of skill and daring among the men, a few knights who had earned it would be admitted to the ranks of the King's Companions, and of course there would be horseracing. Competition among the women was less formal, perhaps, but no less desperately waged. Married ladies displayed their fine clothes, magnificent jewels, and their daughters before one another. Maids vied for the attentions of young men. It was well known that any man, feeling amorous, had only to walk down the lane of pavilions to find his needs relieved. Many maids got husbands in this way, I am ashamed to say.

To my surprise, Elaine had still not married. She had been kept close, it is true, but not without opportunity to make contact with men. I was careful to stay out of the women's quarters for many hours each day, that she might gain some freedom. But when I questioned her guards, I found she had not stirred from her quarters the entire three weeks, and this amazed me. Apparently she preferred to go home in disgrace than to wed a man who was not High King. I could have told her that it might be worth the risk, that sometimes love came after, but she would not have listened to me, in any event.

I tried to pump Ailsa for news, since she knew Grannic well, but all she could discover was that Elaine sang to herself and stitched. That she sang boded ill; either she must be mad, or she had some scheme afoot. But why did she stitch? I had set her no tasks. I directed Ailsa to find out what it was she worked upon. But Grannic did not know. Whenever she was with Elaine, she stitched upon innocent things, cushions and such. But on the few occasions when Grannic surprised her, she was at work upon something quite different, which was always quickly hidden. Grannic knew nothing about it, save that it was blue.

I gave up trying to discover Elaine's plans and attended to my duties as hostess to all the folk who daily arrived in Camelot. Everyone had to be greeted and made to feel welcome, even though many came only to beg favors of the King. Arthur and I spent a good part of every day in audience with new guests. And most nights he spent in council with his Companions, since it was the only time he had for serious talk. This daily routine grew dull and difficult to bear, for I had to smile and curtsy and mouth courtesies and be stared at openly by strangers. But I bore it because Arthur stood beside me and bore it, as well. His recent victory over Melwas made him glamorous in everyone's eyes, and he was followed everywhere by admirers. We both began to look forward to the solstice as to the end of captivity.

Lancelot spent most of his time in the stables, overseeing the final training of the King's entries in the races. I went often to watch, or to visit Zephyr in her paddock. She was a valued broodmare now, having borne four foals to Nestor. The eldest was the fastest horse in the King's stables, and on him was Lancelot's full attention focused. But I liked to stand at the fence and watch Zephyr and the other mares graze in idle content, while this year's crop of foals romped and played about them. One mare, a chestnut, was barren. Usually such mares were kept apart, because they were nasty to the foals and bullied the other mares. But this mare had been accepted because she loved the foals and always watched after them, herding them away from danger, breaking up fights, leading them to their dams when they could not find their way. Whenever a mare was lost in labor, she was given the foal to raise. Her name was Netta. In the three years I had known her, I had never seen any sign of temper in her. She was loved by the broodmares and foals alike. I had brought Zephyr an apple from the orchards, but on second thought, I split it and offered half to

Netta. She took it from me gently and nuzzled me in thanks. I laughed and pushed her away.

"You have a good time, don't you, my girl. Your days are busy and your work is important. You have kept your figure, too. You are content."

Lancelot came over while I was scratching her ears, and patted her kindly. "Good old Netta. I may have found a home for her at last. One of Gereint's sisters—"

"No!" I cried involuntarily. He looked at me strangely, and I blushed. "I beg your pardon. I did not mean to shout."

"What's the matter, Gwen?"

"Is there another mare that would do for Gereint's sister?"

"I suppose, but why? Netta is not needed here."

"But she is! Just because she cannot breed—have you noticed how she cares for the foals? How all the mares trust her? How they do not fight among themselves when she's about? She is the most valuable mare in the stable, if you but knew it. Don't think her worthless just because she cannot breed. I—I have taken a fancy to her, besides."

Very kindly he stepped closer and took my hands in his. There were tears in the corners of his eyes. "Then she shall stay. I had no idea."

"Do not pity me!" I hissed, my face hot. He took me in his arms, there in the open air, with the eyes of others upon us.

"Indeed I do not. But it breaks my heart."

I laid my head on his shoulder and wept. Why I could share my grief with Lancelot and worked hard to hide it from Arthur, I did not know. Except that my failure was not betrayal to Lancelot.

At length I stilled myself, and when I looked up all the grooms had vanished. Lancelot produced a handkerchief and wiped the tears from my face.

"Let time pass," he said gently. "All wounds heal with time."

"Thank you, Lancelot. I—I am not usually so close to tears. It must be the strain of preparations. Please do not tell Arthur. It would worry him."

"I do not talk to Arthur about you. You are the one subject we avoid. By mutual consent."

"May God forgive me. I never meant to come between you. I *must* not come between you. Don't let it happen, Lancelot, I pray you."

He kissed my forehead lightly. "It cannot be helped, Gwen. But the trust stands."

How recently had I heard those very words from Arthur's lips?

* * *

When finally the day arrived, it was glorious. The sun shone in a clear, deep sky and the breeze blew steady and cool. It was one of those days that June is famous for.

Arthur crept into my room at dawn, still dressed, and woke me up. "Good morning, Gwen. Day is dawning."

I yawned and stretched, and finally opened my eyes. "What, are you up already, my lord?"

"I have not yet been to bed. There was no time. I had a messenger late last night from Lothian."

I sat up. "Not Tydwyl? Surely he can handle the remnants of Aguisel's supporters?"

"Not Tydwyl," he said with a smile, and then changed the subject abruptly. "I have come about something else. Kay—"

"Is it so important it cannot wait?" I broke in, smiling, taking his hand and drawing it to my lips.

His face flushed, and he hesitated, then leaned down swiftly and kissed me. "I only wish it could. Ah, Gwen, how little time we've had!"

"It will be over shortly."

"Tonight," he said with fervor, and then straightened. "I was bidden to awaken you. Kay tells me Alyse and Pellinore are camped outside Glaston and are on their way here. What do you want to do about Elaine?"

It was the first time in three weeks he had mentioned her name. I met his eyes. "I will have to tell them. When do they arrive?"

"It shouldn't be much later than midday. You sent for them?"

"Indeed, no. I did not, at Elaine's request. They must be arriving in all innocence. Has Pellinore sent you no message?"

"Only one of greeting and congratulations in the ordinary way."

"Oh, dear. Well, it must be done. Have Kay send them to me when they arrive."

"Bravely done. I will." He paused, half turned to leave, and gave me a long, appraising look.

"The way you look now," he said roughly, "unbrushed and just awakened—five years seems a moment in time."

Then he turned on his heel and was gone.

I gathered up my courage and went to see Elaine. I had feared she would beg leave to be granted her freedom for the day, for her parents' sake, but to my surprise she flatly refused to see them.

"Tell them what you like," she said defiantly. "I will not see them. Say I am ill, or dead. It matters not to me."

"How not? You will go back with them tomorrow, alive and healthy."

Her lips drew back, but it was more a snarl than a smile. "We shall see."

I left her with foreboding in my heart, but even if I had had the time to think about it, I never would have guessed what she had planned.

The morning we spent in church, dressed in our finest clothes of white and gold, adorned with all the trimmings we possessed. Arthur wore his crown, and I wore mine. The bishop blessed us and led all the people in prayers for our happiness and increase. Arthur squeezed my hand, and it took some of the sting from the words. Then we filed out in great procession, with all the lords and ladies following, through the streets of Camelot to the field pavilion. There we sat all afternoon, watching the competitions. Kay had had the cooks busy for days roasting boar and deer in the fire pits, and stewing fowls in great cauldrons over open fires. All afternoon, as the games continued, servants passed meat and drink among the assembled throng, so that all partook of the King's meal. This was a special honor; for only a few hundred could be invited to the feast that night, and in this way Arthur made everyone part of his household. Kay had excelled himself. The food was excellent, the sauces rich. When he finally joined us midway through the afternoon, I complimented him well.

"And if you do not water the wine better," I told him, laughing, "there will not be a man left standing for the King's feast tonight."

He grinned. "Thank you, my lady. I will see to it. The lady Elaine has sent me to ask if she may be permitted to celebrate the day with a skin of wine. She also begs forgiveness for her rudeness of the morning." He said this without expression, for I knew his opinion of Elaine. He had offered for her once, long ago, and her rejection had not been polite.

"You may send it to her, Kay. Unwatered. Perhaps it is best. She leaves Camelot in the morning."

"It is arranged. King Pellinore and Queen Alyse have just arrived, my lady, and have set up their tent in the lane. The King told me I was to bring them to you. Will you see them here, or shall I conduct them to the meeting room?"

I glanced across at Arthur, who was intent upon the contest. "Bring them here, if you please. Let us hope the games engage them."

We made room upon the platform for two more, and when

Alyse and Pellinore arrived I greeted them warmly. Pellinore gave me a bear hug, and Alyse a warm kiss of greeting. They were thrilled with the honor of sitting in the King's pavilion, and I did my best to make them comfortable with food and wine. Pellinore was instantly absorbed in the games; it was Alyse who asked after her daughter.

"Alas, madam, she is not feeling well. She begged to be excused from having visitors today. You may see her in the morning."

Alyse looked at me sharply but said nothing. She had known me from a child and could read my face, but if she scented a lie, she held her tongue. Grateful for her discretion, I turned the conversation to the state of things in Wales.

"I bring you grave tidings from Northgallis, Guinevere," Alyse said slowly. "Your brother King Gwarthgydd has lost his wife and daughters to a plague." She touched my hand lightly. "Do not grieve for him, my dear, for he does not grieve much himself. He is already betrothed to the King of Powys' daughter, a match he ought to have made in the first place, years ago."

"Indeed, I grieve for Gwillim, who has lost his mother and his sisters! This plague, Alyse, this is the first I've heard of it! Is it widespread?"

"No," she replied with a lift of her eyebrow. "'It has affected no one else, even in Northgallis. I have even heard that they died of a curse, and not a plague." I gasped, and her eyes narrowed. "You know something of this, then?"

"No!" I said quickly, "indeed, I do not! And I do not believe people can die from curses!"

She smiled. "May you never cross a druid, and learn differently." Then, as if to atone for this remark, she crossed herself quickly and turned the subject herself. She had heard something of my abduction, and the King's fight with Melwas, and asked carefully about it. I told her what was already common knowledge, but made no mention of Elaine's part in it. I don't know why I put off telling her; cowardice, I suppose, for they would have to know by morning. But in my heart I still expected Elaine to do something to prevent the need of it. If Alyse noticed my uneasiness, she had the grace not to comment on it. Nor did she comment, as had many others, on my slim and youthful figure, cloaking condemnation in words of praise. For this I was doubly grateful and took trouble to answer her questions and talk with her awhile.

At length the horseracing began, and Alyse retired with most of the women, as the crowds grew rowdy. I was one of the few who stayed. There were seven heats, thrice around the field outside the flags, and then the final race between the seven winners. Zephyr's colt won going away, for he had foreign blood in him, but it was a good race, and well ridden. Lancelot was proud of the jockey, a lad of eleven he had personally trained, and of course he was proud of the colt, for whose bloodlines he was alone responsible. The King honored him before the throng, presenting him a new sword with jeweled hilt, made by the smith who made the King's weapons. Lancelot was speechless, and I smiled with joy to see the two men clasp each other so warmly, while the crowd of people shouted and cheered.

We walked back to the castle, the three of us together, arm in arm. It was one of the happiest moments of my life; I knew it then.

We had two hours to rest before the feast, and I bade Ailsa bathe me and comb out my hair. I heard the King in his room and hoped he might come in, but then I heard Lancelot's voice, as well, and knew they were in close conference. I took myself out to my terrace and sang softly while the light slowly faded from the sky, and Ailsa lovingly brushed my hair. At length, when I came in to take my rest, I heard no more voices and thought they were gone. But they had both been listening. For when I had lain quietly awhile, I heard them talking again, but softly, so as not to wake me. Two such noble men! Where else on earth could their like be found?"

At the hour of lamp lighting Ailsa awakened me and shook out my new gown. This had been cut from a bolt of heavy silk Arthur had imported from the East as a Christmas gift. It was a bewitching color, a rich sapphire blue with crimson threads woven in, and in lamplight had a sheen the color of amethysts. I had cut the cloth myself and set my women to work upon it. The lines were simple and straight, with no fancy work or trimmings. I had stitched the bodice myself in purple thread, so the design of interlocking dragons was visible only in lamplight, and even then only at close range. For it was meant to compliment the giver. Arthur had never seen it. Tonight was to be the first time of wearing it.

Ailsa held it out before her and chuckled. "If I were half the size I am, my lady, I could not wear it. It's cut so slim it looks made for a boy."

"Ailsa, ever since I can remember, you have been saying that to me."

"Yes," she said, "and ever since I've known you it's been true. At least," she continued quickly, steering away from dangerous ground, "the bodice is cut low on this one. You're too often shy of that."

"The King will like it, I wager."

"Indeed he will!" she cackled. "Bless the man, the way he looks at you!"

"*And,*" I continued firmly, "it is for evening wear. Such things are now accepted. I couldn't have worn this gown at seventeen, Ailsa. Admit it."

"I don't see why not. He'd have liked to see you in it. He's a full-blooded man, is our King, and always has been—may Bilis take me if I lie—like Uther his father. Now *there* was a man who loved women! Did I ever tell you—"

I sighed and smiled. She was off again on her favorite stories about Uther Pendragon's sexual prowess. There was nothing to be done; she always spoke so when she had had a little wine. I stood still while she dressed me and recited her lurid tales, and said silent thanks that Uther's son showed more restraint than his father. I began worrying about where Alyse and Pellinore would be seated at dinner. Ailsa sat me on a stool and began to dress my hair.

"You should see what the lady Alissa has done with the fabric you gave her," she said suddenly. "Very pretty, to my mind, it is, with trimming on the skirt and a ruffled neckline."

"Ailsa!" I shivered suddenly as a thought struck me. "Did Elaine get any of the leftover silk?"

"Why to be sure, my lady. You gave it to her with your own hands. The color does not suit her, really, her eyes are much too light."

"Do you suppose that is what she was sewing? The blue piece Grannic saw?"

"I wouldn't set much store by Grannic, my lady. She has always had trouble telling blue from green. It's my belief that Lady Elaine made a tunic from the fabric. I doubt there was enough for a gown."

"I wonder."

But I put the thought aside. What difference could it make? My distrust of Elaine had colored all my thoughts. I must forget it.

Ailsa dressed my hair without adornment, for Ygraine's crown was adornment enough. Instead of Arthur's great sapphire, I wore round my neck Ygraine's delicate choker of amethysts and river pearls. Wearing the stones brought out the dual colors in the gown, and the effect in my polished bronze delighted me.

"It's beautiful!" I cried in delight. "He will love it."

"*You* are beautiful," a voice said behind me. "And he loves it indeed."

I whirled around. "Arthur!" Ailsa dropped into a curtsy and backed out of the room.

The King stood smiling by the curtain, looking at me. "Are you flesh and blood? Or did you drop from Heaven? What magic is this!"

I colored at his compliments. "My lord, this is the fabric you gave me at Christmas. I made the gown to please you. I am glad if I succeeded."

"It's not the gown," he said, coming over to me and running a gentle finger down my neck from ear to throat. "Simple silk cannot do such things to a man."

I lowered my eyes. Ailsa, had she been there, would have recognized her Uther in his son's face at that moment. But Arthur was not Uther. He kissed me softly on my neck and stepped back.

"Would I could stop time! I came to see if you were ready. We must go down."

Mischievously I smiled up at him. "I am ready, indeed, my lord."

He spun on his heel and walked away, then turned and grinned. "You are a witch! If you tease me so, Gwen, I shall not be able to help myself. Dinner will be late, and everyone waiting. We will disgrace ourselves."

I laughed. "The great Arthur, beyond control? Perhaps I should like to see it."

His eyes blazed. "By the Bull!" he breathed. "And so you shall!" He drew a long breath and managed a smile. "Later." He returned to me and offered me his arm. "What you will do to poor Lancelot when he sees you, I dare not think. It is cruelty, you know."

It amazed me that he spoke of it. I wondered, with joy and hope, if they had come to some new close fellowship, that they could bear me between them with better ease.

I placed my hand upon his arm. "I will behave myself. Let us go down."

The hall was full when we entered, and the assembled guests rose and cheered us to our seats. The King had placed Lancelot at his right hand, in the seat of honor, while I sat on his left. Alyse and Pellinore were some way down the table, out of speaking range, to my relief. Kay had managed things beautifully. Lancelot's eyes burned like hot flames, but he was too far removed for private speech. Next to me sat Bedwyr, who was my friend. But Arthur was right, Lancelot suffered.

There was something special about that night from the beginning. It wasn't the gown, or the occasion, or the full moon, or the soft June breezes. The very air was alive with promise. It was the smile of God before the bolt was thrown.

The feast was grand and lasted long. Arthur and I went round together to the tables, greeting guests and exchanging pleasantries. When I returned to my seat, Bedwyr sighed.

"You gild the lily with a vengeance, Gwen. Forgive me, but I wish you hadn't worn that gown."

"Not you too, Bedwyr. It's only cloth."

"It's devilment, by Mithra! There's not a man in the room who isn't bewitched."

"Poppycock." I grinned. "Water your wine better, you'll be all right." Then, seeing his face: "Is there truly something amiss? The King nearly told me not to wear it."

"For Lancelot's sake, no doubt."

"Don't, Bedwyr."

He lifted his chin, like a dog testing the air. "I don't know what it is, but there's something afoot tonight."

"You feel it, too?"

He shifted uneasily. "I wish Merlin were here."

I smiled. "There we part company. I am glad he is not. He disapproves of me, you know."

But Bedwyr looked grave. "Not of you, my lady, but of your fate. His only thought, waking or sleeping, is for the King."

I gaped at him, unable to believe my ears. He had deliberately touched upon my wound! My body began to tremble, and I could not still it. "How can I change my fate, sir? Tell me, and I will do it! I would gladly change places with the ugliest slut in Britain if it would bring the King a child!"

My words seemed to ring in the hall. Heads turned. Arthur and Lancelot whipped around.

"What's going on, Bedwyr?" Arthur demanded.

"One moment, my lord." Bedwyr turned to me with quiet gravity and took my hand. "Gwen, look at me." I raised my eyes and looked at him through tears. His face was full of love, and his voice, low and gentle, spoke softly. "You know, you must know by now that it cannot be." Arthur looked hastily away and began talking to Lancelot; others followed their example and once again the hall filled with noise. "Merlin has always known it. But know this, also, that it grieves you a thousand times more than ever it grieves the King. He has no time for children. Listen, Gwen, and I will tell you a secret. Merlin told me once that it is you who will ensure his glory. That your fate, which you curse as betrayal, will leave Arthur standing alone in glory, and because of *you*, his fame will be everlasting."

I stared, wide-eyed, as he told me these things.

He smiled gently. "So you see, even this dark cloud has a gilded lining. Enjoy the King as a man and forget the rest. It is with the gods. As for Merlin—I only wish he were here because I sense something in the air tonight, and I wish the reins were in his hands."

"Everlasting?" I whispered. "Bedwyr, is it possible?"

He shrugged, suddenly shy. "With true greatness it is possible."

I felt Arthur's hand on my arm. "Enough of this. Has he upset you, Gwen? What's this about?"

I turned to him, feeling suddenly light and free of a great burden. To think that I might serve him after all! I raised a hand to his cheek and smiled into his eyes. "Upset me? No, my lord. He has given me a great gift."

He looked amazed. "I can see that he has. May I know what it is?"

I shook my head. "I don't think I can tell you."

He clasped my hand, his dark eyes glowing. "Then I will not ask. It is enough to see you look the way you look!"

Lancelot rose and lifted his goblet. "To the Queen!" he shouted.

All the people rose and cried, "The Queen!" The men stomped and cheered and drank, and I saw tears in the eyes of those ladies nearest us. What, I wondered, had gotten into everybody?

Suddenly Grannic was there with goblets of neat wine, and the King and Lancelot drank my health with it, and then I drank to theirs. There was much cheering and shouting in the hall, and it was some while before the noise died down, and the bard came on. Only then did I think it strange to see Grannic in hall. I looked about and saw her standing by the wall with the other servants. I beckoned her over. She went white as a sheet.

"Why are you here tonight, Grannic? Why are you not with your mistress?"

She curtsied low. "The lady Elaine dismissed me from her service tonight, my lady. She said she had no more need of me. I—I thought it best to obey and to help out in hall." She trembled as she spoke, and two faint pink spots appeared on her withered cheeks. She looked terrified when she saw that I did not believe her, but just then the bard began to strum his harp, and I waved her away. There was plenty of time, I thought, to get the truth from her.

The bard, a master musician from Frankish lands, played fluidly and sang in a haunting voice, perfectly pitched. The wine was good, running through my limbs like gentle fire, and I sat back happily in my chair to enjoy the music. Gradually I sensed a change in atmosphere, as if one of those dry summer storms were approaching, that bring forked fire from the sky but no rain or wind. Colors grew sharper, the bard's balding head seemed haloed with light. I felt a tingling in my fingertips and toes, and a wave of excitement swept my body. I began to breathe in quicker breaths, yet had not moved. Nervously I glanced about, but no one else seemed so affected. I sat back and tried to attend the bard. But I could not keep my thoughts upon him. I kept thinking back to Melwas' cabin, when Lancelot held me in his arms and kissed me, and his hand had touched my breast— desperately I turned to the King, and he turned to me in the same moment. I saw instantly he felt the same, for his father's spirit blazed in his eyes, and his jaw was clenched with the effort of control.

"Sir," I whispered frantically, "I am ill, I think. I must retire."

"Stay a moment," he whispered back.

"But, Arthur—I think Elaine has poisoned the wine!"

His face lit with laughter, and he reached for his water goblet, to hide behind it. "It's but an aphrodisiac," he whispered. "And a powerful one. I can see you feel it. Have you never felt this way before?"

"Why, my lord, I—I—" I stammered, shocked. He waved me silent, and saved me from a lie. Beyond him, Lancelot sat with his arms on the table and his face buried in them, moaning softly. Clearly he had drunk the wine, as well. There had been three cups on Grannic's tray.

"If it is Elaine's doing, it gilds the lily," the King said softly, "for tonight we need it not. Wait till the bard is done, if you can. I promise I shall not be long behind you."

It was about the hardest thing I'd ever done, to sit quietly lady-like while my body burned and throbbed. I tried to think about Elaine, for I doubted not this gift was hers, and why she had done it, but the drug robbed me of thought. I felt like gasping and could not. I felt like running and had to sit motionless. What exquisite torture we endured, to be so tossed by storms of desire and able to do nothing!

On the bard's last note I rose and curtsied low to the king. His was a demeanor long schooled in self-discipline; yet even he could barely drag his eyes from my bodice, to my face.

"With your permission, lord, I will go."

He nodded. "Go," he said stiffly. Lancelot looked up once; my flesh felt scorched where his gaze touched it; he stifled a cry and buried his head again. I fled from the hall. Grudgingly the rest of the women followed. The bard was later well recompensed for the early departure of half his audience. He was assured the Queen had taken ill.

I ran to my rooms and cried to Ailsa for water, for my hair to be undone, for the fretful gown to be unlaced. Yet she did nothing fast enough for me. I paced, and mumbled, and fidgeted, and cursed Elaine, and cursed the King for his slowness. Ailsa said nothing, but I saw laughter in her eyes. I refused my bedgown, but wrapped myself in a robe and dismissed her.

"I will wait in the King's chamber," I announced with as much dignity as I could summon. It can't have been much, for she cackled heartily all the way down the stairs. I waited what felt like six days before I heard his footsteps. In the room below he dismissed Varric in clipped tones and bounded up the steps three at a time. At the door he threw off his tunic.

"Arthur!" I ran into his arms, driven, wild with waiting. He kissed me roughly and then suddenly drew back.

"Wait, Gwen."

"Wait!"

He grinned. "The drug takes hours to wear off, you know. Nothing we are about to do will change that."

"Please, Arthur—"

"Wait. I want to know if you truly meant what you said in hall to Bedwyr. Look into my eyes and say it to me."

I drew a long breath and looked into his beautiful eyes. "I would gladly trade places with the ugliest slut in Britain, if it would bring you a child."

His face softened, and he gently put his hands into my hair. "I would not make the exchange for any price," he whispered. I opened my mouth to speak, but met his lips, and the fire was upon us.

I awoke in the middle of the night with an idea. It came to me complete and in detail, and I am sure its coming was what awakened me. The room was still and dark. Beside me Arthur slept in peace. I slipped into my robe and crossed the room to the water carafe, for the wine had left me with a dreadful thirst. I poured water into the silver goblet and drank deeply. The aftereffects of the drug left me feeling light and drained. I poured a second goblet for the King, when he should awake, and brought it to his bedside. He stirred and opened his eyes.

"Here, my lord. For your thirst."

He grinned sleepily. "I pray you, no more. I feel like an old man."

I blushed at his jest. "It is only water."

"I know. Forgive me. Thank you for the thought." He drank thirstily and then sat back, looking refreshed. "Well, Gwen, what do you think of aphrodisiacs?"

I lowered my eyes, coloring deeply. "I would rather do without," I told him, then looked up hastily, in case I had offended. "Not that I did not enjoy it, my lord—"

He laughed, and took my hand. "Never mind. I know what you mean. I agree with you. It is better without, where there is no need."

I was glad he understood me. I hoped that he would still understand when he heard my idea. Now was the time, for he was relaxed, tired and content.

"Arthur."

"My lady?"

"I would ask a favor of you."

"It shall be granted. Name it."

"Make me no promise until you have heard what it is."

"My dear, if it is you who asks it, it cannot be base. I will do it."

"No, it is not base," I said slowly, "but as it concerns you more than me, you might not wish to grant it."

His attention focused on me sharply. "What is it Gwen?"

I stood on the edge of dangerous ground; suddenly nervousness consumed me, and I clasped my hands tightly together. There was no going back now.

"Arthur, is it true you have a son?"

He froze; not a muscle moved on his face. I stumbled on, hurrying.

"When I was a girl, even in Wales we heard rumors. Of a boy born to Queen Morgause, and hidden from King Lot. A boy conceived at Caer Eden on the night of the great battle that brought you into Kingship. Is it true? Is this your son?"

His eyes drilled me, and in spite of my resolve, I trembled. He had never spoken to me about it; it was his own, dark secret, and I had deliberately, and without his leave, flung it out into the light. I had no idea what he would do. He hardly breathed; but at length he dragged out the answer.

"Yes."

"And do you know where he is now?"

"Yes."

"Then," I said, drawing a shaking breath, "this is my request. Send for him. Bring him to Camelot. He belongs at your side. He must be now eleven or twelve—it is time for him to take his place here. Your Kingdom will accept him, and I—Arthur, I would welcome him as my own."

For a long moment he was deathly still. Then he slowly reached out and drew me to his breast, holding me tightly with his face pressed into my hair. I felt his lips move against my ear, but I heard no sound. He held me thus a long time, and when at last he relaxed his embrace, I saw his eyes were dry and his face alight with joy. It made me wonder if he had been praying.

"Guinevere," he said in a low voice, "you have touched my heart twice tonight, and robbed me of breath. Your generosity astounds me. How could you know how I have longed to ask this very favor of you, but feared to wound you?"

"I did not know it, my lord."

"I would do anything to spare you pain. How can you be sure you can bear this boy near you?"

"I know it, my lord. In my soul. I want him here, if he is yours."

"Oh, he is mine." He spoke with bitterness and avoided my eyes. "Do you know the true tale? Do you know his mother is—my sister?"

"Half-sister, my lord. Yes, I knew it. I asked Lancelot about it when he came to Wales."

His eyes widened at that. "Did you indeed? Before we met? When I was only an intimidating stranger to you? It gave you good grounds to reject me. As your heart lay elsewhere, why did you not do it?"

"He said you sinned in innocence, my lord. Everyone does that. How could I condemn you?"

"But such a sin!"

I shrugged. "Perhaps the magnitude of the sin reflects the magnitude of the man. You could not commit a mean sin, Arthur. It is not in you."

He looked away. "I do not deserve such mercy. Lust drove me that night. She was a stranger to me."

"You were barely fourteen. Forgive yourself."

His look lightened then, and he sighed. "Perhaps when I get to know the boy, that, too, will come."

"Then you will send for him?"

"I have thought of little else since the messenger rode in last night from Lothian. For years I have had a spy planted in his mother's household to search out the boy. But she has kept him well hidden. Last night I finally got word on his whereabouts."

So my thought indeed came straight from God! And I noted, as Lancelot had warned me, that he could not bring himself to speak her name.

"And what made you think of it, Gwen?" he asked. "Why should your thoughts run this way?"

"I don't know, my lord. Unless—unless it was my visit with Netta, and then what Bedwyr said."

"Ah, yes. Bedwyr. He has healed you, where I could not. What did he say?"

I looked down. There was no way to tell him. "He showed me that—that there might be a way I could serve you, other than bearing you sons."

"He spoke about the boy?"

"Oh, no, my lord, you mistake me. He spoke about the future. It—I—I really cannot—"

"Never mind. It is between you and Bedwyr. I care only that you are whole again."

"Have I been so single-minded? I was not aware of it."

He smiled kindly. "It was never far from your thoughts."

"I suppose not."

"Who is Netta?"

I grinned, blushing. "Don't ask me to explain, my lord. But Netta is a horse."

He laughed. "I might have known. Well, let be. I will not ask."

My thoughts returned to the boy, as his must have, also, for when I next spoke he followed my thought as if no other words had intervened.

"What is his name?"

"Mordred. It means, in the Orkney tongue, 'king from the sea.' "

He sounded anxious. I leaned forward and took his hand in mine. "Tell me what you know. What kind of boy is he?"

"By my spy's account, quiet. Reserved. Always watching. The odd man out among princes. The bastard."

"What princes? There are other sons?"

"Four by Lot. Gawaine is the eldest; he must be ten. I know nothing about them but that they are short, favoring Lot in stature, and red-headed, favoring their mother.

"And Mordred? What is he like?"

"He is tall," said the King, warming to it, "and dark. Nimble and swift-footed, with a clever wit and the patience of Job." He paused, his eyes seeing far into the distance. "A throwback, perhaps, to Ambrosius, or even Maximus, with his black eyes and Roman features." His voice died suddenly, and he breathed, "He gets it from both sides, you see."

"Mordred must stand out like a swan among geese," I hurried on. "What excuse is given for his presence? Does everyone know?"

"No one knows. Even Morgause"—and he spat out the name— "does not wish that shame remembered. She gives out that he was fathered by a fairy King, or a demon conjured by her magic, or an Elder Spirit, or a serpent from the sea. Her story changes as often as the tide. Certainly Mordred does not know. He knows nothing. He lives as a bastard half brother to the princes of Orkney. A dogsbody, not a prince. It must hurt like hell." His thoughts were far away, his brow creased.

"You lived such a life once."

That brought him back, and he said brusquely, "Yes, but Ector is a good-hearted, selfless soul, and his wife a loving woman and a Christian. Morgause is a—" He paused, and changed the word. "—a witch."

"Then we must get him out of there."

He nodded slowly. "But it must be done carefully, without anyone's suspecting why. Think, Gwen! Think what I must tell him! How heavy a burden I must lay upon my son! If it is difficult for me to confess it, imagine how difficult it will be for him to hear it. I do not want him guessing before I make it known. There is risk here. God knows he has reason enough to hate me," he said slowly. "Who could blame him? I think I must bring his brothers with him and let them serve as a camouflage awhile."

"Can you do that, Arthur? Can you take her children from her?"

His face hardened suddenly, and his eyes went cold. "It would give me very great pleasure indeed."

Here was hatred, obstinate and possessive. Even the Saxons he did not so despise. Lightly I placed my hand upon his arm. "Arthur," I whispered, "did she do the murder at Dunpelder?"

His eyes slid to my face and then away, and I quailed at the look in them. "Yes." He shuddered and clutched at the bearskin, although the night was warm "And that's not all." I waited, as he struggled to find the words. "She is killing Merlin, even as we speak. She once gave him a draft with poison in it, and although it did not kill him outright, it left the seeds of death inside his body. He is dying, and he knows it. He has gone back to his birthplace in the hills of Wales, to find a cure."

I gasped. "It is true, then? Did Merlin confess it?"

Another sharp glance. "No. He admits nothing. But I know."

I watched his face a long time. It was true, I thought, that an evil deed leaves its mark upon the doer. Long ago, in his innocence, he had sinned a dreadful sin. Now it ate him like a rotten canker and tainted all his thoughts. "He was an entire winter in the Caledonian Forest, with only a cave for comfort and skins for clothes. Surely that is why he lost his wits."

He would not look at me. "What sent him witless into the forest? He had seen the Witch three days before."

"Does Merlin confess this? Does he accuse her?"

"No. But I know it's true."

I took his hand between my own and kissed it. "And the murder," I whispered. "Do you have proof she gave the order?"

"Of course not!" he responded angrily. "Lot gave the order. But once he wed her, Lot never did anything on his own, except in battle. It's what made him so fierce." He shut his eyes suddenly and exhaled slowly. "I see the point of all your gentle questions, Guinevere. But do not bother to pity Morgause. I do not accuse her beyond her deserts. She is evil."

I dared push him no further. He sat still, his eyes far away. I put a hand to his cheek. "Forgive me, Arthur . . . Arthur?" He did not hear me; all the warmth of our loving night was lost in the cold horror of his own tormented hell. "Emreis," I whispered, and at once he turned, surprise and then feeling returning to his eyes. "It is God's will, my love, that Mordred be born to you. What will be, will be. Put it behind you."

He nearly smiled. "Now it is your turn to comfort me."

"I pray I can." I clasped his hand. "Can you bring him here, with all his brothers, without inviting suspicion? I am not the only one who has heard the rumors."

"You put it too lightly," he said with a twist of his lips. "I sometimes think there is no one who has not heard. I will think of some excuse to bring them here." Then he smiled and pulled me closer. "Bless you, Gwen, for charming me out of my ill humor. You have a gift for it." His lips found mine, and I yielded willingly to his embrace. His face had looked like death when he spoke of Queen Morgause; his heat was infinitely preferable to his cold.

Suddenly we heard heavy footsteps pounding through the King's apartments.

"My lord Arthur!" It was Kay's voice, in barely controlled panic. "Arthur!"

"Here, Kay! To me!"

The King leaped out of bed and grabbed his robe, as Kay raced up the stairs and fell to one knee at the door. I had not even stirred from the bed; there was not time.

"Oh, my lord, forgive me, but I bring bad news." In trembling fingers he held out a scroll.

"Tell me," Arthur said calmly, reaching for it.

"My lord, the courier—my dear lord, Merlin is dead."

I gasped. Arthur gave no sign that he had heard. He took the scroll from Kay, broke the seal and read. When he looked up, his face a mask, only his eyes reflected his great grief.

"We leave for Wales. Now." He named the score of knights who would attend him. "Inform Lancelot."

Kay began to shake visibly. Arthur stood as still as stone. "My lord, we cannot find him."

"Look harder," Arthur snapped, with his first display of temper. "Now go. Send Varric to me."

Kay fled, and Arthur did not move. Slowly I arose and went to him. He shrugged off his robe and reached for his tunic in a daze. I recognized his state—I had felt the same just after Melwas left me. Varric arrived, hastily dressed and breathless, and gently took the tunic from his hand.

"No, my lord will want his traveling clothes, not the ceremonial finery. 'Twill be a dusty journey, I fear, at this time of year. A light cloak. Here we are." He talked steadily in a low, pleasant voice and glanced meaningfully first at me and then at the wineskin. Coming to my senses, I filled a goblet and touched it to Arthur's lips.

"Drink, my lord." But it was as if he had not heard me. I touched his shoulder, where the scar from Melwas' blade stood out red and ugly from his browned skin. "Please, Arthur, drink. It will help you."

Obediently he swallowed, then waved me away as Varric pulled the tunic over his head. In minutes Varric had him dressed and booted, and fastened his cloak at the shoulder with the gold enamel Dragon brooch. Arthur walked slowly to the door.

He stared vacantly in our direction, said, "Pray for me," and left.

Varric bowed low to me. "My lady."

"You will attend him, Varric?"

"Yes, my lady."

"Do not leave him alone."

"No, my lady. Don't worry. I will see to him." And he hurried down the stairs in the King's wake.

There had been many rumors of Merlin's death throughout the years. But this one Arthur believed. It did not seem possible it could be true—Merlin had guided Britain through her kings since before either of us was born! I glanced about for the scroll and found it on the floor where he had dropped it. It was a note only, short and to the point. It was from Niniane.

20 ✹ THE SEDUCTION
AND THE SWORD

I woke to a scuffling noise and quick, urgent whispers. "My lady! My lady Queen Guinevere! Wake up, oh, please wake up!"

I opened my eyes and looked into Bran's worried face. With a start, I realized I was in the King's bed, and the morning sun streamed through the unglazed window. I gathered the bearskins tighter around me. The night's events came back to me slowly, but it all seemed dreamlike in its distance.

"Is the King gone, Bran, or did I dream it?"

His eyes were nailed to the floor. "He is gone to Wales, my lady."

"Where is Ailsa?"

"She has been looking for you, my lady. We all have been looking for you."

"I have been here all night."

Bran gulped. Sometimes he still looked fifteen. "No one thought—I mean, after the King left—"

I grinned. I had offended acceptable standards of propriety, I saw, but it did not concern me. "But his bed was warm, and mine was cold," I said, covering a yawn and stifling an urge to stretch. "It's been quite a night."

"My lady, shall I send Ailsa to you?"

"Please, Bran, unless you would care to attend me yourself?" He flushed scarlet to the roots of his hair and backed away. "I'm sorry." I laughed. "I'm feeling devilish this morning—I'm only teasing. I did not mean to be unkind. I would like to speak with the courier who rode in this morning. Tell Kay to send him to me when he is rested."

"My lady, please, they have been hunting the house down for you. Sir Lancelot wants to see you."

"Oh, good, they found him. Well, there is no rush about it. He is the Queen's Protector until the King returns, and he only wants to go over the day's schedule."

Bran shook his head.

"I don't think it's that, my lady. When I saw him, he looked ill. Sir Kay said something was amiss."

"Perhaps he only suffers from the wine we took last night. Send Ailsa to me now, and ask Sir Kay if he will see me in half an hour. Will that do?"

He managed a frightened smile. "I will go tell them you are found."

From his manner, I saw something was indeed amiss. And Ailsa, when she bustled in, confirmed it. She scolded me roundly for sleeping alone in the King's bed and hurriedly bathed and dressed me, chattering all the while about meaningless things.

"Ailsa," I said at last. "What is it you are trying so hard not to tell me? I've never heard you go on so."

Her hand shook as she pinned my hair in place, but she said nothing.

"What is it, in God's name? Has aught happened to the King?"

"No, no," she said quickly. "Not to the King. But—I cannot— Sir Lancelot must tell you, my lady. I cannot."

Then it was that I began to feel fear. But, since Arthur and Lancelot were unharmed, I could not imagine what catastrophe had befallen that everyone feared to tell me.

When Ailsa was finished, I went out to find Kay and met him in the corridor hurrying to my apartments. His tread was heavy and his face long.

"Queen Guinevere." He bowed.

"I know. Lancelot wishes an interview. Take me to him."

Kay hesitated. "He wishes a private interview, my lady. Indeed, I think it is best. I was reminded of your garden."

I stared at him in amazement and growing fear. Kay knew, clear enough, and even he was afraid to tell me.

"Then send him up."

He cleared his throat nervously. "Ah, my lady, I fear it would not look well if he, well, if he entered the King's apartments while the King was away."

Well, that was blunt enough. I had forgotten about the palace gossips. I reached into my pouch and drew out a key.

"Give him this. It is the key to my garden door. Let him go to the south tower, to the postern gate. He has only to get through a corner of the women's garden unseen. I will be waiting."

I set Ailsa and Alissa as guards upon my bedchamber stairs and went out on my terrace in a fever of anticipation. It was another glorious day, fair and warm and sweet-scented. How could anything bode ill on such a morning?

I sat myself on the stone bench behind the fountain, where I had a view of the entire length of the garden, and composed myself to wait.

He did not keep me waiting long. I saw him coming toward me with the reluctant tread of a guilty man approaching his executioner, and I began to fear in earnest. His face and hair were recently scrubbed, his tunic was fresh from the fuller's. Penitence flowed in every line of his body.

He fell to his knees before me and pressed my hand to his lips, kissing my fingers and then holding my palm to his face. Then he looked up. I gasped. He had tears in his eyes.

"What is it, Lancelot? What has happened! Oh, God, what catastrophe is this! Tell me!"

"Oh, Guinevere! I am a miserable sinner," he whispered. "An undeserving wretch. May God in His mercy forgive me. I don't think you will."

I sighed with exasperation. He was forever berating himself with sins.

"Dear God, Lancelot, you are frightening me to death! You are well and whole, are you not? Have you killed anyone? Is your life at stake? Are you in any danger? All right, then. So what have you done? It cannot be as bad as all that."

But he flushed hotly and looked away, holding tight to my hand. What could so deeply embarrass him? Suddenly I remembered his suffering in hall, and Kay's inability to find him in the early morning hours. I nearly laughed.

"I know what it is! You took a stroll down Maiden Lane last night and found someone willing. Am I right?"

His color only deepened. I put my hand on his head and ruffled his hair with affection. It felt like silk between my fingers. "Come, Lancelot, I am not a monster. I can forgive that. If she was willing, it was no sin. The drug was upon you—what else could you do?"

He shook his head sadly but did not speak. I touched his cheek, and he closed his eyes in pain.

"We will honor her," I whispered, "if that would please you, and send her home with gifts. Her father will think it a fair ex-

change for maidenhead. You need not be ashamed. Unless," I said
with a touch of nervousness, "she is highborn." He flinched, and
I swallowed hard. "Even so, it can be arranged to everyone's satisfaction. Leave it to me."

But every word I said was as a knife in his heart, I could see
that, and knew not what to do. So I said nothing, but stroked his
hair, and touched his face, and let him know that he could trust
me with it, whatever it was, for I loved him. And all the while I
wondered who she was, what she looked like, what she wore and
how old she was, sure that however perfect she might be, she
could not have appreciated him.

At length he drew on his courage and steadied himself.

"Guinevere," he began, meeting my eyes at last, and holding
both my hands firmly to his breast, "you light my life. I will
never love another. This you must know and believe before I tell
you the rest. I will pay for last night's lust as long as I live, and
it is right that I should, but she will never have my heart."

My heart beat painfully as I heard my guess confirmed. But
Lancelot never forgave himself easily, and I feared for what punishment he might feel required to endure.

"Before I tell you how it happened, I must tell you—I must tell
you, Gwen—I am betrothed."

"NO!" It burst from me in a hoarse cry; I stared in horror at his
face. But he held my hands firmly, and I could not rise to flee. He
absorbed my anger and held tight to me. "No, it isn't necessary!
You go too far. What is a night only? You need not marry her."

"She is highborn," he said steadily, "and her father and mother
were there when Kay found us this morning. I could do naught
else. I could not dishonor her further."

I felt the tears slip down my face. "To lie with you is no dishonor," I whispered, and he took a quick breath, then let it out
slowly. "Oh, Lancelot, do not leave me, I pray you. I love you
so."

His control broke, and he buried his face in my lap with his
arms around me. I bent over him and kissed his head. In my heart,
I knew it was cruel. He was five and twenty. Most men his age
had sons training to be warriors. He could not go unwed forever;
to ask it of him was unfair. But the thought of losing him was
more than I could bear. He was a man of honor, and he had promised. But it broke my heart.

For a long time we stayed thus, holding each other. With great
effort I managed to speak the words I knew I had to say.

"What you must do, you must do. Have you given your word to her father?"

He raised his head and nodded.

"Then—then there is naught that I can say."

"I have not told you all."

"There is more?" I cried. "How can there be more? You are leaving me—tell me no more!"

He rose slowly and walked back and forth before the fountain. It was not fair to remind me of Arthur. I watched him pace and dared not think ahead. He was unhappy, that was clear enough, and determined, but he was also afraid. Was it possible he could hurt me more than this?

"When the King left the hall last night," he began, "I left soon after. With Bedwyr. He was tired and went off to bed, but I—I could not." I drew breath to tell him I understood it, but he raised a hand and stopped me. I saw he feared he could not say it, if he did not say it all at once. "I never intended to go looking for a maiden. I only meant to walk it off. The night was clear and cool, and I went first to the stables. But the colt was fine, and Lyonel was there. I decided to walk the perimeter of the wall. In fact, I ran." I bowed my head, remembering the frantic drive of the drug. While he had been running, I had been in the King's arms. It was not fair to judge him. "But I tired at last of running, and I had got no relief. I stopped to catch my breath and felt dizzy, and—lost my bearings. I did not know where I was. And so I left the wall and walked toward the lighted torches. I thought that if I got there, I could find my way. In my mind were pictures of my Breton homeland, and the streets of Benoic where I grew up. But when I got near the light, I recognized nothing. There were girls about. One, a brunette, came up and brushed my arm. I could not bear it; even the touch of her fingers set me aflame. How I wanted you, Guinevere! Your face was ever before me, as it had been all night. It seemed to me that you should want me, too, if you loved me, and find a way to escape the King and come unto me." He stopped pacing and covered his face with his hands. "May God forgive me!" he whispered. "That I should ever wish to betray my lord!" Then he turned and continued, forcing it out. "I escaped her and went on, but I did not know where I was going. I was looking for you. I was—driven. To find you. And then I looked up and you were there."

I gasped, and he met my eyes.

"She spoke to me," he said, "in your voice. 'Lancelot,' she

said, 'at last I have found you.' It was so very exactly what I wished to hear."

"She was fair?" I asked hoarsely.

"She was fair and lovely. She wore a blue scarf over her hair, which hid all but a little. But she was fair. And she spoke with your voice."

"And her gown?" I said, shaking, holding hard to the bench. He waited a long time before answering.

"It was your gown. The same I had seen you in an hour before. The gown that drove me mad. It was the same."

I simply stared at him in horror.

"She was standing in the doorway of a tent and beckoned me inside. Her gestures were yours. Inside the lamp was low. There was an inner chamber. She—said very little. But then, I did not give her much chance." He wiped his brow and drew a long, trembling breath. "I will say no more. When Kay woke me this morning, my eyes were clear, and I saw her face."

I put out a hand to stop him.

"Don't!" I jumped to my feet. "Don't, Lancelot!"

"Guinevere, I am betrothed to Elaine."

"Aaaaa!" I screamed, and swooned. He lifted me and held me. But the touch of his hands cleared my head, and I pushed him away.

"You will not do it!" I cried, shaking. "I forbid it! She has duped you, Lancelot, can you not see it? She has duped us all! Oh, God!" I whirled away, holding my aching head, wishing for death.

Now I saw, too clearly, all that Elaine had done. As far back as the Melwas affair she had planned this, when she lay on my floor and whimpered that I could not have them both, Lancelot and Arthur. How clever she had been—making a gown of the same fabric as the one she knew I'd wear; the secret summons to her parents, who arrived in innocence because she had begged me not to send for them; and the drug, her stroke of genius, that would drive us half mad, ensuring that the King and I would leave hall early and spend the whole evening together, and leave Lancelot roaming free and vulnerable. What revenge was this! How she must hate me! But the worst of it was that she did not love Lancelot; she cared nothing for him; she did it only to take him from me. And yet she knew the man. She knew I could talk Pellinore out of holding him to his promise; she had not relied on her parents' presence for that. But she knew Lancelot's honor would bind him to her, when he awoke and found himself in her father's house.

"I forbid it," I repeated coldly, turning back to him. "Do not be fooled by her. You consign yourself to a future of torment. A slut would better serve you and bring more honor to your house. There is not an ounce of goodness in her, Lancelot. I know her better than you. She planned to seduce you—she sent the wine—only because she hates me so. I will speak to Pellinore. You are released from your promise."

He looked pained. I knew what he was thinking—these words were not worthy of me, but he had come prepared to endure a woman's rage.

"Nevertheless," he said, "I must."

"You will not. The King will not allow it. You must have his permission."

"He will be back within a week. I will ask him then."

And suddenly I understood. Arthur would let him do it. Arthur would think of his home in Lanascol, held now in his name by his brother Galahantyn since their father died. Arthur would consider his future as an ally king, and what good could come of a strong arm in Less Britain. Arthur would look ahead to the training of Lancelot's sons as his own loyal knights—but at the thought of Elaine bearing Lancelot's sons, I cried aloud in anguish.

"NO! It will not be! I cannot live with this! You will kill me, Lancelot, as surely as you stand there! Oh, have pity on me, my love, and do not do this thing!"

He leaped forward and took me by the shoulders. There were tears in his eyes. "You don't understand! You were not there! I—I took her thrice, and she was virgin!"

"Lancelot!" I cried, clapping my hands over my ears. "Spare me the details! What do you want of me? I cannot bear it!"

"Understand me!" he cried hoarsely. "I am not a brutal man, but—but I caused her pain and suffering, through my impatience. I was no gentleman. I am responsible."

"She has her reward!"

"I owe her more than that."

"Not your life!"

"My name, at least. To save her from shame if she bears a child."

"Oh, God!" I closed my eyes on that, and fought back tears. "She would feel no shame. She has no sense of it."

"Gwen." His voice was very soft. "It is not like you to be cruel. I have hurt you very deeply. I am sorry."

I began to weep quietly, but his very tenderness made me angry.

"Don't pretend you love me!" I cried. "You knew it was not I who beckoned you. You knew I was with the King."

But it only hurt me more to wound him; he would not fight back, but only accepted shafts, one after the other, without complaint. "Yes," he said slowly, dropping his hands to his side, "I suppose that deep within me I did know it. I saw the way you looked at Arthur. That was why I left the hall when he did. I could not bear the thought—but let be. You have come to love him, and God knows that is as it should be. He has the gift of sowing love. And last night you wanted him. That is what made me so—fierce with Elaine. How I longed to hold you in my arms and lie with you! I confess it before God. So when I saw someone who resembled you, I shut my mind to the truth and believed the lie. I am responsible," he finished simply.

I fell to my knees and reached for his hand, splashing it with tears and pressing it to my breast. "Oh, noble Lancelot! Forgive me, I pray. I am only a woman, and wounded to my soul. I had no right to speak so!"

He lifted me in his arms and carried me to the bench. I wept on his shoulder, my arms about his neck. He held me on his lap and waited.

"She is not worthy of you," I whispered, "and you will regret it." But I knew he had made up his mind. When my sobs subsided, he spoke again.

"I will take her to Less Britain. I have been too long away. But she tells me you two have quarreled, and her movements are restricted. I must ask you, Gwen, to let her go."

I drew back and looked at his face. Then it was I realized he knew nothing of Elaine's part in the Melwas affair. And how could he know, unless the King had told him? For I had not, and he was on Ynys Witrin when her treachery was revealed. Here was a weapon to my hand, I saw it instantly. I could prevent his leaving if I told him what she had done. He would never marry a woman who had betrayed me into Melwas' hands. I opened my mouth to speak, when I saw the other side of that coin. And how would he feel, when he knew? He would feel as if he had lain with a snake, and the shame of it would eat at his very soul, as the shame of Morgause ate at Arthur. I knew then I could not do it. But the agony of wanting to brought back anger.

"Did she tell you why we quarreled?"

"Yes." I gasped, but he went on. "She said you discovered her great love for the King and accused her of hubris, which she admits."

"Lancelot," I beseeched him, "does that sound like me? All the world loves Arthur. Would I lock one woman up on account of it?"

He looked puzzled, and then shrugged. "Before this interview, I would have said it was unlike you. But I—I confess I do not understand women well. If that was not the truth, then what was it?"

I was well revenged for wounding him. He cut me to my core. I had behaved abominably. And now, what could I say?

"It is partly true," I said at last. "But there is more to it than that. She—took advantage of her closeness to me to further her own ends and sought a private interview with the King. I don't know exactly what happened, but the King was angry and asked me to see to it that it did not happen again. It was more than foolishness, I fear, and I had intended to send her home to Wales. Today was to be the day of her departure."

"Then she is restrained on Arthur's orders?"

"She is not restrained enough!" I cried, then bowed my head. "No, the orders were mine. I—I felt personally betrayed. It is the kind of thing women do not forgive one another."

"Well," he said gently, "she has not your judgment, Gwen, or your control. But if the cause of this embarrassment is her love for the King, can you not forgive it? I will take her away, where she will never see him again. Then it is solved."

"She does not love you, my dearest, and she never will."

The ghost of a smiled crossed his lips. "And I will never love her." My heart ached for him; it was a future of dust and ashes. "Will you release her, Gwen? For my sake? Let her go to her parents until the wedding. You need not see her, if it pains you so."

The tears slipped out again, and I leaned against him, exhausted and relenting. "Yes," I whispered, "I will give the order."

He held me closer. "When Arthur gets home, I will ask formal permission. I will leave before the autumn winds close the seas." I shut my eyes. It was over and settled.

"Will I never see you again?"

"Of a certainty you will," he said, pulling away and drying my cheeks. "I will be back when the seas open, bringing Galahantyn with me. I will stay with you for three seasons out of four, while the King is about his business. He is my liege lord as well as my friend. I owe him service. And I desire his fellowship." He almost smiled and gently touched my hair. "But more even than Arthur, I need you. I will return."

At last he kissed me, and I clung to him, desperate with longing. His lips were warm and eager, and for a moment only I thought of nothing else. But it was only a sweet ending to the horrors we had suffered. It changed nothing.

By the time the King came home, the whole of Camelot was abuzz with rumors about Lancelot and Elaine. I had released her to the care of Alyse and Pellinore, who kept her close, sensing trouble. I could not see that Lancelot spent much time with her, a courtesy call in the evenings perhaps, for almost every minute he was with me. He certainly showed no inclination to return to her bed. But he had been to see the bishop, and so the rumors ran wild.

As for Arthur, here also rumors ran ahead of fact. Merlin was dead. The King had gone to the old enchanter's hilltop cave in South Wales, and found him lying cold and blue, as Niniane had said. The magic of the place had kept corruption from him, and Arthur spent three days and nights at his side in the hope that he still lived and might awaken. At length, facing facts, he filled the cave with treasures beyond counting; all round the countryside the folk brought gifts, and the King gave him everything he had at Caerleon, to send him to his gods. Then, to protect the grave from robbers, they levered the stones above the cave mouth and brought down an avalanche to cover the entrance and bury him deep in the hill. So it was done. And the King had not spoken a word to a soul after it was accomplished, but rode home in silence and would see no one.

It was the same when he rode into Camelot. Kay and the home guard awaited him on the steps. I watched from Alissa's window, which gave onto the forecourt. It reminded me of the first time I had ever seen him, except that now he moved like a man in sleep, and not like a leader of men. He spoke to no one, but dismounted, dropping the reins, and climbed the steps without seeing them. Kay gave him formal welcome; the King did not reply, but walked past him and into the castle without turning his head. The lady Niniane had ridden in behind him and sat her horse watching the king with a worried face. Even Pelleas, who rode beside her and would wed her within the month, could not turn her gaze from the King. The soldiers all looked puzzled, and Lancelot, standing beside Kay, glanced quickly toward my window and shook his head.

I retired to my chamber, to be there if the King felt need of me. Standing by the curtain, I heard his steps come up the stairs. His tread was slow and heavy. I heard Varric's voice and Bran's, and movement within the chamber, but the King did not speak. Then all was silent. I waited for a long time, hearing nothing. I was not sure he was even in there, except I had not heard him leave. I determined to go in, for had he not said himself that I was always welcome? Gently I pulled aside the corner of the curtain, but what I saw stopped me where I stood, and I went no further. He had stripped to the waist and knelt like a penitent next his bed. His back was to me, his head bowed against the coverlet, his long arms outstretched and his hands clasped. He was praying.

I went to Lancelot. The Companions had just broken up from council, and Lancelot briefed me on the news. While Wales was quiet enough, a courier from Rheged had come to the King at Caerleon while he collected treasure for Merlin's burial. The King had heard his news but had given no direction; indeed, Bedwyr said it was difficult to know whether or not he had understood a word the man said. King Urien sent to say that Caw of Strathclyde had died, leaving his kingdom in chaos. Although he had been a graybeard, his death was unexpected. He had sired twelve sons and five daughters; the eldest boys were twins, thirty years old and wild. His sensible son was third born, one Hapgar, and the old king's favorite. But Caw had died quickly and had not had time to bequeath his kingdom into anyone's hands. Urien, whose lands lay next to Strathclyde, reported that the young men were fighting it out among themselves, and no one's life was safe out of doors. Urien's own sons by his first marriage were riding patrol upon their borders; his seven-year-old daughter Morgaine, Queen Morgan's child, had been kidnapped on a short journey near the border and held for a week by Heuil, the eldest twin, and raped repeatedly. He had her back now, but his wrath was high, and if the High King did not step in, there would be war.

This was black news indeed. But what was worse, Bedwyr despaired of the King's recovering from his grief in time.

"He was like this when Merlin disappeared, years ago, just before his first Queen died," Bedwyr said, twisting his hands together. "We thought the enchanter dead, and the King grieved deeply for months. We had the Saxons, then, and he came out of his fastness only to fight them. But this is worse, Lancelot. This is internal strife of a kind only the High King can settle. Caw had sworn allegiance, but none of his sons have bent a knee to Arthur. This is not a thing that you or I could settle in his place."

"Is there danger that the Saxons, sensing division within Britain, could test our strength again?" I asked him.

Bedwyr's frown deepened. "I had not thought of it," he confessed, "but knowing Saxons, it seems more than likely."

"Cerdic watches the borders closely," Lancelot remarked, "and I hear he has good spies. I doubt not he knows already of this news, if it is five days old."

Bedwyr shrugged. "He would not be hurried. He sent the old man off in proper style, I will grant him that, but it took ages. He could not leave him. For half a day he stood outside the rockslide, alone, as if he could not bring himself to say good-bye."

I touched Bedwyr's arm. "Remember," I told him, "that none of us has ever known life without Merlin, the King least of all. It must seem to him that he has lost a father, a friend, a trusted advisor, and more—a confidant of his heart. He is alone now, for the first time in his life, I think."

Lancelot straightened. "He is not alone."

I looked him in the face. "You are off to Lanascol, my lord, come fall. He has Bedwyr, Kay and Niniane, and me. And none of us is to him what Merlin was."

Lancelot took the slap without flinching. Bedwyr looked on with interest, but said nothing. No one but I knew Lancelot's plans, until he had confirmed them with the King. And that now seemed unlikely to happen soon.

Two weeks went by, and nothing happened. The messages from Urien grew more urgent. Border fighting had broken out; Urien kept his actions to defense, but his army cried out for blood to avenge the princess. The King hardly stirred from his room. He took his meals there and did not appear in hall, although Varric reported that he did not eat enough to keep a bird alive.

The rest of Camelot seemed to march in place, waiting. The people were afraid; the soldiers worried. Although relieved of his role as Queen's Protector now that the High King was home, Lancelot served as Arthur's proxy in Council and in hall when the King did not appear. I sat beside him in hall, but conversation was strained. Alyse and Pellinore attended every night, looking bewildered, and I could not bring myself to speak to them. Elaine kept away, not from shame, I was sure, but to avoid my fury. It was still in my power to foil her plans, and this she must have known.

I remember the morning when Ailsa told me, as she brushed my hair, that Elaine was deathly sick in the mornings. Grannic was full of the news, it seemed, and all the women were talking. I whirled on the stool, clutched her hand, and tore the brush from her grip.

"Leave me!" I shrieked. "Get out! How dare you bring such lies into my chamber! Go! I cannot bear the sight of you!"

But dear Ailsa merely cowered against the wall as I stormed about the room, cursing the cruel fates and begging God to take my life from me. At length my anger passed into despair, and I fell to the floor, where Ailsa held me and whispered sweet endearments while I wept most bitterly.

"It isn't fair! That she should—in one night—and I, Ailsa, *all these years*! I hate her, I hate her! Let me see her but once," I cried, "and I will kill her!"

"Now, now," Ailsa crooned, stroking my hair from my face, "would you, indeed, and bring dishonor on all the ones you love? That is not in you, my lady. Everyone looks to you for strength."

"To *me*?" I whispered. "Dear God, then we are lost, for I have none!"

"You are stronger than you know," she replied. "My little Gwen, in five years this will seem a small thing, looking back. Don't let it hurt you so."

"A small thing! Oh, Ailsa!" I sobbed, clutching her garments. "It can never be a small thing! She will have his child always by her—Lancelot's child!—and what will I have?"

"You are Queen, my lady. Oh, Gwen, my precious Gwen, even could you bear, you could not have his children. What are you asking of him? That he should stay unwed and childless for your sake?"

"No," I whispered. "Yes. No. Oh, Ailsa, I must be evil, for deep in my soul I do want that very thing—his heart is mine—I do not want to share him. There is no love between them, Ailsa—all this is wrong, so wrong!"

"Is it right that he should forgo his future and deny his kingdom heirs, to stay in Camelot and worship a woman he cannot have?"

I closed my eyes and pressed my face into her shoulder. "Stop, I pray you! I know I cannot ask it. I do love him, but this—this is so unfair!"

Gently she kissed my brow and hugged me. "If you truly love him, the way the King loves you, you will let him go and take what joy he can with her. You will always have his heart."

"I have not Arthur's forbearance," I cried, "nor his mercy. And he—he could not feel like this!"

"He keeps his pain inside, my lady. But it is there." She sounded very sure. It steadied me, to think of Arthur, and made me feel ashamed. I had completely forgotten about the King, suffering in the next room. That he did not come in when I shrieked and wept was a telling sign of his illness. How could I have forgotten?

"But I am only a woman," I whispered, "and I have not his strength."

"You are his right hand," she asserted, "and you must control your tears for his sake. I will make you a posset that will let you sleep. We must have those tear-tracks gone before hall."

Ailsa performed what magic she could with potions and charms and hairbrush, but when Lancelot met me outside the hall, he knew at once I had been weeping.

"Gwen, what's amiss?" he asked gently.

I shook my head and placed my hand on his arm. "I cannot tell you. It will pass. Let us go in."

But as we entered hall and everyone rose, I stopped, frozen in my tracks. Elaine stood between her parents, smiling and smug, her hands placed protectively upon her little belly, looking right into my eyes. She did not care that he loved me; she only wanted me to know she had conceived his child at his first bedding of her, and that however close I kept him to me, he was hers. I felt the blood drain from my face, and I gripped Lancelot's arm.

"What is it, Gwen?"

"You—you promised me, my lord," I whispered fiercely, trying desperately to keep my tears at bay, "you promised I should not have to see her again. Either take her away or lead me out. I cannot abide her in the room with me!"

He was shocked, but I would not move, and everyone was waiting.

"My God, Gwen, how can I? They are all assembled."

I raised my face to his and met his eyes. "Choose, Lancelot. Choose between us. One of us must go."

At length he nodded, and said wearily, "I will take her out. Let me seat you first."

He led me to my place, but I did not sit, and all the hall stayed standing. Bedwyr took my arm, to still my shaking. I looked straight across the hall, out the windows, but from the corner of my eye I saw Lancelot go down the table to Elaine, speak softly to her and to Pellinore, and offer her his arm. Alyse was affronted, Pellinore bewildered. Elaine smiled triumphantly, made a pretty curtsy in my direction, and leaned upon his arm as he took her out. Utter stillness blanketed the hall. Bedwyr tugged gently at my arm, and at last I sat, and the meal was served.

Elaine kept out of my way after that, and everyone trod lightly around me. With Lancelot himself I was alternately furious and penitent, coldly indignant and self-indulgently forsaken, a ship without a rudder, while Arthur was not there. How Lancelot bore it, I do not know. That he did not despise me for my tormented behavior, nor chastise me for my cruel words, is a testament to the quality of the man and the deep love he bore me.

At last two couriers arrived with the news we dreaded. Urien's forces were shaping for attack; the King of Elmet and Tydwyl, Arthur's appointed governor of Lothian during Morgause's exile to Orkney, were being drawn into the dispute. It looked as if the whole north of Britain would be torn asunder within days. And Cerdic, King of the West Saxons, was quietly amassing a force near the border of his kingdom. So far they were patrolling only, but their numbers were growing. They waited, like wolves outside the boar's den, ready to pick apart the winner, weak from battle.

The Companions were beside themselves with frustration and worry. Niniane had tried to see the King, but he would not bear her name mentioned. Kay, Bedwyr, and Lancelot, who all had tried repeatedly to see him, and had all been turned away, drew me into conference. They begged me to go to the King and see what could be done to awaken him from his trance.

"But, my lords," I told them, "on the second day of his arrival he sent me word through Varric, ordering me to stay out of his chamber. It was not the request of my husband, but the command of my King."

Lancelot took my hands, his face white. "We are asking you, Gwen, to disobey him. For Britain's sake. He is so deep in his grief he knows not what he risks. He will thank you for it when his mind is healed."

They were so distressed, I agreed to try. Indeed, the state of the Kingdom was growing desperate. It was something Arthur could so easily have solved, three weeks ago, simply by showing himself in Strathclyde. But now, who knew? It might already be too late.

"Get me his Sword," I said, thinking hard, "and his sword belt. Have Varric bring me his best cloak, with the Dragon brooch."

They glanced quickly at one another.

"What is your plan, my lady?" Bedwyr asked cautiously.

"I don't know yet, really. But I have an idea. I will not appeal to his heart, but to his honor. I will threaten to lead the troops myself."

Kay gasped. Bedwyr froze. But Lancelot smiled, approving.

"But you cannot! You are a woman! You may not touch the Sword!" Kay cried, distressed. "No one may draw it, but the King himself!"

"Why is that?" I asked him. "Did Merlin put a curse upon it?"

"No, no," Bedwyr said quickly, "Merlin never dealt in curses. It is just tradition. The Sword was made for Arthur, a hundred years ago, and only he has ever touched it."

"Nonsense. It is the Sword of Maximus, who was my ancestor as well as his. Merlin has held it, and no doubt countless servants, as well . . . Well, I will risk it. Perhaps the sight of it in my hand will shock him as much as the very thought of it has shocked you. What think you?"

Kay was calmer when he realized it was a ruse only, and that I did not really intend to lead the High King's troops to battle; Bedwyr and Lancelot thought it might work.

"Should it fail," Lancelot said, "and we should have to go north without him, we will take you with us. For I think your idea has more merit than even you believe."

Kay was aghast, but Lancelot turned the talk to the specifics of the plan. It was arranged that everything would be sent to my rooms during supper, when the Round Hall was empty and the Companions would not miss the Sword, which hung on the wall above the High King's chair. Then, in the evening at the time of my choosing, I should try to see the King.

They left me, then, alone with Lancelot. I was nervous about the plan and wished I had not thought of it, or they had not agreed. But I could see no other way. We talked for some time about what should happen if the plan failed. Lancelot was second in command, and to him would fall the leadership of the High King's troops. He would go north to Urien's aid. But the Saxon threat could not be discounted, and the King's fighting force must be divided, with a strong contingent left at Camelot under Bedwyr's command. They must make themselves visible along the Saxon border and discourage attack until Lancelot could return. It was risky. If Cerdic were clever, he would know what the display signaled, and he might attack.

We talked this way and that, and then at length prepared to go. At the door I stopped and turned to him. In three weeks we had said a good deal to one another, but Elaine's name had never been mentioned. I did not know if he had even seen her, except to remove her from hall.

"I must congratulate you, Sir Lancelot."

He looked blank and startled by the formal address. I saw he did not even know.

"On what?" he asked. "I have done nothing."

"Did you not know your betrothed carries your child?" I whispered.

He started as if struck and paled. I was both gladdened and saddened to see that it gave him no joy.

"How in God's name do you know?" he breathed. "They have said naught to me."

"I know. I would know even if I had not seen the triumph on her face. Ask her if it is not true."

He swallowed hard and shook his head. "No. If it is true, I will know soon enough. Let them keep it quiet until this fracas is behind us. Next to this it matters not."

I softened to him then and spoke gently. "I told you in case you wanted me to mention it to Arthur, if I can make him hear me. You have waited three weeks already to ask permission, and if we are to go to war—if you wait too much longer, all the world will be able to see why you are marrying her."

His eyes were shining, and he lifted my hand to his lips. "You are a noble woman, Guinevere. But I do not want you to plead my cause with the King. Not in this. I will do it. If you can bring him round, I will speak to him. As for the rest, I do not care if all the world knows why I marry her."

I smiled at that, and we parted on good terms.

When I ascended to my chamber after supper, I found everything arranged. My best riding clothes were laid out upon the bed, along with the King's own cloak, and his gold and enamel brooch. I ran my finger over the smooth surface, the Red Dragon of Britain, from which he took his name. And it came to me again, that sense of shock, that this one man should be so important to the world. He was the center, and we all, like spokes, moved around him.

On the little needlepoint bench lay the great Sword. Up close, it looked huge. The scabbard was old leather, so old and well oiled it felt like silk to the touch. The thing lay balanced on the bench, dwarfing it, the great gem on the hilt winking in the lamplight. The jeweled belt it hung on lay carefully on the floor beside it. But the Sword itself must not touch the ground—that much I knew. I reached out a hand to touch it, but withdrew it. I dared not. It was a thing of magic and power, lying there so still in the dim light, shining with a glory of its own. It was not for me.

So I turned and thought again about my plan. Perhaps it was not wise to do this. I thought that I should first find out what the King had in his mind, and how he was. I would try womanly persuasion first and see what happened. With a sense of relief, I called for Ailsa to take down my hair and prepare it for night. I would go to him in the gown I had worn on his wedding night, the white one Elaine had sewn. Perhaps it would remind him of another time and distract him. At any rate, I knew what I was about in this and felt more comfortable. When I was prepared, and my hair was brushed and hanging down my back, the way he loved it, I bade Ailsa wait in my room. I went to the curtain. I heard nothing. Lifting it slowly aside, I took a deep breath, and went in.

I did not see him at first. The room felt empty. The fire was out in the grate, the wicks had not been trimmed, and the triple lamp burned smokily. Nothing moved. I was just about to turn back, disappointed, when I saw him standing at the far window, looking down. I nearly cried aloud. Was this the King, this pale shadow of a man? How could three weeks of fasting change a man so? He was still dressed as a penitent, in a loincloth only, and his flesh, once hard with muscle, now displayed his bones. His collarbones threw shadows on his shoulders; I could only count his ribs.

"Arthur!" I said it on a sob, and he jerked toward me.

"Go away. I do not want you here."

"That's as may be," I whispered, "but I cannot obey you." Turning my eyes from him, I took flint and got the fire going. When the coals were burning, I put out the lamp, trimmed the wicks, and relit it. It shed a golden glow, and the room felt warmer. I fetched a wineskin from my own room, and I hung it to warm over the coals. The water carafe was empty, and I filled it from my own. Clearly he had not allowed Varric to attend him.

By this time Varric had arrived in the antechamber, and I whispered down to him to bring me a bowl of beef broth, a heel of soft bread, some cold chicken, cheese and fruit, and hot water, soap, and towels. He spread his hands out helplessly.

"My lady, I have tried. But he will not allow me in the room." He felt shame, I am sure, for the King's state.

"Never mind. Bring them to me, and I will see to it."

I swept the room and made up the bed with clean sheets that Ailsa brought me. I never looked at him. He would have to try a conversation if he wanted to speak to me. But he had turned back to the window and said nothing. Varric arrived with Kay, Bedwyr and Lancelot close behind. I would not let them mount the stairs, but went down myself into the King's antechamber and took from them the basin of hot water, which was heavy, and the towels and soap. I struggled up with them myself and set out the towels beside the low stool.

"Come, my lord," I said at last. "Sit here, if you will. It is time you had a bath."

Wearily he turned from the window. "Leave me, Guinevere."

"No, my lord. I cannot."

For the first time, I saw a spark of anger in his eyes. "What means this defiance? I said, leave me."

"Come sit here, my lord. You need a bath."

"And you are not a bath slave. Let it be."

"You will allow no one to attend you. Thus it must fall to me."

He looked at me sharply, and then came and sat. I suppose he thought I would not do it. But I bathed him, from his dirty hair to the soles of his unwashed feet. I toweled him dry, and rummaged in the trunk for his day robe.

"There," I said, when he stood clean and dressed. "That is closer to the lord I serve."

"You have shown me your devotion. Now go."

"No, my lord. I cannot." I carried the basin of dirty water to the landing, where Varric took it from me. The tray of food was waiting, covered by a clean cloth, and I brought it in and set it on his writing desk.

"I order you to go." His face was a study. He was angry and indignant, at the same time grief-stricken and powerless.

I took a deep breath. "Eat the meal I have brought you, my lord. Sit here, and I will serve you."

I lifted the clean cloth to let him glimpse the food.

"Guinevere! I am your King! Obey me!"

I lifted my chin and faced him. "You were my King. But you have not done much work in that line lately. You have put down the burden and left your friends to pick it up. I obey *their* orders now."

He looked startled, but then gave up the fight. I ached to see that submission. It was so unlike him.

"You do not understand."

"Sit and eat."

"I will not."

"Then I will not go."

We stood facing each other. I was reminded of childhood fights with Gwillim, which usually ended with some adult coming between us to settle things. But there was no one to settle things for us now.

He walked slowly to the table. "If I eat this, will you go?"

"Yes."

He sat down and began to consume the meal. At first he ate slowly, and I gave him only water, but then, as he felt better, and had more interest, I gave him watered wine, as well. At length he finished, and dipped his fingers in the waterbowl and dried them on a napkin. Then he looked up at me. There was nothing in his eyes but grief.

"Leave me now, Gwen."

I sat upon the edge of the table. "I have promised, and I will. But first tell me what it is I don't understand. Why are you doing this? It is not like you to stand idly by while Britain falls to ruin. The patient work of the last five years is about to go for naught. There must be a reason. What are you waiting for?"

To my amazement, he answered me.

"A sign," he said. "A sign from God. From any god."

"What—what kind of a sign?" He astonished me; then I remembered he had grown up under Merlin's cloak and must be familiar with wonders. "Is it an omen you seek?"

He shook his head. There was a haunted look about his eyes, a touch of fear. That was what made him look so different—I had never seen fear in him before.

"Why do you not ask Niniane about it? She has his power now."

He shot to his feet, instantly angry. "I forbid you to mention her name. She has betrayed him. At the last, she betrayed him."

I took a deep breath and spoke calmly. "How do you know this, my lord?"

With a heartfelt groan, he held his head in his hands and turned away. He sat heavily on the bed, bending forward, resting his elbows on his knees. I followed him silently and stood beside him, grieving for the grief and pain he suffered.

"Merlin told me," he whispered finally. "He said it was his destiny, to die betrayed by a woman. He said it was his fate."

"And yet he went to it willingly, did he not?" I trembled at my own temerity, but he only shrugged. This was not what tortured him so. "What is it, Arthur?" I asked softly. "What else did Merlin foresee?"

It was a wild guess, but it hit its mark. He jumped up and strode back to the window. I thought for a moment he was going to order me out again, but all grief is easier to bear if shared, and after a struggle, he told me.

"He foresaw that he would go living to his grave," he said, the horror of it making him shudder. "It was the only thing I ever knew him to fear. And—and it was I who buried him. If—if I have buried him alive, the man I loved more dearly than a father—I waited three days, to be sure. He did not breathe, but neither did he rot. I knew not if it was magic, if the god he served protected his flesh, or if—if perhaps he truly lived but the life signs were hidden from me. But I could not keep the people waiting and had to come to some decision." He paused and swallowed. "I buried him so none could get at him, deep within the hill. But if he is alive—" He stopped. This was the fear that consumed him. "He will never get out."

"I see." Indeed, it was a horrible thought. And Merlin's foreknowledge, as everyone knew, had never been wrong. "And so you have asked God to send you a sign that he is truly dead?"

"God. Mithra. The Mother. The Elder Spirits. Any who will listen."

"What kind of sign will it be?"

"How do I know? But I will know it when it comes."

"Can you not—can you not accept, my lord, that Merlin knew what it was he went to, and that you could not prevent it? If he foresaw it, it had to happen. I see no blame here."

His smile was bitter. "Do you not? You had better go now. I wish to be alone."

I was near the curtain but did not turn to go. "My lord, the Kingdom is divided. Urien is at war. Leave this brooding and take up your arms. Britain needs you."

But he turned his back to me. "Britain will have to wait."

I gasped. But he had only shared his grief with me, not set it aside. I saw I would have to do more. I went back to my room and bade Ailsa help me change into my riding clothes and dress my hair for the road. She obeyed in silence. I had told her nothing of my plan, but although she saw the King's belongings in my room and must have been filled with curiosity, she said nothing. I think it was the Sword that kept her silent; indeed, its very presence filled the room with an awful majesty, and I did not say much either, and then only in a whisper.

When I was dressed, I donned the King's cloak. Ailsa's fingers shook as she fastened the Dragon brooch on my shoulder. The cloak was heavy, and so long that it dragged on the floor. I gathered the extra folds over my left arm. But we had trouble with the sword belt. It was too big and could not be made small enough to hang on my narrow hips. More than once the Sword itself nearly touched the floor.

"Never mind," I whispered at last. "I see no other way. I will have to draw it and carry it in my hand."

Ailsa clutched her amulets, her eyes wide with fear, but said nothing.

I held the scabbard and put my hand to the hilt. It felt smooth and cold. Gently I drew the Sword, and we both gasped as the living blade caught the lamplight and threw it back, filling the room with a glorious light. It was heavy and trembled in my grip like a live thing, seeking action. Now was the time, or never, and I pushed the curtain aside and strode into the room.

"King Arthur!" I cried, and when he turned, I lifted the Sword to my forehead in salute, as I had seen his soldiers do.

He stared, dumbfounded.

"If you will not lead your troops to save Britain, I will do it in your place. I will not let her go down into the dark, even if I am only a woman. I can sacrifice my life as easily as you, and the men will follow me."

"Put down the Sword." He could not take his eyes from it, and the sight of it in my hand shook him to the core.

I held it aloft, where its weight was better balanced, and did not strain my arm so. "No, my lord. If I let it go, it will drop to the floor. Come and take it from me."

In four quick strides he was at my side and roughly took it from my hand. Then he went still. My arm felt dead, but his had come alive. It was as if the power from the blade ran up through the hilt and into his body, awakening the flame that had gone out. His face changed; the doleful marks of grief gave way to the eager quickness he was known for; his eyes lit with joy. He looked down at the Sword with awe and crossed himself. Tears of thanksgiving sprang to my eyes unbidden. He took it for the sign, as I hoped he would.

"What have I done?" he said suddenly.

Across the room, on the landing beyond the door, Bedwyr, Kay, and Lancelot were kneeling, open-mouthed. He saw them and bowed low.

"My lords. If you can find it in your hearts to forgive me, I beg you will. I had no thoughts of abdication, but I see now it is what I have done. I was weak and allowed myself to be blinded. But this woman has opened my eyes."

He turned to me. He addressed me as he did them, man to man.

"My thanks, Guinevere. We will speak of this after. And now, if I may take your cloak, which drags upon the ground?" His mouth twitched, and his eyes were smiling. I fairly tore the cloak off, as his knights ran into the room, all talking at once, and Varric threw open the trunk to find his traveling clothes.

The trumpets sounded as they left, and the signal fires were lighted to give warning of the High King's coming. He took Lancelot with him and sent Bedwyr to command the patrols along the Saxon Shore.

"This Queen," he had announced to all, "is her own protection."

21 ✹ the farewell

The High King arrived just in time. Urien was an experienced leader and knew the value of patience. He had waited as long as he could. When it became clear that Heuil intended to assume the kingship of Strathclyde and had got his twin's support, the other brothers came together and chose sides. Most joined Heuil, figuring once they had Urien off their backs, they could treat with Heuil for power. But Hapgar fled to Rheged with two younger brothers and allied himself with Urien, being disgusted with Heuil's rank injustice and his greed. The High King arrived on the eve of a pitched battle between the kingdoms. Hapgar knelt before him, swearing allegiance, and Arthur knighted him.

Against such war leaders as Urien, Lancelot, and Arthur, the Strathclyde forces had slim hope, and indeed, many of the soldiers fled as soon as they saw the Pendragon banner and realized who was there. Heuil and his brothers fought bravely, having the most to lose. The twins were killed in battle, and Hapgar was set upon the throne. All the brothers swore allegiance to the High King at day's end, and friendship with Rheged.

So those long weeks of worry ended swiftly. The Saxons, knowing their enemy well, did not attack, and Bedwyr was home before the King. All was quiet in Camelot. King Pelleas married Lady Niniane, but they stayed in Camelot. For she would not leave to the Lady's shrine on Ynys Witrin or to Pelleas' castle in the River Isles, until she had seen the King. I spoke to her about it once, wondering how she felt about Merlin's going and whether she knew what the King thought of her.

"I know he prophesied betrayal at his end," she admitted in her quiet voice. "But Merlin gave me everything himself. Not his power only, but his memories. Everything that was in his mind is now in mine. I have the knowledge in me. I know the King thinks

I betrayed him, but I do not know what he means by it. Whether it was the taking of the last thoughts, while he lay dying . . ." She paused, and I shuddered. The image she conjured up was not a lovely one. "Or whether he means I took Pelleas to my bed while Merlin still lived. Both could be counted as betrayal. But truly, Guinevere, there was no harm in either. I have loved Merlin dearly, as father, counsellor, teacher, and man. I did what he bade me do. He wanted me to take it all from him, and time was short."

If she felt she had to justify herself to me, it seemed she was not free of guilt in this regard. I watched her closely.

"Then he is truly dead, and not sleeping?"

She turned to me, shocked. "Of course. How not?"

"You know not the other prophecy, then? That he should go living to his grave?"

She took a quick breath, and her eyes filled with tears.

"So," she said slowly. "That is what it was. I felt, at the very least, that he kept something from me. There was a wall. Even with his power, I could not reach beyond. The god stood there." She rose, trembling, visibly upset. "It cannot be. I felt his death come. May the Mother give me strength—Arthur will never forgive me and never trust me, if these things are true."

"Niniane, you are only human. Let me speak with the King when he returns, before you go to see him. I know your distress is real. Let me prepare the way for you. He will need you beside him in the future, and after all, that was Merlin's plan."

She nodded. "You have my thanks." Then she looked at me sideways and said hesitantly, "Do you know why the king has sent a ship to the Orkney kingdom?"

"Yes. To fetch his son."

She exhaled slowly and smiled at last. "I am glad you know."

"I asked him to do it."

"Indeed?" She raised an eyebrow. "That is generous of you. I wonder if you know what you are doing."

"If he is Arthur's, then I know I want him here."

She shrugged. "So be it. But don't start feeling sorry for his mother. Be sure he keeps the Queen Morgause in exile. To bring her into contact with her sons again would be disaster."

"Niniane, you are cruel! They are her children!"

She looked at me with cold, dark eyes. "She has no more mother love than an adder. The sooner she is dead, the better."

"She is of the King's blood. Can she be evil?"

Niniane's smile was bitter. "Yes," was all she said.

* * *

The King came home one hot morning past midsummer, and all the town turned out to greet him. He had a month of work to make up, a month's worth of petitions to hear, and reports to take from his commanders and knights errant. He was busy all the day.

The knights errant he heard first, always. These were those of his Companions whom he trusted most, and who understood his justice. They traveled across Britain for months at a time, visiting petty kings and lords, hearing their complaints and the petitions of the people, and dispensing the High King's justice throughout the land. They carried the King's seal and a writ of appointment for a term. But lest they should become corrupt with power, the writ was always dated, and any man who complained of their judgment was free to seek the High King's in Camelot. In this way, Arthur hoped to change the vagaries of laws, which had always varied from kingdom to kingdom, depending only upon the whim of the king, into something along the lines of Roman law, the same for all.

When a knight returned from his travels at the expiration of his writ, he gave a full report to the King in Council, so the King could judge how things stood. Then he received couriers, or sent them if need be, and then he heard petitions from all who came, high and low, to get justice.

All day Niniane and I waited to see him. But he worked steadily until midafternoon, then called the Companions to Council. This lasted until dinner.

When I met him outside the hall, I thought he looked a different man. He had put on flesh, though still was thin, but his love of life was back. He had come to terms with his fears, and looked serene.

"Welcome, my lord," I said, dropping into my curtsy. "We are glad to have you back!"

He smiled at me and slipped an arm about my waist and drew me near, although others were about. "How are you, Gwen? It's wonderful to see you. I would talk with you awhile, if you can await me, but it will be a late night, I'm afraid."

"I will await you, my lord."

"Have you forgotten my name?" he whispered, bending down to kiss me.

"I will await you, my lord Arthur," I replied, grinning.

Lancelot, behind us, coughed gently as the doors swung open. Arthur laughed and, releasing me, offered me his arm.

"I am reminded of my manners," he said with mock gravity,

then beckoned Lancelot to come up on his other side, and threw an arm across his shoulders. "The King of Lanascol saved my life yet once again in Strathclyde," he said, looking at me. Then, turning to Lancelot: "My thanks again, friend."

So we three went into hall side by side. But my heart was heavy. By referring to Lancelot as the King of Lanascol, Arthur had let me know that Lancelot had made his request and that it had been granted. Although I had fully expected it, I grieved to know it, and I could not share the King's joy.

After dinner, he sent for Niniane. He had stopped three days at Caerleon on his trip south from Strathclyde and had ridden over to Merlin's cave again. He had shouted, but heard nothing but gentle echoes through the hills. All had been quiet, still and peaceful. It gave him ease of heart, and when he left, he was master of his grief. They were together a long time.

Afterward he called a meeting of the Companions, where Lancelot announced his news to all, and the date of his wedding was fixed.

During all this time I walked in my garden, for the night was hot, and a cool breeze eddied around the fountain. The moon in her first quarter rose late and yet sailed high in the night sky before the King came to me.

He walked along the path with an easy stride and, when I rose to greet him, took me in his arms and kissed me. "Hello, Gwen. Thank you for waiting."

"How did you deal with Niniane? She loved Merlin dearly and did not mean to betray him, if that is what she did. I spoke with her, my lord. She knew nothing of the prophecy you feared."

He led me to the bench, and we sat down together."

"I know. You need not champion her cause. I have apologized for my wrath. I've had time to think it through with a clearer head, and I see well she is the last person to wish Merlin ill. If she says she did not know, then she did not. Merlin must have wanted it that way. Anyway, that's not why I sent for her. I wanted to hear about his last hours . . . and get her advice on what to do about Morgaine."

"Yes?" I had been thinking the same thing myself. She was the King's niece, and there must be some way we could help the poor child.

"Urien had us to his castle after battle. He showed excellent sense in his handling of Caw's sons, and I did him all the honor I could. While I was there, he took me to his daughter." In the dim moonlight, his face was dark, but his voice was full of pain.

"She is so afraid, poor child. She fears anything that moves. She fears her own shadow. She fears all men, even her father. He is afraid, and not without cause, that she will never recover her wits. I asked Niniane about the Lady's House of Healing, where Lancelot recovered from his grievous wound. I wanted to know if she thought the women there could help the girl."

"And what did she say? Surely they can do something?"

"She said it could be done, but it must wait. Time must pass. Certain things must happen."

He sounded uncomfortable, and I deduced that Niniane had had a vision in his presence. "What did she see?" I asked.

"Is my mind an open book to you, Gwen?"

I smiled. "I know you well."

"You do indeed. She bade me be patient. 'All things come to him who waits,' she told me. One of Merlin's favorite lines. I wonder if she knew she was stealing . . . well, I will wait and keep the child in mind. She is young to be taken from her mother, even though Morgan is more interested in witchcraft than in childcraft."

This was news to me. "Did you have speech with Queen Morgan, my lord?"

"No. I had no wish to. She has not made Urien's life a pleasure to him, and he is a good man. She has made him suffer for the honor of being my brother-in-law."

I realized there was no reason why Arthur should feel close to his sister. They had been raised apart and never met until he was made High King. Still, it made me shiver to hear him speak of her with coldness.

In the darkness, he was a shadow darker than the rest. I reached out, and held his hand. "Niniane told me you have sent for the Orkney princes."

"Yes." His voice went flat, and I felt his tension in his grip. But their mother, I have ordered to stay in exile. She is a witch, Gwen, and her power over men must be seen to be believed. Even men with judgment, who know her to be evil, will do her bidding willingly, and not know why. I do not trust her here in Britain. If I brought her south, I might be forced to take steps I would regret."

"You would not kill her! And bring a blood feud down upon my head? No, by God. I want Lot's sons to be my soldiers, to fight for me, not against me. I will give Lancelot the training of them. They will hold the north for me when they are grown. If they are Lot's sons, they will take to it like ducks to water. But

I must get them young, or she will warp their minds against me. If she hasn't already."

"And Mordred? Will you single him out, or treat him like the others? What will be his status here?"

"Ah, I know not, till I have seen the boy. So much depends on him."

"When will they get here?"

"Give it two months at the outside. I wish—it is hard to wait, knowing they are coming. I feel the need to make up for the lost years."

"But you said yourself, you could not have had him by you," I whispered, hearing a father's love in his voice and feeling again the old, familiar pain. Arthur knew me. He sensed it instantly, and put his arms around me and drew me onto his lap.

"Gwen," he said softly, "he is your gift to me. Whatever happens between us when he gets here, whether or not he can bear me as his father or his King, I will always love you dearly for this gift. Without you, I never would have known him."

"But for me, you might have known him sooner." I was trembling, thinking that had he not feared to wound me, had I not been so sensitive, he could have asked me years ago to welcome his son.

"Never think it. Had my wife borne children, I would never know him at all. He would be lost to me." His arms tightened about me, and I rested my head on his shoulder. Strength and peace flowed from him into me, and set my heart at rest. "Had you been other than you are, Gwen, everything would be so different. My Kingdom would not be whole. I have not yet thanked you for that."

"I am not alone responsible," I told him. "Everyone tried to get at you, Bedwyr, Kay, Niniane . . . Lancelot. We made a plan together."

"But you had more courage than all of them," he said quietly. "You disobeyed me to my face and gave me truth I could not swallow when you told me I was no longer your King. I cannot tell you what that did to me."

"It was not what turned you, my lord."

"No. But it planted the seed. And you alone had the courage to draw the Sword. No one else would have dared. My soldiers think you must have magic power, and I—I know not what to think."

"I acted in ignorance, my lord. I did not know it was such an awful thing to touch the Sword. I merely wished to shock you."

I sensed him smiling. "You succeeded. But I was amazed you could hold it, that it stayed in your hand."

"It was heavy," I said, recalling the feel of it, "and hard to carry, for a woman. I was glad you took it from me. It trembled like a live thing and sought your grip."

He let out a long breath, I thought in satisfaction. "So, you felt its life. I wondered, but feared to ask. All soldiers believe that good swords carry the breath of life in the blade. But that one—this is known—that Sword carries the spark of the god. It is no wonder my knights were afraid to touch it. I wonder they let you try."

"I put it off as long as I could. But something had to be done."

"Yes. God knows, that is true. I forced you to it."

He was quiet awhile, and I knew he felt more thanks than he could express. And then suddenly, softly, out of the dark it came.

"Guinevere, can you bear this—this parting with Lancelot?"

I froze. I wished heartily I were not sitting upon his lap, where he could feel my trembling and my every intake of breath.

"My lord," I whispered. "Don't."

"He told me what he told you. And I deduced that you had forborne to tell him the real reason Elaine was in disgrace." He waited, but I could not speak. "I gave him permission to wed her and take her away. But I grieved to do it. Not only for his sake, but for yours."

"My lord." I shook as the tears fell, and he hugged me gently.

"Why did you not tell him, Gwen? It would have kept him here. It would have foiled Elaine. It is a thing a man might wish to know about the woman he intended to marry."

I shook my head. "He—he had already lain with her. It was too late. If—if I told him, you know him, Arthur, where his honor is involved. He would never have forgiven himself. The shame would have eaten at him all his life."

"Ahhh. That is why I did not tell him myself." He held me tightly, and gave me a chance to control my tears. "Perhaps it is better this way," he said at last. "I asked Niniane about it, but she had seen nothing concerning it. But it may turn out well. He will be back . . . The wedding is fixed for next week. He asked me to tell you."

"Please," I whispered, touching his hand, "please, Arthur, don't make me go. I cannot—it is such a travesty—I cannot watch as he binds himself to Elaine."

"You are excused. I will be there. But I shall not enjoy it, either."

"Thank you . . . when does he intend to leave?"

"In a month. Perhaps later. It depends upon Elaine. Do you know, after she schemed for this, she is surprised that he is taking her to Less Britain. Apparently she expected to stay here and be a thorn in your side for the rest of her days. Lancelot says she is angry at having to leave."

Had I not been so unhappy, I could have laughed.

"She counted on his honor to bind him to her. Now she must obey his honor's demands. All the sons of his house are born in Lanascol. She should have had longer sight. But that is Elaine."

He sighed. "So, you know. It was the last thing I had on my mind to tell you. I did not speak of it to Lancelot, but the news has been buzzing about my ears since I rode in. Bedwyr confirms it. She is with child."

I bit my lip hard. "I knew it before he did."

"Well, then. I see you understand." The tone of his voice changed, and I felt his lips against my hair. "All I ever wanted in a wife was someone pleasant, kind, and soft-voiced to come home to. When I saw you, I thanked the gods for the gift of beauty, as well. But such sense, such loyalty, and love, these I never counted on. These are your gifts to me."

"My lord," I breathed, blinking back tears, "they are easily given to such a man as you."

He pulled me closer and touched his lips to my face. "It is over a month since the solstice," he said softly. "So much time I have wasted!"

Lancelot and Elaine were married with Arthur in attendance. I gave out I was ill and stayed away. It fooled no one. From then on, Elaine sat on his right hand at table. It was her right, and I could not prevent it. She said very little to him, but I could say nothing at all. Alyse and Pellinore stayed in Camelot as the King's guests, until the time of departure. This was put off until mid-October, when the winds were right, but it could not be put off forever, and at last the day arrived. The King had promised me an hour alone with Lancelot before he left, but in the bustle of preparations I feared there would not be time. And Elaine seemed determined to keep me from him; thrice in the last three days I tried to steal a moment of his time, and thrice she thwarted my desire. She followed him everywhere and hung on him shamelessly, looking helplessly up at him with her great blue eyes and never letting him forget his obligation.

I paced about my chamber in despair as the last morning

dawned, my head so full of things to say I feared I should burst if I could not say them. At last a page arrived to say Lancelot awaited me in the King's library, and I raced from my apartments, eagerness overcoming sense, toward our tryst. When I reached the library I found it still and empty. But the garden door stood open, and I stepped out into the cool morning sun and called his name. Nearby, the gardeners worked preparing beds for winter; the chief gardener rose and ducked his head.

"I'm sorry, my lady, but Sir Lancelot is not here." He sounded apologetic and stared nervously at the ground. "We've all been here since sunup and have not seen him. I've heard tell he is with the King."

"And where, then, is the King?" I demanded crossly, wondering who had sent the page with such a message. He shrugged, and all the men looked sidelong at one another. Was it possible, I asked myself, she had duped me yet again?

"Never mind, good sir. I beg your pardon for my manners. Thank you kindly for your information; it is not your fault it is not what I would hear. I will find the King myself."

I hurried back to my chamber, this time more mindful of my dignity. I had not liked the knowing looks in the gardeners' eyes.

"Ailsa!" I called when I reached her doorway. But no one answered. Swiftly I mounted the steps to my chamber and stopped dead upon the threshold. On my terrace, wrapped in a traveling cloak and as cool as she could be, stood Elaine. Her back to me, she looked down upon my garden. I blinked twice and shook my head but she was not an apparition.

"Elaine!" She whirled, saw me, and smiled slowly in contempt. "What are you doing here? Get out! How do you dare?"

The smile only deepened. She reached out a soft-gloved hand and pointed to the bed. "I came to return your gifts."

Every single thing I had ever made for her or bought for her or given her lay upon the coverlet. I walked closer, unbelieving. There lay the yellow gown—her favorite—which I had embroidered with stars eight, ten years ago? And the woolen sash I had made with her name stitched at the edges, to keep her warm in the long Welsh winters. The seashell I had found on the beach and polished for her, which spoke with the sea's voice when she held it to her ear, the leather pouch I dyed and sewed to hold her little treasures, the leggings, the pillow cover, the bracelets, pendants, and trinkets, the cushions and the slippers, all were there. I reached out a trembling hand and took up the comb of horn I had carved myself—how lovingly!—in Northgallis the winter my father had taken ill. I had made it to please my new cousin, whom he said I must befriend. My shaking finger touched the "E" carved at the crest; childish work, perhaps, but heartfelt, with love and hope in every stroke—yet even this she did not want.

Carefully I replaced the comb on the coverlet. "If you don't want them, I will keep them. They still mean something to me."

"I don't want them, obviously." She turned away with a careless shrug and looked once again down at the garden.

I walked out to her. "Did you send the page to draw me away?"

"Of course."

"Well. You have done what you came to do. Now get out. You are here without my leave."

She paid no attention, but fiddled with her glove. "I care nothing for your leave. You are too full of yourself, Guinevere. Being High Queen has gone to your head. I await my husband, who is with Arthur."

I followed her glance and saw, at the end of the garden, Lancelot and Arthur. Arthur's arm was slung around Lancelot's shoulders, and Lancelot held Arthur by the waist. They walked and talked together in close conference. I would have smiled to see them, if Elaine had not been there.

"Await him somewhere else."

"And let you have speech with him? Indeed, I will not."

"Why do you fear it? What are you afraid I will tell him?"

Slowly she turned and met my eyes. The autumn air, or perhaps her pregnancy, gave her pale skin a glow of health. With golden curls framing her aquiline features, she looked young and very pretty. But there was nothing soft and yielding in her face. Already one could see the woman she would become: hard, cool, and unforgiving.

"I fear you not, Guinevere. You dare not tell him now. I keep him from you merely because you wish to see him."

I caught my breath and stepped back. "Elaine, what has happened to you? You never used to be so cruel!"

"I am as I have always been. It is you who have changed. You have forgotten your beginnings."

"And what is amiss with my beginnings?" I bristled.

She shrugged and smiled again that cold, unfeeling smile.

"Northgallis is a small, dark, and pagan kingdom. You came from thence into the light and power of Gwynedd, a Christian land. Had you not made that journey Arthur never would have noticed you. Yet you have never given us our due. Once here, you turned your back upon us and forgot our gifts to you."

"How can you think so! Why, Pellinore is—"

"I speak," she cut in coldly, "not of Pellinore, but of my mother and myself. You have turned the King against me to serve your selfish ends—"

"*I* turned the King?"

"—and your dreams of power. You would have served him better by stepping aside. You have consigned him to a future as barren as your own, and for what? So that you might be Queen!"

"That is not true! Ask Arthur yourself, if you dare! I—I—I cannot help my fate, but Arthur has chosen his of his own will!"

This time she smiled in pleasure and stepped closer to me, backing me against the balustrade. "Indeed he has. He has chosen more than he knows. Listen closely. I have something of importance to tell you before I leave. I have an informant on Ynys Witrin—this you knew—who serves the Lady's shrine when she is not in Melwas' bed. But for the gold I pay her, she would not stay to serve that insufferable Niniane. However, her information is beyond price. Have you ever heard of the Lady's Oracle?"

"Do you mean—in Northgallis we called it the Sacred Speaking, when—"

"—Every thrice three years when the full moon rises on the night of the equinox, the chief priestess climbs the Tor, sacrifices upon the Black Rock, and holds the sacred crystal to the moon's face. In it, if she is worthy, she sees a vision of the future."

"Yes. I know of it. So was Arthur's coming foretold."

"Well." She leaned closer until I felt her hot breath upon my cheek. "A month ago Niniane saw a future that she will not tell the King. The whole shrine is alive with whispers. Niniane secludes herself and speaks to no one."

I knew Elaine to be capable of every sort of falsehood; I knew her motives and the depth of her dislike; yet this revelation struck like a cold knife in my belly, and I shrank from her. Since the night of Arthur's return, no one had seen hide nor hair of Niniane.

Elaine's voice sank into a singsong whisper. "The wheel is turning and the world will change. Those who are weak shall grow in power, and the mighty shall be cut down. A dark prince from the Otherworld shall arise and slay the Dragon; a great serpent shall wade forth from the sea and swallow the Dragon's remains. The Dragon himself will be borne across water and buried in glass. Forever." I covered my ears with my hands to blot out her words. "And all this, Guinevere, is a result of the King's choice to keep you."

"No! No!"

"And a son of Lancelot," she hissed at me, opening her cloak and spreading her hands upon the hard mound of her belly, "shall, with a bloody sword and a righteous fury, renew the Light in Britain before she goes forever down into the dark. You will live to see it all. You will be spared nothing!"

I staggered back; my knees would not support me. "It cannot be! Dear God, it cannot be! You say it only to wound me—well, wound me, then, and have done. But Arthur—Arthur must be spared!"

She began to laugh softly. "This is not my vision, fool. Pleading with me changes nothing. I tell you so that you may know what fate you have brought upon him. You should have listened to me when you had the chance."

"I don't believe you! I will not believe you! You want him still, and look only for a way to hurt me—get out, Elaine, I can bear the sight of you no longer!"

"Believe what you like. I need not obey you. When my husbands calls me, then I will go. You will not have speech or comfort of him while I live. And once we are gone, Guinevere, you will never see him again."

I gasped and clutched at her arm. "He has promised! He has promised the King!"

She flung off my hand and smiled, sliding her hands across her belly. "He has promised me, as well. And I have ways of keeping him."

I cried out at that and saw her face grow dark. "You greedy little whore, you want him still! You want the both of them!"

Too quick for thought, I slapped her face.

"By God!" she screamed. "After I am through with you, neither of them will ever want to see your face again!" She tore off her gloves and showed me her hands. Her nails had been sharpened to claws.

"Go ahead!" I shouted. "Do it! You do me a service to mar me! Oh, God, why do you hesitate? Do it now!"

She raised her arms to strike. I lifted my face for the blow, when Arthur took her suddenly from behind. Lancelot, aghast, raced after him up the stairs.

Caught in Arthur's grip, Elaine turned and pressed against his body, fastening her mouth on his. He recoiled and pushed her away.

"You should have chosen *me*, my lord!" she cried.

"Not," Arthur said darkly, turning his head to wipe his lips against his sleeve, "for the price of my soul."

"My God, Elaine!" Lancelot pulled her roughly away and she whirled, snarling.

"Don't touch me! I'll lay your face open!"

"What ails you? Are you in pain? Come to your senses!"

"Do *you* accuse *me* of lack of sense, my lord?" She began to laugh. "What a hypocrite you are! You lust for the Queen and lie with me—is that sense?"

"Elaine!" I gasped. "How can you?"

She turned to me, the cruel smile still upon her face.

"If I am forced against my will to leave Britain, you will see how quietly I go. Defend him at your peril, Guinevere. He is your lover, and the whole world knows it, but the King."

Both men froze. Falling to my knees, I covered my face with my hands. "Sweet Christ, what do you want of us?"

"Whatever thin tale you have told to save your honor, *I* know the truth of what went on in Melwas' cabin. And I shall see the whole world learns of it, if I am forced to leave."

"Arthur!" Lancelot gasped, crimson-faced. "I swear by the Book of God I never—"

Arthur waved him silent. "I know it well. And so does she."

"If you *ever* say a word against the Queen," Lancelot cried, standing before her, "I swear you shall pay for it with you life!"

"How brave you are!" she spat.

He took her arm; she flew at his face. He was quick, but not quite quick enough. One nail ripped a bloody gouge across his cheek.

"Let me be!"

He ignored her and roughly pinned her hands behind her back.

"Take care that wound does not fester!" I cried. "Those nails were meant for me—they may be tainted!"

"You are my wife, Elaine," Lancelot said solemnly. "Try to remember it."

"Because I love you so," she replied with venom, struggling against his grip.

I shut my eyes and looked away. "Oh, God! How could you marry her? Lancelot, how could you do it to yourself?"

Arthur's hand came down upon my shoulder, and I shoved my fist into my mouth to stop the words.

"Lancelot!" Elaine hissed, great, slow tears creeping from her eyes. "Always Lancelot! Does no one care how *I* feel? Dragged from the land where I was born, exiled from my parents and my King—and for what? Because this man of honor you love so dearly has no more command of his flesh than a rutting stag!"

"That's enough!" Arthur said sharply. "I feel for your condition, but not your fate. You chose this, Elaine, with both eyes open. Don't pretend that you are cruelly treated. It fools no one. And it might so easily be worse." She heard the veiled threat and lowered her eyes. "Go now and get some rest. The journey will be a long one for you."

Elaine looked up and flashed him a look of open longing.

"Arthur," she whispered, "let her go! She is your death!"

Lancelot clapped a hand across her mouth but she pulled away. "Tell him, Gwen! Tell him, if you dare!"

Angrily, Lancelot picked her up and carried her back across my chamber.

"Lancelot! Is this farewell?"

At the door he cast me a swift look of longing and regret, and then he was gone. I bent my head and wept.

"Gwen." Arthur came to where I knelt and knelt beside me. "Dry your tears. You will see him again. He will be back."

I brought his hand to my lips and kissed his ring. "My lord, forgive me. I should never have brought her here!"

"It is not your fault, Gwen. I forgive her for it—poor girl, young and highborn as she is, she will find no happiness in life. She does not know how."

"I will *never* forgive her for it!"

"Yes, you will, in time. Let time pass."

I raised my head and looked into his dark eyes, warm and comforting. "Hold me, Arthur. Give me strength." He put his arms around me and held me gently.

"What is it," he said softly, "you must tell me?"

"Nothing! I don't know what you mean."

He laughed quietly. "What a terrible liar you are! Like it or not, you have the gift of truth, and I can read your face. Elaine told you something she wanted me to hear. Something you fear to tell me."

I looked up at him and wondered how he would feel when he knew. His arms tightened gently about me. "Tell me."

"Niniane is the one who should tell you."

"Ahhhh." Still his face was calm. "It is about the Speaking. I thought as much."

"Has she come to see you?"

"Not yet. But she will."

"Are you sure?"

"Very sure. Don't distress yourself, Guinevere, she has seen nothing Merlin did not see before her. Be brave and tell me."

"Did he see a great change coming? And a serpent from the sea? And a—" I gulped and clutched his tunic. "—a dark prince of demons who will—who will slay you?"

He caught his breath and let it out slowly. Still his face was calm, but his eyes looked far away. "Yes," he said at last, "all this he foresaw."

"And did he tell you—this was all because you chose to keep me? No wonder Merlin hated me all those years ago!"

"What nonsense is this? Merlin hate you? There was never hate in that man, even for my enemies. Is that what Elaine told you? Well, my dear, consider the source."

"Then—it is not true that you will die because of me?"

He laughed outright. "Certainly not. Quite the opposite. My fate, if Merlin is to be believed, was written in the stars before ever you were born."

"Then what does the Speaking mean, my lord? Will you be drowned at sea? Oh, Arthur, don't ever take ship again!"

He smiled at that and shook his head. "This is a distant future, Gwen. Let it be."

"And—and Lancelot's son, did Merlin see that, too?"

He frowned and his focus sharpened. "What about Lancelot's son?"

"He will wield a bloody sword and bring the Light of righteousness to Britain—before she—no, that's all."

"To my knowledge, Merlin saw nothing regarding Lancelot. Are you sure this was part of the Speaking, or was it something Elaine perhaps invented?"

"For all I know, she invented everything."

He smiled and kissed me gently. "Britain will not go down into the dark. You need not fear to tell me what it is you fear the most."

"You knew?"

"I've heard whispers. But this, Guinevere, Merlin has seen, and often. It is a true Sight. Someday, when we are no more than memories in a bard's song, Britain will be the greatest land in all the world. And you and I, if we are constant, will have a hand in making it so."

I thought again of Bedwyr's words. "Everlasting?" I whispered. His eyes were shining. "If you like. Long-lasting, at any rate.

No King could ask for more. So you see why I do not worry about the future."

I looked up at him and smiled. "Even *you*, my lord, even you believe in visions when it suits you!"

He grinned. "Every king does. It's wise policy."

"Oh, Arthur, bring your son here quickly! If we are to build a lasting legacy for Britain, we must train him now!"

Something moved behind his eyes, and he drew me closer.

"He is coming." He paused. "Let us pray God he makes a King."

Haemas blinked.

Between one breath and the next, the warm dining hall had gone cold as the winter-wrapped mountains outside—and silent, so mind-numbingly silent. The crackling fire in the great stone hearth had burned down into red coals, and the platters heaped with roast ebari and baked whiteroot were mysteriously half-emptied. Two of the delicate green crystal goblets had tipped over, and red wine stained the tablecloth like blood.

She saw her father's ornately carved chair tumbled on its side, and an icy knot of fear formed in her stomach. Only a second ago she had been sitting across the table from her stepmother and cousin, half-listening as they discussed the boring details of last night's gathering at Rald'ayn. She slid out of her seat, confused, then stopped as her toe bumped something soft and yielding.

She looked down: her father sprawled at the foot of the table on the plush maroon rug, one gnarled finger grazing her boot. Her throat ached. She wanted to run, to scream, to do anything but just stand there, gazing down at his white and empty face.

"What's the matter, skivit?" her cousin Jarid asked from behind her. "Having second thoughts?"

She tried to turn around, but her body wouldn't answer.

Jarid walked into her field of vision and nudged her father's shoulder with his boot. The gray-haired head rolled loosely. "Going after your own father like that." He crossed his arms and smiled his familiar crooked smile, as always, in perfect control. "And at such a tender age, too, only fif-

299

teen. Not even properly Named. Whatever will the Council say?"

Every muscle in her body ached with her effort to move. "I don't understand." Her voice was only a hoarse whisper. "What's wrong with him? What—what happened?"

Jarid arched a golden eyebrow. "You killed him, of course. I always knew it would come to this."

A drop of ice-cold sweat trickled down her temple as she fought to move and failed. Jarid must have a mindlock on her motor centers. "Let me go!"

"Before the Council arrives?" His voice was mocking. "I think not, my girl."

She closed her eyes and reached for every bit of psionic strength she possessed, trying to break Jarid's hold. Time blurred as she hurled herself against her cousin's will, but he was so much older and better trained that she found herself lost in a red haze of pain.

"Damnation!" She heard his voice from a great distance away. "Who would have thought it?"

"What are you going to do now?"

Alyssa, Haemas thought, sliding down a long blackness. That was her stepmother's voice.

Jarid answered, but she could not make out the words.

"Then do it!" Alyssa's voice was also fading. "Let the Barrier k . . . her, the sooner, the bet . . ."

The Desalayan mountainside, littered with jagged gray rock, sloped sharply down from Haemas's feet. Her boot slipped and the sound of falling scree echoed hollowly across the mountains. Her startled breath puffed white in the chill air. Shivering, she hunched against an exposed rockface and stared about with bewildered eyes.

The orange sun hung low in the west, the sky a riot of rose and gold. She thought she recognized the rolling, soft green valley far below. She must be about halfway down the outward face of Kith Shiene, the sheltering mountain that stood between the Highlands and the outside world, but only a second ago she had been in the dining hall with Jarid. She tried to remember how she had come here, but a fevered pounding began behind her eyes and the details retreated behind an impenetrable curtain. She felt sick, dizzy, unreal. Then, out of the confusion, one compelling certainty leaped at her: she must get away. When the Council learned she had killed her father, the punishment would be death.

Below, pale-blue psi-active ilsera crystals had been embedded in the mountainside, each one as big as the head of a full-grown man. Since the first handful of Kashi had realized what their developing Talents meant and seeded themselves into these mountins in order to remain apart and stabilize their gene pool, the non-Talented chierra had remained below, breeding themselves randomly and overrunning the land. The Barrier had been erected to prevent the chierras' superior numbers from invading the Highlands.

The crystals shimmered as Haemas approached, triggered by her brainwaves, and her heart began to pound. She had entered the Barrier once before, several years ago, as part of her training, but it had been a wrenching experience.

She clenched her hands and edged into the pulsing blueness, trying to shield her mind from the Barrier-generated pain as she had been taught. At the first touch of the light, though, she doubled over and struggled for breath. A raw, scalding agony burned through her body, relentless as an avalanche. She clenched her hands and fought against the pain, but it was as though she'd never learned to shield, as though she weren't Kashi at all.

Her breath came in aching gasps as she inched downward, focusing on the need to keep moving above everything else. The frigid mountain wind blasted through her thin indoor clothing, but she was quickly drenched in sweat. With each step, the pain thickened until a red haze swirled behind her eyes. Every comfort she had ever known in her life, every affection, every certainty, seemed distant and unreal.

Her foot slipped. She lost her balance, slid, then tumbled several yards over dirt and loose rock, her right shoulder coming up hard against a jagged outcropping. Throbbing and bloody, she clung to it until her sight cleared slightly; then, taking a ragged breath, she lurched back onto her feet and stumbled on. When she finally reached the far edge of the blue shimmer, the false agony gradually faded, but the pain in her wrenched shoulder remained.

Shivering, she edged ever downwards.

Ten hours now, Jarid thought, and still the Lord of Tal'ayn lingered on that indistinct sill between life and death. Jarid's aunt by marriage, the Lady Alyssa, had sent for the best healers from every High House, but they all said nothing more could be done.

Jarid watched as the remaining eleven High Lords stood around his uncle's bedside in tense silence, their bent heads ranging from sun-bright gold to the palest silver.

"And you say the seneschal is dead, my Lady?" Lord Rald turned to the young white-faced mistress of Tal'ayn.

Alyssa nodded, her golden eyes narrowed with anger. "Jarid foung the body in the same room, not even cold, and my husband was as you see him." She reached down a trembling hand and brushed the cheek of the unconscious gray-haired man in the great canopied bed.

Lord Senn patted the woman's slender shoulder. "What of his daughter, the Lady Haemas?"

"Gone." Alyssa's bitter voice choked. "I have Searched for her myself, but she seems to have fled Outside."

"You're sure it was her?" Rald leaned one arm against the mantel and shook his head. "If I remember correctly, the child is only fourteen or fifteen."

"She's fifteen." Aaren Killian's pale gold eyes met Jarid's for a heart-stopping second, then turned away, dismissing him. "Tal and I have already agreed on a marriage contract. She will marry my oldest son, Kimbrel, as soon as she's Named in a few weeks."

His oldest son. Jarid's jaw tightened. Someday he would make Killian regret refusing to acknowledge his birth. He shoved through the onlookers to Alyssa's side and took her arm. "What difference does it make how old my wretched cousin is? I *saw* her do it!"

"Jarid Tal Ketral, isn't it?" Rald nodded at him. "I remember you from the Council's last Temporal Conclave. You were quite promising, if I recall correctly."

So the old fool had noticed him, Jarid thought behind his tightly woven screens. He was careful not to let the inner smile reach his lips. The rest of these old fossils had better learn to pay attention to him as well, or he'd displace the whole lot.

Rald drew his ebari-leather gloves out of his belt and thrust his right hand into one. "Well, of course she must be found. I'm sure we're all agreed on that. We can't afford to have even a half-trained traitor of that age running wild among the Lowland chierra. Who knows what ideas might get into their

302

heads? It could even breed rebellion. They're barely kept in check as it is."

The others nodded. Senn turned back to the younger man. "Then we will trust you, Jarid, to look after things here at Tal'ayn." He hesitated, gazing down at the ashen face of the injured man. "Both of your uncle's brothers are dead, and the line has thinned out so much in recent generations that, with the girl missing, the question of succession is unclear. In spite of everything, you might even have a claim on the estate yourself."

Jarid's face burned. He felt the simmering rage that rose to the surface every time the question of his parentage came up. His mother, Danih, had been a weak, sentimental fool, and it seemed the whole Highlands knew how she had cuckolded her husband, then foisted an unwanted Killian bastard on her brother, Lord Tal, before having the sense to die.

He glanced at the bold profile of the Lord of Killian'ayn. Killian was tall and angular, with piercing pale gold eyes much the same shade as Jarid's. The other man peered intently down at the still figure on the bed, seeming not to even notice Jarid.

Alyssa held out her hands to Lord Senn and bent her head to be kissed.

"You have my blessing in this time of sorrow, Granddaughter," Senn said softly. "I grieve that such tragedy comes so soon after your marriage into this fine old House." He pressed his old lips to her smooth forehead. "Twenty-three is terribly young to be widowed."

Alyssa tightened her fingers over his hands. "Perhaps, the Light willing, that will not come, Grandfather."

Senn looked around the circle of powerful men, all fellow Househeads. "A Searcher must be sent to the Lowlands to bring back the girl."

Again the heads nodded. Jarid watched them closely without detecting the least shade of suspicion in their surface thoughts.

The Council filed out, Senn waiting until last. He touched Alyssa's cheek. "I'll contact Shael'donn and arrange for the Search," he said quietly. "You just tend to your husband."

She nodded, seeming to swallow back her tears, and gave him a wan smile.

303

Senn patted her arm. "It will be all right." He opened the door and followed the rest. Jarid walked beside him up the main stairs to the family courtyard.

The mountain wind drove chill raindrops into their faces as, one by one, each Council member stepped onto the covered platform, inset above and below and on the four midpoints with pale-blue ilsera crystals, then wrenched the energies into alignment with his destination and disappeared.

Jarid turned around and saw Alyssa's green-gold eyes staring at him from the open doorway.

"They *knew!*" She drew her thick black silsha-fur cloak closer around her body as he approached.

He took her shoulders in his hands and drew her back into the covered stairwell. "They did *not* know." He pushed a lock of burnished-gold hair out of his face. "And watch what you say out here. You know the walls have ears."

Alyssa jerked away from his hands and glided down the worn stone stairs. *Chierra ears,* her voice said in his mind. *Those can be quite easily taken care of.*

Don't take them so lightly, Aunt. Jarid followed, his heavy outdoor boots echoing hollowly down the long stairwell. *It was chierra ears, after all, that spoiled our plan.* He held the door open at the base of the stairs and she brushed past into the main house.

A chierra serving woman, stooped over her scrubbing, moved hastily out of their way, bowing her head.

Jarid caught sight of her reddened eyes. It was old Jayna, Pascar's wife. Still mourning her husband, the seneschal, he supposed. Alyssa jerked off the heavy cloak, threw it across the wall rack, and swept by the old woman without even noticing.

Jarid followed Alyssa's black-clad back along the corridors to the family wing. Inside the spacious apartment, he cast his mind about for other presences, but there were only Alyssa and himself, if one didn't count old Tal and the chierra nurse in the main bed chamber.

Alyssa gripped her fingers together and glared at him. *I told you this would never work!* She paced to the window and looked out into the growing dusk. *They could read us—they know!*

Don't be such a coward! Jarid walked into her private bed

chamber, then threw himself backwards onto the rich, gold-worked spread. *Are you sure you're really a Senn?*

Lineage is your problem, my dear, not mine! She followed him inside, locking the heavy door, then pressed her back against it, watching him like a bavval on the hunt.

Blood pounded in Jarid's temples, but he held onto his anger, hiding it deep inside. Alyssa was an idiot, but he couldn't afford to let go, not yet, not with so much at stake. He took a steadying breath. *They didn't know. On my part, I radiated shock and outrage, and you, of course, were properly subdued and grief-stricken.* He folded his hands behind his bright hair and smiled. *In a little while, we can send Uncle on to the Light, and then I will simply make myself indispensable running this great House and all its lands.*

And our marriage? She fingered the embroidered red flowers on the collar of her black gown. Her narrowed golden eyes, shot through with green streaks, followed his every move.

In time, he replied, *after my uncle has been properly mourned.* He reached up and seized her wrist, pressing his lips to her warm white skin. *Now—my boots, wench!*

She resisted his strength for a moment, then collapsed against his broad chest, laughing and knocking him back across the wide bed.

He laid a finger across her soft red lips. *Although we must be careful for now, we can still enjoy ourselves.*

She stood back and braced herself, tugging on one of his gleaming black boots. *And the brat?*

Lying back, Jarid sighed as the boot slipped off. He wriggled his liberated toes. *My sweet cousin? Don't worry about her.*

Alyssa dropped the boot to the floor, then took hold of his other foot and strained backwards, stumbling as the second boot gave. She threw it to the floor beside its mate.

Jarid pulled his long legs back up on the bed. *We'll make certain to find her before the Searcher, and then she'll meet with an unfortunate accident, too. Such a sad story.* He stretched and settled comfortably on the pillows.

Alyssa sat on the bedside looking down into his face. Then she leaned over and snuggled against his chest.

Jarid took her shoulders and flipped her roughly over

305

on her back. His eyes, pale as newly drifted sand, bored down into her more golden ones. *Everything is going as planned.*

Hunched on the downward side of a scraggly, wind-stunted tree, Haemas tried to think. Her shoulder still throbbed and her right arm was all but useless. She pressed her cheek against the tree's rough bark and told herself she had to go on.

Far below, a tiny glittering ribbon of silver threaded the broad valley floor. A river, she thought, trying to imagine it something like the rushing mountain streams she knew, only much wider. The darker blue-green of trees dominated the sloping sides of the alley, with the valley's center a patchwork of bare brown fields and green pastures.

Her eyes drifted shut as she tried to imagine the people down there. They would look like the chierra who had served her all her life, but these would be free, paying tribute to the Kashi Mountain Lords, but not service. They would be uniformly dark, none of them possessing golden eyes and hair, the genetic tag heralding the presence of Talent in her kind. Their eyes would be brown, unreadable chierra eyes. They would have only five fingers and five toes, not six like the People of the Light, and they would be both head-deaf and head-blind, as she seemed to be now.

Left-handedly, Haemas pulled herself onto her feet and started downward again. Before her, the early evening sky was a creamy gray-green, the suspended sun orange and huge. Through the pain in her shoulder, she thought she could feel that the air already seemed warmer, but she might just be imagining that.

Far above she suddenly heard the sharp crack of falling rock. Glancing upward, she saw nothing, but she quickened her pace. The darkness thickened as she picked her way down. Scattered stars pierced the night sky, cool and disinterested.

Then she felt just the slightest feathery brush against her thoughts. Heedless of the rocks, Haemas hurled her aching body to the ground, stretching out in the chill dirt and grass, trying to blank her mind, thinking only of dirt and rock and the cold evening air, trying not to remember her father's still, white face.

Somewhere up above in the Highlands, someone was casting a mental net for her, but she dared not look. She could only press against the cold ground in the darkness until, at some point, she fell asleep.